A Collection of Short Stories

Gareth Davies

To Sarah Jane.

Hope you enjoy

Gareth Davies

A Collection of Short Stories
Gareth Davies

All rights reserved. No part of this publication may be reproduced, stored in any retrieval system or transmitted in any form or by any means, electronic, mechanical, photocopying, recording or otherwise, without the prior written permission of the copyright holder for which application should be addressed in the first instance to the publishers. The views expressed herein are those of the author and do not necessarily reflect the opinion or policy of Tricorn Books or the employing organisation, unless specifically stated. No liability shall be attached to the author, the copyright holder or the publishers for loss or damage of any nature suffered as a result of the reliance on the reproduction of any of the contents of this publication or any errors or omissions in the contents.

ISBN 9781912821341

A CIP catalogue record for this book
is available from the British Library.
Published 2019 Tricorn Books
131 High Street, Portsmouth, PO1 2HW

Printed & bound in the UK

Contents

A Rose by Any Other Name	5
The Castle of the Kings	20
Alexi's Journey	24
The Loyal Assistant	163
The Chosen Ones	175
Dirty Gutter Rat	188
Three Lives	197
The Picture Restorer	211

A Rose by Any Other Name

With his arm around the sobbing woman Father John escorted her to the entrance of the church, after a final word of comfort from him she began her sad walk home. He stood with the echo of her tears still ringing in his ears. Surely one of the saddest sounds in the world is a mother grieving for a lost one. He had spent the last hour comforting her after the death of her youngest son Aldo. He had won a large sum of money in a casino, only to lose the money and his life in an alleyway sometime later that night. Of course no one knew who had done the evil deed, nor was it likely that the law would ever find them. For this had happen in a place where there was no law. Sadly, he was not the first and almost certainly he would not be the last to die there.

He stood and watched her until she disappeared for sight before turning to sit on his favourite bench overlooking the valley. The sun was just above the horizon casting long shadows across the land below

He remembered Aldo well, as a baby he had baptised him, It took a moment for him to remember he had also baptised his mother. He shook his head as he said out loud. "Have I been here that long?" He knew he was not the man he used to be, his body told him that every day. Perhaps it would be better if I stood aside for someone younger? But the thought quickly passed. Who was he to say when his work was done; the Lord would let him know when it was time to pass the burden to another. Until then the people were in his care, and as a shepherd would look after his flock, he would look after them for as long as his faith burned within him, and that was still strong enough to singe the devils beard given the chance.

His mind drifted back to when he had first come here as a young priest, then the only danger seemed to be from the minor earth quakes that still occasionally occur. It would have been unthinkable for something like a killing to happen. He still remembered the first time he'd sat here on this spot and looked out on his new parish. It was called "Valle de la Tolerancia" (The valley of Grace.) with the church build on a hill high enough to see all the surrounding lands.

Fifty years ago the town below was a village, no more than just a few houses scattered on both sides of the only real road that linked them with the outside world. The valley then had only horse and cart tracks that covered the land from one end to the other.

Far to his right was another hill, where for some reason nothing would grow on its upper sloops. It was known as "Dead Men's Hill." and none of the locals would go there. It was said to be haunted by the ghosts of three young men who fell asleep there on the night before one was to be wed, and the next morning all three were found dead, but without a clue as to the cause.

It would turn out to be a place of more infamy then he could have imagined, but that was for the future. Back then all he could see was a patchwork of fields, each one a different colour depending on the crops planted there. And with the passing of the days those colours would slowly change as one season followed another. The beauty of it took his breath away, and even after all these years it still did. The light was beginning to fade, but he could still see in the far distance the high mountains that surrounded the valley on three sides. In the winter those mountain took the brunt of the weather keeping the valley mild. Then In the spring and for most of the summer the melting snow would flow down and irrigate the crops below.

The first decade of his priesthood had passed quickly with the valley having only rich harvests. But then an avalanche in the mountains changed the course of the river cutting off almost all of the water and the valley quickly began to die. A few had moved away as the crops failed and the rich soil turned to dust, but many were reluctant to leave the place that had been home for many generations and tried their best to scratch a living. Everyone pried to God to save them from their suffering, and finally their prayers were answered. A mining company found some large copper deposits only a few miles away and needed men to dig the ore out.

Almost all of the men left their lands to work there. He remembered the joy he felt at the turn of events, now the people at least had money to buy food, even if they could not grow their own.

But the money brought much more than just food, for the first time cars and TV's began to appear along with and all the other trapping of modern society. And to complete the recovery a few years later a dam was built high in the mountains to supply hydroelectricity, and one of consequents' of this was the river returned to its old course thus making the valley fertile again. Now many left the mines and returned to their first love... the land. But they were quickly replaced by others, and almost overnight the village became a thriving town. But not all the newcomers wanted to earn their living by farming or copper mining. At first they tried to build their saloons and gambling dens in the town. But his influence had been too powerful and the town council had thrown them out. But if he and the townspeople thought they had won a complete victory they were mistaken. Those that were expelled travelled just a few miles outside town to "Dead Man's Hill," land that was not owned by anyone which made it perfect for their needs. Soon another town began to take shape, but this one had no church, schools, or police to give it law and order. This town only dealt with gambling, drugs, and prostitution. It was said that if you were rich enough there was no form of sinful pleasure you could not buy there.

Now the hill had a new name, Patio del Diablo (The Devils' Playground) and for the last five years he had seen the creeping tide of evil invade almost all their lives. Before the outsiders had come the town had been a pleasant and safe place to live; now women could not venture out after dark without an escort. Even young men in their prime often carried a weapon for protection from the many drug addicts and alcoholics that now roamed the streets. No doubt some had once been decent people, even to the point of having families and jobs. But that was long ago, the booze and drugs had sucked everything that was good out of them, like a sponge sucks up water. Now they would slit your' throat for the price of a drink, or drugs for their next "fix." The police would sometimes make an arrest, but never enough to make a difference. He had fought hard to keep his congregation safe, but as the years rolled by his defeats mounted quicker than his successes. The young were especially at risk, and many were seduced by the bright lights and easy money that could be earned there, it was at the devils playground that Aldo had been killed.

He thumbed in one of his coat pockets and after a brief fight with the pocket lining his hand emerged with his old watch. A smile lit up his face, it was nearly time for his friend Dr Eduardo Charles to pay his weekly visit, and he was always on time.

He'd barely had time to take his coat off before the knock on the door announced the arrival of his oldest friend. He could clearly hear the joy in his house keep's voice as she hung up his coat. A moment later they greeted each other with no more than just a silent nod and a wry smile, but the pleasure of being in each other's company was plain to see. What happened next was a ritual that had not varied for many years. First the chessboard with the pieces unmoved from the last visit was carefully lifted from their usual resting niche and placed between them on a small table. His housekeeper Chiqita came in with a bottle of wine and two glasses, and when the wine had been poured they relaxed in two big comfortable chairs. Eduardo still liked to smoke a pipe and within minutes the room was filled with the haze of smoke and contentment as he sipped his wine and planed his next move. He looked at his old friend with a frown on his face, "You look like you've lost another pound or two Father. We should be putting on weight at our age, not taking it off" He tapped his pipe to remove some ash "You must start looking after yourself, If anything happen to you, then where could I find someone who serves such excellent wine and is so easy to beat?" Father John give a gruff reply "Easy to beat am I, I'll show you who's easy to beat. Just because you've won the last two games" Eduardo pointed his pipe like a finger "You mean the last five games I've won" both men burst out laughing. "Alright" stuttered Father John "The last five games." Eduardo looked at him over the rim of his glasses "You may try to make a joke of it my friend, but I think it would be wise to pay me a visit at the hospital to give you a good check-up". He filled and relit his pipe as he spoke "After all, we worked hard enough to have it built." Father John shrugged his shoulders "You have many more needy than an old man like me" He could see Eduardo was about to give him an argument and added quickly with a gesture of surrender "All right, all right, I'll come as soon as I can." Eduardo looked at him steel in his eyes "When?" Father John thought for a moment "Tuesday next week." Eduardo nodded "Don't forget or I'll come and drag you there myself" Satisfied that he had won the argument he returned his attention to the chess and the silence of contentment again filled the room.

The true wonder of their relationship was that it existed at all. Dr Eduardo had first come to the valley about five years after Father John, and was a very bitter man. He had spent his whole adult life fighting against corrupt authorities who lined their own pockets at the expense of others. He was also of the opinion that with so much suffering and injustice in the world there could not be a God, and even if there was one, he was not worth following. All the churches should be turned into homes for the homeless and any wealth in them shared between the people. He was very outspoken in his views, and in a strongly Christian population was not at first liked. He and Father John rarely met, but when they did the discussion between them could go on for hours. But neither could change the other's view, and it would have stayed that way but for a tragic event. During the bad times of drought and famine a flu epidemic had swept through the valley, and with most of the population already in poor health many succumb that in better times would have survived.

Both men worked tirelessly against the epidemic, and gradually a mutual respect grew between them. Father John soon realized that with or without a god Dr Eduardo was a true humanitarian who pushed himself to the point of total collapse to save his patients. Dr Eduardo in turn recognized that armed only with faith Father John had kept many alive when logic said they should have died. But with no hospital and few drugs there was little they could do. When it was all over 67 people had died, many of them children. Even before the last victims were buried both men made a promise that never again would they be so unprepared. Somehow they would find the money to build a hospital, and the medicines' to stock it. It took them five long hard years of begging, bullying along with threats of God's anger on those rich enough to donate before they fulfilled their promise, but fulfil it they did, and along with building a hospital they built a friendship strong enough to last ten lifetimes.

The time seemed to fly by, as it always did when they were in each other's company, and all too soon it was time for the good doctor to depart. As Father John walked his guest to his car he mentioned the tragic news of Aldo's death, Dr Eduardo remembered him well "A sad loss to his family" he buttoned up his coat against the chill wind "I will call by his mother's house tomorrow, no doubt she could do with something to help her sleep." Father John nodded "a kind thought Eduardo." As Eduardo was about to closed the car door Father John added "I will also pray that God will lift the heavy sadness from her heart, and ask again for his help to rid the valley of the evil that exists so close by, who knows, if it is his will perhaps this time some good will come of it."

Eduardo nodded his head briefly in agreement, he was still true to his atheist views, but both had made an unspoken agreement many years ago to respect the other's beliefs, so with just a wave of his hand he drove away.

Father John went back inside the church, he felt very tired as he often did these days, but determined to fulfil his promise of prayer.

He knelt before the altar and was about to begin when he heard the sound of shuffling feet. He turned to find his elderly housekeeper Chiqita hobbling towards him. "I'm sorry to disturbed you Father, I just came to tell you that I'm going to bed, but I've made you a cold supper as you asked, it's on the kitchen table." He nodded his thanks "I will come soon, but first I must pray for a graving mother." He smiled as he added "and also for his help against The Devils' playground. I will eat your supper after I have made my peace with him" Chiqita shook her head from side to side. "I don't know why God doesn't just burn it all down, that place has caused more heartache and grief than hell itself." The priest give a gentle laugh "I would gladly give my life for than to happen, and if it is Gods wish perhaps one day it will, now go to bed and rest your poor legs" He bowed his head and began his prayers. Chiqita walked quietly and painfully away; she worried more about him with each passing day. He hardly ate a full meal anymore, or slept for more than a few hours and was beginning to look very gaunt. She muttered to herself "That place really should be burned to the ground. The worry of it is making the Father ill. I've a mind to take a match to it myself if only my poor body would carry me that far." And so still muttering to herself she went to bed.

Chiqita rose at her usual time the next morning and again as usual the first thing she did was have a cup of coffee. She was joined a moment or two later by Dalmira, a much younger girl whom the priest had given a home to in exchange for help with the housekeeping. She had protested at the time, saying she did not need any help, but the priest had insisted, and he had been right. The advancing years had taken their toll on her, and she had become more and more dependent on Dalmira. Now the two women had a mother/daughter kind of relationship. Chiqita then noticed the plate of cold meat she had prepared the previous evening still on the table…untouched. She give a deep sigh, "The Father is so busy looking after everyone else he forgets to look after himself." Dalmira nodded agreement "He's a good man who only thinks of others" Chiqita stood with her hands on her ample hips "We'd better cook him a big breakfast to make up for missing supper." A little later with the meal prepared she knocked lightly on his bedroom door, but there was no answer, she knocked again, but still no reply. Now she became concerned, the Father never failed to wake up when she knocked twice. She opened the door slightly and peeked in, the room was empty and the bed unslept in. They found him a few minutes later in the church. He was still on his knees as if prying to his God, Chiqita touched his hand, and felt the coldness of death. Hurried phone calls were made to Doctor Eduardo and members of the church council, the doctor arrived first. He quickly confirmed that his old friend had been with his maker for several hours. He could not be 100% sure, there would have to be an autopsy, but it looked like a heart attack sometime last evening.

By the end of that day everyone in the valley had heard the sad news. Many cried and wept at his passing, and even those that were not strong in the faith felt sadden by his death, but there was one only a short distance away who celebrated his demise.

Benicio Calderón owned more of the place called The Devils' Playground than anyone else. His "Lucky Seven" saloon sat at the very peak of the knoll and was the biggest and grandest gambling house to be built there.

He liked to give the impression of a man of high breeding and culture, but the truth was very different. He was born to a drunkard mother who had no memory of who his father was. She died when he was still little more than a youth, but even at that young age his feet was already set firmly on the path of crime. Now he sat in his private suite listening to Mozart while drinking a glass of champagne to celebrate the priest's death.

Five years ago he had tried to build his gambling house in the town itself, but the priest had roused the people and besieged the town hall, forcing the council to refuse him entre. But if they all though they had beaten him, they was wrong. Benicio Calderón does not give up that easily. From the very first day of his exile he worked on a plan that would someday allow him to return. They say that every man has his price, and Benicio was an expert in finding that price, be it money or something else. The first to fall were the ordinary policemen, with poor pay they were easily seduced. Then the higher ranking officers followed one by one until all were in his pay.

Now that he had corrupted the law to his side, he set about doing the same with the town council. But surprisingly they proved to be a harder nut to crack. Most of the council were farmers or active members of the church, and at first they nether wanted or needed anything he could offer them. But five years is a long time, long enough for many to either succumb to the endless bribes he offered them, or to be blackmailed for some act of indiscretion. And now just as he had secured enough votes on the council he had the added bonus of the death of his biggest obstacle...the priest. From now on, the town council would do his bidding without too much persuasion. In his safe was all the sordid evidence and secretly taken photos that could ruin the reputations and lives of them all.

He would wait until the priest was buried and people's emotions' had calmed down before doing anything. Then he would make them call a special Council meeting, and at that meeting they would lift the ban for his return. The cover story for the general public would be that in gratitude for allowing his return he would fund the cost of a new school, and who knows, perhaps one day if he became rich enough he might even fulfil his promise. The thought of having a school named after him appealed to his vanity, yes, the "Benicio Calderón School" had a nice ring to it.

Tomorrow he would contact all the other owner's and offer them an opportunity to set up their business alongside his. Of cause he would charge a "fee" for this "opportunity," a small cut of their action, say 50%. He had no doubt that some would refuse his offer, but he was also sure they would change their minds when he pointed out that as soon as he took control of the town, one of his first acts would be to use the police to close down any who did not accept his offer. So they had a choice, they either move with him, or move far away from him, he would not stand for any competition close by. But that was all in the future, for now he would relax, and enjoy the moment and his champagne. It had taken five years, much longer than he had first hoped, but now total victory was in his grasp. With the help of his police force he would be free to do anything he wanted. He smiled, the town was about start paying the price for throwing him out the first time, and his price would be high, very, very high.

Two days later the body of the priest had been returned to the church, the cause of death was confirmed to be a heart attack. The funeral would take place tomorrow. It would be attended by all the dignitaries in the area, and the service would be conducted by the Bishop himself. Chiqita and Dalmira were pleased with the honour being shown to the old priest, but it did not lift the sadness they felt. Now they sat in silence at the kitchen table preparing food for the day's meals. For both the future was full of uncertainty. Chiqita had been the priest's housekeeper for over thirty years. If the new priest brought his own housekeeper, or found her to be unsuitable then at her age the future would be bleak

For Dalmira the position was better, she was younger and could find other work if she had to, but the loss of Father John had hit her hard. She had loved the priest as if he was her real father, now he was dead, one of the few men that had ever showed her real kindness.

Chiqita gave a little sigh, "It was the worry of the Devils Playground that killed him, I could see it in his eyes the night he died, she then repeated almost word for word the conversation between then. Dalmira sighed deeply, the greatest sorrow in her life was caused by that evil place, and now it had also played a part in the death of the priest.

Dalmira's started to chop up some onions, but they were only partly to blame for the tears in her eyes. Even after many years she could not think or talk about the Devils Playground without touching what was still a raw nerve. In truth Dalmira was what people call "A fallen woman." She had gone there the first time almost as a dare, but she met an older man full of charm who had swept her off her feet, and with words of love quickly seduced her. Her parents had been horrified when it became obvious she carried his child and quickly disowned her. She had gone to see her lover, but he too had rejected her. In desperation she had come to the priest. He arranged for her to have her baby in a nunnery far away where no one knew her. In due course a baby boy was born and passed on to a young couple who could offer him the home she could not. She returned to the valley still grieving for the child she had given away and with nowhere to live. But again the priest again came to her aid by offering her a home, and now after robbing her of her innocents that place of evil had also played a part in his death, the tears were now flowing freely, and the onions had little to do with the reason for them.

Both women would have been horrified and even more fearful for their future if somehow they could have heard what was happening at that very moment in the cellars of "Lucky Seven"

Benicio Calderón and his second-in-command Sanchez Diaz were making their way slowly between racks of wines, pausing for a moment at each rack. "Just remember Sanchez I want all our men to be in or around the building when the meeting starts." The other man nodded, "What time is it set for boss?" "Six o' clock tomorrow evening, after the funeral but before our paying customers start to arrive" he took a bottle out of one rack for a closer examination before he went on. "I've arranged for our friends from town to be here, they will tell the other owners about the benefits of moving there" Even without seeing you knew he had a smirk on his face as he added in a sarcastic voice "Everybody will drink a toast to the dear departed before we get down to business" "Are you expecting any trouble?" Benicio shrugged his shoulders. "Who knows, some may get upset when I tell them the terms for moving with us, and what will happen if they don't. Anyway, it's better to be prepared just in case things get ugly." For the next few minutes more sound of clinking bottles as Benicio restocked his personal wine cellar. "Two more red, and three more white." Sanchez noted the figures down "How many owners are coming Boss?" Benicio give a little grunt of a laugh "Every one of them, and all their men. It seems they don't trust me to come alone, they have to bring their whole armies with them for protection."

He pointed to certain bottles as he went on "Don't order any of these again, they're terrible wines. We'll give them to our guests,' with their uneducated palates they won't know the difference." The sound of laughter echoed around the cellar as they both enjoyed the insult "Don't worry boss, every man we have will be ready for them, and if they're stupid enough to start anything, it will be the last thing they ever do."

Chiqita woke the next morning feeling depressed, and with a headache. For the past two days both the women had worked long into the night preparing for this day. After the funeral the Bishop and several members of his party were staying for a meeting, and they had been asked to supply meals for them. Chiqita sipped her morning cup of coffee before she went about her business. She felt the air was heavy, as if a storm was close, but she looked out of the window only to see a clear blue sky. She shook her head as if trying to clearer the cobwebs out, but that only made her headache worst. She began to make her way to the hen house, but before she was half way there the sound of loud clucking was ringing in her ears. She turned the corner and was greeted by the sight of some very agitated chickens running up and down in panic as if trying to escape. A few minutes later she returned to the house to find Dalmira standing in the open doorway. "What's the matter with the chickens? I could hear the noise from here?" Chiqita shook her head slowly "I don't know, but something is upsetting them, they've not laid a single egg between them" again she looked up at the clear sky "I thought it might be a storm coming, but…. Chiqita body shook as a shudder ran down her spine. "Something….something big is going to happen today, and I don't just mean the funeral. I feel it in my bones; this will be a day we will all remember for the rest of our lives." Dalmira waved an arm skywards. "Well come on, we've much to do today, and if the day is to be remembered for something, I don't want that something to be our fault."

By mid-morning all of the church council had arrived in time to greet the Bishop. His Holiness rested in a back room after his journey as the final preparations for the funeral were made. The service itself went off without a hitch, but in a very subdued tone. Father John was to be buried in his favourite spot where he used to sit and look out over the valley. The Bishop himself led the procession out of the church. As they stood at the graveside, the sound from above made everyone look up to see an astonishing sight. The sky was dotted with flocks of birds, some of less than a dozen, others numbering in the thousands, and they were all flying in the same direction, out of the valley. At the end of the service those that knew the meaning of this behaviour left quickly. The birds had given them a warning that danger was approaching, now all wanted to be back on their farms or in their homes before it arrived. Chiqita touched herself with the sign of the cross as she made her way back inside, now more convinced than ever that a great storm was coming. The afternoon passed slowly as the meeting between the church council and the bishop dragged on and on. The Bishop was himself an old man and not in the best of health, he had to frequently take short breaks for rest and refreshments. It was not until early evening that they left to return to their homes.

Dalmira and Chiqita sat at the kitchen table sipping their coffee. Both were exhausted but happy that for the first time in days they could relax without any pressure on them. Chiqita particularly was content, she had fretted all day that something bad was going to happen but the day had proved her wrong.

The clock on the kitchen wall marked the time at five minutes past six when the celling light began to flicker and a distant roll of thunder reached their ears. Chiqita looked out of the window, already clouds as black as night covered part of the sky blotting out the early evening light. She turned to Dalmira "I knew it, I just knew it, I told you this morning we were in for a storm and its coming fast." Now both women watched as the clouds marched across the sky, within minutes they had almost reached them with streaks of lightening that crisscrossed the sky constantly, heavy rain and strong winds began to lash at the window frames making them rattle.

A tree just a few hundred yards away burst into flames as the lighting struck the trunk into splinters. Both women retreated to the safety of the pantry and sat there terrified as the flashes of lighting grew brighter and the claps of thunder grew louder and louder. And then it was on top of them, all the windows were filled with a blinding white light and the church shook from a clap of thunder so loud they thought the very sky was falling on them. A few seconds later another almighty clap, but not quite as close, followed by another, but mercifully each one a bit further away as the storm began to pass them by. But then a new sound emerged, a sound even deeper and more powerful than the thunder still ringing in their ears. The room started to shake; Chiqita kissed the cross that hung around her neck as she cried out in fear "O Mary mother of God now we have an earthquake as well as the storm." The shaking lasted just long enough for a heavy pan to fall off the wall and land on Chiquita's' leg and she let out a yell of pain. And then as suddenly as it had started it was over. Dalmira helped Chiqita hobble out of the pantry; the pan had cut her leg just below the knee. There were some broken dishes and other items that had fallen on the kitchen floor, but apart from a fine layer of dust in the air the earthquake had been too mild and not lasted long enough to do any real damage. They made their way outside to the fresh air. It was still raining slightly but thankfully the lighting and thunder were dying away as the storm moved further up the valley. Dalmira let out a gasp and pointed "Look Chiqita, the Devil's Playground is on fire" Both women watched as the thick clouds seemed to hover over the hated place, lighting forked to the ground, and almost every time it did a building seemed to explode or burst into flames to light up the evening sky. Chiqita forgot the pain in her leg as she danced a jig of joy "It's happening just as Father John wanted, God is punishing the evil doers with fire" Dalmira shook her head "No, it's more than that, the night he died he said he would gladly exchange his life for the destruction of that evil place." Chiqita nodded "Yes, I remember" Dalmira returned her gaze to the burning inferno "Well don't' you see, God took him for his word, that is the hand of God punishing those in league with the devil, but that hand is guided by Father John." They stood and watched in silence as the fire spread from building to building, and the rosy glow in the sky grew brighter.

Andres Garcia had been a fireman all his working life, for the last six years he had been in charge of the local fire station. He was a man dedicated to the fighting of fires and the saving of lives. So when the phone call came that the devils' playground was on fire he did not hesitate even though it was outside his territory. Fifteen minutes later he was driving up the hill to where all the casinos were. He was greeted by a sight he had never seen before in his life. Flowing down the main road towards him, was a stream of water from the rain still falling, alongside the water was fire that seemed to spring up from the ground itself as it also slowly made its way downhill. He watched as sometimes the two intermingled, but always the flames refused to die. A large building just in front of him exploded throwing burning debris high into the air. Two large pieces of burning timber fell on the Fire engine, one on the bonnet breaking the windscreen, the other fell near the back injuring one of his men. He had no choice but to retreat back down the hill, this was like no fire he had ever seen, and if a sky full of rain could not put out the inferno, then there was little he could do.

At the bottom of the hill other services were arriving including some police and ambulances, but there was little anyone could do beyond evacuating the area below the fire line and helping the few injured people so far found. A skeleton crew from each service stayed there all night, but it more out of a sense of duty than anything they could achieve.

With the coming of dawn the full extent of the damage could be seen for the first time. The top half of the knoll that had been "The Devils' Playground" had completely gone, nothing, not even a stick of wood remained. The main fire had burned itself out in the early hours of the morning, but small fires continued to break out and then die until after first light. So it was not until early afternoon that Andres Garcia declared it safe to begin the grim task of finding those who had perished. The hope was that with the bad weather and the fire happening so early in the evening the death toll would be low. Slowly the fireman and other rescue workers began to search for those who had lost their lives. At first they made good progress with no bodies found, but as they approached the place where the "Lucky Seven" had stood the number quickly began to rise. In one part alone there were over twenty bodies. It took two days of careful searching before they could be certain they had found them all, and in the end the death toll reached over a hundred.

From the start it was clear that none of the owners of The Devils' Playground or any of their underlings of importance had apparently survived, this in itself was a mystery. All the survivors were in agreement that the "Lucky Seven" had been the first to be hit by lightning, and had exploded with the force of a bomb. But all the other casinos further down the hill had survived for several minutes before they became engulfed in flames, and all of the ordinary staff from these had survived. To add to the confusion the chief of police and several of his officers, along with many from the town council and prominent citizens were reported missing by their families. And then, a day after the fire all their questions were answered. At the hospital it was found that one of the few to be rescued was none other than Sanchez Diaz, Benicio Calderón second-in-command. When the "Lucky Seven" had exploded he had been outside checking that his men were following orders. The force of the blast had thrown him clear of the building, he was found before the fire reached him and carried to safety. His injures were very severer, and he must have sensed that death was very close, so he did what many would do; he sought redemption from his sins. He named all the police, judges, and politicians that had been in Benico' pay, many almost from the start. He went on to tell them of all the rotten deals, and all the rotten people they were made with. When he has finished they had all the names and information needed to cleanse the town of every crooked person who lived there. Many were horrified when it became clear just how corrupt their town had become, and this had been before Benicio Calderón had taken control, what future horrors had lain in store for them and their families could only be guessed at. Now they were filled with a new resolve and wasted no time in correcting the situation. Within days all those on the list who had not died in the fire were either in jail or had escaped to pastures new.

One question that would need answering was what kind of fire could still burn in the middle of a storm with heavy rain falling. Andres Garcia had over thirty years' experience and he'd never seen a fire act like this one had, so a request was sent to higher authorities for someone who could solve the mystery.

Two months later a new town council met to hear the results. Three geologists appointed to the task sat facing them across the table. They were told that the hill "The Devil's Playground" had been built on was not a true hill, but a bulge forced up by the pressure of gas deep below the surface. From time to time if the pressure became too great, or as on this occasion an earthquake took place, small fissures could open up and the gas would escape. It was undoubtedly the first time this had happen since the hill had been built on, and with so many sources of ignition it was inevitable that the gas would catch alight. The reason some building had explode was due to the gas gathering in their cellars first and then igniting. They went on to say that once lit it would have been almost impossible to put the fire out until either the pressure dropped or the fissures closed.

There was also evidence that this cycle of events had happen many times in the past, although without a fire, and this was the reason why little vegetation could grow there. They concluded the ground that "The Devils' Playground" had been built on should never be used again for any kind of dwelling, and should be left as it is. The three finished their presentation and asked if anyone had questions. Silent greeted this offer, so with no questions from the council they gathered up their papers and left the room

Dr Eduardo had sat listening to the report from the geologists with a sense of unease.

He had called to treat Chiqita's injured leg, and both women had told him that on the night Father John had died he had offered his life in exchange for burning down that place of evil, and they believed God took him to his word. At first he dismissed their story as just fanciful thinking, but now he was not so sure. The number of coincidences had grown to a point where logic said it was impossible to believe. He ticked them off in his mind. First…There was the meeting with everyone connected to the devils playground there. Never had such a meeting taken place before, and most likely it would never have happen again. Then… the timing, 30 minutes earlier or an hour later and all those at that meeting would still be alive today. And he sobered to the thought that Benicio Calderón would probably be running this meeting and certainly running the town…. And the strength of the earthquake, a miracle just by itself, strong enough to open the fussers, but not long or violent enough to frighten people into leaving the meeting, He shook his head, it was impossible, his thoughts were going round and round, there were just too many coincidences to be just coincidence. And he hadn't even mentioned the storm and the….. He stopped and took a deep breath. His mind was in turmoil, he had to reverse a lifetime of thinking and think the unthinkable. And the unthinkable was there had to be some other force at work here, and that force was greater than anything mankind possessed.

The councillors' were talking among themselves about the information they had just been given. One voice was just a bit louder than the others, "Well, now we know, it was an act of God that burned the place down." The words echoed in his head like the ringing of a bell "An act of God" His jaw took on a firm line as he made up his mind and said in a

clear voice loud enough for all to hear "You are right my friend, it was an act of a God, but he may have had some help," A hush filled the room. The shook of hearing Dr Eduardo admitting to an act of God stunned them into silence. It took a few seconds before a voice rose from the back. "We all know what your views about religion were in the past Doctor, even Father John could not change them, why you change your tune now." Dr Eduardo give a rue smile "Change my tune you say, no, I do not change what I never had. As for Father John, he and I were friends before most of you were born, but for me it was always the singer I respected, not the tune he sung. But now I listen with more open ears, and I think the tune may also have some merit to it" He went on to tell them what Father John has said the night he died, and that some already believed it was he who guided Gods hand the night the disaster happened. When he had finished, many believed it to be so.

He was not surprised; it had taken him until this moment to realize that people needed to believe in something greater than themselves, something, or someone powerful enough to turn to for help in times of trouble, as a child would turn to its mother or father. For him it was logic, but for others it was religion. Maybe there was a kind of force in the universe, certainly after this incident there was room for doubt. And what did it matter if some called this force God, or Buddha or anyone of dozens of other names, a rose by any other name is still a rose. Soon the story about Father John and the hand of God was spreading from one end of the valley to the other. Within days everyone had heard it, and enough believed it so that within weeks it would become set like concrete in the folk-lore of the valley, and there it would stay for as long as people lived here.

Dr Eduardo stood by the grave of his old friend, a bunch of freshly cut flowers lay across it. He had been here many times in the last six months, and there were always fresh flowers here.

He had just paid a curtsy call to the new priest, he looked so young, but then everyone seems too young for their post these days. Even the doctors he worked with in the hospital looked like they should still be in school. He had also paid his respects to Chiqita and Dalmira, for them life goes on as before. Chiqita particularly was in fine fettle, not only had the new priest accepted her as his housekeeper, but would seek her advice as to how Father John would handle certain situations. He looked out over the valley below; it really was a beautiful view from up here. Far to his right the black scar that was the remains of "The Devils Playground" could still clearly be seen. It was deserted now as the people there along with many from the town had moved on. And with their going crime had become a thing of the past overnight. Already the memory of the bad times was beginning to fade as the valley returned to its old ways of years ago. "The valley is a better place now Father, thanks to you." He paused before adding. "And by the way, I may be partly responsible for making you famous, now everyone thinks you guided God's hand to destroy the Devil's playground." He laughed out loud, "There's even talk that you are to be made a saint.

He returned his gaze again to the view, the many colours of new crops, the sparkle of the sun on the river below. And everywhere the silence's only broken by the singing of the birds in the nearby trees. He give a sigh that almost sounded like envy "You picked a fine spot to rest Father, perhaps, just perhaps mind you, one day I may join you." The afternoon sun felt warm on his face, he looked at his watch, there was just enough time to visit that new tavern down by the square, it was said their wine was like nectar to the taste. He smiled as he added "But not today old friend, not today", he turned and slowly walked away.

The Castle of the Kings
A Short History of the Island Kingdom of Santross

In a time millions of years ago, long before man first trod this earth, a single volcano broke the surface of the sea for the first time. Slowly over the following centuries the lava won its battle with the waves and spread out to became an island. The first volcano was followed by another at the northern tip of the island and its size doubled. Over millions of years the pattern continued until a chain of volcano's over four hundred miles long formed the spine of the island. The volcanoes were numerous and many still active enough to make any crossing of them a hazardous journey. Only on the southern plain was it possible to travel from the east to the west coast with safety and ease. At its own pace, the island became populated with vegetation, birds and many animals, the means of accomplishing the journey a mystery known only to nature. It was to this pristine island that a storm delivered the first human beings ever to walk on its shores. They called themselves the Darosi, a warrior race where before the age of puberty the male children were taken from their mothers to live the harsh life of a soldier. They were taught to have no fear of death, their only goal in life was to become warriors superior to all others. Over the generations these traits had become ingrained in their character to such an extent that when they were not fighting their enemies, they would fight each other. Their empire grew quickly, and as it grew so did their reputation for brutality and slaughter. They became so feared that on many occasions cities would surrender as soon as their army appeared at their gates. Those that chose to fight but lost suffered a terrible fate. Only the survivors who were able to work were spared, the very young and the very old were ruthlessly put to the sword. But in time their own success led to their downfall. They become too reliant on those they had conquered for their daily needs. Throughout their kingdom the slaves now outnumbered them many times over. Their end came when some newly captured slaves who still had the spark of freedom rebelled. After killing their guards they began to free and arm other slaves who immediately joined them in the fight against their cruel masters. By chance they had chosen a good time to stage an uprising, the main Darosi army was hundreds of miles away fighting to conquer more lands. They soon numbered in the tens of thousands and the rebellion spread with such speed that the Darosi who were left were quickly overwhelmed. The result was that those who did not flee died in their thousands, most in their own homes, some even in their beds. They were killed in the same ruthless way they themselves had killed. So an empire that had existed for hundreds of years disappeared almost overnight. The surviving Darosi escaped by sea, intending to sail to an island a few days journey away for sanctuary. But they were destined never to reach those friendly shores. On the night they sailed a great storm fell upon them. Their small fleet was made even smaller as many ships were lost to the torrid seas that battered them day after day. It was a weary few who after many weeks of drifting aimlessly found the uninhabited island that was to be their new home. They called the island Santross in honour of the kingdom they had lost. When they first arrived they had little more than the clothes then stood in, and had to survive only on what the island had to offer. But they vowed to keep alive as many of their old traditions as they could, and never forget how great and feared the Darosi had once been. Over several generations they settled on the southern half of the island. The geography of the land meant that only at the very tip of the island was there any contact between east and west. Slowly two Darosi cultures began to emerge. They were still tied by blood, language and religion, but began to differ in their everyday lives and attitudes. Then one day an event happened that would change all their lives forever. Many times in the past after great storms they had found the wreckage of ships washed up on their shores, but never any clue as to where they had sailed from. Now for the first time a ship was driven aground with many of its crew surviving the ordeal. The people came from land only three or four days sailing to the northwest. Without navigation aids they always sailed in sight of land, so for centuries each had lived only a few hundred miles apart, but without the knowledge that the other existed. Now the Darosi learned of other kingdoms to the north and east, and soon a thriving trade existed. But almost from the start the boats brought not only items to trade, but people as well. The lands across the sea to the north and east were ravaged by endless wars that caused death and chaos. The people of Gottan were not warriors, but people of the land. Their religion and culture forbid them to make war against others, in the past they had been safe, all the kingdoms surrounding them had been too small and weak to invade. But then the northern kingdom of Hatta began to expand their empire, they sent a powerful army south which quickly conquered all before them. Now many of the Gottans' farms and villages were burned to the ground, and their occupants killed or enslaved. Those that had fled heard stories of a new-found land only a few days sailing away. A land that was empty of people, and with soil that was fertile and ready for the plough. So they came to Santross. Only a few at first, but soon the few became hundreds, and the hundreds became thousands. In a short time they had settled all over that part of the island untouched by the Darosi. But if they thought they had found a safe haven they were soon proved wrong. It did not take long for the Hatta to find them, and again their settlements and farms were being plundered and their families killed or taken into slavery.

At first the Hatta moved south as if to conquer the whole island. But they quickly found that the Darosi were not pacifist like those of Gottan, and were far superior to them in armed combat. They suffered defeat after defeat and quickly retreated north again. On seeing the Hatta fleeing from the Darosi, those who spoke for the Gottans' turned to them in desperation for help and protection. At first most Darosi leaders were unsympathetic, they saw all outsiders as little more than invaders steeling their land, and the Gottan's had little in the way of gold to pay them for their services. But those who were wiser soon realized they had something more precious than gold to offer..food. In all their time on the island, the Darosi had made poor farmers. They had tried to grow crops, but even with the rich soil they had little return for their efforts. In their culture all forms of manual labour was considered the work of slaves, not warriors. They preferred to live by hunting game and gathering the fruits that nature provided. This meant that in winter sometimes there was not enough to eat. Now they had been given an opportunity to end their constant search for food and banish hunger for good. With others willing to till the soil they could secure a steady supply of food all year round. So after much debate they agreed to fight the Hatta, and protect the outsiders so they could farm the land in peace. In return they had to acknowledge that the land only belonged to the Darosi, and to provide them with a share of their harvests each year. The demands were harsh, but the settlers had little chose, they could either die or be enslaved at the hands of the raiders, or agree to a life of servitude in return for the safety of their families.

Although still outnumbered the Darosi took the fight to their enemy. They would send a small number of men to attack the Hatta, but they would quickly retreat as a larger force of Hatta advanced. Then at a set point the Hatta would be attacked by an overwhelming force of Darosi soldiers from both flanks . Time after time the Hatta were lured into these well set ambushes from which none escaped. The conflict soon came to a head. The last great battle saw what was left of the Hatta army trapped between a Darosi army attacking them from the south, and another who had outflanked them and was advancing from the north. When the two Darosi armies met the Hatta were forced on to a peninsular with high cliffs on all sides. With ruthless efficiency the Darosi now moved slowly forward behind a wall of shields and long spears, stepping over the dead bodies of their fallen enemies as they advanced. They ignored the many cries of surrender and pleas for mercy until finally the last Hatta fell to their deaths on the rocks below. After this crushing and merciless defeat any Hatta that survived quickly fled back across the sea. Soon it was known by all the tribes of the northlands that the new found land was home to a tribe of great and fearless warriors who took no prisoners in battle. Now none dared to challenge such warriors and suffer almost certain death. So Santross was left in peace, as in the old kingdom, the Darosi had again spread fear amongst those who would be their enemies.

At first the agreement between the two cultures worked well. The Darosi called the new people the "Outsiders" and they proved to be as good at farming as the Darosi were at fighting. Soon food was so plentiful that they began to export the surplus to the northlands. Here only the lowlands give a good return, the further inland you went high mountains made much of the landscape barren and the winters long. Even in the good years there was barely enough food for all. Now the Darosi prospered by living on an island where the volcanos had made the land fertile. The Darosi of the east were more liberal in their attitude to the outsiders. Most but not all accepted that the outsider's reluctance to fight was due more to their culture and religion than a lack of courage. Those of the west were harsher in their opinions. They had remained closer to the old ways and considered them to be no better than cowards, a great sin in the eyes of all Darosi. They had little respect for anyone unwilling to fight to defend their homes and families, and treated them almost as slaves. As time when on they began to take more and more of the harvest for themselves to exchange for gold. The outsiders protested at the ever increasing demands made upon them, and slowly at first but then in increasing numbers began to emigrate to the friendlier east. The western Darosi grew alarmed as the people who created their wealth became fewer in number. To end the exodus they revered totally to their old ways of brutal and total dictatorship. They openly made slaves of all those who lived on their side of the island. Any who resisted were killed, and those they did not kill were only allowed to live in return for their labour. And they did not stop at just enslaving them, they took away every vestige of their past. Anyone caught speaking anything other than the language of the Darosi was beaten without mercy. All evidence of their culture and history before the time of their capture was destroyed, and they were forbidden to make idols or worship their own Gods. Their spirits were chained as thoroughly as their bodies. The Darosi did this in the hope they would never rise against their new masters. The result of all this turmoil meant that two very different ways of life developed for the outsiders. In the western half of the island a culture of slavery existed. In the rest of the kingdom they had their freedom, but without the right to own any land.

As time passed a new danger began to emerge. At first there had been many small kingdoms in the northlands, each fighting to conquer their neighbour. None were strong enough to invade Santross on their own, and they mistrusted each other too much to form an alliance. But it was inevitable that sooner or later one king would triumph over all others. Now all the land to the north was conquered to become the kingdom of Kmaree, ruled by King Sennon. He quickly became jealous of seeing a great sum of gold disappear into the pockets of the Darosi every year, and began to look at the wealth of Santross with envy. He set himself the task of adding to his empire by conquering the island kingdom. The Darosi had long foreseen this danger and the certainty that one day they would again be invaded.

Remembering what had happened in the old kingdom, on both sides of the island the Darosi leaders built strong castles with high walls to protect themselves from any future rebellions or invasions. Those lower in the social ladder with lesser wealth built more modest dwelling but still with an eye on defence. But there were a small number of Darosi who lacked the ability or desire to live in such a way. They followed the old ways and lived the life of a warrior, traveling from one part of the kingdom to another, selling their sword to anyone willing to pay. The richest of these became known as knights of the Kingdom, the poorest became soldiers in the service of those rich enough to employ them. Eventually all the Darosi of high rank became known as the nobility of Santross.

End of History

Chapter 1
Alexi's Journey

The early morning sea mist was just beginning to thin as the sun rose above the distanced mountains. Now the last of the night only lingered in the shadow of the high cliffs that formed the entrance to the bay. Alexis stood by the prow of the ship as it slowly rounded the headland on the light breeze, he was eager to catch the first glimpse of his destination, and with good cause. This was no ordinary castle he sailed to, this was Castle Kingshome. The castle of the Kings. When his ancestors had first arrived on the Island, this place had become their first place of refuge, and was now regarded as the spiritual home of his people. At last the dark sombre shape of the extinct volcano that the Castle was built on came slowly into view. He felt a shiver run down his spine, whether caused by the morning chill or the dread of his new home he was not sure. Not for the first time he pondered on the circumstances that had brought him here. This was a journey he had never expected to make, it should have been his brother Bart sat here, not him. Bart had been first born, and it had always been the custom that the eldest son of families of nobility could be called to serve the King for up to five years, to refuse was treated as treason. This had the twin effects of insuring the family's loyalty to the crown, and swelling the ranks of the kings' army if any uprising did occur. A few weeks before a kings' messenger had delivered the call to duty, and Bart was ready and eager for it. Even their father Damon, who as a young man had been a Commander in the King's Guard, could not match him with sword. Everyone was sure he had a glorious future before him, but the Gods can play some cruel tricks on mere mortals, and so it would be for Bart.

Two days before he was due to leave he fell off his horse as he jumped a fence he had jumped a thousand times before. A broken neck they said, a life stuffed out in the blink of an eye. And so the task of serving the King and upholding the family tradition had fallen to him. But Alexis and Bart had been as opposite as fire is to water. When they had been children, Bart had forced Alexis to practice with him using wooden swords. Bart was two years older than his brother and strong for his age. Alexis was the opposite, small and lightly built. The result was that Bart always won, often inflicting great pain while doing so. Alexis was only six years old when the beating started, and soon grew tired of them. The sword quickly becoming a hateful symbol of pain for him that was best avoided. In the end he refused to fight, and would run away and hide. In a normal family, the father would have realized his younger son was overmatched and needed protection, but this was not a normal family. This was the family of Baron Damon Monrell, a proud family of warriors. And the Baron did not see Alexi's refusal to fight as a call for help. He saw it as a mark of a coward, and with that thought in his mind their relationship soured from that time onward. As he grew older his brother Bart also undermined his confidence on a daily basis by constantly telling him that he would never be a true Darosi. The family of the Baron continued to grow in the years that followed as three more sons and two daughters were added. As each of the males was born, Alexis moved further down the pecking order. He grew to manhood unsure of his true status in life, and was now totally ignored by his father. Alexis slowly became almost invisible in the background. He would spend most of his time in the company of servants, who treated him with a kindness that he never received from his family. Free from the close control of his father, he would sometimes go out into the fields and talk or even work alongside the farm workers. Over time he grew to like and respect the people who toiled on his father's estate, unlike his father and the rest of the family who treated them all with contempt.

He took an interest in how everything worked, and his curiosity knew no bounds. He would sit and listen to those with the most knowledge for hours on end, and ask question after question as to why certain things were done in certain ways. As the years passed and his general knowledge grew he would often make a suggestion of a better way to do things, and more often than not they worked. His education was of a more practical nature and much broader in scope than it would have been under normal conditions. One of his favourite people was Hyman. He saw to all the castle's needs on behalf of his master the Baron Monrell. He was a kind and wise man who taught Alexis much about life and people. As Hyman grew older, Alexis began to help him run the castle and estates, and upon his death he took full control and responsibility for such tasks. He had hoped it would please his father, but his efforts changed nothing. His Father only had eyes for Bart and his others sons. Bart would spend hours every day with sword and shield. He was every inch a soldier, both in looks and attitude. Alexis had none of the dash of his older brother, and his girth confirmed that his most strenuous task was writing with pen and paper. Although he proved to be a superb administrator and organizer it mattered little to the Baron. In his eyes the tasks he performed were more suited for a servant, and not a true Darosi. Alexis knew that his father considered him to be a failure both as a man and as a son, and unworthy to be a valid member of his family.

He still remembered the look on his father's face as he bid him farewell. It was a mixture of anger and fear, anger that it was he standing before him and not Bart, and fear that he was totally unsuited for the task ahead and was almost certain to bring shame and dishonour on the family name. He offered no fond fatherly embrace, no wish for him to keep safe, just a warning of what was expected from him.

"Remember, for many generations we have always served the King with honour. Our ancestors have fought and sometimes died for the King, and you must be prepared to do the same"

There was an edge of pride in his voice as he went on.

"Always remember your name is Monrell, of the house of Monrell, one of the oldest and greatest warrior families in the kingdom"

He wrapped his coat against the winter chill before adding with a firm nod of his head.

"I would rather have a dead son who died doing his duty, than a live one who dishonoured the family name"

He turned and walked quickly away without a backward glance. The first part of their journey was to travel to the major port of Adenor. This was one of the main ports in the east where much of the grain and other food supplies started their journey to the markets of the north. Although their destination was far to the south, it was too late in the year to take the land route to Castle Kingshome. The first heavy snows of winter had already fallen in the mountains, making the high passes treacherous and many blocked. So it would be easier to complete their journey by ship. Alexis had two companions with him when he left that morning. One had been squire to Bart, a tall big boned man called Gant. He had two outstanding attributes, one was his skill in the use of weapons, second only to that of Bart. The other was less flattering, he was without doubt one of the ugliest looking man you were ever likely to meet. His face looked to be made up of parts from different people. Nothing matched, each of his eyes was a different shape and size as was his cheekbones, both were most prominent, but one appeared to be lower and smaller than the other. All this give him an evil and menacing look, but in character he was a gentle man with a soft voice. The other was his personal manservant Huggle, a man always with a happy disposition, and a shape that showed his love for good food. He had been his manservant for many years and always looked after him well. Their journey was less than a day old when the horse the squire was riding stumbled on the rough road and threw him to the ground. At first he appeared to be unhurt apart from a small cut on his leg, he remounted and the incident was quickly forgotten. A few days later, just after they had sailed he complained about his leg for the first time. Alexis examined the wound, puss was beginning to flow freely from it and the leg had swallowed to twice its normal size. The Captain sent the nearest they had to a ship's doctor to treat the illness. The man cleaned the wound and rapped it in clean linen, but it was too late to save the squire, the infection had gone too deep. By the next morning he was delirious and full of fever and died later that day. They buried him at sea within minutes of his demise. Any kind of fever is always a great concern to a ships' Captain. He ordered Alexis and his servant to remain in their cabin, just in case something other than the wound was the cause of death. Alexis did not object, now that his squire was dead, he had lost his main source of protection. For almost every day of his life Bart had told him how useless he would be in any kind of fight, and in time Alexis had come to believe him. His confidence in such matters was so low that he doubted he could ever defend himself with a sword. He decided to take a precaution that to him seemed like just common sense, but many Darosi would have been considered an act of cowardice. He discarded his normal form of dress and wore the same ill-fitting clothes as a commoner to hide his true status, and lessen the chance of any attack. Now if any of the crew or fellow passengers saw them they would think them to be just some poor travellers not worth the robbing.

Chapter 2
The Bay

The high cliffs at the headland were behind them now and Alexis watched as the gently sloping ground allowed the rising sun to come into view. It gave no warmth to the feel, but was a welcome sight after the dark and cold of the night. The heavy mist was now thinning and he turned his attention to the place that would be his home for the foreseeable future. The steep cliffs surrounding the bay made it a safe anchorage, only the narrow entrance could cause any concern. It would be easier to enter and leave with the tide in your favour. Still partly shrouded in the early morning mist the whole bay and the castle had the most depressing feel about it. Almost everywhere you looked you were greeted by the colour black. Black cliffs, black rocks. And most of all, a black castle that dominated the whole surrounding. In truth the whole island was made of the same black lava rocks, but that had been long in the past. In most places the black had been eclipsed by the natural growth of vegetation, so that green had become the dominate colour. Now the only place where black still held sway was on the upper slopes of the few volcanoes that still occasionally erupted. The volcanoes stretched right across the island from Castle Kingshome here in the south to the constantly active Temple Mount at the northern tip of the island. And to a large extent the high volcanoes also controlled the weather that each part of the island received. In the winter, the winds blew from the northwest, so that part of the Kingdom took the full brunt of the weather. The high Volcanoes were often covered in snow, sometimes for many weeks. They protected the land to the east, so here away from the high peaks the winters were mild and the summers warm. This far south snow was almost never seen, and the weather warm enough to allowed crops to grow for most of the year. His gaze followed the coast line past the castle. Half way along on the far shore of the bay there was a small harbour with a few fishing boats swinging at anchor. High about the water mark there were some smaller boats, their bright colours stood out clearly in contrast to the small black grit that formed the only beach he could see. Behind them in the thinning mist the outline of many houses began to appear, with smoke beginning to rise from their chimneys as the occupants greeted the new day.

The extinct volcano that the castle was built on stood a little way from the shore. On the seaward side he could see a pier that stopped just short of the castle proper. A large drawbridge at the castle entrance would be lowered to join the two. The pier itself jutted out about a hundred paces into deeper water, thus allowing ships to load or unload without waiting for the tide. Now as his ship slowly turned on the wind he could just see the landward side. It was just as his father had described it. The only permanent link from the castle to terra-firma was a narrow causeway not much wider than a cart. When the tide flooded the castle was surrounded by sea on all sides. Slowly the castle drew closer as they passed into its shadow, now it was less than a hundred paces away. He studied it more closely, everything was as his father had described it many times. The steep sides of the volcano rose at least three hundred cubits or more, and then the battlements of the castle built above that. He held the side of the ship to steady himself and looked up, from sea level the castle soared as if to touch the sky.

The clamour of chains unwinding reached them across the water as the castle drawbridge was lowered to receive them. He could not see beyond it, but again he knew he would find not one, but three heavy portcullis guarding this entrance. The ship gently glided to within a few feet of the pier wall. Shouted orders were given, ropes thrown back and forth, and within minutes the vessel was tightly held with gangways placed for passengers and cargo to disembark.

Minutes later he and his manservant stood on the pier, a little unsteady on their feet after spending so much time on a moving deck. The journey by boat should have taken less than a week, but because of gales and unfavourable winds it had taken over twice that long. Now they stood by their belonging, wondering if they should wait to be greeted by someone, or make their own way to the castle, a loud call from behind made their mind up for them.

"Make way there, make way I say"

A sailor rolling a large barrel eyed him as he passed and spoke as if giving an order.

"Don't stand there me' lad. There's work to be done before the tide turns and you'd be right in everyone's way"

Alexis was not used to be spoken to in such a gruff manor, but could not in fairness blame the sailor. He had stayed in his cabin for the whole voyage so his face was unknown to the crew. And he was still wearing the clothes that give no hint of his true station in life.

Chapter 3
The Welcome

Just then men from the castle arrived to help unload the ship. Huggle bid two of them to carry their belonging to the castle. They were reluctant at first until Huggle told them they belonged to the son of a Baron. Then they were only too eager to obey thinking of what could happen to them if they ignored the request. Alexis told Huggle to go with them to make sure their belongings were not touched while he made some inquiries as to their new quarters. He approached one of several guards standing by the drawbridge and asked in a polite tone where new recruits' were meant to go. The soldier looked at him with humour in his eyes, then with a smile on his face turned to his companions

"We've got a proper little gentleman here lads, he even said please"

Another said

"Christ, does the army think this fat little porky would frighten an enemy?"

The soldiers laughed for several seconds, as they gathered round him, one stepped closer to Alexis and felt his tunic

"Nice and soft, just like a woman would wear"

Another thrust out a hand and pinched Alexis on his cheek

"Soft skin too"

Again the soldiers laughed

The one who had touched him winked and said

"Come over here little boy and give us a kiss"

Alexis had always tried to treat people fairly, but these soldiers had dared to act in a disrespectful manor that he had never experienced before, and he did not like it. They had acted above their station and for that he would make them pay. He was just about to make his displeasure known when a shout from the castle entrance brought all the soldiers to attention

"Can't I leave you lot alone for a minute, you are supposed to be guarding the bloody castle, not pissing about with young boys"

The first soldier spoke with laugher in his voice

"He's not a young boy Sergeant, He says he's a new recruit"

The Sergeant stopped in his tracks and shock his head in despair

"Bloody hell, if they get any younger we'll be expected to wipe their asses for them"

He looked at the new recruit as he approached and was clearly not impressed. The youth had a face with three double chins of fat, and a girth twice the size of a normal man. If you had to guess what abilities he might have, a priest or a scholar could be a possibility, but the thought that he could be a warrior would certainly not enter your mind. He shook his head from side to side as he silently came to this conclusion, he doubted it would be worth even *trying* to make a solider out of him.

"Well, I suppose we'll find something you can do, the cooks are always asking for more help, and judging by your girth you must know a lot about food. Do you have a letter of any kind?"

With great effort Alexis held his temper in check as he took from his tunic the letter his father had given him. The soldier unrolled it carefully. He instantly recognized the coat of arms, and could read well enough to know the name of the man who had written it. His eyes opened wide, and without looking up he asked Alexis

"Are you the son on Baron Monrell?"

Alexis nodded.

"Yes I am"

Now the Sergeant spoke with respect in his voice and bowed his head in greeting.

"It is an honour to meet you my lord, you are most welcome. I most humbly apologize for my remarks and the conduct of my men. But you were so well disguised in your manor of dress that we did not recognize you for who you are. Please forgive us my lord, we are but common soldiers and know no better"

He nodded towards the soldiers who had taken the hint from the Sergeant's spoken words and tone of voice and came smartly to attention.

"They're a good lot really,"

Alexis' anger slowly calmed down at the sergeants words of apology. The sergeant pointed to one of the soldiers who had not been involved in any way.

"Escort the young lord to the parade yard"

He made a gesture with his finger to emphasize his next order.

"And make sure he is properly received"

He turned to face Alexis and with another slight bow said

"If you would follow his man up to the parade yard my lord, you'll find the Master-at-arms there who will see to your every need"

Alexis thanked the Sergeant. He was still a little shaken and angry with what had just happened, but due to the sincere sounding apology, he decided it better to forget the incident. As he followed a pace or two behind his guide he reflected that again he had acted in a way that would have caused his father to think him unworthy. At the very least the Baron would have the men flogged. Or if he had really felt offended, he would have instantly killed the one who had dared to touch him in such a manner. But because he was not dressed in his usual fine clothes, and he had not introducing himself by name, he felt that perhaps part of the blame was his. With this thought in mind he was forgiving them without even the threat of punishment. They crossed the drawbridge and through the first open portcullis, and just as his Father had said, there were three of them, each in turn bigger and stronger than the one before.

The remaining solders watched him disappear, one asked

"Who the hell is he Sergeant?"

The sergeant was still looking at the entrance, his helmet in his hand as he mopped the sweat of fear from his brow.

"Only the son of Baron Monrell, Lord of all the lands to the north and east of the river *Yeel*, and one of the wealthiest and most powerful families' in the kingdom. You better pry to the Gods that he holds no grudge against us. Or come morning I'll be back as a private, and you lot will be shovelling shit for the rest of your lives"

He put his helmet back on his head

"That's after we would have had the skin removed from our backs by a good flogging. Some of the old ones' still speak of his father to this day. A Commander of the Kings Guard no less. It is said that he saved the Kings life in battle on more than one occasion. A real hero lads and a fine soldier at a time when soldiers *were* soldiers"

Chapter 4
The New Squire

Alexis knew from his father's teaching that he was in one of only two passages that went from sea level through three hundred cubits of almost solid rock to the castle above. The only light now came from the many oil lamps fixed to the walls every few feet, He touched the stone side as he passed, it was as smooth as smooth could be. Maybe the old saying were right, perhaps they had been made by the Gods. There were steps cut into the floor as it rose in a spiral pattern, the echo of their footsteps followed them as they made their way higher and higher. He judged that they had climbed more than two hundred cubits before he asked his guild to pause for a moment so he could catch his breath. His lack of hard work and abundance of good food meant his body was unprepared for such efforts. As they started their journey again other passages leading off the main one began to appear, each had a heavy steel door, some were open and sounds of people and much activity echoed round the walls from inside. He carried on for another fifty cubits or so before natural light began to appear, and suddenly they were out in an open courtyard of some kind.

The clash of steel on steel filled the air. Row upon rows of men were practicing with swords and shields while others walked up and down the lines constantly shouting instructions.

"Keep your arm straight when you thrust, and put the weight of your shoulder behind the blow"

"YOU THERE!! What the hell do you think you're doing, my fucking GRANDMOTHER could gut you like a fish the way you're holding that shield."

And sometimes the words of instructions were followed by a blow from a thick batten to drive home the point. His guild approached three men standing a little way to the side and saluted

"Sir, I am ordered by my sergeant to introduce the son of Baron Monrell to you, he has come to join us sir"

With another salute he stepped aside.

For Alexis the moment the man had started speaking he had changed from being just another soldier to someone of interest, he spoke with a strange accent that Alexis had never heard before. He tried to see the man's face, but the faceguard of his helmet hid most of his features apart from his eyes. They were keen eyes like those of a hunter, and they were looking directly into his. The middle man of the three bowed his head in greeting.

"You are most welcome my lord, I remember your father well, I was a young recruit when he was Commander of the King's Guard, it will be an honour to have his son server with us"

If he was disappointed with Alexis's appearance in any way it did not show. He turned to one of his companions.

"See that some food and drink is taken at once to his lordships' quarters"

He returned his gauze back to Alexis.

"We have arranged lodging for you in the west wing my lord, we have already sent your servant there so he can prepare for your arrival."

He nodded to the man on his right

"Show Lord Monrell to his quarters"

The man gave Alexis a bow of respect.

"If you would like to follow me my lord I will show you to your rooms"

It felt like they had walked for hours through a maze of passages and Alexis was again becoming short of wind as he struggled to maintain the pace when his guide stopped and opened a heavy wooden door.

"These are your quarter's my lord, and your manservants and squire can lodge next door"

Alexis was casually looking around the room as the man spoke.

"My squire died during my journey here. I would be obliged if you could furnish me with a replacement until my father sends another"

The man bowed, "I will see to it at once my lord"

And with that he left the room. Alexis thankfully sat on the bed to recover from his efforts, it was rough and of poorer quality that what he was used to, but felt comfortable enough to sleep on. After a moments rest he opened a small window and looked out. In two directions he could see as far as the horizon. He just stood there for several minutes enjoying the grandeur of the view, silently thanking the Gods for giving him such a room. He had been afraid that he may have been given quarters in that part of the castle below ground, without normal daylight and fresh air. The adjacent door opened and his servant Huggle entered carrying a suite of his clothes.

"I thought you may want to change into something more suitable my lord"

Alexis nodded

"Thank you Huggle, as usual you look after me well, I will change after I have eaten"

Just as he spoke there was a knock at his door. He nodded to Huggle to open it. Two people stood there, one was a servant holding the promised tray of food and drink. The other was the same soldier who had been his guide. The servant entered first and placed the tray on a small table by the window before bowing and retreated the way he had come. The soldier waited for him to pass, then brought himself smartly to attention.

"If it pleases you my lord, I am to be your new squire"

Again his accent made Alexis curious about this man. The castle of Baron Monrell always had visitors and traders from faraway places, often with skin of different colours and always with different languages, and Alexis thought he knew the sound of them all. He had always prided himself that he could place any man to his homeland just by his accent, but never had he heard anything like this soldier.

"Why were you chosen to be my squire, do you have any knowledge of that position?

"I was not chosen my lord, when I heard you needed a new squire I volunteered. In my homeland I trained many to serve their masters in such a manor"

Alexis asked him where his homeland was, but the soldier could only shake his head

"I do not know my lord, I came to this island as a castaway, all I know is that it must be very far from here, for no one I have met has heard of it"

He said the name of his homeland, but the word meant nothing to Alexis, yet another curiosity about this man to add to his accent. He also had an air about him that conveyed a man of higher standing than a common soldier. Alexis knew from a life worth's of experience that servants would never make eye contact with him when he looked or spoke to them. They would always look down, or to the side, but never at him. But this man did, then he had introduced him to the Master-at-Arms he had made direct eye contact with him, only afterwards did he lower his gaze in a submissive way. Now if he accepted him he would be his squire, with time enough to find out all he wanted to know. After a brief moment Alexis nodded his head

"How are you called?"

"All people find my real name hard to say my lord, so I have been given the name of Halsey"

Alexis nodded, the name of Halsey was very common and widely used.

"Very well, I will accept you for the moment, your knowledge of the castle will be of help to me, as for your worth as a squire, time will tell if you are suitable"

The man bowed his head

"I will try to please my lord in my duties"

"Then I give you your first order, take my manservant Huggle to the kitchens so he can have some decent food and drink"

He waved an arm at his servant

"Go with him Huggle, and wash the foul taste of ships' food from your mouth, I can do without you for an hour or so"

Like his master Huggle was of ample proportions that confirmed his love for good food, so his face lit up with a broad smile, he eagerly nodded his head

"Yes my lord, at once my lord"

Even as he spoke he hurried the new squire through the door, Alexis could hear him urging him on just before the door closed.

"Lead the way Halsey, lead the way, I have a hunger bigger than this castle"

He turned his attention to the meal the servant had brought for him, a good helping of well cooked beef in rich gravy with greens and fresh crusty bread, all to be washed down with a full flagon of ale, he would have preferred wine, but after two weeks of ship food he would not complain.

Chapter 5
To serve the King

The next few weeks were spent getting to know his new surrounding and the routine of the castle. Alexis was one of many sons of nobility serving the King. He soon found that they was not expected to train as other soldiers did, in fact it quickly became clear that nothing of importance was expected from any of them, and their present here was little more than a gesture to tradition. On a lighter note Alexis was also surprised and relived to find that not all the sons of nobility followed the path that Bart had. After a few months at court at least two were almost as plump and unfit as he, while most of the others showed no sign that they would be mighty warriors.

They ate every evening in in the great hall, a place of little comfort with its cold stone floor and long wooden tables. Its walls were covered with banners in various stages of decay, from the very old that were little more than colourless tatters of rags, to the newest with their colours and fabric still bright and intact. They were the banners of all the nobility that had died in the King's service. Alexis knew that if he looked close enough he would find the colours of two of his ancestors hanging among them. The King had stopped attending the suppers a little while ago with an illness that now kept him in his chambers. In place of the King the heir to the throne Prince Robert would dine with them most evening and engage some in polite conversation about their homes and family. Alexis liked him from the first time they meet, he had felt at ease in his company and both had got on well. Now many weeks later he had again been invited to sit next to him during the evening meal.

"The King has bid me to ask about his old companion Baron Monrell, how was the old solider when you left home?"

"In body my father was well your majesty, but in mind he is a sad man"

Alexis told the story of the death of Bart, and how he had trained all his live to be of service to the king.

"Your majesty lost a worthy warrior then he died, he was a much better solider than I will ever be"

The prince shook his head.

"The Gods in their wisdom did not make one path for all to follow, each of us has his own destiny to find. Your brother was to be a warrior, do you know yet what your calling is to be?"

Alexis replied that he organized the day to day running of the castle along with all provisions, and controlled the finances of his fathers' estates.

Prince Robert was openly impressed that a Darosi should wish to undertake such duties, and even more so that one so young was equal to such a difficult task.

"For some time I have had to oversee those same tasks myself. The last man who successfully carried out those duties carelessly allowed a wild boar to have him for supper rather than the other way around. And those who have followed him have found the task not to their liking"

He sipped his wine slowly as if in deep thought for a moment before continuing

"I think you are the solution to a problem that has vexed me for some time. The royal affairs take most of my time, so there is little to spare for such matters. These duties cry out for someone to give them more care than I can offer, and every day they bring endless new disputes that even the Gods could not solve. So my young lord, as from this moment I make you a minister of the crown, and I order you to perform the same duties for the King as you did for your father. He took another sip of wine and looked down at the other sons of nobility, unable to totally hide his disapproval of their conduct. They were noisily eating and drinking their fill with enthusiasm, and seem quite content with their life of idleness.

"You will be a rarity among us, someone who came to serve the king and is actuality doing something worthwhile, rather than just sitting around doing nothing…… like some of your kind"

Alexis nodded his head in reply

"You do me a great honour your majesty, I am not sure that I worthy of the post, but I will try my best. I will start my duties tomorrow morning"

Prince Robert made an open gesture with his hand,

"It will be an easy start for you, all the harvests have been gathered in long ago, and now that deep winter is upon us nothing of note will happen until the spring, it is then your real duties will start"

The prince held his goblet of wine and offered it as a toast to Alexis

"You are truly one of a rare breed my young lord. The kingdom has plenty of men who only want to swing a sword, but precious few who are interested in bring order out of chaos. I wish that if someday I do reign it will not be soldiers by my side, but men like you, because that will mean the kingdom is at peace"

Chapter 6
The Castle

True to his word, the next morning Alexis began the task Robert had set him. He had Halsey to show him around those parts of the castle that normally he would never visit, and for the first time he began to realize just how much was inside the mountain. There were many passages and spaces, some big enough to gather and feast in. Man had made some small alterations, but they were no more than cosmetic and did not go beyond a few heavy steel or wooden doors with some bolt holes to fire out at attacking enemies. They started at the lowest level of all, and Alexis had the biggest surprised thus far. A large cavern, so big he could not judge its true size in the poor light and filled with water. Several men passed them leading asses loaded with barrels of water. Halsey answered Alexi's unasked question.

"They never stop my lord, they trudge up and down these passages all the day long to keep the castle supplied. Halsey filled a cup and offered it to him, Alexis took a small sip, it tasted clean and fresh.

"This water is as sweet as I have ever tasted, where does it come from?"

Halsey pointed to the rocks,

"From the castle itself my lord, it is rain that fell in the past and slowly made its way to this cavern"

As to prove his point they stood in silence for a moment and out of the darkness Alexis could hear the cascade of water falling on water. Alexis asked how deep it was, but Halsey shook his head

"I do not know, but it is much deeper than a man is tall, and no matter if summer or winter the water is always the same to the touch"

They moved on, all the other passages on this level and the next one up were set aside as storerooms, some were empty while others held vast amounts of the thousand and one items need to maintain the castle. Then higher up were the quarters of all who serviced the castle, and above them the soldiers who lived permanently in the castle to guard it. All the accommodation above ground level was reserved for visitors of importance and nights of the King. He was most impressed the first time he stood on the high ramparts. It was not hard to see why the castle had never fallen in battle. The high walls give an uninterrupted view as far as the horizon over the mainly flat countryside. It was dotted with many small farm houses, which in turn were surrounded by many fields, they were mostly bare now, but come spring would be full of colour depending on the type of crops planted. Away to his right was the fishing village he had seen the first misty morning he'd arrived. Now in the clear light of day it looked much bigger than he had first thought, more like a small town than a village. He pointed to several building of substance a little way inland.

"What are those Halsey?"

"They are the stables my lord, only one or two horses are kept in the castle, all the others are kept there."

Alexis could see the logic in keeping the horses on dry land, it would be much easier to feed and keep then fit, there was nowhere for them to have a good gallop in the castle. He pointed to other building a little further to the left.

"And those?"

"That is where the rest of the permanent army of the king are barracked my lord, not many, perhaps less than five hundred men. In normal times they are garrisoned there, in times of unrest they would all live inside the castle"

Alexis was surprised at such a small number.

"I expected the King to have more men"

Halsey shook his head.

"In peace the number is more than enough. In times of unrest if more soldiers are needed they come from the private armies of the Barons and other nobility who are pledged to server the King, at the moment many are far to the west fighting with Prince William"

Further away and to the side were what appeared to be collections of ramshackle building thrown together without any skill or care. Smoke rose from a multitude of chimneys to show they were occupied. Again the question was asked, Halsey's reply surprised him.

"They are the homes of the wife's and families of the soldiers, they live there to be near their husbands."

He gently tappet the ramparts' as a show of displeasure before continuing.

"The Darosi do not see it as their duty to provide them with proper quarters, and the soldiers pay is so poor they cannot always afford proper lodgings. This is the result, they are forced to live where they can"

Alexis felt a pang of despair inside, most of these people were descendants from the ordinal Darosi who landed on these shores hundreds of years ago, but now such is the arrogance of the nobility that they are treated little better than the outsiders. Alexis give a sigh of sadness, why must ordinary people be treated in such a shabby way? He was disappointed that the Kings' horses were deemed more worthy to have a decent roof over their heads than the wives' and children of his soldiers. He made a mental note in his mind that if he could even do something to correct the situation he would.

Alexis returned his attention to the layout of the land from a defenders point of view, and even to his non-military eye it was as near to perfect as could be. Any forces moving to attack the castle could be seen miles away. He looked over the edge of the battlements, from this height of four or five hundred cubits the causeway below looked very small with only a few feet showing. With the tide coming in the part that reached to the shore was completely submerged under several feet of water, another advantage for the defenders. It meant that to have any chance of success from land the castle could only be attacked for the few hours when the tide was out. Any attackers would also be under a torrent of arrows and other missiles thrown at them from a great distance and height. It would be many minutes before they would be close enough to return fire, and even then there would be little they could have done to harm the people inside. The castle was so high and far from the shore that it was out of reach of most if not all the weapons of war. No one had dared attack it in living memory, and whoever held the castle, held the throne. His present sovereign was King Eric of Tierees, He had ruled for many years, and when future history judged him he would be remember as a good King who taxed his subjects lightly and did not interfered in their daily lives, unlike many of his kind.

Alexis followed the ramparts round until he faced the sea. There were two towers large than any others, and both towers were joined at their base by a large garden. Alexis asked who lived in them, Halsey pointed to the taller one on the right first.

"All of the upper floors are the Kings private quarters and sleeping chambers, the ones directly below are where Prince Robert and the Princess Livia live. The lower levels of the smaller tower along with the garden are reserved for the Princess Aquilia and other ladies of the court. They do not attend the feasts in the great hall, but have their own place to eat, and only leave their living quarters on special occasions. The upper levels belong to Prince William, along with a very privilege few. I have been here over two years and have only seen Princess Aquilia once"

Alexis first looked at the larger tower of the King. The family Tierees had held the reins of power for many generations. Six royal banners hung in the great hall, each remembering a king now dead. And rumours' that he had heard since his arrival said there would soon be another. King Eric was now an old man, his health slowly in decline. It was clear that sometime in the not too distant future there would be another to whom they would have to pay homage.

Next Alexis looked at the Princess Aquilia tower with more interest. It seemed strange to find a garden of all things high up in the middle of a castle. Some movement among the greenery caught his eye. A few of the ladies were taking a stroll around their green oases. They were too far away so see their faces clearly, but one had long golden hair, a rare colour amongst the Darosi, and mainly found only in those of royal blood. Her hair made her stand out clearly from the others. Alexis immediately felt a degree of desire for her. She walked with a grace and elegance that in his mind could only come from youth and beauty. He stood and watched with a smile on his face as she completed her walk and disappeared back inside. He stood in silence for several seconds. It was suddenly very important to him to find out all he could about her. For a moment his imagination formed a picture of both of them together as if they were lovers. He shook his head in denial, he could never be that lucky, still, he could dream, and who knows what the future holds. Alexis made a small grunt as his moment of daydreaming ended. He turned to look out over the land again, he spent several seconds scanning the horizon.

"In which direction is the port of Egion?"

Halsey pointed far off to the left

"Over that way my lord, you cannot see it from here, it is on the other side of that range of hills on the horizon, but you can just see the hamlet of Greenfield, just to the right of the low ridges in the middle distance. Egion is just a few leagues further on. When I came here two years ago Greenfield was just a single farm with a small alehouse to one side. Now the towns and hamlets grows so fast I think that soon one of them will reach to the gates of this castle"

Alexis nodded his head, now he knew in which direction to look he could just make out the faint outline of building in the far distance.

"I see it, I must go to Egion soon, I promised my younger sister that I would send her some imported lace from Akrei for her birthday"

Chapter 7
The Changing Kingdom

The Darosi had never made good sailors, their world had always been that of the land, so at first there were no ports anywhere on the island. It was only when they had begun trading with other kingdoms that the need for them arose. At first all of them were small, little more the a few wooden piers where ships could unload their cargo, so they attracted little interest from the Darosi. Then almost overnight the trade with the northlands increased many times over, this brought more and more ships and sailors to Santross. Soon the sea fronts were full of many taverns which quickly grew rich by catered for all their needs, but still most Darosi lords paid them little heed. Their eyes were firmly set on their estates that produced the food. Over a very short space of time the ports grew to become more powerful and prosperous than the lords who owned them. Now when it was too late to act some Darosi lords tried to take back control of them. In the reign of King Leavos Lord Tambar had tried to increase his wealth by levying higher taxes on the port of Histria. The people refused to pay such a large sum, so he threatened to burn the port down. The people quickly banded together and hired an army of Darosi Knights and mercenaries big enough to defeat him. Afterwards the port simply added the lands of the now dead lord to their own. No Darosi had dared try to impose a large tax on any port since.

Because Egion had been blessed with a safe and deep harbour it had grown from being a small fishing village to a major port as quickly as a boy could grow to a man. It was said that with enough money there was nothing a man could not buy there. It was also another good example of the way Santross was changing. When the people from Gottan had first arrived to Santross, the Darosi had been equal to them in number, now the population of the Kingdom had increased many times over, while the numbers of Darosi had not. With the outsiders now greatly outnumbering them, it was inevitably that the power of the Darosi grew less as they slowly ceased to be a major part of the population. But the biggest threat to Darosi numbers came not from the outsiders, but from the Darosi themselves. The smallest of insults, whether real or imaginary would often end in a fight to the death. Another weakness was their love of gambling, and the boastfulness of their character. This meant that sometimes they would make reckless wagers with money they did not have. The result was that many lords now walked the land as paupers, when once they walked their castle ramparts. Others were so heavily in debt from overspending that any income was welcome, no matter how it was earned. Alexis sometimes despaired at his own people. The Darosi were slowly being whittled away, and it was the Darosi themselves who were doing most of the whittling. They were less in numbers now than years ago, and without a doubt would be even fewer in the future. His big fear was that the Darosi may already be too weak to successful defend the Kingdom. The warlike tribes of Kmaree just a few days sailing away to the north had looked at Santross with envy for many years. In the rein of King Sennon they had sent an army to conquer the island kingdom. But the Darosi had been warned of where and when they were coming and had set a trap for them. The result was that the invasion had failed. Most of the enemy soldiers had died as soon as they had come ashore. To press home their advantage the Darosi in turn invaded the north and killed the troublesome King Sennon who had tried to conquer them. His son in return for sparing his life had agreed to stop all raids on Santross. That was many years ago, and the man who had made that promise had long ceased to be of this world. Now the threat of invasion from the north was growing again. Their armies became stronger with each passing year. Some time ago the raids had begun again, slowly at first, but grew more frequent and daring with each passing year. Now even towns and hamlets away from the coast lived in daily fear of the men from the north. It could only be a matter of time before they again tried a full-scale invasion.

After this appointment as a minster to the King, Alexis and Prince Robert sat together on many evening as their friendship grew. Their conversations would last the whole evening covering many subjects. Robert would tell him in some detail of his hopes and plans if or when he should become King. Alexis could see the wisdom in his words. He was a man of great passion, and perhaps more importantly for a King to be, a man of great compassion. They found a great deal of common ground between themselves. Both held views that went against many of the customs and teaching of the more traditional Darosi, and both feared for the future of their race. They knew that change had to happen, but neither knew how this change could come about. On one occasion Alexis mention the slavery that the Darosi of the west imposed on the outsiders as a suitable example of one of the evils that must end, but Robert disagreed.

"I think maybe that would be a step too far. Let sleeping dogs laid my lord, it has been so for hundreds of years, and in a way the outsiders are rewarded for their efforts, we keep them safe from harm and there are more important issues to resolve"

They both agreed however that the kingdom was trapped in the past. From the time the Darosi had made the outsiders bend to their wishes they had rejected progress in all its forms. Now almost every part of their lives was governed by rituals, some of which went back to the old kingdom. Society had also stagnated, in the old kingdom a Darosi had to prove himself in battle before he became a leader. Now those who ruled Santross passed on their titles from father to son, and it did not matter how inept the son proved to be. Even the Darosi themselves could no longer rise in rank, a common solder must stay a common solder to matter how great his abilities were. On the other side of the coin, no matter how talented and able an outsider proved to be, he was still an outsider and could never rise above his station in life. On a lighter note, Alexis was also surprised by Robert displaying a mischievous sense of humour, an emotion that was totally absent from most Darosi. As he came to trust Alexis's discretion this part of his character came more to the fore. He would often act and gesture in a manor you would not expect from a person who would someday be king. Alexis would discover with time that this made him disliked by many. In their eyes he was too flippant in his attitude and paid too little respect for the honour and tradition that was expected from a King.

King Eric had many daughters, but Robert and his brother William were his only sons. The boys were not identical twins, but when they were young many could not tell one from the other. The confusion ended when William had fallen from a tree. The accident left him with a small scar down one side of his face that would remain with him for life.

Some years before Robert had married the beautiful Lady Livia, so far he had been blessed with three daughters but no heir to the throne, an issue that grew more serious as the years pasted. William had spent most of his adult life fighting with the army. He had fought many times and had never lost a battle. Along the way he had also found time to sire several children, but without the legitimacy of marriage they would have no rightful claim to the throne. He was away at the moment with part of the army lying siege to a troublesome lord's castle who had attacked neighbouring estates and refused to pay homage and taxes to the crown. The thought came to Alexis that in many ways the relationship between the two Princes was similar to the one that had existed between Bart and himself, only on a higher level. Like him, Prince Robert was the organizer, who ran and controlled the kingdom on behalf of his father the King. And like Bart, Prince William was a soldier, whose sword dealt with those who would destroy it. The birth of the princes was so well known and dramatic that it had entered the folklore of the nation. The night they were born the lives of two Queens were lost. First to die was their mother, the Queen Alaine, she gave her life in exchange for theirs, and within moments the mother of the king, Queen Helois had also joined her in death.

Chapter 8
Halsey

Now with Halsey in his company every day he gently probed the man about his background, and slowly his knowledge increase. Halsey had been many things in his life, as a young boy his family had been killed, and he had been sold into slavery to a blacksmith where all day he pumped the bellows to draw the fire. After only two summers his master had been killed when a warlord destroyed the settlement where he lived. He had only saved his life by hiding from the attackers before running away. He had spent all his youth and early manhood in a holy place and learned the ways of the priests. He would have been content to spend the rest of his life there, but again the horrors of war had found him. The monastery was destroyed and many of the priests killed and again he had to flee to save his life. Using the skills the priests had taught him he became a bodyguard to anyone who would pay for his services.

Eventually he joined a band of traders as one of the many guards they employed to defend them on their travels. After he had proved his courage and honesty on several occasions, one of the traders who had become too old to travel had offered him a partnership. After a year or so the old man had died and he took over the business himself. For the next ten years good fortune and a willingness to travel further and seek harder than anyone else made him one of the wealthiest men in his Kingdom. But soon he became bored with a life of ease and sought a new challenge. At heart he was still a trader and had heard of a cloth rich in many colures and so fine and smooth that it flowed through your fingers like water. It was to be found many miles away in a land beyond the Sea-of-Red. He became obsessed with finding this prize and hired a ship and a crew to look for it. At first the winds had been favourable and they made good progress. But then a great storm blew down on them for several days and carried the ship many miles off course. Their voyage ended on the rocks of Santross. Once again the Gods had smiled upon him and he was the only one to survive. He managed to find a few items that washed ashore from the wreck, but nothing of great value. All the gold and precious gems he had brought with him for trade now belonged to the sea. Penniless, he had eventually come to Castle Kingshome and became a soldier of the King. His reasoning was that any visitor from a foreign land would come to pay his respects to the King. And perhaps one of them could ether be from his homeland, or know how to return there. There was one question Alexis was particularly keen to know the answer of. He asked him why he volunteered to be his squire, and for once Halsey give him an answer freely.

"Because on the day we met you proved to me that you were a just and honourable man"

Alexis shook his head in bewilderment.

"How so, what did I do than made you think of me in such a way?"

"The soldiers at the gate my lord, they are my friends. I was afraid they could be in very serious trouble for the way they had mocked you. When I took you to the Master-at-arms I expected you to at least give orders for them to be flogged for the disrespect they showed you. But you said nothing. You accepted that part of the misunderstanding was due to your appearance. No other lord I have met would have acted in such a fair manor"

Alexis shrugged his shoulders

"Yes, I remember it well, it was the fact that I was dressed as I was made me decide to overlook their conduct"

Halsey continued

"You are unlike all the others of your kind my lord. You are fair in your dealing with others, even if they are of lower rank. While all of those you call nobility are anything but noble in their thoughts and deeds. They are arrogant with no thought or care for others, and are not well liked my lord. Later when you asked for a squire, I saw a chance where we could both profit. I offered myself as a reward for your kindness in sparing my friends. And as your squire I became closer to any person that might help me to return to my homeland"

Alexis was embarrassed by Halsey's less than favourable opinion about the Darosi. But he respected his honesty in saying so. And he had said nothing new. He had known for almost all his life the true thoughts of the people towards his own kind, but had paid little attention to them.

Halsey went on

"Do you remember your first order to me?"

Alexis shook his head

"No, I was tired and out of sorts after my journey here"

"The first order you give was to see that your servant had a good meal. Only a man of honour and caring for others would act in such a way. You treat people as fellow humans being, and not as slaves. For such a man I can serve for as long as I remain here"

It pleased Alexis that he had been right to think of Halsey as more than just a common soldier. If they had met in his homeland it would have been as men of equal standing. This made the fact that he was being used as little more than a stepping stone easier for him to accept. It was what Halsey thought of him as a man that hit home the hardest. There was a core of truth in his words. He had known from a young age that he lacked the arrogance of his father and brothers. They believed it was their birth right to be the masters and treat others as they wished. While he believed it better to treat all people in a fair manor. Halsey admired him for the very same qualities that his father had used to condemn him. To Baron Monrell, the most important duties that any member of nobility could perform were to rule with an iron hand. To live his life with honour, and fight in battle with courage. For him, this was the highest accolade that any man could achieve, and it was of little important if you lost your life doing so. In his eyes Bart had been a true Darosi with the courage to be a soldier. He was ready to die in battle if it was to be his fate, a true member of nobility. To act in any other way marked you as unfit to be called Darosi.

Alexis remembered what Prince Robert had said the night they had dined together that the Gods in their wisdom did not make one path for all to follow, and that each of us had to find his own destiny. His words summed it up better than he could. Up until now he had tried to be the kind of man his father wished, but his efforts to do so had only brought him a life of sadness and inter turmoil. Now he must find the courage to be his own man. From this day forward he must live his life according to his own conscience and sense of justice, and not try to be a shadow of his Father. With the decision made, for the first time he could remember he felt at ease with himself. They say that in life, when one door closes, another one opens, and so it had been with Alexis. Because his family had shunned him so much in his childhood he had been blessed with an education that give him more knowledge and a much broader outlook of life than normal for a person of his position. He did not know it when, but such an education in time would be a great help to him and the Kingdom of Santross.

Chapter 9
Egion

A few weeks into his new post Alexis had all of his duties in order and up to date, the only supplies the castle was receiving at the moment came by sea. Later when the royal estates began to produce his job would become much more time consuming, but for the moment he was free to do as he wished. He decided it was time that he and Halsey paid his planned visit to Egion. It was a sunny morning and not too cold when they set out, the road was clearly marked and for the most part flat and easy to travel along. Without tiring their horses too much, they arrived there by late afternoon. Alexis was amazed at the number of people still milling about on the streets. To him they seemed to number in the thousands and he joked to Halsey that there were not enough houses in the whole kingdom to accommodate all of them. His joke almost turned out to be the truth as they searched in vain for lodging for the night. Finally they found an inn with spare rooms, and it turned out to be a great disappointment in every way. The only outstanding memory about the place was the cost. The meat in their evening meal was badly cooked and full of gristle, and the ale was as flat as the road they had travelled on that day. As they finished their meal, Alexis looked around at the other people eating, some were dressed in clothes little better than rags. In view of the high cost of his lodging he wondered how they could afford to pay such prices. He came to the conclusion that they were either richer than they looked, or he had been grossly overcharged, he quickly decided it was the latter. He smiled as he made a promise to himself that next time he came he would again dress as a commoner, his clothes would not fit or look so well, but he was sure the price would be much cheaper. The next morning they searched for the lace from Akrei that Alexis had promised his sister. Now in the light of day it was even more crowded, and each street they travelled down was lined with merchants selling everything a man could want. The bustle and noise was so great it soon made his head ache. There were many gold and silversmiths with necklaces and all kind of jewellery, and all offering their wares to anyone they thought rich enough to buy them.

"Gold, gold, the finest in the land, look how it sparkles in the light. No woman could refuse you if you give her such a gift"

He held a chain out to Alexis

"For the one you love sir" and with a wink of his eye added "Or perhaps the one you would *wish* to love you"

They could not move more than a few feet without being accosted by traders trying to sell them something.

"Come buy my cloth, the finest in the kingdom, try it sir, feel the quality, I can see you are a man of great taste and importance sir, so for you I give a very special price just for today"

It was the same everywhere, and so crowded you could walk at a shuffling pace or be constantly bumping into others. Street after street were all the same, but then Halsey spotted something that was of interest to him. He handed a small amount of the black tarry substance to Alexis.

"I know of this my lord, we call it "Ah-pen-yen" where I come from, but most call it opium. If you take a small amount it can ease any pain, and makes you feel happy and well, even if you are not"

Alexis laughed as he handed it back to him.

"Perhaps one day when I am old and full of aches I will use it"

It took the rest of the morning, but finally Alexis found what he was looking for at a price that was only just short of robbery. They stayed at another inn that night on the edge of town, but it was no better than the first, and cost even more. It was a deeply thoughtful Alexis that rode away from his first visit to a town of this size. The next morning he opened the window of his bedroom and took a deep breath. The air smelled sweet after that of the town, where one street would smell of exotic spices, while the next would have the stink of rotten cabbage. He wondered if all towns smelled the same, or if it was just Egion. He looked out over the castle ramparts with contentment, this was his world, and this was where he belonged. A much different place to the one he had just visited, but in his heart he feared that this world could easily disappear. It was as if there were now two kingdoms on Santross, the new kingdom of Egion and all the other towns like it, and the old kingdom of the Darosi. If they did not join, then one must triumph over the other, and he feared it would not be the Darosi who survived. The days when a man only needed his sword to rule over all others were coming to an end. Power in the future would belong to those who commanded and made use of all the resources of Santross. It must not just include the few thousands Darosi, but the towns and outsiders as well. All must join to make the kingdom as one, a strong kingdom free from the threat of invasion.

Alexis shook his head in despair, his father and all others of his kind would never think like that. They were rooted too deeply in the traditions of the past. And although they did not yet know it, too few in numbers to have any hope of controlling the future, even if they tried. The Darosi might still own large stretches of land, but they only held the land by tradition. If the people rose against them, they would be brushed aside as easy as a handful of dust. He had seen more people in his short visit to Egion than lived in half the kingdom of Darosi. And Egion was only one town, there were many others almost as big. There was *one* positive result to his visit, he had remained true to his word, and on her birthday his sister Akantha received enough Lace to trim a dozen dresses and half a dozen veils.

Chapter 10
Safe Return

A week after their return the castle was suddenly filled with excitement, a rider had raced ahead of the army to bring the news that Prince Williams had completed his mission and was returning home. The troublesome lord would trouble no more, unless he could find a way to do so without his head. A week later Prince William appeared at the castle causeway riding at the head of a tired looking column of men, Prince Robert rode out to greet him, and both men embraced before riding back across the causeway. That night in the great hall, a great feast had been arranged in honour of their safe return. But before the celebrations began, a sombre tribute was paid to those who had died in battle, and six more banners joined the others hanging on the wall. Alexis shook his head in despair, another six of their number lost, and that was without counting any from their former foe. Their estates would be pasted onto their heirs, but there always seemed to be at least one lord who died without issue. His estate would quickly disappear, either to the Money Leaders if he own debts, or to the strongest of his neighbours who would claim the land for their own.

But the mood changed and the dead quickly forgotten when the wine began to flow freely, and the music and dancing carried on at a reckless pace. The two princes sat at the high table, and for the first time Alexis saw the Princess Aquilia, she was the oldest of the Kings daughters and had almost as much influence in royal matters as the King himself. She had married an Earl who had been a Commander in the Kings Guard, soon after the marriage a fever had taken his life and she had never remarried. She was the only daughter still living in the castle and was rarely seen outside her chambers. Now she spent most of her time attending to her father the king. Many said of all Eric's daughters she had been the most beautiful, and seeing her for the first time Alexis agreed that although well past the first flush of youth, she still had the looks and dignity worthy of a princess. The return of the army marked this as one of those very special occasions when she consented to join in the festivities. Next to her was the Princes Livia, and further along the table sat the ladies of the court who attended the princesses. At the end of the table sat a beautiful young girl with gold colour hair wearing a blue dress. Alexis immediately remembered her from her walk in the tower garden. He had been taken by the elegant way she moved and the colour of her hair. Now seeing her close up her beauty took his breath away, and for the first time in his life Alexis had trouble controlling his manhood. He could not take his eyes off her. Lord Ashdown was sitting next to him, and quickly noticed his interest. He nudged Alexis with his elbow.

"Isn't she a beauty, I am to marry her in the summer, and best of all she is rich, very rich. We have already agreed a dowry and she has consented to the match"

He laughed in a jolly way that made his ample stomach shake like a branch in a gale.

"A good wench beneath me and money in my pocket, what more could a man ask for?"

Alexis bit his lip, he had just found the girl of his dreams, only to find she was already pledged to another. Now that he had started on his favourite subject Lord Ashdown could not stop talking about her.

"We have met several times, and on more than one occasion I have arranged for our chaperon to be otherwise engaged"

He tapped the end of his nose with a finger to hint that something underhanded had taken place.

"And I found the lady very obliging to my touch"

Again his finger touched his nose as he roared with laughter.

Alexis was shocked, he had never thought that a lady of breeding was capable of an indiscretion before a marriage had taken place. Again he looked at what had been the object of his desire until just a few moments ago. She looked so pure, so innocent that he would never have thought she was capable of acting in such a manner. Lord Ashdown used his napkin to remove a drop of gravy from his tunic that had escaped his lips.

"Her wealth and her looks are a rare find, come sir, do you not agree she is a beauty?"

Alexis sadly nodded his head in agreement.

"Yes my lord, you are a very lucky man, I wish that I may be so lucky when I seek a bride"

Ashdown took a large bite out of a chicken breast before he went on.

"Tis a match made in heaven my lord, I could never resist a good looking woman with hair as black as night"

Again a nudge with his elbow followed by a roar of laughter that lasted many seconds before he added.

"Especially a rich one"

Alexis took a moment to fully understand what had just been said. He looked again at the high table where the ladies sat, and next to the girl of his desire sat a much older woman in a green dress of the same kind of proportions as Lord Ashdown, and with shiny black hair. He decided to make sure he had heard right

"And I like the colour of her dress my lord, it is a very pleasant shade of blue"

Lord Ashdown made a sound of displeasure.

"Blue, did you say blue my lord. I fancy you have had too much to drink already. The dress is green sir, and I should know, I bought it."

He added quickly

"With her money of course"

Another laugh that made his belly shake like a jelly.

Alexis had a smile on his face as he answered

'Of course my lord, I meant to say green, a slip of the tongue, I must have been distracted by the lady sitting next to the love of your life"

Lord Ashdown wiped the tears of laughter from his eyes.

"What was that you said, the lady in the blue dress?"

He looked again at the high table and studied her for a brief moment.

"What, that slip of a girl?"

He grunted to show his lack of interest.

"No my lord, she is not to my taste, far too small and skinny."

He paused to take another bite of chicken before continuing.

"I like to feel a woman of substance beneath me, and she is all bone and no meat. With her it would be like lying on a log. And narrow hips, just look at them, narrow hips are no good in a woman, they hinder childbearing.

He emptied his cup of wine before adding.

"Mark my words, take a woman of substance for your wife, they make for a comfortable ride, and in bed they have warn feet on a winters evening"

Again a roar of laughter with a banging of a fist on the table that made all the wine glasses near to jump. Alexis smile again.

"As you say my lord, the hips are too narrow"

Chapter 11
Lord Ravenhead

With the thought of how easy it would be to lose her, he was more determined than ever to first find out who she was, and secondly to make her his wife. After the meal and before the heavy drinking began to take effect both the Princesses left the hall, and the objects of both their desires left with them. Soon after they left Prince William began to show the twin effects of the huge amounts of wine he had drunk, and the long tiring journey he had made and appeared to fall into a drunken sleep. Prince Robert sipped his wine slowly as he watched the festivities with a sober eye. Alexis was now standing with a few of the others lords drinking and listening to tales of the battles just fought when one of the dancers jolted his arm, his wine showered the man sitting just in front of him. He jumped up and turned to Alexis, his face and voice full of anger. He was a mountain of a man, big even by Darosi standards and towered over the much shorter Alexis by two hands or more.

"You bumbling oaf, this tunic is made of the finest cloth, you will pay twice the cost of it, once to buy another, and as much again for your sloppy manners"

His tone upset Alexis, who shook his head in denial.

"It was but an accident sir, my arm was jolted by a dancer, but to keep the peace I will pay for another"

The offer did not calm the man's temper

"You will do more than just pay for another, you common cur"

He raised his arm to strike Alexis but the booming voice of Prince Robert stopped him in mid stroke.

"Do not strike the blow Lord Ravenhead, there has been enough violence in the Kingdom of late to satisfy even a warrior like you. What has this man done to deserve such anger?"

Lord Ravenhead held his wine splattered tunic for all to see.

"Look your majesty, this fat oaf threw wine over me, he insults me and I demand satisfaction"

Prince Robert asked Alexis if this was true

Alexis shook his head in denial

"No your majesty it was but an accident, I meant no insult, someone bumped into me from behind causing the wine to spill"

Prince Robert asked if anyone saw this.

Lord Ashdown who has been standing next to Alexis raised his hand.

"I saw it all your majesty, it was as young Lord Monrell said, nothing more than an accident. In the excitement of the evening his arm was jostled from behind causing the wine to spill"

Prince Robert nodded his head

"There you have it Lord Ravenhead, the deed was not meant, your honour has not been insulted. Now I command you to put your anger away, I will not tolerate any violence tonight"

He held his arms out wide

"Let the feasting continue, for tonight I command everyone to celebrate the success of our troops and their safe return"

His words brought a great cheer from all present, and the music and dancing started again with even more vigour than before.

But not all cheered, Lord Ravenhead was still angry at the tipping of the wine, and even angrier that this fat idiot had caused Prince Robert to rebuke him in front of so many. He strove out of the hall still clearly in a foul mood. Alexis thanked Lord Ashdown for his support as he watched Lord Ravenhead leaving. Lord Ashdown had a worried look on his face as he touched his arm

"In Lord Ravenhead I fear you have made the worst possible enemy in the entire kingdom Lord Monrell. He is from the west, and like many from that part of the kingdom he is eager and willing to make enemies of anyone he dislikes"

Alexis watch him disappear through the entrance of the hall.

"Surly he would not seek my life for such a minor incident"

Lord Ashdown shook his head as he replied.

"I fear he will, most people at court try to avoid him due to his quick temper and his willingness to shed other people's blood. You would not have been the first to die by his hand. I am certain he will not forget tonight and even now may be planning his revenge against you. You would be wise to walk with friends and carry your sword by your side from tonight onwards"

Alexis remembered the wild look in his eyes as he was about to strike him, and for the first time in his life he had felt fear, and then he became angry with himself for feeling the fear. Could he be the coward his father had always condemned him for? He had never thought of himself as a coward, but there again his life had never been in danger before. He returned to his quarters that night in a sombre mood, afraid of the future, and afraid of the fear that may live inside him. Even the large amount of wine he had drunk could not bring a good night's sleep. He woke the next morning still tired and in a foul mood. Before sleep had finally come Alexis had resolved to learn how better to defend himself, tomorrow he would go to the practice yard and spend an hour or two with his sword.

Chapter 12
Childhood Memories Returns

Huggle had been Alexis servant long enough to know his ways well, but he had never seen his master in this kind of mood before.

"What troubles you my lord, you seem out of sorts today?"

But he got no direct reply, but as Alexis ate his breakfast he asked Huggle to send Halsey to him.

"Tell him I have need of his services"

Minutes later Halsey stood before him

"You sent for me my lord?"

Alexis nodded his head

"I have decided to improve my sword skills Halsey, we will spend some time in practice each day from now on."

Halsey had not known Alexis for long, but it was long enough to know that his master was troubled in some way, but he held his peace and said nothing.

So a daily ritual was establish, each day for an hour or so in the yard below Alexis would practice sword play with Halsey. It took a great effort from Alexis to hold a wooded sword in his hand after so many years. Even now as a man the memories of the pain suffered in childhood would sometimes return to haunt him. The squire proved to be a good teacher and knowledgeable in the art, and Alexis improved a little with each day. If they had been given enough time Alexis would have become a good swordsman, but fate decreed otherwise. Less than two weeks into the training a familiar figure approached them, it was Lord Ravenhead.

"So the young pup has decided to learn how to defend yourself, you would have profited more if you learned to drink wine instead of throwing it over innocent people. Come, let us see how you perform with a sword in your hand instead of a glass"

He took a wooden sword from a nearby rack and pushing Halsey aside immediately attacked Alexis with blows of power. Thanks to his new found skill Alexis parried the first blows, but it could not last. As soon as he began to tire blow after blow found their mark. He was a seven year old child again, taking a beating, and come the morning his body would show where every blow had landed. His defence was now in tatters as a heavy hit to his sword arm made him drop his weapon, followed by one even heavier to the head that brought him almost to his knees. And Lord Ravenhead laughed and clearly enjoyed each time he struck home. The torture would have gone on but for the intervention of the Master-at-arms. He stepped between them and with a simple flick of his wrist parried Lord Ravenhead's sword aside.

"That is enough Lord Ravenhead, the wooded sword should be used only to practice the art of swordsmanship, not used as if a stick to beat someone with"

Lord Ravenhead reluctantly took a step backwards, even though he was a lord, it would not be wise to make an open enemy of this man. His skill as a swordsman was best not to be challenged. Of a greater worry was the respect and unshakable loyalty that all the soldiers in the castle held for him. Many would willing do his bidding without question, and for someone as hated as he that could be a danger. In the dark of night a knife does not care whose throat it cuts, even one that belonged to a lord.

He gave a loud grunt of satisfaction as he threw the wooden sword to the ground and walked away with a swagger in his step. He had set out to gain revenge, and he had. His only regret was the sword was made of wood, not steel, but next time the young pup may not be so lucky. The Master-at-arms watched him go before turning to Halsey.

"You best help your master to his quarters, and get him to soak in a hot bath, it will take away some of the pain"

Halsey helped the injured Alexis back to their quarters. He lay on his bed with a sigh of relief. The beating had been so bad that it three days before he could stand and walk again. And for all of those long three days the anger grew inside him until there was no room left for fear. He had once made himself a promise that if anyone inflicted a beating on him again he would seek revenge, and he meant to keep that promise. Lord Ravenhead now became the prime object of hate in his life. He would someday repay him in full for the pain and humiliation he had caused, not only for now, but for all his childhood beating too. And he did not care what the price of revenge would be, even if it was to be his life.

But revenge was not the only thought on his mind, he remembered something that Halsey had said when he first became his squire. It was early afternoon when he confronted him

"When you offered to be my squire you said you did it as a form of reward to me, do you remember?"

Halsey nodded his head

"Yes my lord, I remember"

"So why do you consider yourself worthy to be a reward for sparing your friends?"

Halsey shrugged his shoulders

"Because the holy men taught me ways to attack and defend myself in a manner that no one in this kingdom could counter"

Now it was Alexis turn to shrug his shoulders

"They could not defend themselves well enough to save their lives"

"That is true my lord, but their teaching were meant to protect them from robbers and bandits. Alas it was no defence against an army with arrows and battering rams. But they did not die alone, many times their number also passed with them into the next world that day."

Halsey could see Alexis was still not convinced, in the corner of the room was Alexis's wooden practice sword.

He handed it to him and Alexis reluctantly took the offered weapon.

"Come my lord, you know only too well the harm a wooded sword can do, I will be unarmed, try to strike me with it"

Alexis shook his head, his body still ached from the pain this weapon had inflected on him, but against an unarmed man even with his low level of skill it would not be a fair fight.

"I cannot do that, the risk I might hurt you is too great"

Halsey took off his heavy leather jacket and flexed his bare arms, then stood facing Alexis on the balls of his feet.

"You need proof as to my skill my lord, do not worry, I have no wish to end the day with my body covered with bruises as yours were"

Alexis reluctantly turned to face him.

"So be it, but if harm comes to you do not try to blame me, you bring this upon yourself"

Even as he spoke the last word Halsey made a move of such speed that the next instant he was lying on the floor with Halsey standing over him. He stared up at him angrily.

"That was not fair, I was not ready to begin the fight"

Halsey helped him up.

"I am sorry my lord, I will let you strike the first blow next time so that I will know you are ready"

The slightly mocking tone in Halsey voice made Alexis angry, it made him even more determined to land a blow to stop the peacock crowing. He swung the sword aiming at his shoulder, the result was the same as before. Even as he began his move his legs were taken out from underneath him and he was back on the floor looking up at a smiling Halsey. The uneven fight went on, and the longer it went on, the more angry Alexis became.

Halsey tried to calm him

"You cannot win the fight with anger my lord, anger will make you fight without skill, you must keep your mind clear to control your body"

But Alexis continued to swing and thrust the sword widely without effect, and try as he might he could not lay a blow on his squire. Finally, after ending up on the floor again Alexis called a halt.

"Enough, I am convinced, you have skills I have never seen before"

Alexis looked at his squire with new respect, never had he seen anyone fight in such a manor, and with such skill and speed. It was as if Halsey knew the next move he was about to take before he did.

"The holy men taught you well, could you teach me as they taught you?"

Halsey nodded his head.

"Yes my lord, but first you must learn to control the mind, only then can you learn to control your body. It will take you some time my lord, but it can be done."

Chapter 13
Against the Rules

Alexis asked him if there were any other wonders he brought with him from his homeland. Halsey left the room and returned a minute later holding a rolled up blanket. He took from it a bow of a type Alexis had never seen before and handed it to him. It was a lot stronger than the standard bow commonly used, and made of different material.

"It will shoot further by half as much again than the best archer you could find my lord. In my country it is used both by those on foot and mounted on horse"

Alexis gave a little gasp at the thought of archers mounted on horseback, no such soldiers existed in any army on Santross. He asked how they could be sure to hit the man and not the horse. Halsey shook his head.

"They cannot my lord, nor do they try to do so. In my country the horse is not sacred as it is here, nor is it so feared, and to kill a horse is not a sin"

Alexis frowned at his words

"Why is the horse not feared in your country, surely no men on foot can stand before a charging line of knights and horses"

Halsey took from the blanket a heavy weapon shaped with a vicious cutting spike

"Because of this my lord"

He handed the spike to Alexis.

"Normally this would be on the end of a heavy pole, perhaps twelve or fourteen of your cubits long. It is sharp enough and strong enough to stop a charging horse. Men standing shoulder to shoulder with this weapon firmly anchored in the ground could stop any charge by knights and horse"

Alexis looked at the weapon with awe.

"I have seen a something like this before, the people of Tashmar have them. Over the years they have fought many battles against the armies of Lalang. The Lalang always fight on horseback, and a weapon like this has been their defence against them"

He shook his head

"We have nothing like this, and even if we had, we would never use them to kill a horse"

Even thou Alexis was not as steeped in the tradition of battle as his father or brothers were, to harm a horse was a thought too far even for him. When the kingdom of Santross was first settled, the Darosi did not have any horses, it was not until they started trading with people from Lalang that they imported them to the island. For the first few years trade had been brisk between them until the Darosi had enough stock and knowledge to breed their own. Soon the horse became both a sacred symbol of power, and a stature of wealth and rank. There were many rules of war that were never to be broken. One was that only the nobility would be mounted in battle. And another said it was perfectly fair and proper to remove a man's head from his body, but it was considered a crime against the Gods to harm his horse. There were archers in their army, but because they could never be sure to hit man and not horse they were never used against mounted knights. The bow was only used against foot soldiers, or to pass orders along the line of battle by firing arrows with different colour ribbons attached. The main body of common soldiers carried long spears with large shields for defence or swords and a smaller shield for offensive, and always marched on foot. Mounted archers that paid no heed to whether they kill horse or rider went against all the rules of war and tradition, but Alexis could see the devastation that such troops would cause on the battlefield. A company of such soldiers could easily tip any battle in their favour, even if they were outnumbered by the enemy. It was plain that in the right hands this could be a formidable weapon, but one he was not ready to use.

"For the moment we will keep your bow and the pike a secret between ourselves, I have other matters on my mind. I think we are both going to be very busy men from now on Halsey, you will teach me the new skills here in this room. I do not wish to give Lord Ravenhead another chance to practice his sword play on me until I am ready for him"

And so Alexis' training began, not only how to fight in unarmed combat but also with a staff about six feet long. Halsey proved himself to be even more deathly with the staff then he was just with his hands. Alexis' admiration for his squire grew almost daily as he demonstrated speed and sleuth to dispose of any enemies that stood in his way.

Halsey smiled a quiet smile to himself, the young lord was behaving just as he hoped he would. Even his best friends though little of Alexis as a fighting man, but if the young lord remained true to his word, they and Lord Ravenhead would get a very big surprise at some time in the future. For the remainder of the winter and early spring Alexis spent all his spare time working with Halsey, sometimes for as much as four hours each day. He very soon became faster and stronger in his actions as his large supply of puppy fat quickly melted away.

Chapter 14
An opportunity Lost

As the spring slowly turned to summer the crops from the royal estates began to arrive, and with them came the discontent and problems that Prince Robert had hinted at when he had been first offered the position. Some of the farms were complaining that they were sending their products to fulfil their quota, only to have their goods rejected as sub-standard. Just as Alexis was about to visit some of the outlying estates to investigate he was invited by Prince Robert to go with him on a hunting trip. Alexis gladly postponed his own journey when he learned that Princess Livia and the lady with the golden hair would accompany them. The camping lodge that was to be their base was high in the mountains and many days ride to the east. As they travelled Alexis and the Prince often rode side by side.

Robert look across at the young lord, he looked much thinner than when they had first met. At first he was afraid the loss of weight was due to illness or worry, but the young lord looked the picture of health. He asked him if was well and content with his life. Alexis knew the true meaning of his enquiry. Everyone knew of the beating Lord Ravenhead had inflicted on him, and many had noticed his reluctance to be anywhere near the man. A few though it prudent for him to act this way, most others thought him a coward. Alexis took a moment to reply before speaking in a clear and determined voice.

"I am well your majesty, and growing stronger with each passing day"

Prince Robert smiled both at his reply and the manor it was spoken.

"It pleases me to hear so, I know of the harm Lord Ravenhead inflicted on you. He is Prince Williams's man and I have asked him to inform Ravenhead that such behaviour against one of my ministers displeases me, and I will not tolerate it. If he tries to repeat the deed I will find someone better suited for him to test his sword on"

Alexis give a slight nod in reply

"I thank you your majesty, it was kind of you to think of my welfare, I need a little more time to prepare before I am ready, then we shall see who harms who"

Prince Robert let out a roar of laughter and slapped his thigh with his hand

"Oh oh, my young lord, I look forward to that day with the appetite of a staving man. It is well pass the time when someone should have taken that ill-tempered bully down"

They rode on further, with Prince Robert still laughing from time to time as he pictured Alexis's revenge, and would occasionally pause to suggest a particular method to increase the level of pain inflected. Alexis laugh at his outrageous suggestions, and for the next hour each tried to outdo the other in thinking of the most painful or humiliating ways to gain revenge.

On a more serious note, Alexis wasted no time in finding out all he could about the object of his desire. The ladies name was Gaia, and had just come into womanhood. Her mother had been Lady Annabelle, a lady-in-waiting to the Queen before her death. After Queen Alaine died King Eric never married again, but a man needs the comfort of a woman from time to time, the result was he sired four children with three different ladies of the court. The Lady Annabelle had given him two children, a son called Denis, and Gaia, who was the youngest of the four. Fortunately the Darosi still remembered when selective breeding was part of their culture. In the Book of Knowledge it is written that it was not uncommon for a warrior who had proved himself in battle to father dozens of children, so they treated children born in such a way with more reverence that most other peoples. While they were not given full rights of inheritance as were true born, they were not despised or made to feel inferior in any way. The other half-brother was called Giles, and he was already near the end of his training and had fought with William in the last battles. The other girl was called Aelian, a shy girl a year or so older than Gaia. Some say she is dull of wit and never seen outside the Princess Livia chambers. When Giles and Denis come into full manhood they would be given minor titles and join the Kings Guard. The half-sisters were ladies-in-waiting to Princess Livia, and would also be given a title along with a modest dowry. They carried no shame as to their birth, so all were eligible for men or women of nobility to wed. The brothers would particularly be much sort after. They carried the blood of Kings in their veins, a useful aid to any family seeking to raise their status in the pecking order of nobility. The visit to the mountain retreat lasted six weeks, but much to Alexis's disappointment while Prince Robert and he along with several others went hunting most days, in the evening the ladies kept themselves apart. Only on a few occasions did he find himself in her company, and found himself so tongue-tied and red of face that he could only stutter a few words before lapsing into silence. His embarrassment and lack of skills in the art of courtship give Prince Robert much amusement, and Alexis became a target for many of his light-hearted jests. But there are more ways to express your desire than just by words, and when the feeling is as strong as his the eyes can say words of love as clearly as those spoken. So everyone, including the Princess Livia knew what was in the young lord's heart when he looked at her, And Gaia was also touched by his attention to her, and she responded in a demure way that clearly hinted of approval. Her acceptant of him as a suitor was clear for all but Alexis to see. He was so blind in the ways of love and women that for the moment the seeds of her willingness fell on stony ground. The weeks pasted quickly, so if the budding romance was to bloom, it would be at a later date.

Chapter 15
Trouble down on the Farms

On his return to the castle, Alexis began to organize the visit he had planned to the outlying royal estates. Some of them were constantly complaining about not being credited for the goods they supplied to the castle. Many of these farms were almost a week's ride away, and remembering Lord Ashdown's words of warning he thought it prudent to take a few soldiers to accompany him on his journey. At Halsey's suggestion he chose the sergeant and men who had mocked him when he had first arrived.

"They are good men my lord, as honest as most, and more loyal than many. If you treat them well, they will defend your life even if it costs them their own"

Alexis had learned to trust Halsey's word and judgment, so the next day he sent for the sergeant who had first greeted him.

"I am in need of an escort while I preform my duties to the King, and Halsey has suggested you and your men"

Sergeant Caius gave a slight bow as he replied.

"My lord, Halsey has told us that you are a fair and godly man in your dealing with others, and that he would lay down his life to protect you. I promise you that we will do no less, and I thank you for giving us the chance to redeem ourselves for the error of our ways when we first met"

Not for the first time Alexis felt surprise and embarrassment by his squires opinion of him.

"Very well sergeant, then it is done. We leave tomorrow morning. I have never taken this journey before so I am unsure how long we will be away, better carry food for five days, after that we can replenish as we go along"

The next morning Alexis rode out of the castle at the head of a dozen men all smartly turned out and on their best behaviour. It took a few days to reach the first farms of those that were complaining. Alexis managed to speak to three farmers, they all complained that they would send farm products to the castle, only for them to be rejected as sub-standard, but the next wagon was passed, even thou it came from the same crop. The next day's journey ended with the same result. By the end of the week as many as a third of farmers had told him the same story, some of them had suffered several times. Many in the past had travelled to the castle to complain, but nothing had been done. Now because of the rejections many were barely able to fill their yearly quota, and without any surplus to sell it meant they had worked for a full year without any reward for their efforts. A few had already given up their farms to work for other lords, and there were many more close to doing the same if the situation was not resolved. Alexis was in a sombre mood when he returned to the castle. He thanked his escort for a job well done before returning to his quarters. The problem of rejection that was causing the unrest had to be solved. The wealth of all nobility came from the land, so good farmers were always in short supply. The royal estates had already lost some of their best with the threat that more would follow. He was determined to find out the truth, and started with the account books that registered what each farmer had sent and credits made to them. Both the number of wagon loads and the amount of goods tallied, if someone was robbing the farmers there was nothing in the books to show it.

But Alexis was so sure that something was wrong, he widen the search to all the account books. He spent many days and more than a few nights studying them, a lesser man would have given up long before a pattern finally began to emerge. There were far too many deliveries with almost the same items and amounts to be a coincidence, but to hide his fact they were entered in the books many days apart. It was unlikely anyone just glancing at the accounts would spot the truth. The facts were now clear to him, on many occasions the castle was paying twice for the same items. He had found a crime, but it was not the crime he was looking for. He had the Head Clerk in charge of accounts brought to his quarters, the man collapsed into a snivelling heap on the floor when he realized he had been found out and begged for his life. Alexis looked down on him with eyes of steel.

"Who else benefited from the Kings money, speak the truth or I'll remove your thieving head from your body where you lay"

It did not take long, once the man started talking the words flowed from his mouth like a torrent. It seems the deception had started as an error. From an independent source he had entered the same delivery twice by mistake, but his old master, the one who had ended up as a meal for a wild boar had been drinking heavily and signed the note for payment. When he died it became even easier. All those that had followed him, including Prince Robert never looked at any of the accounts and simply signed any documents put before them. Alexis shook his head in disbelief, the Prince had showed the same weakness that all the nobility had, including his own father. Each had an arrogance that placed them above dealing in such common matters. He asked the clerk about the rejection of products from the royal estates as being sub-standard. Yes it was true, many times he had rejected supplies that were of poor quality, but he had never taken any money from the estates, only the royal purse. Even with the threat of instant death he denied all further knowledge. If it had not been for the days and nights Alexis had spent examining the accounts the clerk could have carried on for as long as he wished, and would almost certainly never have been found out. He gave a share of the money to the purser in charge of the royal kitchens, who in exchange signed that the non-existent items had been used there. Alexis ordered Halsey to lock the man up in the dungeons while he interviewed the purser. Alexis was pleased to have stopped thieves stealing from the king, but it did not answer the question of how someone was robbing the farmers. But that mystery was also answered within minutes of the purser coming before him. He offered little resistance when he found the Head Clerk had already confessed to his part in the crime. Now under the threat of the sword the rest of the truth came out. Not content with what he received from the clerk, the purser had his own idea of how to make money. He would buy old produces from the market in the town for little or nothing and mark them as received from one of the Kings estate. He would then show the produce to the Head Clerk and tell him which farm they had supposedly come from. The head Clerk would reject them as sub-standard and refuse payment. Finally, the farmer's real produces would be entered under a false name and he would pocket the money for himself. So one thief was stealing from another thief, and it was the second mans greed that was the undoing of them both. Alexis could not have discovered the crime at a better time, both men planned to soon "retire" from the Kings service and take their ill-gotten gains with them. Now in an effort to save their lives both men reviled their hidden horde, which amounted to a very considerable sum. The turn of events quickly reached the ears of Prince Robert, along with his embarrassing part in allowing the thieves to prosper. So for him there was great relief when the money that had been stolen was returned to the royal coppers. As a reward for his efforts Alexis was immediately elevated to the High Council. He attended his first meeting with high hopes of doing good deeds for the benefit of all, but was disappointed to find that most of the council strongly disapproved of his appointment. All were at least twice his age, and some even older. They resented his swift appointment to the council, and considered him to be too young and inexperienced for such high office. It was the start of a troubled relationship between them that failed to improve with time.

At first Prince Robert also wanted the money that had been stolen from the farmers, but Alexis argued that as it was stolen from them, it should be returned to them. He won his case and the money was returned to the farmers on their next visit. This instantly made him a hero to all the workers on all the king's estates. At last there was a member of nobility that treated them in a fair and honest way. Up until now, Alexis had worked unaided, now he transferred a servant from Castle Monrell to help him. His name was Conway, an outsider that he had befriended when still a young boy. Now in adulthood he had found his ability in most subjects to be as almost as great as his own. He had promoted him to as high a position as was possible for an outsider to be, and trained him to a level where he was capable of running the estate if necessary. This made Conway a devoted servant who was fearlessly in his defence of Alexis, and would never betray him in any way. Later he added one other, a Darosi called Stephan who due to a childhood illness was unable to walk unaided. Not surprisingly he was held in very low esteem by everyone, including his family. Stephan gratefully accepted the appointment, and found Alexis to be so honest and honourable in his dealing with him and all others that he soon joined Conway in his admiration for him. To protect the estates from ever suffering the same crime again, three representatives were chosen by the farmers themselves. One was to be present at the castle at all times to check all incoming deliveries to make sure they were of good quality. The number of disputes dropped to almost zero, and thanks to Alexi's efforts the exodus of discontented farmers ended. To speed the healing process, Conway persuaded Alexis that for the coming year he should lower the quotas of those who had suffered. It would ease the anger that some still felt towards the crown, and allowed them to keep more of their yields for themselves. Many would sell their products in Egion for a good price. The money gained would be a useful addiction to their income. In the eyes of the common worker Alexis now assumed almost god like stature, even the King himself could not command such loyalty. He had learned long ago with his own estates workers that if you treat people fairly whatever their rank nearly all will respond in a positive fashion. His ideas did not go unchallenged, at the time it had caused much annoyance between him and his father. Baron Monrell believed a lord should rule with an iron hand, and considered those who worked his fields not as the freemen they were, but as much his property as the horses in his stables. But time had proved Alexis right as with the goodwill of the workers yields had increased year upon year.

Chapter 16
Promises Made

The summer turned to early autumn, and with the changing of the seasons so did the mood in the castle. Now with the return of Prince Williams and his men there were many more every night in the great hall, and slowly, at a pace that was not noticeable the men gradually gathered around the Prince they favoured the most. The victory against the troublesome lord had turned out to be far greater than was first thought. Prince William had led his troops into battle against not one, but three lords who had banded together. Although outnumbered he had won battle after battle, until the last lord had lost his head. He was a natural leader in every way, and it was a view widely held that in terms of warfare William was truly a military genius, a true Darosi in every way. Robert on the other hand was considered to be an empty headed fool who drank too much, and with little regard for the traditions and values of his people. It was inevitable that now with the failing health of the King common knowledge many began to think about his successor. It was from this point onwards that a dark cloud formed in Alexi's mind as he began to hear whispers softy spoken that Prince William should be king. The dark cloud grew even more menacing when he learned that the lords who had fought with William all came from the west, and they commanded armies many times larger than any in the east. They still gather around each night drinking and cheering as they relived the battles.

It was clear that if William did make a bid for the throne, those of the west would support him. Robert would be heavily outnumbered in any battle as far as ordinary troops were concerned. And to make matters worse a few of the lords who had been his friends also joined the swelling ranks of Prince William supporters. The best hope for Robert was the Darosi nobility themselves, for once the honour that was so dear to them worked against William. As long as Robert was the clear heir to the throne, the vast majority of them would remain loyal and keep the crown far out of William's reach. There were a number of knights who roamed the kingdom whose allegiance could be bought, but their number was not thought to be great enough to make a difference. As the autumn continued the split between the groups became clearer. Prince William hinted that if he was King, he would make all the outsiders throughout the kingdom serve nobility without any rewards. They would become total slaves to be dealt with as their masters saw fit. He would also deal with the towns one by one and bring them all to heel. And if any of the people refused to pay homage and taxes to the crown, they would lose all their valuables, their homes and their lives. The money lenders were the most hated of all. Prince William promised to cancel all debts owed to them and take back all the money that in his eyes they had stolen. The very worst would lose their lives, all others would be driven from the kingdom. But to his disappointment his promises had little effect, most of the Darosi still remained true to their code and refused to change sides. Only a few more rallied to his banner, not because they thought he would make the better king, but because he promised to cancel any debts they owed, and their debts were so large they outweighed any other consideration. But they were mainly of minor nobility and brought little to the cause. The supporters he did have at court now openly began to cheer for him whenever he appeared, and each day the whispers as to who should be king grew louder until they stopped being a whisper and became the spoken word. The atmosphere between the groups became so bad that Robert asked his brother to speak to his followers to try and calm thing down, but Williams only answer was to leave the royal table and join his supporters below. The rift between then was now in plain view for all to see. Prince Robert was left with only a few of the older men at his table, and this made him look even more isolated, and for the first time he took the possible threat of William seriously.

The dark cloud in Alexi's mind had now taken shape and substances, it was time to plan for the future. He raised the issue of living conditions for the families of the garrison's soldiers, pointing out that with all the unrest and possible future conflict, they could end up as the only large body of men on Roberts's side if William did challenge for the throne. At first Robert was reluctant to spend money from the royal treasury on such matters, but Alexis persisted in his efforts to change his mind.

"It could turn out to be a wise investment your majesty, and a lot cheaper than trying to bribe them with more money if we needed them to fight on our side"

At the use of the word "cheaper" Roberts' ear's become more receptive

"A lot cheaper you say, how much cheaper?"

Alexis replied

"A great deal cheaper your majesty, one gold coin for each man would not be enough to win their loyalty. We could be so heavily outnumbered it could cost two, three or even five gold coins to give each man the courage to risk his life. That could be well over two thousand guilders, maybe as much as five thousands, a goodly sum your majesty. We could build them new family quarters for much less, and what man would not fight to protect his home?"

Robert could suddenly see the sense in what Alexis was saying, make better homes for the soldiers' families, at a small cost, and they were certain to fight to protect them. He gave permission for Alexis to go ahead and undertake the task himself, but in a quite manor, and always with an eye to the pennies being spent. He did not want William to know that money from the royal purse was being used to build homes for the families of common soldiers, normally the Darosi would never be concerned about such matters. If William found out he would claim it was just another sign of his brothers weakness, and that he not worthy to be a King.

It was now plain that the only way to save the kingdom from civil war was to resolve the question of succession, and that it must be done while the king still lived. Many feared that his death would bring the end to peace in the kingdom, and it would be a long and bitter time before it returned. Finally the possibility of civil war had reached the King's ears. Now weak and frail he summoned the two princes to his chambers. He demanded that William must swear allegiance to his brother as king after his death, or he would be banished instantly from the Kingdom. William had no chose but to agree, so for the moment peace appeared to return between the brothers.

Alexis meanwhile quickly set about his task of building better homes for the soldiers' families to live in. A fine autumn morning saw a long column of carts with over a hundred men slowly begin their journey to the forest of Teal, an area some twenty miles away from the castle on land too steep and rocky for any kind of farming, so was still rich in good timber. On the journey there one of the soldiers made a comment about how grand it would be to travel to the battlefield in such a way, so they could arrive fresh for the fight, rather than tired and worn out by a long march. His words set Alexis thinking, it was not possible to transport an whole army in such a way, there were not enough carts in the whole kingdom to do that, but to transport a few, say a force of a few hundred quickly over a short distance, or to cover a longer journey much quicker that a march, and it could be done. In his mind he had created the idea of mobile infantry. He was not sure of how to use such a force, but was equally sure that time would show him a way. With the willing help of every soldier to build their new homes, they took shape very quickly, and in just a few months the task was complete. Each had solid walls and doors with a good roof to keep out the cold and the rain, and a stone fireplace to cook hot meals on. And they finished just in time, the winter came with a harsh wind from the north that brought the castle and surrounding land a covering of snow for the first time in many years. As the winter grew deeper it was so cold that for the first time in living memory the sea began to freeze around the castle, but all the families were snug in their new homes. Now the ramshackle outbuilding that had once been their homes were quickly torn apart and the wood of the old became a useful supply of fuel for the new. As the snow had begun to fall, Alexis celebrated his first year at Castle Kingshome , a year in which much had happen. He had become a different person from the one who had first arrived. Then he had felt to be a lamb among wolves, with little or no ability. Now all that had changed. He had become free from the daily disapproval that had constantly undermined his confidence. And in its absence along with all the hard work with Halsey he had grown into a man, both physically and mentally. A man who was so sure of his own thoughts and judgment, that now he stood tall and at ease among Kings and Princes.

Chapter 17
A New way of thinking

Several weeks into the winter, the Master-at- arms paid Alexis a visit to thank him on behalf of his men for supplying the new homes.

"You stand very high in the regard of all the soldiers my lord, it is well known that it was by your efforts that they were built. You could not have found a better way to earn their loyalty and respect. Many of us have known for some time of the fairness you treat all people with. Unlike others who do not think the welfare of soldier's families is any of their concern. But you saw the need, and everyone knows that with a winter as harsh as this it would have cost many lives by now. I think I am safe in saying that there is not a man, married or unmarried who would not willingly fight by your side, to the death if need be"

He turned to leave

"And I include myself in that honoured company"

Halsey heard every word spoken, and smiled a quiet smile to himself and said nothing.

When Alexis had first been given control of the castle supplies, he had diligently conducted a survey of all that was in the castle storerooms. Now Robert asked Alexis for it to be done again. He thought the promise his brother made to the King was too easily given, and it would be prudent to be prepared. Alexis happily agreed, like many he still had the fear of war on his mind, and if the castle did need further supplies now was the best time to get them. Alexis soon warmed to his task in more ways than one. Due to the harsh winter he began to spend his nights below ground as well as his days. No matter how cold it became above, in the passages the air always remained at a moderate temperatures. Finally he presented the accounts of stock to the Prince. He suggested that they needed some extra supplies of certain war items, with them the castle could withstand a siege lasting a great many months. He began to read out the list of items needed, but Robert just held his arms up as a sign to stop.

"Spare me the details my lord, I give you full permission to buy whatever is needed"

Alexis looked at the long list in his hand.

"The needs are many your majesty, and some will cost a pretty penny. Are you so sure of my judgment that you need not know the details?"

Robert waves his hands.

"Yes, yes a thousand times yes my lord, do whatever needs to be done"

Alexis bowed acceptance.

"As you wish your majesty, I will do whatever needs to be done"

It was while he was writing out his list of war needs that he remembered the weapons Halsey has showed him many months ago. He had thought then that a company of archers on horseback could tip the balance in any battle, but had dismissed both the weapons because they went against all the rules of war. But now the position had changed, with almost all of the army against him, and the possibility that many of the nobility would also change sides, Robert could be so outnumbered that defeat was more than just a possibility. Alexis was also sure in his own mind that if William came to the throne and tried to carry out his pledges, the Darosi would be under two threats at the same time. First, if he attacked the towns, they were likely to hire foreign mercenaries to defend themselves, and with enough soldiers against them the Darosi could easily lose the battle. But even if they won, when the armies of the north found out that Santross was divided they would quickly invade. Either way the Darosi would disappear from the face of the earth. Now that Alexis was sure in his own mind that war was coming, he thought it prudent to create a force able to use the bow, even if Prince Robert chose not to use them. He asked Halsey to show him his bow again. Alexis turned the weapon over in his hand, he tried to draw the bow, at first he could not succeed. It took all his strength to draw the bow less than half way and he could clearly feel the power it produced. He nodded to Halsey

"We will take a ride tomorrow to some quiet spot and see how it preforms compared to one of ours"

The next day, on the stump of a tree they set up both steel and leather breastplates of the kind of that most knights would wear in battle. Using the Darosi bow and an arrow with the standard tip it failed to pierce the leather armour cleanly from more than a few paces away. Then they tried Halsey's bow, the extra performance was staggering, it was clearly many times more powerful than the normal bow and with a specially formed tip it pierced the leather every time up to a hundred paces away. Alexis could hardly believe what he was seeing. The difference between the bows was as great as that between a wooden sword and a real one. To kill an unarmoured horse would be easy and could be done at a much greater distance. For the few knights that would be wearing full armour the bow was less effective, the arrow would not pierce the steel breastplate from more than fifty feet away, but only the richest Darosi could afford such expensive armour, and their horses could be killed just as easy as any other, and without their horse the weight of their armour would render them helpless. Alexis was impressed, with this weapon even an army that was outnumbered could easily win a battle. He asked Halsey what the bow was made of.

"The bow itself is made of animal sinew, bone and birchwood my lord, along with a few other ingredients"

"Could you make more such as these?"

"Yes my lord, given the time and material, and a place to work in"

Alexis was silent for a moment as he thought the project through.

"Can men really be taught to shoot arrows from a galloping horse and still hit their targets?"

Halsey nodded his head

"Yes my lord, back in my homeland they learn from an early age, and by the time they are men they can strike any target up to 300 hundred paces away. But any man who can shoot a bow and ride a horse can learn. They perhaps would not be as good, but with practice and with the firing of many arrows some would still find their mark."

Alexis was impressed, to hit a target at 300 paces while on horseback was unheard of. You could not expect men of lesser skill to achieve such distance, but even if they could manage 50 paces it would be a surprise to any enemy.

"To find you the materials and a place for you to work without prying eyes is easy. I control all the supplies and storerooms in the castle, I'm sure we have an empty one out of the way somewhere, It would be difficult to hide such an undertaking from Stephan or Conway, but they are loyal and would never betray my trust in them. You say you need animal sinew, bone and wood, what else?"

Halsey rubbed his chin

"A large amount of fish to make glue, and as large a pot as we can find to boil the bones in until they become soft and pliable, and some horse skin for the gut"

Alexis nodded his head,

"I will fund you from my own pocket for the moment, I don't want anyone to know what we are about. Take Conway with you and go to Egion to buy all you need, it was draw less attention there than at the fishing village. And before you buy you must change out of your soldier's uniform, with plain clothes and the colour of your skin no one would think you a soldier"

To help with the task of producing more of the deadly bows, Halsey suggested that Sergeant Caius and his men should become Alexis' personal bodyguards. Alexis made a request to the Master-at-arms and he readily agreed to the change. He sent for Sergeant Caius and he was most happy when told of his new status. Along with his new duties Alexis promoted him to the rank of Captain and made him head of his personal troops and escorts.

So after being sworn to secrecy some were given the task of helping to make the bows, while others made the arrows. Captain Caius told Alexis there were many men who would willingly join their ranks. Alexis agreed, but reminded the Captain to recruit only those he knew he could trust. Halsey also made a confession that there was another reason why he wanted Sergeant Caius and his men to join them. It turned out that when he had been just an ordinary member of the squad, he had taught many of them some of the skills he had learned from the holy men. None were at the standard of himself or Alexis, but with further training they could become a formidable force in any fight, and would make excellent bodyguards if there was ever a need. Alexis allowed him to train a few of the men each day, as long as it did not hinder the making of the weapons. The work and the training went on day after day all through the remaining winter months. Both Alexis and Halsey were never satisfied, they always wanted more, despite the fact that their numbers steadily grew as more and more men were added.

Chapter 18
To Find an Army

To make the bows was only half the task, Alexis needed both men who could shoot the weapon, and a supply of horses for them to ride. This was a problem he spent many hours trying to solve. Then one evening while working on the estates accounts the answer came to him, the farm workers! Each farm that made up the royal estates had many strong young men capable of shooting a bow, the only weapon they were allowed to use for killing vermin. And what farmhand never rode the plough horse home at the end of each day. So the farms had at least one of the two ingredients he needed most…men who could ride. And they had a very good reason to fight if there was a war. If William won he would lose his life, a quick thrust of the sword and his suffering would be over. But for them, a victory for William would condemn all outsiders to a life of slavery, a fate far worse than a quick death. Now with others to help him in his duties, he had often made trips to visit the royal estates to the point where now it was considered normal behaviour. The cold of winter was still with them, but no more snow had fallen, so travel was possible. His first call was to a farm owned by a man called Ben Tiller, he had been one of the three elected to represent the estates at the castle. He was also one of many who had profited by Alexis returning the stolen money. Both men liked and trusted each other, so Alexis told him freely about his fears for the future if there was a war between Robert and William. He also told him in detail that William planned to make him and all the other workers and their families' slaves if he came to the throne. He told Ben he needed two things to happen quickly, one was to find out how many men and horses could be mustered. And the other to arrange a meeting with those who had influence over the workers, he would attend and tell them his plans. Time was very important, but to keep their deeds secret was of even more importance, no one must know what they planned. Two weeks later, accompanied by Halsey and fifty of the new bows he met again with Ben and the men who could speak for all the estate workers. Alexis told them all that if William came to the throne he planned to make slaves of all of them.

"You would lose your freedom, your children, perhaps even your wives could be sold to another Nobleman on the other side of the kingdom. And if you resisted it would mean death for you and perhaps your family. This will be your future, and your children's future if we lose the battle I'm sure is coming. I need to know that if war comes, will you fight alongside us for Robert, and I tell you now that it is almost certain we will be greatly outnumbered and many of you may die. But if we are victorious I give you my oath that as a reward I will try to make a better life for all who survive. I will wait outside while you decide"

He and Halsey retreated to the kitchen, and both men sat and waited for the worker reply. Halsey looked at his young lord with respect in his eyes.

"You spoke well my lord, your voice carried the mark of command, truly you grow in stature and wisdom with each passing day"

Alexis had long ago given up trying to rebuke his squire for making such statements, or trying to find a suitable reply and just sat quietly waiting for the outcome of the meeting.

Twenty minutes later Alexis were called back into the room. Ben Tiller spoke first.

"My lord, you have proved to be a good friend to all of us in the past. You we trust above all others, and we believe what you say will happen to us is true. Each of us is willing to fight by your side to win a better future for our families, but what can we do? We are people of the land, we know nothing of the ways of war, and we have no swords or armour."

Alexis nodded his head in agreement

"That is true, but if the fight comes we could be so heavily outnumbered that we will fight in a new way, and not follow the rules of the past. You will not need to learn how to use the sword, or the shield, or any other weapon you are not familiar with"

He unwrapped one of the new bows.

"I know all the people of the land already know how to shoot a bow, and shoot it well. There has been more than one cooking pot filled with meat killed by such a weapon. And I have no doubt that many a wild animal paid with their life for fancying one of your chickens for supper, but you have never used a bow like this"

"I have many more of these in the cart outside, this will be your weapon, and we will use it in a manner that it has never been used before. Now that you have given your word to fight, within days you will receive as many more as I have to give. You must keep this weapon and how we plan to use it a secret, no one apart from those of us committed to the cause must know about it. My squire Halsey will give some of you instructions on how to use the bow and how to care for it. Those he teaches will then pass on their knowledge to others. The men must start practicing to ride and shoot with this bow as soon as possible. Choose the best horsemen to train first. We will need an army of many hundreds of such men if we are to have any chance of winning"

A loud murmur rose from all present, to ride and shoot at the same time? Most thought it impossible. Alexis held one in his hand

"This will pierce a suite of leather armour at a hundred paces, and carry for over four hundred"

Another murmur from all present, but this time louder, a chorus of voices all spoke at the same time.

"Pardon me my lord, but did you say FOUR hundred paces?"

"How do you know this?"

"There is no bow that could pierce leather armour at one hundred paces"

Alexis smiled as he answered.

"The answer is yes to all your questions. Yes, it will carry for four hundred paces, and it will pierce armour at a hundred. I have a leather breastplate in my quarters which has more holes than plate, most of them made by my squire, and one by an arrow I shot myself"

He gave a small laugh as he added.

"I must confess my aim was so poor it took me a dozen shots before I found my target. But once found, the arrow went through easily"

His confession was greeted with smiles and a little laughter. He continued on a more serious note.

"I know that all of you shoot better than I. With the skill you have you could kill a dozen men with this bow before they could come close enough to do you harm. And if they were on foot, and you rode a horse, you could ride around them keeping your distant and kill as many as the number of arrows in your quiver"

Another murmur, but this time accompany by smiling faces as they realized the potential of the new way of fighting. Alexis continued

"I doubt that we will have enough horses for all, so we will need many carts, at least a hundred or more that are big enough and strong enough to carry men to the field of battle"

He looked to Ben.

"Do you have the count of men and horses that I asked for?"

Ben nodded in reply

"We have over five hundred men, but only some forty horses, and most of those are only used to plough, but Josh knows where we can get more horses from"

An elderly man near the back of the room stood up

"Within a day's ride from here there are three farms that to not grow crops, but only breeds' horses for the Nobility, and another four or five a days' ride further. Each has at least twenty horses at any given time. I have spoken to the men who control these places, and they are willing to join us and bring all the horses with them if any war happens."

Another man stood up and joined in the discussion

"All the workers of Lord Carsell will join us, some fifty men and four horses."

Now it seemed that everyone wanted to add to the score. By the end of the count the workers of over twenty lords were ready to fight for Robert, and more would join with each passing day. Alexis had his army, over one thousand men and counting would stand by his side if war came, but the low count of horses was of some concern, they would need upwards of a thousand. Ben spoke to him when the meeting ended.

"You must know they do not fight for Robert my lord, they fight for you. If it had been only for the King I doubt if you would have had more than a few dozen, but for you, such is the respect of the people than by the time the battle comes, if it comes, half of all the outsiders will be by your side"

Not for the first time that evening Alexis was speechless and could not find a reply. Halsey was at his side and heard every word spoken, and he smiled a quiet smile to himself, he said nothing, but thought much. From the first time he had met this young lord he knew he was different of all others of his kind. He had met many Kings and other people of importance in his travels as a trader and had learned to recognize those with the mark of greatness. They are often humble in their manor, but so mighty in stature that they can command men and armies to unite and follow them without question. Such men of vision can shape the future and perform great deeds that lesser men would not think possible, and for Alexis the journey to that future had only just begun. Within a week Halsey delivered over two hundred of the new bows to Ben Tiller along with thousands of arrows from their winters work. He stayed for over a week, first giving instructions on how to alter their saddles to make it easier to ride and shoot at the same time. And then how the bows were made, along with the special shape of the arrow head to pierce leather and metal. As he left to return to the castle, Ben promised him that before the new moon came to the full, he would have fifty men working to increase their stock of both, and to tell Alexis the training of archers had already started.

Chapter 19
The way forward

Now Alexis had the making of his army, he turned his attention to the task of how to use them. The mounted archers were the key to his plans, if they proved their worth then victory was just a possibility. Now he had to solve the problem of how best to use them. One good point in their favour was that the horses they needed did not have to be big and strong like a warhorse. They were bred to carry the weight of a knight and his armour. No, what the archers needed was speed, fast mounts that could run faster and further than those of the Darosi, and as many as they could find. Pickings would be slim on Santross, to buy a horse entailed great expense. But a week's sailing to the east was the kingdom of Thanjab, and beyond that the lands of the Lalang. The Lalang were a tribe who lived by breeding and selling some of the finest horses to be found anywhere. He needed to arrange for one or more ships to sail to Thanjab and return with as many as they could. So there were two tasks to fulfil, one to arrange such a convoy. And of equally important, someone who could he entrust with such a task? There was a thought in the back of his mind that may resolve one, but not the other.

At last the cold winter was loosening its grip, and there was a hint of spring in the air, and with it an invite that Alexis had to read many times over before he believe it to be true. He was to have supper with Robert and Princess Livia in their private chambers. The thought that he might catch a glimpse of the Lady Gaia at such close quarters made his pulse race. Almost from the time they had returned from summer camp he would sometimes stand on the high battlement in the hope that he might see her walk in the garden, but without any luck. But there was one lady of the court who noticed his frequent visits, and she had a good idea of why he was there. Lady Anna had first noticed Alexis' interest in the Lady Gaia at the feast to celebrate the return of William, now with the help of Lord Ashdown, it was made known to Alexis that if he should find himself on that part of the battlements at a certain time and day he might find his visit fruitful. And so the young would-be lovers saw each other from afar almost every day, but never more than a wave passed between them. Now it was an excited but very nervous Alexis escorted by Prince Robert who climbed the steps to the royal chambers. The Prince smiled at Alexis's obvious nerviness. He had liked this young lord from the first time they had met. Over the last year he had come to feel a deep kinship for him, and if the truth be known, he felt more brotherly love for him than William. He had asked more and more of Alexis with the passing of time, and he had never let him down. He had served him and the Kingdom well from the first day he entered the Kings service, and despite being of young age, his was the voice he listened to before all others on the High Council. This did upset some of the older members of the council, but they had no grounds to complain. The fact was that up until now he had invariably been proved right, so what was planned for tonight would be a fitting reward for him. They entered the royal chambers, the walls were covered by drapes of the finest quality, and the floors with thick carpets that made no sound at your passing. Alexis looked around in wonder at the luxury surrounding. They sat in comfortable chairs with a glass of good wine in their hand and waited for the Princess Livia to appear. A few minutes later she entered, and Gaia was at her side. The smile on Alexis face could not have been broader. He was going to get much more than just a glimpse of the Lady Gaia, she was to join them in their meal. To Alexis she looked more beautiful every time he saw her. Minutes later the four of them sat down to the meal, with Gaia sitting opposite him. And so the evening continued, with both thinking that no one would know the secret thoughts they said to each other without speaking. But they were wrong, when two people love each other they do not have to speak their love, they wear it like a badge on their sleeve for all to see. And Robert and his wife smiled as they enjoyed played cupid to the young couple. Gaia had known of Alexi's interest in her from the first night when they had celebrated the return of the army. It was the first banquet she had attended since coming into womanhood. At first she had been flattered that the son of one of the richest and most powerful Barons in the kingdom was showing an interest in her, and although she was not overly impressed by his appearance, he was so obvious in his desire for her that she blushed inside, and felt excited to be thought of as an attractive woman. Lady Anna sitting next to her noticed Alexis's interest, and whispered in her ear that she had made her first conquest. She said nothing, but smiled in reply. All girls of her age dream of a young handsome man to sweep them off their feet and carry them away to his castle. It was true Alexis was young, and rich enough to have his own castle, but that was all. He carried far too much weight just with his own body to be strong enough to also carry a woman, and with his three double chins he could not be called handsome. But by the time of the summer camp the three double chins had disappeared, along with much of his weight to the point where he could be called handsome. And the force of his desire for her was even greater and completely overwhelmed her, it awoke in her a desire that only comes with womanhood, and from that moment onwards she wished only to be his wife. Having decided to give herself to him in both body and soul, much to her disappointment nothing happen. Alexis lacked any skill in courtship and never pressed her in any way, so the opportunity for them to be together had passed them by. She had spent the winter months looking at Alexis from afar, unable to tell him of her love for him. And every night before sleep she would run her hand down the empty side of her bed and imagine him lying beside her. She promised herself that next time they met she would be more open in her love for him. Even the Princess Livia had commented on the change in her behaviour and questioned her about it.

"Tell me Gaia, what troubles you, you sulk like a lovesick puppy, are you well?"

Gaia did not have the courage to give the true answer that she had fallen in love and wished to be wed. But the Princess knew full well the reason for her malaise, and it was an illness for which there was only one cure. And now that cure was here, just a few feet away across the table. She could almost feel his love and desire for her reach out across the table to touch and caress her. To Gaia, he was now the most handsome man she had ever seen, his transformation from an ugly duckling to a beautiful swan was complete. She wished they were alone, so he could take her in his arms and….she blushed at her own thoughts, only brides should let a man touch them in the way she had just wished. And all the time unknown to her Alexis was thinking the same thoughts and making the same wishes, but with the boldness of a man, he did not inwardly blush.

Chapter 20
The Floodgates of Desire Open

As the meal ended a messenger appeared, The King wished to see both Robert and Livia at once. Robert made a gesture towards Alexis.

"There is no need for you to leave, please stay and entertain the Lady Gaia, It may be some time before we return"

Alexis and Gaia found themselves alone for the first time. Alexi's heart raced with excitement, he little knew that Gaia's heart matched his beat for beat. They made their way to the small garden Alexis had seen all those months ago from the high ramparts. Now the cold of the winter had finally gone, and with the scent of spring in the air it was a perfect night for lovers. A new moon hung low on the horizon, and the stars sparkled in the dark heavens above like the diamonds Santross was famous for. Gaia pointed to a bright star just above the headland.

"Tell me my lord, do you know the name of that star?"

Alexis stood close behind her to better follow her aim, his hands rested on her shoulders. He brought his head down until their cheeks almost touched. The sweet smell of her hair fuelled his desire, he closed his eyes and put his arms around her waist, and for a moment held her so close to him that their cheeks touched. It all seemed so natural, as if this was the way it was meant to be. They turned their faces to each other, and as one they kissed. It was a long gentle kiss, slowly they adjusted their position until they stood face to face. And the real kissing began, and with each kiss the passion increased. Now the floodgates of love were open Alexis was driven on with a passion greater than any he had ever felt, he kissed her as if he wanted to consume her, to take her within himself so the two would be one. It took many minutes before the passion died enough for the kissing to pause. Finally they just held each other in their arms, he ran his fingers through her golden colour hair.

"I have loved you from the first moment I saw you on the evening of the banquet, I have wished and prayed for this moment to happen from that day forward"

He held her at arm's length

"I love you Gaia, with a passion that will last a lifetime, I ask with all my heart that you consent to be my wife. This I want more than life itself, please, please say yes"

Gaia touched his face gently with her finger tips

"Yes of course I will"

She giggled in a very girlish way as she added

"Every night for many months pasted I have dreamed of us being together as man and wife"

Alexis laughed loudly, he jumped up and down. Then he looked up at the night sky, his arms outstretch as if reaching for the stars.

"Yes! She says yes. To all the Gods I give thanks. May you reign forever in your heavenly realm, Thank you, thank you. A thousand times thank you"

Then he turned to face her and put his hands around her waist.

"Now all my dreams have been answered, all my wishes are to be fulfilled. You are so precious to me I will guard you so that not a drop of rain will fall on your head, no cold wind will ever ruffle your hair"

He caress her hair again with his fingers

"This beautiful, beautiful hair"

He buried his face in her long golden locks

"I love your hair, and I love your cute nose, and your blue eyes"

He laughed again

"Oh those beautiful blue eyes that put the colour of the sky to shame, and your neck, it calls out to me that it must be kissed, and…."

He ran his hands gently down both sides of her body to rest on her hips.

"I love you from the highest lock of your hair to the tip of your toes"

He laughed as he added

"And all in between"

He picked her up in his arms and swung her around so her feet left the ground

Gaia laughed at his behaviour

"Stop Alexis, please stop my love before you do harm to both of us"

He gently lowered her to the ground, but he could not stop his love for her, he held her face in his hands and gently kissed her eyes and her ears, before working his way down her neck.

Gaia began sighing with enjoyment, his kisses made her neck tingle, then realizing where his lips may go she hurriedly pulled away.

"No my love, I beg you to go no further while I still have the strength to ask"

Alexis stopped his downward plunge, but the kissing went on for several more minutes before he stopped for breath.

"And we will have children, many, many children, we will fill the castle with them"

Gaia laugh,

"Yes, yes many children"

Again they held each other in their arms, now the kissing continued at a gentler pace. After a while they just stood, their arms wrapped around each other. Gaia was the perfect height for her head to fit neatly on his chest. He gently kissed her forehead, he wanted this moment to last forever, but it was not to be. The sound of approaching voices carried on the night air, and suddenly they were transported from their own magical world back to the real one. Alexis looked into her eyes, had it only been a minute ago that he had held her in his arms for the first time? It seemed like they had been lovers all their lives. Robert and Livia walking arm in arm appeared from behind some bushes.

"Ah there you are, we were wondering where you had disappeared too"

Alexis and Gaia still holding each other's hands walked towards them. Alexis open the conversation with a bow.

"Your majesties, if it is your pleasure, we would like to be married"

He slid his arm around Gaia waist.

"The Lady Gaia has consented to be my wife"

Robert cheered loudly, while the Princess Livia just smiled. Robert asked in a mock stern voice it Alexis could keep his half-sister in the style she was accustomed to. Without waiting for a reply he stepped forward and slapped him on his back

"Well done my young lord, well done to you both"

"Does that mean you majesty's will let us wed?"

Robert laughed again

"Let you wed? let you wed you ask? I will lay the flat of my sword across your backside my lord if you try to withdraw. It is done, you shall be married as soon as a date can be arranged. We have known about your love for each other for the best part of a year. We were beginning to wonder Alexis what we had to do to loosen you tongue enough to ask the girl. So tonight was arranged for you to be alone together, and the plan worked"

It was a very happy four that returned inside.

Chapter 21
The Sad Event

The next few weeks left Alexis in a daze. The worry about the war that may come were banish from his mind, his thoughts were only of Gaia. He saw her every day for as long as his duties would allow. He soon found out the truth of Lord Ashdown's words that chaperon's are a great inconvenience to those in love. They did manage a secret kiss or two, but Alexis, with a stern look or word from Gaia managed to contain his passion and desire…most of the time. Gaia would say in a hushed voice full of happiness

"Save it for the wedding night my love"

And with a giggle added.

"You must not tax yourself in any way before then"

Alexis replied that with her beauty to inspirer him, he would have the strength and desire of a lion that night, and for very night that followed, and Gaia openly blushed at his reply. They laughed together all the time, with chaperon or no chaperon they were the two happiest people you could even meet. Gaia talked constantly about the wedding. The Princess Livia herself was attending to the details. In less than a month they were to be wed, and then they would spend the rest of their lives as if in heaven.

But there was one task from his past that Alexis wished to finish before his wedding. On top of all his other duties he had still practiced with Halsey each day. He had doggedly stuck to his task well, now when they fought he often won. They had just finished for the day and were wiping the sweat from their bodies when Halsey said

"You have learned well my lord, I can teach you no more. You could beat any man in the kingdom now"

Alexis continued to dry himself, due to his hard work with Halsey his body was lean and muscular. He still lacked the bulging muscles that his brother once had, but his speed of movement made him a much deadlier foe. He nodded his head in agreement.

"Yes, I have waited long for this day to come, it is time Lord Raverhead paid his debt to me, perhaps tomorrow we might accidently find ourselves alone in a quiet place"

He had been ready for this task for many months, but Raverhead had been absent from the castle for all that time and had only just returned.

But Alexis would have to wait more than just a day. That evening the event that everyone feared was announced, the King was dead. For months he had laid in his bed growing a little weaker each day. Everyone knew his death was near, but still it came as a shook to many. Prince Robert announced a week of mourning for his father, and for once William did not argue. And so a week later, in the presents of as many of high rank as could travel there in time, King Eric of the house of Tierees was buried with all the honour and ceremony due to a King. Later the same day his royal banner joined the others on the wall of the great hall. One day after the funeral Prince William and several of his men including Lord Ravenhead rode away from the castle. The castle was awash with rumours about the purpose or destination of their journey, but no one knew for sure. A casualty of the king's death and the events that were to follow was the postponement of Alexis and Gaia's wedding. They met the news with great disappointment, but confident that their time would come. Alexis made the joke that it was like serving dinner late, the more hungry you are, the better the meal would taste.

Meanwhile the minsters of the crown set about organizing Robert's coronation. All the Baron and lords of the Kingdom were called to attend to recognize Roberts' right to the throne and swear their loyalty to him. Over the past year, Alexis had truly become the right hand man of Robert. He was now entrusted with the task of organizing accommodation for the guests of real importance. Slowly over the next month or so all the important men of the kingdom began to arrive and for a while Alexis became a very unpopular man. He had to ask many people to move to less favourable lodgings to accommodate those of higher rank. On a few occasions the request had to be made into an order, but in the end everyone cooperated and thanks to his efforts all ended up with a bed to sleep on. Alexis' father, Baron Monrell had further to come than most and was one of the last to arrive. Alexis was shocked at his appearance, he had aged noticeable in the one and a half years since he'd left home. Gone was the straight back of a warrior, now his back was bent and he needed a crutch to help him walk. He was accompanied by his younger brother Leon, next in line after him. Alexis greeted his brother first, he was struck by how young he looked compared to himself. Then he realized he was the same age as he had been when he had first arrived at Castle Kingshome, it was no wonder the soldiers had first thought him to be just a young boy. Baron Monrell seem confused the first time Alexis approached him, as thou he did not fully recognizing him

"Is it you Bart?"

Alexis shook his head

"No father, it is I, Alexis"

Baron Monrell shook his head

"You look different, I thought for a moment you were Bart"

Alexis could hardly believe his appearance.

"What has befallen you father that you need a support to walk?"

Baron Monrell shook his head, and replied with bitterness in his voice.

"A dammed horse"

He waived his free arm

"I will tell you later, now all I want to do is lay on a bed. My back gives me much pain when I stand for too long"

For the first time in his life Alexis felt pity for his father. He immediately ordered two soldiers to bring a litter and carry his father to his quarters. Alexis had given up his own rooms to his father and brother and had moved his belonging to the chamber below ground that had been his home during the winter. He gave orders to Huggle to fetch some wine and a hot meal for his father and brother to eat. Twenty minutes later, with his father lying comfortable on his bed he told him of how his injuries came about.

"I bought a fine looking chestnut filly from Baron Lomax. He told me that he had tried but failed to break her spirit and that she was too wild and too cunning to ride. But I would not listen, I set myself the task of proving to be the better horseman. We spent hours breaking her in, and after a while I thought we had tamed her wildness. She rode well and in an obedient manor, but then the wretched animal showed her other face. The face of cunningness, she waited until I relaxed in the saddle and threw me at the first opportunity"

He moved to a different position on the bed to ease his pain.

"May the Gods forgive me, but such was my pain and anger that the next day they carried my bed to the stables and I slit her throat with my own hand"

Again he shifted position on the bed.

"They told me after that I had broken some small bones in my back, along with my hip. And from that day to this I have never been free of pain"

Baron Monrell spent most of the following days in bed, unable to move. For the most part Leon stayed with him, but did sometimes venture around the castle accompanied by Halsey to show him the way. Once or twice he met with Alexis, but the brothers found little to talk about. Leon was only interested in stories about the battles that had taken place the year before. It was plain that Leon was following Bart rather than himself in his outlook on life. He had no interest in any of the duties that Alexis preformed, and with the typical arrogance of a true Darosi told his older brother he found him "boring" To Alexis relief he found some of the other young lords in the kings service more to his liking and he spend most of his free time with them. Alexis came to see his father at least once every day. A few days before the coronation was due Prince Robert came to pay his respects to the Baron. The two sat and talked for most of the afternoon as Damon recalled the time he had been a Commander of the Guard to the late King. In turn, Robert told him of the high esteem he held for Alexis.

"I could not do without him now Baron Monrell, he is my right hand man in many matters. You should be very proud to have such a son'

The Baron was surprised and proud at the same time. He stuttered a reply.

"I ..I..had always hoped that Alexis would carry on the high traditions of our family in serving the King. You make my heart leap with joy with your words of praise your majesty, and I thank you greatly"

Prince Robert patted him on his arm.

"It is I who thank you baron, you have also served the Kingdom well by giving me such a son for my aide"

Baron Monrell bowed his head in thanks.

"If Alexis has served you well then he also has my praise. He has done all that I asked of him"

Chapter 22
The Crowning

At last the day of the coronation had arrived, and every space in the hall was filled with all the great and noble of the kingdom, all wearing their finest robes and honours, but no swords. The Darosi had found out long ago that due to their volatile nature many a gathering of nobility had turned into a wake before the day was out. So now by tradition all weapons were banned from any ceremony. The only outstanding worry on the mind of many was there was still no sign of the return of William and his men, but the proceeding could not wait. Now with pomp and ceremony, Prince Robert, with Livia at his side began their slow march down an aisle formed by all the Barons and Earls of the realm towards the twin thrones. The Princess wore a stunning pale cream dress with a front covered by diamonds and other precious stones, the long train of her gown carried by Gaia and her sister Aelian, who wore matching dresses, but on a lesser scale. Alexis beamed with pride as his bride to be arranged the gown so the Princess could sit on her throne. When done, both young women retired backwards to stand alongside the others gathered there. Gaia gauged her retreat to end up next to Alexis, they stood close together, discretely holding hands behind their backs as they shared this moment of history. Over the next hour oaths were sworn, and vows spoken before the Holy Keeper of the Book of Knowledge slowly began to lower the crown on Robert's head. The act was nearly done when movement and shouting came from the back of the hall. Suddenly Prince William broke through the mass of people standing there. He marched down the aisle flanked by some of his men crying out at the top of his voice.

"Hold Fast, I claim the throne is rightfully mine, you crown the wrong man"

The Keeper of the book of Knowledge raised his voice in surprise

"What you say Prince William is treason unless you prove your words. By what deed of truth do you claim the throne of Santross?"

Prince Williams made a sign to one of his men, a moment later two elderly women were brought to his side. William spoke to them in a harsh voice

"Tell them, tell them how you and the others robbed me of my birth right the night my brother and I were born"

He pointed a finger at them as a sign of warning

"And speak in a voice loud enough for all to hear"

He looked at Robert.

"Loud enough for even my brother to hear"

Both the women were sobbing as they stood holding each other.

An elderly man from the crowd standing closest to them let out a cry

"I recognize these women, they are Lady Cassian and Lady Flavia.

The man bowed before them,

"It is an honour to see you both again my ladies. It is many years since you were Ladies-in-Waiting to the late Queen"

The Keeper of the Book asked again

"What is your proof of claim Prince William?

William turned to the Ladies again

"Tell them of your crime, and make it quick"

Now as the tension began to rise the only sound to be heard in the great hall was the voices of the women. It was well know that two Queens had died the night the Princes were born, but few knew the sequence of events. Lady Cassian started the narrative.

"There were five of us attending the Queen that night, plus the Kings mother. Queen Helois who loved Alaine as if she was her own daughter insisted at being present at the birth, despite being in such poor health that she was on the point of death herself. At first the birth of the princes went well, but slowly. It took many minutes before the first child could be handed to Queen Helois and taken to the next room to be washed and swathed in cloth"

She broke down with a burst of crying as the memories came flooding back. Alexis grew concerned, the passion of the situation was growing by the second, and there were half a dozen men all heavily armed standing feet away from Robert, while there was not a single sword among all the others present. And he was not the only one to feel concern. The Princess Livia also felt her husband to be in some danger, she moved to his side, ready to give her own life to save his. Alexis had other plans to save all from trouble, while all the attention were drawn to Lady Cassian he slowly let Gaia hand slide from his grasp Gaia had a look of fear on her face as Alexis pulled away from her. He smiled to reinsure her that all will be well. Then he held a finger to his lips for her to remain silent as he silently made his way to a door at the back of the hall. He opened it gently, a castle guard stood a few feet away. Alexis quickly explained the situation and ordered that the Master at arms with as many men as could be quickly found should be sent with the greatest speed to guard Robert from harm. He returned the way he had come and gently closed the door again. He had move only a few feet when he felt a tug on his arm, Denis, Gaia brother whispered softly

"What would you have me do my lord?"

Alexis shook his head.

"You are unarmed, were you to try anything it could mean your certain death"

Denis grabbed his arm harder and again whispered, but this time with a touch of anger in his voice

"You are also unarmed, yet you go to aid the King, I am just as ready to die for my sovereign as you are my lord, and I have an extra reason, don't forget Robert is my half-brother"

Alexis nodded

"I am sorry, I did not mean to offend, my words were said without thought. Try to make your way around to the front, and be ready to stand between Robert and William. The castle guards are but moments away. With luck no one will be harmed"

Finally Lady Cassian had recovered her composer and continued telling the events of that fatal night.

"The trouble started with the second child, he did not lay right in the womb. Queen Alaine began to lose a little blood and quickly grew very weak. At last the second child was born and handed to the queen mother to wash as the first. But now the blood began to flow freely from Alaine, and no matter what we tried we could not stop it"

Again Lady Cassian burst into tears, even after many years the trauma of that night was still burned fresh in her mind. The Lady Flavia spoke for the first time as she continued the story

"We truly tried all we knew, we loved Queen Alaine as we loved our own, but it was in vain. Queen Helois was called to her side and held her hand until she passed into the next world. The Queen mother's sorrow was so great, and her health so poor that she could not stand the strain and cried out in anguish, and still holding Alaina's hand it took but a moment for them to be joined in death. We were so stunned that all we could do was stand by the bedside and cry for them"

And so it was again as both women held each other for comfort and began to cry and sob as they relived those sad moments in their life.

Both the women were still sobbing loudly as Alexis quietly edged his way to the front to stand again by his love. Again he smiled at Gaia to indicate that all will be well as he began to work his way around to the back of the thrones. At first Gaia tried to stop him, but he shook his head to indicate that he must go. He whispered in her ear

"Do not worry my love; all is in hand, the castle guards are but moments away. I only need to keep Robert safe until they arrive and all will be well. Now I must go to the King's side"

William was pacing up and down, waiting impatiently for the women to end their tears and continue. Finally his patience was exhausted. Again he confronted them angry.

"Come ladies, you may cry for as long as you wish, but only after you have told all of the truth."

Finally the Lady Flavia composed herself enough to continue her story.

"We became aware of the sound of the new born babies from the next room, then we entered they were being attended to by a servant girl. It suddenly occurred to us as we looked at them that we did not know which would be the future King. We asked the girl who was first born, but she appeared to be dull in wit and did not answer. We looked at the babies, one had been washed and properly dressed, the other was not, and still had some blood on its skin. We reasoned that the first born would have had the most care and attention, so we decided he would be King"

Prince William confronted them both, and pointed an accusing finger at them said.

"So with the most flimsy of evidence YOU decided who would be King. Yet you still do not tell the whole truth, do you? Did that servant girl when asked again point to the other child, the one you had chosen NOT to be King?"

Both the women looked at each other. Lady Cassian answered.

"Yes you majesty, but only after been asked many times. She was dull of wit your majesty, I doubt she even understood the question, I'm sure she only give an answer because we pressed her to"

William held up a parchment for all to see.

"This is a deathbed confession made by the Lady Faustina of the house of Grimswick who was one of the five ladies present during that night. She left clear instructions before she died that it should be deliver into my hands. She clearly states that when asked who was first born, the servant girl pointed to me. She did so not once, but many times"

Again he pointed a finger at the two sobbing women.

"But you ignored her, you refused to change your minds as to who was first born"

Aloud murmur rose from all those assembled. Someone at the back asked

"What of the others your majesty, what do the other two ladies say about that night?"

William shook his head.

"Nothing, they say nothing because they are both dead. I have spent the last month riding the width and breadth of the Kingdom searching for the truth. I was alerted by this"

Again he held the parchment high.

"A deathbed confession no less, made by someone who wanted redemption for the crime she had committed, and now you have the admission of these two that the servant DID point to me as the true King"

Again a stirring of murmurs, a deathbed confession is held in high regards by most. The atmosphere in the hall began to change and the confession from the ladies admitting the servant girls chose William made many think a miscarriage may have taken place. William spoke again addressing himself to the Barons and others of high rank

"All of you knew my father well, he was a great warrior. He proved himself in battle many times, as I have also done. We both led our troops into battle as any true Darosi would"

He pointed to Robert.

"How many battles has he fought, how many times has he acted as a true Darosi would have? I will answer for you….NONE. So I ask the question, which one of us is more like the true son of Eric. Which one is the more fitting to sit on the throne?"

There was a low muttering from those assembled. Many thought Williams spoke the truth, and began to think thoughts that would had been unthinkable only a few moments before.

Chapter 23
Princess Aquilia intervenes

Suddenly another voice could be heard above all the chatter.

"There was another present that night that you have not heard from"

The Princess Aquilia stepped forward to stand beside them

Prince William shook his head

"You are wrong, there was no one else there, I have looked in every direction, followed every lead, and found nothing"

Princess Aquilia shook her head.

"I was there that evening, I begged my mother to let me attend the birth, but she refused. I was only twelve and not yet into womanhood, and she thought it unwise that I should witness what could sometimes be a painful event. I think she was afraid I would shy away from motherhood as a wife. But my grandmother Queen Helois did not see the harm, so she smuggled me in through the servants door on the understanding that I stayed in the outer room until the births were complete. I agreed along with the promise that I would be allowed to tend the babies as they arrived. I wished to forget the saddest evening of my life, and have never told anyone that I was there when our mother and grandmother died"

She turned to Robert

"It was I who washed you clean after your birth, and dressed you in fine blankets to keep you warm"

She then turned to William

"I was still washing you when those who were attending our mother called out that she was dying. The Queen mother called for one of the servants to take me back to my room. But I persuaded her to let me stay by the door so I could hear what was happening. I started to cry when they both died, and did not resist when I was quickly led away. This is the first time I have spoken of that evening in all the years that have followed"

She turned to both the Ladies-in-waiting

"The servant girl was unable to answer the question you asked because she did not know. She had only entered moments before I left with jugs of warm water, and had not attended the babies in any way. She was confused, and only picked William because she was afraid she would be beaten if she did not give an answer"

William shook his head

"No, no, no what you say is too neat, far too neat. You speak now to help Robert securer the throne"

Robert spoke in anger.

"Do you call your own sister a liar?"

William nodded

"Yes, yes I do, you were always her favourite, I see it all now. When we were young it was you she mothered as if you were her own child. If she was there that night why have we not heard of this before? Like I said, this is all too neat"

Robert stood down from the throne, Livia tried to stop him approaching his brother by holding his arm, but Robert shook her free and confronted his brother face to face.

"Just a few short months ago you pledged to our father that you would accept me as your King. Does your word mean so little that now you try to win the throne for yourself?"

William shook his head in denial

"I did not know then what I know now"

William pointed his finger at Aquilia.

"And it is plain to me now that it was you who used your influence over our father to make such a demand of me. Even then you were trying to secure the throne for Robert."

Robert spoke with a mixture of anger and sorry in his voice.

"You have become twisted in your mind brother, and your heart is set on the throne before all else. You have heard from our own sister the sorrowful events of the night our mother died. Her own words condemn you to be second born, I am willing to forgive you if you swear allegiance to me. If not, then in the name of peace I must banish you from the Kingdom"

The tension now was so high it was as if the air was charged with electricity. William shook his head.

"No, no, it is all a trick to rob me of what is rightfully mine. It is you who must swear allegiance to me, and you must do it now or…"

The sound of a great intake of breath filled the hall as his hand grasped the hilt of his sword. Those closest to him said afterward that they saw the sword move slightly as he begun to draw the weapon. But before the act could be completed the silence was shattered as a strong voice cried out.

"Do not draw your sword Prince William!!"

There is a natural reaction in almost all people that if they are given a command in a forceful tone, for a moment at least they will obey, Alexis' intervention had that required effect, the sword remained undrawn, and William loosened his grip on the handle. Alexis had now reached Roberts' side, and his concern for his safety was greater than ever. He stood only feet away from his brother, and within easy reach of William's sword. With slow gentle steps and his hands in a posture of prayer not to cause any reaction he moved just in front of Robert, a movement on the other side of Robert caught his eye. True to his word, Denis stood next to his King, as ready as Alexis was to lay down his life if necessary. Alexis said to William in a quiet calm voice

"I'm sure that with good well this matter can be resolved without blood being spilled"

William's eyes flashed with anger as he turned away from Robert and confronted him.

"You dare to give me orders?"

Alexis gave an apologetic smile in reply

"I do not mean to offend you in any way your majesty, but there are some deeds that once done, cannot be undone"

William said in anger

"But you do offend me, even the sound of you breathing offends me. Compared to me you are little more than a dung heap. Now be silent, I do not wish to hear another sound from your lips"

He turned again to his brother, but thanks to Alexi's intervention the moment of high tension had passed.

"I will not swear allegiance to you, not now, not ever. If it takes me a thousand days and ten thousand lives, I will sit on the throne, and you will either bend your knee to me or be in your grave"

Chapter 24
Revenge at last

Just then one of his men stepped forward, because he had concentrated so much of his attention on Prince William, Alexis had not even noticed that Lord Ravenhead was among the half dozen. Now the hated lord stood before him.

"You dare to stand before my King and give orders? You common cur, you yellow bellied coward"

He turned to all present and pointing to Alexis spoke in a loud voice.

"This is just one more reason why William should be King,

He again faced Alexis.

"Cowards like you would find no welcome in *his* court. Just by living you offend all true and brave Darosi, my King would wish not to hear you breathe"

He took another step forward and drew his sword in the same movement. He held it high above his head ready to strike a mortal blow and shouted at the top of his voice.

"I grant him that wish"

The Princess Aquila and Livia screamed, a loud gasp came from all others, and Robert made a movement towards the young lord, but none were close enough to hinder the blow from being struck.

But the blow never landed, now all his months of practice with Halsey served Alexis well. He stepped aside from the blow with ease and grabbed Ravenhead's wrist as he lunged passed. With a sharp twist he forced the sword from his hand. Then in one seamless movement he held his arm behind his back and swept his legs from under him. Both men landed as one, Alexis on top with his knee firmly planted in Ravenheads' back. Ravenhead was not a small man and with the extra weight of Alexis and his armour he made an almighty clamour as he hit the floor. The force of his landing was so great it took all the wind out of him and send his helmet cartwheeling away to stop at the feet of Robert. Without loosening his hold Alexis took Ravenhead's own dagger from his belt, then holding the point to his throat he said in a voice edged with anger.

"Try to touch your sword again my lord and I will carve you a new mouth"

The whole incident had taken no more than a second or so.

Both Robert and William had the look of shock on their faces, but Robert's was tinged with a smile. He held a hand out in a gesture to stop.

"Hold fast my lord, I do not want any death on the day I ascend my throne"

The smile became more prominent as his mischievous sense of humour got the better of him. He moved to Ravenhead's side, and looking down at the fallen lord said in a voice loud enough for all to hear

"It appears you are wrong in your judgment my lord. The man you call a cowardly cur is more like a lion, and a mighty lion at that. So mighty it appears that even if he is unarmed, he can still take your life anytime and anywhere he wishes"

He looked up at William, and nodding towards Alexis said.

"He amounts to a great deal more than just a dung heap brother, would you not agree? Perhaps next time you might address him in a more respectful manor. It would be very undignified for a person of royalty to end up as…."

He did not finish the sentence, but looking down at the helpless Lord Ravenhead, his meaning was clear

Those close enough to hear and understand the true meaning of his words could not resist a smile and a gentle laugh that helped to lower the tension a little more.

Robert turned and again mounted the throne. Princess Livia again moved to his side and held his arm firmly. If Robert tried to confront his brother again he would have to drag her with him.

Those that lived at court and knew the history between Alexis and Ravenhead were shocked into silence. Although they would never openly admit to it, many feared Ravenhead, thinking him to be a great warrior. To be defeated in the blink of an eye by someone who was unarmed, and supposed to be without any fighting skills, was too much for them to understand. Those who lived afar, and were unaware of the magnitude of this event were also stunned, not because one man had defeated another, but the manor and speed of the defeat. Although it had happen before their eyes, the speed was such that most had no idea of how it had been accomplished.

Now with perfect timing the castle guards entered the hall with swords drawn and surrounded Robert, more appeared on both sides of William and his men. And to complete the entrapment, the Master -at-arms with a dozen more men approached them from the rear. If William had intended harm to Robert the chance had passed. Now, under the threat of so many blades, and with their own swords still undrawn, William and his men had no choose but to surrender their weapons. Alexis helped Ravenhead to his feet, he whimpered loudly as the point of the dagger drew a small trickle of blood.

"Move slowly my lord, I would not like to ruin the royal carpet with a stain of red"

Alexis turned towards Robert

"What shall we do with this boastful wretch your majesty"

Robert knew what this moment meant to Alexis, his revenge had been long in coming. He decided to make Ravenhead suffer a little longer, and again his humour came to the fore as he answered. He spoke loudly so all could hear his words.

"His fate is of little interest to me, no true Darosi would attack an unarmed man. You defeated him Lord Monrell it is for you to decide. But please, if you are to slit his throat choose a time other than at my coronation"

He waved a hand in a casual manor.

"And do it somewhere where it will not matter if the stain of blood shows"

Lord Ravenhead eyes bulged with fear that they should discuss his life in such a trivial fashion. Now he stood on tiptoes and gave another whimper as Alexis pressed a little harder with his dagger. After a moment he lessened the pressure allowing Ravenhead to return to a normal stance.

"As you say your majesty, any day I choose"

Chapter 25
The Tide Turns

Now the mood in the hall was firmly on Robert's side. Thanks to Princess Aquilia intervention for many William had lost his argument about who was first born. And because of Ravenhead's hot-headed attack, swiftly followed by his defeat, William had lost the initiative. Now unarmed and surrounded by guards it was he and his men who looked under threat. Once again Robert appealed to his brother.

"I ask you again, for the good of the Kingdom well you accept me as your King. You can sit by my side in high office as befits your rank, or you may live in your own castle on your own estate if you wish. I do not want to spill the blood of Darosi to hold that which is mine by right"

William had stood speechless and in shook that one of his most feared warriors had been defeated so swiftly. Now he senses returned, along with his anger. The anger was all the greater because he also felt the change in the people. He was losing the argument on all fronts, but he refused to give up.

"Never, the throne is rightfully mine, and I will have it. If needs be from your dead hand'

Robert gave a deep sigh.

"Think brother, think. If you refuse to honour me as king, then you leave me no choose. I must banish you from my kingdom"

Robert looked intensely at him, hoping to see some sign that sense would prevail, but for the moment William stood with a defiant look set hard on his face. Perhaps some time to think would help him see the truth.

"You have until the morning to change your mind and believe the words of our sister the Princess Aquilia. I give you this last chance because I still have brotherly love for you, and do not believe for one moment that Ravenhead was acting on your orders. If I thought that then all of you would spend the rest of your days in the castle dungeons"

Robert sat back on his throne, Princess Livia knelled by his side, but still held his arm tightly.

William took a step forward.

"I do not need the help of others to do my killing, Ravenhead acted as Ravenhead always acts, without thought. If I chose to kill any of you, I would do the task myself. This affair is not ended, the throne is rightfully mine and I will have it"

He turned toward the nobility gathered there and spoke in a voice loud enough so that all could hear his words.

"And when I have the throne, I will restore the Darosi to their rightful place. The towns and ports would be conquered one by one. And all those who are not Darosi would be slaves, and forced to kneel before us. We will be great again as we were in the old kingdom"

Robert spoke with sadness in his voice

"You will be held under guard in your own chambers for the night to ponder on your future. If by first light you do not accept me as King, you shall be taken to the port of Egion and placed aboard a ship. You shall be banned from this kingdom. If you return without the promise of peace between us then the price of trespass will your life"

He gestured to the Master-at-arms

"Have Prince William escorted to his chambers, and place a guard at his door. No one is to have contact with him without my permission"

He waved an arm to Williams men.

"You have a choose, you can swear allegiance to me now, in which case you will all go free, or you can spend the night in the castle dungeons, and follow William into exile come the morning"

Lord Lucose stepped forward.

"I will pledge allegiance to you your majesty. I came here with William because I honestly believed him to be the rightful king, but having heard the Princess Aquilia speak of that night I know I was wrong to think such thoughts"

He quickly knelled before Robert.

"I most humbly ask for your majesty's forgiveness, and pledge my sword to your cause from now on"

Robert held a hand out in his direction.

Lord Lucose kissed the royal ring on Roberts's finger.

"Arise my Lord Lucose, I do not wish to take the life of any of my subjects that does not need the taking. I forgive you for the error in your ways, may we both live long and prosperous lives"

"I thank your majesty for your kind judgment and understanding, from now on I will be a man for the true king and no other"

Robert looked at the others who had come with his brother.

"Lord Lucose has decided to accept me as his King, do any of you wish to follow him?"

His question was greeted with silent until one of the lords stepped forward

"We are King Williams's men, we choose the dungeons every time before swearing allegiance to another"

The others nodded agreement. Robert sighed.

"So be it, Master-at-arms, escort these men to the dungeons and make them secure"

As William and his men turned to leave, Robert gestured to Alexis to release Lord Ravenhead, who bent down to retrieve his helmet, as he turned he was confronted by Alexis now with his sword in one hand and his dagger in the other.

"Your sword and your dagger will remain with me my lord. I will keep them as souvenirs, and every time you hold their replacements, it will remind you of his day"

Lord Ravenhead slowly backed away, he had been too humiliated to argue, so with his head bowed he silently turned and followed closely behind the others. When they disappeared Alexis handed both weapons to one of the guards for safekeeping.

Now that the danger had passed, what remained of the tension disappeared like a puff of smoke on a windy day, and the hall exploded with loud muttering. Each asked his neighbour to confirm that the events they had witnessed had really happened. All agreed that never in living memory had there been such a coronation as this. Most sentences started with the words "Did you see" referring to a fight so short that if you blinked you had missed it. The thoughts of all present fell mainly into three camps. Some believed that Robert was the true heir, and accept the throne as his birth right, while there were a few who still had doubt as to the true King. But there was another line of thought that for the moment only lived secretly in the minds of many. They saw Robert as someone not worthy to be King, he did not speak or act in a true Darosi manor. They would prefer William to sit on the throne, even if he was not first born. After all, he had promised to take control again of all the towns and ports, this would insure an avalanche of new taxes and wealth as the Darosi emptied the purses of the rich who lived there. As an added bonus for many he also would reduce the peasantry to the stature of slaves. But these thoughts were not for discussion now, they still had a crowning to perform. But at the back of the minds of all was the thought that the story would not end here. Everyone doubted that William would give up the throne so easily, the future could still hold a great deal of sadness and death before peace would return to the land.

The Keeper of the Book of Knowledge had quickly faded into the background out of harm's way. Now he stepped forward again and in a slightly pompous voice addressed all gathered there.

"Let us put the unfortunate events of the last few minutes behind us, let the crowning continue"

Chapter 26
Just Rewards

The rest of the ceremony passed without a moment of concern, and it was almost an anti-climax when the crown finally rested on Robert's head. All proclaimed Robert as their King, shortly followed by the crowning of Queen Livia. It was a much relieved Alexis who now with his proud father hanging on to his and Leon arms for support followed his new King and Queen from the hall. Gaia was just a few feet in front of him, and even after the stressful events just passed, and surrounded by all the high nobility, her elegant walk and the gently swaying of her hips brought love and desire to his mind in equal share. Between the brothers they more than half carried their father back to his rooms. Damon immediately lay on his bed, he had taxed his strength to the limit by standing for so long a period. Alexis poured him a full glass of winter wine quickly followed by another as he sat by his bedside. Alexis could see the pain etched on his face.

"Do you have nothing to ease the suffering father?"

The baron moved a little to find a position with the least pain.

"Sometimes I chew the leaves of the Bay laurel tree, but at best they only dull the pain, and I have used all I had"

"Rest easy father, I will consult with the court doctors, I'm sure some can be found for you"

As he turned to leave, the Baron reached up and held his arm.

"I judged you wrong Alexis, and for that I am sorry. I asked you to uphold the family tradition and serve the king, and you have done all I asked of you. Today you showed me your true worth, you are more worthy to be my son then I am your father. I hope in time you will forgive me for being so blind to your virtues"

Alexis blushed inside, he had never expected ever to hear such words of praise from his father, and for a moment he was speechless, a very common occurrence of late. His father sunk back on the bed, his face twisted with pain.

"Thank you for your kind words father, I only ever wanted to please you, now I will see that you have something to ease the pain"

Alexis left Leon to help their father as best he could. He called to see one of the many court doctors that had attended the late king. His father was in luck with the Bay laurel leaves, the king had also used them to relieve his pain. A good supply would be send at once to the Baron's room. As he returned to his own quarters he remembered about the substance they had found in Egion, if Halsey rode hard, he could be back in less than two days.

While Huggle helped him out of his coronation robes he gave him orders to ride as fast as he could and purchase a good supply of the 'Ah-pen-yen" (opium) to relieve the pain for his father. Alexis had just finished changing into new clothes when a message arrived from King Robert. He wished to see Alexis at once in his chambers. Alexis wondered what could be so urgent, but it suited him to go, he wished first to speak with Robert, then to Gaia to reinsure her that all was well.

King Robert was now safely installed in his new chambers and on entering Alexis bowed before his new sovereign

"You sent for me your majesty, how may I serve you?"

Robert smiled

"You have already served mightily today my lord. I am told it was you who summoned the guards to the great hall to protect me and my Livia. I must confess I was so taken up with William that the thought to send for the guards never entered my mind. But best of all was your magnificent defeat of Ravenhead, Where in the world did you learn to fight in such a manner? You took all the wind from Williams sails, and made him and his men look small by your valour"

He gave a little laugh as he recalled the events

"You must teach me that trick you played on Ravenhead"

He laughed again as he added.

"There are a few on the High Council I would dearly love to treat in similar manner. But your revenge on Ravenhead was truly superb, and the look on his face when I bid you not to stain the carpet, I have not stopped smiling all afternoon with the memory. I have never seen a man go from *so* brave to *so* humble in *so* short a space of time. Truly Alexis, I doubt that a King was even better served by one of his subjects. And I do not forget young Denis, he showed courage and loyalty today and should not go unrewarded, I think an Earldom somewhere would be a fitting reward, but I will leave that for you to decide. As for you my lord, the Queen and I have discussed what would be a fitting tribute. We have decided to reinstate a position that existed for many years until the time of my grandfather. We will announce your new appointment at the dinner tonight. We tell you now so that it will not be a surprise to you. From this day onwards you will be known as 'The Kings Chancellor" second in authority only to me. Your word will be obeyed as mine would. And we have one more wish, that you take our old royal chambers for your new home, now if you wish, or when you and Gaia are married"

Alexis was stunned into silence

"You pay me too great an honour your majesty, for the second time today I am rendered speechless by events".

Robert smiled

"What other event could possible match the one I have just given you?"

This time it was Alexis who smiled.

"It was my father your majesty, for the first time in my life he asked for my forgiveness. He admitted that he had misjudging me as a son, and told me how proud he was of me"

Robert could not contain his amusement, he chuckled for a moments before saying.

"I am not surprised you were rendered speechless, my late father spoke of Baron Monrell many times. He often told me he was the most stubborn man he ever knew. They often had words together, sometimes in anger, and the Baron would never admit that he was wrong or in error in any way, even to his King. A truly mighty event my Lord Chancellor, but one you richly deserve"

Alexis give a bow of thanks.

"I will attend to the matter of Lord Denis your majesty, there is another point that needs our urgent attention. The transfer of William to a ship"

Robert looked bemused.

"Why does such a simple task need our attention? Just send a strong escort, it is less than a day's ride to Egion, and surly with enough coin it will not be too hard to find him a passage?"

Alexis shook his head slowly.

"William could have troops close by in large numbers your majesty, we could be sending the escorts to their deaths. I have an idea that may outdo any plans William's allies may have to recuse him"

For the next ten minutes he told Robert his plans. Robert agreed that it was unlikely that anyone would think of transferring William in such a manor, but wondered if such a plan was necessary. He thought that Alexis was being overcautious, but gave his Chancellor permission to proceed, he added with a smile.

"I think you have surprised many today my lord, including Livia and myself. I remember you telling me long ago that you need time to deal with Ravenhead, but your revenge was so great and overwhelming that it left all who saw it in awe of your fighting skill. I doubt there will be anyone at court now my lord who would dare to draw their sword against you"

Again he laughed, Alexis just smiled in reply. He was already thinking about the consequences that were sure to follow today's events, he again bowed.

"Thank you your majesty, now that I am here I wonder if it would be possible to see the lady Gaia for a short moment. Like all of us she was upset at the events this afternoon, and I would like to reinsure her that all is well"

Queen Livia smiled,

"I thought you might like to see your bride to be"

She pointed to a door a few feet away.

"Lady Gaia waits for you just beyond that door"

Alexis bowed his farewell

"Thank you your majesties'

He entered the room, and there she was, sitting in a chair looking more beautiful than ever. They quickly embraced, words tumbled from their lips in between the kisses.

"O Alexis, I was so afraid for you, my heart was in my mouth when Ravenhead attacked you"

Alexis made light of the attack

"You need not have worried my love, that bumbling oaf is so slow I'm surprised his armour does not freeze with rust every time it rains"

Gaia beat his chest with her tiny fists

"You should not take your life so lightly, he could have killed you"

She reached up again to kiss his lips

"And if he had killed you, he would have also killed me my love"

The kisses grew more passionate, both were aware they were alone. For a moment the passion overcame them, and Gaia did not protest or resist. It was Alexis who recovered his senses first.

"No my love, I wish with all my heart to take you now, but we must wait. You must be pure on our wedding night, and I must be patient"

The passion slowly died, Alexis held her in his arms.

"Soon my love, soon we will belong to each other for the rest of our lives"

At the feast that evening King Robert announced the new appointment of Alexis as the Kings Chancellor. For almost all, it was his defeat of Ravenhead that made the appointment acceptable. Before this event many had thought him a man of little ability. But his courage in defeating Ravenhead while unarmed had changed all that. He had proved his worth, and so the position was well earned. Many were still reliving with words the events of the afternoon, and still could not understand how it was accomplished. All agreed they had never seen a man fight in such a manor. Some of the older men more steeped in tradition thought it ungallant to fight in such a way, but they were few in number, and their voices small. Not all the nobility were invited to the feast. Even as the celebrations were getting underway, a few had already begun their return journey to their estates. But Lord Lucose did not take the road home, he rode with all speed to the north, to a point just a few leaguers away where a force of men along with Baron Fairchild were camped. The Baron would wish to know what had happened in Castle Kingshome that day. He rode hard and reached the Baron's camp a few hours later. Fairchild was angry when he heard the news. He had counselled William not to confront Robert without an army at his back, but the young prince was too hot-headed to heed his words, and had raced ahead to stop the coronation. Now he must set about rescuing him, without William to lead, no army would rally to his banner.

Chapter 27
The Trap is Set

In the small hours of the morning, long before dawn showed its first light, two columns of mounted men rode away from Castle Kingshome, each had a separate duty to perform, the largest headed in the general direction of Egion, the other turned a different way. The cock had crowed and the sun had risen when another smaller column containing only six or eight men and one covered coach left the castle ahead of the rising tide and took the road to Egion. The coach moved at a slow pace, and the men sang as they went, as if had not a care in the world. It was a fine late spring day, and at around midday they stopped to take a drink. From a distance the men looked at ease, but close up they showed a different face. They eyes constantly moved as they scanned the road and land close to them, they were all on high alert, as if knowing events were about to take place. And suddenly it happen, a force of men, some forty strong appeared out of the woods a hundred paces ahead of them. The escort immediately abandon the coach and wheeling their horses around rode back toward Castle Kingshome at full gallop. The attackers cheered their easy victory and surrounded the coach. Baron Fairchild was fifty paces behind his men as one of them opened the door. The man instantly cried in surprise.

"The coach is empty my lord, we had been duped"

The Baron immediately turned his horse and rode away, shouting over his shoulder.

"It is a trap, ride for your lives!!"

But for almost all of his men it was already too late to flee, most had dismounted expecting Prince William to alight from the coach. Now from both sides of the road companies of the King's guards burst from cover with swords drawn and fell on them from behind. The fight lasted barely ten minutes, five of the Baron's men were captured, another five or so escaped with the Baron, the rest lay dead where they fell. The Kings Guard suffered barely a scratch, now along with their capture's they rode back to Castle Kingshome .

Later that day, in the company of Queen Livia, The Commander of the Kings guard Lord Duncan gave a full report to Robert. He ended with the words.

"It was just as you said your majesty, they were waiting for the coach which they thought contained Prince William"

He added.

"At least we know the source of their information your majesty, the body of the traitor Lord Lucose was among the dead, he will never swear a false oath again. We outfoxed them this time your majesty, but for your plan I fear William would already be among his allies plotting to steal your crown"

Robert silently nodded agreement, but the plan was not his, once more he was indebted to his Chancellor for wise council. He thanked Lord Duncan, and with a wave of his hand. The lord bowed and withdrew. Queen Livia had sat and listened to Lord Duncan make his report without understanding any of it.

"You mean Prince William was not in the coach? Then where is he?"

She turned to her husband for help,

"Am I going to be kept in the dark? Please explain the details to me my love, where is William, have we lost him?"

Robert made a calming gesture with his hands.

"No, no my love, we have not lost or misplaced William. Our Lord Chancellor foresaw the attempt William's allies would make to rescue him. So he devised a plan to foil both their attempt to rescue William and a trap to catch any that tried, and it appears he has succeeded on both counts"

Queen Livia waited for further details, but Robert lapsed into silent. Finally she asked in frustration.

"Well where *is* William! And what of Lord Alexis? Tell me that no harm has befallen him"

Robert shook his head in admiration.

"I doubt that any harm has befallen him, when Lord Duncan said we had outfoxed William's men he was telling the truth better than he realized, Alexis has the cunning of a fox, and the fighting skills of a lion. Even now in all probability he has begun his return journey. As for William, I am equally sure he is already sailing into exile."

He looked at his wife and smiled.

"Our Lord Chancellor sailed with William and his men not long after midnight from the nearby harbour in two of their larger fishing boats. You know that Egion is a full day's ride away by land, but by sea it is less than three leagues away. I should think he had already reached his destination before the coach was even attacked"

Queen Livia breathed a sigh of relief and sat with a contented smile on her face.

"You do not know the calmness Alexis brings to my mind Robert. I feel the respect and brotherly love that you both have for each other. With him by your side I am sure you are blessed by the Gods and they will keep you both safe from any harm"

Alexis returned to the castle a few hours later and gave a full account to Robert.

"Prince William sails to Brimmeon your majesty, by chance I met a ship's Captain I've have had dealing with in the past, he was about to sail and only too willing to earn a few extra gold gilders. I stayed and watched until the ship was below the horizon. But I fear we may not have seen the last of Prince William. His last words to me were that he would return, and claim the throne for himself. They were spoken with great determination and anger"

Robert shook his head in sadness.

"I pry to the Gods that he will change his mind my Lord Chancellor, we must do everything possible to avoid such an event from happening"

Alexis was silent for a moment.

"William's allies will quickly find out he is no longer in the kingdom. Even as we speak they could be asking questions around the seaport, seeking news of what ships sailed from Egion on this day and their designation. And there is always the possibility that someone saw something and is willing to tell all for silver or gold"

He paused in deep thought.

"I fear William could be returned to Santross within a month your majesty, perhaps six weeks at the most. What of the men who tried to release William from our care, do they say who ordered the attack?"

Robert shook his head.

"Not so far, each claim to be acting on their own, but it is noted that all come from the northwest of the kingdom"

Alexis nodded his head.

"As we thought, from that part of the kingdom dominated by Baron Grimswick and Fairchild, two of William's strongest supporters. And nether attended your coronation to swear allergens to your majesty, claiming that they were too ill to travel"

Robert massaged his forehead with his fingers as though he had a headache.

"Lord Dungan fancies he saw Baron Fairchild in the distance but he was too far away for him to be sure. I could summon them to court, but I fear they would refuse claiming they were still too ill to travel"

Alexis shrugged his shoulders.

"I agree with you your majesty, but there is no need for the Barons to be summoned, with a little thought we already know who our enemies are"

Chapter 28
The Teacher is Appointed

The next morning Alexis was up early. Despite the fact that William was by now many leagues away at sea his vision of the future was still filled with darkness and death. In his heart he knew that somehow this affair was destined to end in war between the brothers, and it would mean the certain death of one of them. His first visit was to Andras, the Master-at-arms. He wanted to know the strength of the garrison and their readiness for battle, the news was a mixture of good and bad. The bad news was the number of men was less than five hundred, the good news was they were regarded as the best trained troops in the whole army. Alexis asked if there was any way to quickly increase their number. Andras shook his head.

"I doubt it my lord, there may be a few knights of the Kingdom who would fight by your side, but I have found them only to fight well when they outnumber the enemy, they are less reliable when faced with a larger force"

Alexis presided

"What about the soldiers that fought under Williams command, would not some of them prefer to fight for Robert?

Again Andras shook his head in a doubtful manor.

"Those that are Darosi by birth are good troops, I trained a few myself. If I could talk to them I'm sure that many would join us, but even if they did we would still number a lot less than William could have. Most of the armies of the west are mercenaries hired from the northlands. They would be more interested in booty rather than loyalty my lord. They can be bought, but would quickly change sides if they saw a better reward elsewhere. In that respect they are no better than the knights"

Alexis pondered for a moment

"We must do all we can to increase the number of men at our side. Can you let it be known that any man, no matter what his past will be treated well if he joins us?"

Andras nodded his head in agreement.

"We can post in all Darosi villages, sometimes the endless toil of trying to live off the land can wear a man down so much that even a soldier's life seems attractive. And word has a habit of getting around my lord. It is already widely known of the kind deed you did for the soldiers' famines in giving them good homes to live in. If the Barons do declare for William, It would not surprise me if some of their Darosi solders would come over to our side"

Alexis secretly smiled inside, it had given him much satisfaction when he had built those homes, and now there was a chance that his good deed could give him more of a reward than he first thought. An idea had come to him a few days before, the Master-at-arms was skilled in the training of others, if he could be recruited to perform such a task with the outsiders their chances of success would multiply, he decided now would be a good time to ask.

"How long would it take to train men well enough to give a good account of themselves in battle?"

Andras shook his head

"It depends on the men my lord, if they are eager and not afraid to lose their lives they can learn to defend quickly. To learn how to march and hold formation for attack requires more skill and training"

Alexis looked at the Master-at-arms intensely.

"I think we all know that with William unwilling to give up his claim to the throne there is a war coming, I also know you are a godly man of good character and loyal to Robert. Are you prepared to do all you can to save Robert's crown"

Andras answered with a touch of annoyance in his voice

"I serve King Robert to the full my lord, with my life if necessary and no other"

Alexis nodded

"I'm sorry Andras, I did not say the words to mean any disrespect, but I will ask you to perform a task that is outside your normal duties, and it will require a man with great determination to carry it out"

Over the next twenty minutes or so Alexis told him all about his undertaking with the estate workers and outsiders, and the use of the bow as the main weapon of attack and defence.

"They are willing to fight William, and to die in doing so if it is the will of the Gods. They fight to save themselves and their families from slavery. But they lack skills in warfare. If you and some of your instructors could help them, you would be saving many of them their lives, and costing William many of his own men in the doing of it"

The master-at-arms said nothing for several seconds.

"Is it the Kings wish that I undertake this task?"

Alexis shook his head

"I have not yet told the King of these men, I wish them able to display some skill before I offer them to him. Otherwise he may think them unworthy to stand by our side in battle"

Andras was silent for a moment

"You do all this for the King, and he does not know of it?"

Alexis nodded his head in agreement.

"Yes, but the King is a man of honour, he may not agree to use the weapons I offer, or to use them in the manner I plan to. In the past, nobility has always fought nobility, and the common soldier fought common soldier. But I plan to fight a different way, the bowmen will attack all our enemies and not worry if they kill horse or rider. To the Darosi the horse is sacred and must never be deliberately injured, so all this may be for naught. But the outsiders will still fight, be it by Robert's side or on their own. They cannot afford not to, if William wins he will make slaves of them all. And there is one more point to consider. It does not matter who wins the coming battle, when the armies of the North find out the Darosi are divided, the whole kingdom will quickly disappear under an avalanche of foreign armies. The only hope for the future safety of the kingdom is a victory for Robert, and the support of the outsiders to boost our numbers"

After a moment thought, Andras nodded his head.

"I will help train your army of farmers and herds men, but to what degree I cannot promise"

Both men shook hands, Alexis quietly whispered

"For the King, and the future of Santross"

Alexis reasoned than Williams' allies would show little aggression until his return, so he choose this time to travel north and visit those few Lords who in the past had strong links with the throne and might declare for Robert. To be so close to his possible future enemies carried some risk, but it was one he was prepared to take to booster Roberts' following. His journey had been mainly fruitless, apart from a few half-promise's none of the lords he had called on would openly declare for Robert. Now he was travelling south again on Edmonds Way, one of the major roads between north and south, and the most likely route that William would take if he invaded. They came to a place where the road divided, to the left Edmonds Way continued, to the right was a lesser known route called Tennyson's Way, named after the lord who had built it many years ago. He decided to take this road home for no reason that he could later remember. After less than a league the road wound its way through a deep rocky gorge. A land slide from some time in the past made the last few yards so narrow that only a few horses could pass at a time. Then the land quickly opened up again to become several hundred paces wide and stretched in a straight line slightly up hill for as far as the eye could see. An idea began to form in his mind, that idea took shape when they next came a field planted with wheat that was still many weeks away from being ripe enough too harvested. The road at this point took a sharp turn to the left and formed the front border of the field, a small bank formed the side nearest the road and joined with a steeper bank that formed the back edge and stretched for its whole width. Without warning he reined in his horse and looked around, now in his mind he could see the whole battle. He could see where the pike men would stand, where the mounted archers would ride, and where he would stand with Robert and all the other Darosi. In a few seconds he had found the perfect place to fight the battle, and more importantly, the manner in which to should be fought. Now all he had to do was find a way to pursued William to walk into his trap. He sat for a moment in deep thought, but nothing stirred in his mind. Maybe the Gods would give him some help later, for now he had to be content to have found a place where the battle could be fought, the means of bring William here would have to come later. Now on his return to Castle Kingshome he sent Captain Caius and several troops to travel north. Half would go to Castle Grimswick, the others to Castle Fairchild. They would join with the outsiders already there to first watch for the return of Prince William, and secondly to gather information on how many Darosi were calling on the Barons to swear allegiance for the coming war. Captain Caius and his men would look with a solders eye on Robert's enemies, they would notice small things that others could overlook. He reminded him again of his strict orders.

"You are not to expose yourselves to any danger, keep hidden at all times.

There is a village called Hempfield less than two leagues from Castle Fairchild, go there and seek out a man called Will Halfready, he has arranged suitable vantage points for each castle. The outsiders will supply you with food and drink and hide you if it is necessary"

Chapter 29
Three ships to sail

A few days later Alexis with a small escort rode out of Castle Kingshome and headed in the direction of Egion. He had arranged to meet a ship owner called Captain Callan there in one of the many inns that lined the waterfront. He had often traded with the Captain for goods when he had run his father's estate. Within half a day a deal was made to hire his ship plus two others to sail to Thanjab, and safely bring back a cargo that was much needed. He rode through the night back to Castle Kingshome, and after only a few hours' sleep was up and about again.

His next task was to send for Lord Denis, Gaia's brother, he had proved his worth by standing with him to confront William and his men. The young lord entered

"You wish to see me my lord?"

Alexis nodded

"Yes my Lord. In the Kings' and my eyes you have proved your loyalty by your deed at the coronation. I have an important task that I wish you to carry out. You know William will not give up his claim to the throne?"

Denis nodded his head in agreement

"I think everyone had fear of that. Do you think there will be war my lord?"

It was Alexis turn to nod in agreement.

"Yes, yes I do. Even as we speak, his allies seek to return him here, and when they do, they will gather an army for him"

Alexis left his desk and stood looking out of a window. He had taken up the offer of Robert and moved along with his father and brother into the much larger royal chambers directly below those of the king. The move suited him for more than one reason. The most important being that now he controlled all the passages to the Kings' chambers. Already he had replaced the normal castle guards with men from his own personal bodyguard. They had strict orders that no one was allowed to enter without his permission. The other reason was of a more personal note, being higher up, his view of the castle ramparts was even more spectacular than before, and such a view always lifted his spirits. He half turned round to look at Denis as he spoke.

"And I fear that war is much closer than we think"

Denis ran a finger over the pommel of his sword as if to show he was ready to use it.

"What would you ask of me my lord?"

Alexis turned to face him.

"I want you to sail to Thanjab, then travel on to Lalang and offer to buy as many horses as you can. Make it a condition of the sale that the Lalang must deliver the horses safely to the ships waiting in Thanjab before they are paid"

He smiled as he went on

"I have traded with the Lalang many times, and found they can be quite forgetful if you pay them before the goods are delivered"

He returned to his desk, and placed a large bag of gold coins before him.

"Here is the money for them, remember we do not need warhorses, I want you to buy horses that are swift and strong of wind, and Lalang has many of these. You will have many of the men from the kings' stables with you to help pick the best stock and tend to then on the return journey. You will also have my assistant Conway with you. You must heed his advice and let him take the lead in most things. He knows the Lalang well and speaks their language. Some of my own specially trained soldiers will also be with you for protection. Never send them away, always have them by your side, you will live longer."

Denis looked puzzled at such advice, but nodded his head in agreement. Alexis continued

"There are three ships waiting for you in the port of Egion. The name of the man you seek is Captain Callan, he will be staying in a tavern called "The Mary Best" Conway knows where it is. When you get to Thanjab, Captain Callan has arranged for a guide to show you the rest of the way. Your return to Santross will also need to be discreet. Three days ride to the east is the small port of Godspit. Many years ago it was a busy port with a good size harbour, but it silted up and now can only be used when the tide is full. There are less than fifty people living there now and they are all related to Conway who was born there. He is sure that our arrival there is a secret that will be kept. I will arrange for you to be met there by enough men to herd the horses inland"

He sat down again at his desk and stated writing.

"The king has also asked me to find you a suitable reward for the courage you showed at the coronation. I can tell you now that I have decided that on your return from this mission, the King will knight you, and you will be given the title of Earl of Greenburg"

He looked up at Denis and smiled.

"The King does not know it yet, but he will also grant you the sum of five thousands gilders to fund your new estate"

Denis was clearly pleased with the news.

"I thank you my lord, both you and the King are generous in your reward. I will do my best to deserve the honour, and serve the king, with my life if necessary"

Alexis handed him the written note.

"Here is a written order for you. God speed my lord, and a wish that you will be successful and return with a full cargo"

A few days later Alexis again paid a visit to Ben Tiller to arrange for a company of men to me sent to Godspit. Andras and his other instructors had already begun the task of making order out of chaos as they trained their men from morning to night. Alexis told Ben the bad news that even as William had set foot on board the ship that was to take him into exile, he swore to return and claim the crown from Robert.

"Even as we speak he sails further away, but I fear his friends will find him and return him to Santross, of that I am certain. When he returns, he will most likely stay with Baron Grimswick, or Baron Fairchild until he can raise an army. He will not want to wait until next spring, so I think he will strike before the winter is upon us"

Both men stood on the edge of a wheat field. Alexis absent-minded rolled an ear of wheat between his fingers as he had done so many times before. Due to the long winter and cool spring it would be a late harvest this year, the wheat was a month or more behind what it should be for this time of year. As the seeds fell to the ground he wondered if there was some way he could make use of this fact to help his cause. These days his mind never stopped thinking about the battles to come, and how best to fight them. He had a hundred ideas a day, only to reject all of them after further thought, but he must keep trying. William was a proven commander who had fought many times in battle, while for Robert and himself it would be their first test. The use of mounted archers was his main hope of surprising William, a form of fighting never seen before on Santross, but it would do no harm to have one or two other tricks up their sleeves to surprise him with. He brushed his hands clean before adding.

"I'm sure that before summers' end we will all know what our fate is to be"

He stood for a moment in deep silent.

"I think it could be dangerous for the cause if I come here too often, any spies that William will send will no doubt follow my movements closely. From now on I will visit you less often, and be more discreet when I do. If you need to send me urgent news then use the delivery of estate products to the castle as cover. I will arrange for one of those I trust to make contact with them"

He looked around the encampment.

"The longer William does not know of these men, the better our chances of surprising him on the field of battle"

Ben nodded his head in agreement.

"A good thought my lord, if William does not know about us, he cannot plot against us"

Ben sighed in disappointment.

"But is sad news about William still wishing for the throne my lord, but if we are destined to meet in battle he will find we have not been idle these last few months. We now have over fifteen hundred men in this camp who are willing to fight for Robert, and a dozen or more join each day. We work the men hard, and most use the new bow, we have just over a thousand at the last count, and the number rises with each passing day. I don't know how many arrows we have, but by the time they are needed there will be more than enough"

Alexis nodded his head at the good news

"What about the mounted archers, how do they fair?"

Ben became very enthusiastic as he replied.

"It has been a revelation my lord. We have almost six hundred men training to fire while mounted and they have mastered the skill much quicker than many of us thought possible, and I include myself in that number. Many can hit the target three times out of four at fifty paces. We could train more if we had the horses. The number now stands at just over a hundred, they came to us in ones and twos at a time. Where they came from I have no idea, and thought it better not to ask."

He could not stop smiling

"They will give a good account of themselves my lord, of that I have no doubt. Would you like to see some of them training?"

Alexis nodded his head in agreement

"Very much so, lead on Ben"

It took over two hour's hard riding to reach the camp where the mounted archers were being trained. Both Halsey and Alexis greeted each other warmly.

"It is good to see you again my Lord, how goes Huggle these days, does he still eat enough for both of you?"

Alexis laughed loudly.

"He is still the same, only now he eats half of my meals instead of yours. I have come to see the progress our mounted archers are making. How soon do you think they will be ready to fight?"

Halsey smiled as he answered

"They could fight now if need be, but to what degree I cannot say"

He held his head low, as if in deep though

"Three more months my Lord, give me three more months and they will be a force to be reckoned with"

Alexis replied

"Let us hope William will oblige us. Now let me see the results of your labour so far"

They moved to a meadow flanked by thick trees to stop prying eyes. Each rider rode at a full gallop as he fired his arrow at the target, some missed the target completely, others missed the outline of the rider, but clearly would have hit his horse, either way the knight would have been rendered helpless. Without a mount, even those with a heavy suite of armour would be an easy target for any bowman. Alexis congratulated Halsey on the work he had already done, and stayed the night. The next morning Alexis and Ben returned to the main camp. As they rode Alexis asked Bed if it was possible to send people north to keep them informed of events

"When the time comes, we will need to know when William plans to march on us, and the route he is to take, could the people of the land tell us such things?"

Ben ran his fingers through his hair

"I think it would be possible my lord, we could easily find out when he plans to march, no doubt he will use some of us outsiders to load his wagons and supplies. As for his route of march, that is harder to know, unless he takes some outsiders with him, there are many roads he could take"

Alexis pondered for a moment

"Then we will need to post men on every road to inform us of his movements. Will you pass on to all your people in the west that if they see any of his soldiers to somehow get word to us?"

Ben nodded, and smiled as he answered.

"There is little that goes on in both sides of the Kingdom that we do not know about my lord, I think I can promise that you we will know more of his movements than he will about ours"

Alexis nodded.

"Good, if we can find out his plan of march we may be able to find land that would be an advantage to us in battle"

A week later Alexi's received a message from Ben Tiller that gave him good news. Three days before the ships of Lord Denis had returned with over three hundred and fifty horses. He added that he will sail again as soon as the ships can be made ready. He has already agreed a price with the horse traders of Lalang to buy over three hundred and fifty more. When he arrives there the horses will be ready for him. If the next shipment is as good as this, they would have over eight hundred mounted archers.

Chapter 30
The State of the West

When the island of Santross had been formed the lava had flowed mostly in a westerly direction, so this side of the island was almost twice the size of the east and the most heavily populated part of the Kingdom. But it was more than just a chain of mainly extinct volcanoes that separated one part of the kingdom from the other. The river Hunggot marked the boundary between slavery on one side, and a degree of freedom on the other. On all the land north and west of the river the outsiders had always been treated as slaves. They were not thought of as people, but as property to be bought or sold according to the whims of their masters. They and their families were forced to work the land without pay or reward, kept there by an army of guards who did not hesitate to kill those who tried to escape. From the start those estates closest to the river Hunggot and the mountains would lose a few slaves each year as they made their dash for freedom. The Darosi would climb the mountains or cross the river to try and recapture them, but sometimes if the original escapee was hard to find, they would just take the first outsider they found. They would also sometimes cross the river and raid deep into the east to kidnap any outsiders unlucky enough to cross their path. This made the Darosi on the free side of the river very angry, and sometimes they would return the raids and try and free their workers who had been taken. At one time he raids increased almost to the point of an all-out war. That possibility was only adverted by the intervention of the King. He declared that any Darosi of the west found guilty of raiding in the east would be put to death. At the same time he ordered that any slaves who escaped but found must be returned to their owners. But still each year many escaped and were not returned. The Darosi of the west accused those of the east of encouraging the outsiders to escape, even hiding them from capture. This had caused an ongoing rift to develop between the two sides of the kingdom that never fully went away.

The outsiders themselves also helped those in slavery. They set up escape routes and found shelter for those who managed to avoid capture. Alexis had taken an interest in all this when he found out that a brother of Conway called Talan had organized such an escape route. The ones who organized and run these escape routes were always under threat of betrayal, the Darosi of the west offered a high reward for their capture. In the end this is what happen to Talan and he was quickly executed. With the pasting of time the plight of the people in that part of the kingdom had come to weigh heavily on his conscience, in his mind it was just one of the many things that needed to change if Santross was to have any kind of future.

Now although it was not yet plain to see, the north and west were slowly dying. The Darosi never became involved in the actual running of their estates, all the work was done by the outsiders. And to keep them from escaping they had to employ an army of guards, this was why the armies of the west was so much bigger than those of the east. This expense was a great drain on any estate. Over many years the skill needed to produce the best harvests had been lost and now with a mainly unskilled and unwilling workforce even with good weather the harvests were barely able to produce enough income. For the last few years bad weather had produced a series of poor harvests so that when Baron Fairchild and Baron Grimswick had approached the cash-poor nobility many were forced by circumstances to join William's cause. The harsh winter that had just pasted added greatly to their problems. It had caused more hardship than usual, and many of the poor and frail had died due to the cold and starvation. The north did not have the supplies needed to keep an army in the field for a long period, so they must wait until Williams' return before they could begin to gather. The problem then would be that there were few roads in the north, and those that did exist were badly maintained and little more than dirt tracks, it would take time, and time was something they did not have. William would need to move fast, or his army would quickly become more interested in seeking food than battle. The reports that followed over the next few days confirmed that events were turning out as Alexis had predicted. The Darosi were rallying to William's banner in large numbers. The age of unconditional Darosi honour was over, now it had a price, and William and his allies was promising to pay that price with the untold wealth of that would come from the conquest of towns and cities.

Many evening now Alexis and Gaia would dine with Robert and the Queen. Now they sat together as they again discussed their delayed wedding plans, and for the first time they had a disagreement. Alexis wanted to postpone the wedding, at the back of his mind for the fear that if they married now, Gaia could be a window in a few short weeks. She argued that there was no point in waiting, and wanted the marriage to take place as soon as possible.

"Let us not waste precious time by worrying what the future may hold for us my love. But let us take all that life can offer while we can"

She had a serious look on her face as she continued.

"I know why you hesitate Alexis, you think of me and wish to spare me the anguish that our marriage may be a short one, but I would wish us to wed even if it was for a single day, and you cannot yet be sure that there will be a war"

Both Robert and Livia agreed with her, with such powerful allies Gaia got her wish, so reluctantly Alexis agreed for the marriage to take place, hoping the date would be far in the future. He was taken back when Queen Livia declared the date would be only a week hence. Alexis made one last desperate attempt to postpone the wedding.

"That is too near your majesty, you could not possible make all the arrangements is such a short space of time"

Both Queen Livia and Gaia eagerly said it was. Robert just smiled as he said.

"Your last hope of a postponement is lost my lord, the ladies have out-maneuvered you. I'm afraid my Queen Livia and your bride-to-be have been working on the arrangements for many weeks passed without your knowledge, everything is ready and in place"

Alexis could do nothing but accept defeat with good grace. If it was the will of the Gods that he should marry then so be it. In truth the distraction of marriage would be a welcome rest from the heavy workload he had been under for many months past. He spent his remaining days of bachelorhood in the castle. He still received almost daily reports from Ben Tiller and none said that Prince William had yet returned to Santross. Free from the thoughts of an immediate war his love and desire for Gaia again began to dominate his thoughts. From the first moment he had seen her it had been his one great wish that they should be married, and now that wish was about to come true. Gaia had been right, the truth was now clear to him. It *was* better to love even for a day, than to have no love at all. The day dawned bright, it was now midsummer and the long days with warm sunshine made an ample reward for the hard winter just past. Just as the bell of noon sounded, Alexis stood before the keeper of the Book of Knowledge, the sound of trumpets filled the great hall as Robert escorted Gaia to Alexis' side. Alexis looked across at his bride, she looked utterly stunning in a long pale blue dress, her long blond hair covered by a veil interlaced with flowers cascaded down her back to her waist. Never had she looked more beautiful. They both knelt at the alter as the service began. The vows were spoken, the promise of safe-keeping and honour were made, and finally the symbolic wedding bond of rich cloth was placed around their wrists as the words were uttered

"You are now bound for life, the two become one before the eyes of the Gods"

The keeper leaned forward and whispered softly.

"It is done, you may now kiss your bride"

And kiss they did, with a tenderness and obvious love that made all the women present sigh as they remember the day they too had been wed. At the back of the assembly a married woman of long standing placed an elbow with some force into her husband's ribs, his gasp of pain echoed faintly around the hall as she asked him in a whisper why he no longer kissed her in such a manor.

And so it ended, they all followed Alexis and Gaia as they left the hall. That evening the wine flowed freely and the singing and dancing never stopped. Much to Livia annoyance Robert could not restrain himself from hinting of the night to come for the newlyweds. Both Alexis and Gaia took his jests in good spirits, but spent a good part of the evening with embarrassed looks on their faces. The evening finally came to an end, and with loud cheers from all their friends the young couple departed. We need not go into details about the events that followed, it is enough to say that Alexis *did* have the desire and strength of a lion, and by morning Gaia was a very happy and contented wife in every way.

Chapter 31
The Return

Although Alexis did not know it, on the day of his wedding William returned to Santross to be met by Baron Fairchild. He landed at the small northern port of Baruron with the few men he had been exiled with. Without delay they rode with a strong escort to the safety of Castle Fairchild, once there Baron Fairchild and Baron Grimswick informed him that almost all the nobility of the north and west were ready to join him in his quest to seize the throne from Robert. Their reward would be a sizeable share of the gold that would come with the conquest of the towns. William reluctantly agreed, he had eyed the wealth of the towns for his own treasury, but without an army he could not have the crown, and he wanted that more than money. The Baron Fairchild also told him of his failed attempt to secure his release.

"We surrounded the coach, only to find it empty. Then we in turn were surrounded by the Kings guard. I lost over thirty good men, and barely escaped with my own life"

William gave a sound of displeasure.

"That accursed Lord Monrell took me to Egion by sea. I must confess my brother surprised me with such a cunning plan, normally his head is more full of wine rather than clever thoughts. I was already aboard a ship before your attack on the coach. I am sorry you lost so many good men, but we will make Robert pay with his own life for their deaths"

Baron Grimswick stroked his beard.

"Lord Monrell is now Chancellor Monrell, second only to the king himself"

William slowly nodded his head.

"Robert probably gave him the post as a reward for what happen at his coronation"

Fairchild looked puzzled at William.

"What did happen at the coronation? Lord Lomax told me of the intervention of Princes Aquilia, and the way you were taken prisoner, but he was vague about how Monrell defeated Lord Ravenhead saying it must have been done by some kind of magic"

William shook his head.

"I saw it with my own eyes, and I am still not sure how Monrell won the day. It happened in the blink of an eye, one second Lord Ravenhead was about to deliver a fatal blow, the next he was on the floor with his own dagger at his throat. He now claims that he put so much power into the blow that he overbalanced and fell to the floor, stunning him and allowing Monrell to take his dagger"

Grimswick made a sound that suggested he was not fully convinced.

"Do you believe him your majesty?"

William again shook his head.

"I am not sure, in all my time at Kingshome I thought little of Monrell as a man. Many think him to be a coward with no fighting skills. I myself have seen him almost run away when Ravenhead approached him. I find it hard to believe that such a man could suddenly change into a great warrior, so that Ravenhead claims could be the truth"

William made a cutting movement with his hand to signal the end of the subject.

"Let us move on to more important matters, I do not fear either Robert or Monrell, in my eyes they are both small men of little account, if it comes to a battle we will brush them aside without much trouble."

He looked at Fairchild and Grimswick

"How many friends do we have in the Castle Kingshome that will do our bidding?"

Fairchild looked a little sheepish as he answered

"Eight, if we do not included your men, there were nine up until a week ago, but Lord Cecil challenged another knight to a dual, but the stupid man was so drunk he fell on his own dagger"

Lord Cecil had picked a bad time to remove himself from this world. But the man had spent more of his life drunk than sober, so he was not surprised at the way of his demise. Only he knew the names of the people Fairchild had referred too, and it only took a moment for him to decide that they should remain hidden. William drummed his fingers on the table.

"Eight armed knights should be enough for the task I have in mind. My brother is a trusting fool, he never has more than a few solders' guarding his chambers. We have one chance to assassinate him, if it fails, then you can be sure from then on he will be surrounded by guards day and night. His loving wife Livia will see to that, but if they succeed then the kingdom will be mine, and the war will be over before it has begun"

He looked at them both.

"Let it be known to all, I will pay 100.000 guilders to the man or men who can rid me of this accursed brother who has robbed me of my rightful throne"

Grimswick and Fairchild both smiled and gave a grunt of approval, Grimswick put their thoughts into words

"A most generous amount your majesty, there are many men in the kingdom who would kill their own mother for a fraction of that amount."

Fairchild nodded his head in agreement before adding.

"With such a sum on his head, Robert will live every day in fear. He will see assassins behind every bush, every curtain, each holding a knife ready to plunge into his back"

He laughed as he added.

"And one day it will be so, the sum is too great to be ignored"

William smiled, there was always those who would risk everything for a large sum of money, perhaps even someone close to Robert would want to claim the reward. He pondered on that though for a moment before adding with an evil sounding laugh.

"I throw many seeds of greed to the wind, who knows where they will land and take root"

Again he laughed

"Now let us assemble our army, if the assassination plan fails, the battle to come is certain to give us the conquest that will make me king"

The three men laughed loudly, they were supremely confident that if there was to be a coming fight, it could end only one way, with victory to William, and death to Robert.

Chapter 32
An Army Gathers

The week following the wedding was bliss for the couple. Alexis signed no documents' or become involved in any undertaking. All his duties were performed by Stephan and Conway while he enjoyed total rest and the company of Gaia. All this came to an abrupt end when Captain Caius returned with news of William. It was as Alexis had suspected, William had made Castle Fairchild as his base. The Captain completed his report by saying

"I left Sergeant Moro, and privates Kimon and Tellis to keep watch on the castle my lord. One will ride to tell us if William leaves before my return, while the others would follow him."

He added quickly

"There are many Darosi joining William's army my lord, and not all of them are from the west. I saw the banners of Lord Carsell and several others from the east who have joined their cause"

He hesitated for a moment.

"I also saw Lord Giles, Lady Gaia's half-brother, he rode with Baron Fairchild"
He bowed his head.

"I am sorry to bring you such bad news my lord"

Alexis shrugged his shoulders, the news was disappointing, but not totally unexpected. He told the Captain to eat and rest overnight, but tomorrow he should return to Castle Fairchild. Again he reminded him to be careful.

"Do not take any chances of being found out, send a rider each time you have something to report. I need to know what William's strength will be for the coming fight"

Alexis was sure there would be many more Darosi who would now change sides. They would use the doubt as to who was the rightful king as their excuse. But he would worry about that later, first he must let Robert know that his brother was gathering an army. The King greeted the news in a sombre mood, he had hoped that William would give up this quest for the throne. If William was gathering an army, then he must do the same. Riders must be sent to the four corners of the kingdom calling all loyal Darosi to arms. Robert was confident that all would respond, Alexis was also sure they would all respond, but was less sure on whose side they would respond to. Without any hesitation Baron Monrell declared for Robert, but due to his state of health was staying here. Instead Leon was dispatched to inform all the nobility of the East and the northeast and gather all his troops at Castle Monrell before returning with them to Kingshome.

Alexis received an urgent message from Ben Tiller, disturbing news had come from the north and it was important that he should know about it as soon as possible. He was still making the occasional visit to Ben Tiller, but now much to the annoyance of Gaia he would leave in the dead of night. After much persuasion Alexis convinced her his journeys were to visit some of the Kings estates, and his early start was due to the distance involved. Now Alexis left with only two of his men as escort and carried no colours that showed who he was. As dawn broke he and his two companions, Sergeant Amos and private Griffin stopped under a large tree to rest their horses. Even before they had time to dismount Sergeant Amos declared they were being followed.

"They rode on for a second or two before they realized we had stopped. I counted two, maybe three horses my Lord"

Alexi's instinctively looked behind. He could not see nor hear anything amiss, but not for a moment did he doubt the sergeants' word. It was well known that for most of his early life Sergeant Amos had been a poacher, and to listen to his tall stories, he must have been a good one. He claimed that in his village he had filled the cooking pots of all those who had grown too old to fend for themselves. Whether that was just a boast or the truth no one knew, but one thing was certain, he could live off the land better than most and had remarkable eyesight and hearing. He had only joined the king's army to avoid a good flogging or worst when his Lord found out who had been taking his game.

Alexis took hold of Griffin's long spear in exchange for the reins of his horse. In a whisper told him to ride on holding the reins of all three horses. He would hide in the undergrowth on one side, while Amos hid behind the tree on the other. He gave instructions to his sergeant.

"I will attack the first man, and you the second"

Amos had a smile on his face as he asked.

"And if there are three my Lord, then what do we do?"

Alexis answered in a light-hearted way.

"Then we better be very good at our task Sergeant, now let us be silent and await our guests"

With seconds Alexis could hear the sound of horses' hoofs on the rocky ground. Amos saw them first, with a sour look on his face he held up three fingers. As they drew level Alexis could see that all three had the coat of arms of Baron Grimswick on their tunics. The first two were riding side by side. He ran hard at them, using the long spear as a pole-vaulter would he soared through the air feet first and knocked both men from their mounts. The nearest one to him had taken the full impact and lay still, while the other stumbled as he tried to regain his feet. Against a man with Alexis training and speed he was far too slow. A powerful thrust with the spear to his chest ended his journey through life. As he looked down at his dead foe Alexis realized what he had just done. He had killed his first man, and had done so with a deathly efficiency he did not know he possessed. Meanwhile Amos had dispatched his opponent with equal ease. Amos looked at the pain on Alexis face, and guessed the reason for it.

"It was them or us my Lord. We only did to them what they would have willingly done to us"

Alexis nodded, what the sergeant had said was the truth, he should not feel any shame for defending himself against those who would do him harm, but he was still shocked that he had taken a life so easily. There must be more Darosi in him than he realised. They turned their attention to the third man who was still unconscious. The sergeant splashed a few drops of water on his face. He came around slowly, when fully awake, he reached for his sword, only to find it had been removed. Alexis looked down at his capture.

"The penalty for spying is death, if you wish to save your life you must tell me what I want to know"

Not wishing to die, the man spoke willingly, but knew little of importance. He told Alexis that he was one of many who were sent to spy on Robert to find out all they could before the coming battle. And if possible to kill any high official who served the king. Alexis asked how they had known about this journey, he pointed to the dead man that Alexis had killed.

"Only he could have answered that, all he told us was that a bright star from the west had showed him the light"

Alexis frowned, that could mean that someone from the castle had given a signal to announce his departure. That worried him deeply. It would have to be someone in daily contact with him and the king to able to observe him that closely.

They reached the encampment by late afternoon. Alexis handed over his prisoner, along with the added bounty of three good horses and saddles for their cause. He suggested to Ben that it would be a good idea to have a few lookouts posted a little distance from the camp, just in case others tried to follow in future. Ben nodded his head.

"It will be done my lord"

Chapter 33
To kill a King

On meeting, Ben told him the news that William had offered 100.000 guilders to anyone who assassinated Robert, and that Alexis would be wise to take extra steps to keep his king safe. Alexis thanked him for the warning. He had already anticipated that there could be one or more attempts' on Roberts' life. He was sure that there were many in the castle who would wish both him and the king dead, and the events of the morning had proved that not all were from the west. When he had first moved into his new chambers directly below Roberts' he'd made certain arrangements' to increases the Kings safety. He had placed several of his now enlarged force of personal bodyguards to the approach's and entrance of the king's chambers. Now on his return to the castle he would double the number of guards on duty, and keep a reserve close by. But with such a large sum of money on offer, his task had just become much harder, the number of suspects had multiplied many times. From now on he must trust no one, and suspect everyone. Now that the possibility of assassination had become a reality, it would be better if he warned Robert of what his brother had done. He was far from being a coward, and he was sure he would just laugh at the threat. But Livia was a different matter, she would be greatly upset at the extra danger her husband was now in, so the extra guards would have to be very discreet in their duties.

On a happier note he could see the encampment growing larger with each visit. This army was now well over three thousand men strong, and still their number grew daily as knowledge of their existence spread. Alexis knew that at some point it was probable that William would find out about this camp, and the efforts of the outsiders to resist being made into slaves. But he was counting on the famed Darosi arrogance to dismiss the idea of an army of outsiders as of no value. The majority of all Darosi still considered the outsiders to be cowards afraid to fight in battle, even to save their own homes and family.

Now the skill of Alexis as an administrator and organizer was plain to see. When men had first began to arrive he had formed a council of a dozen men or more and allocated a separate task for each one to perform, the result was that from the very beginning it had been a well-run camp where all the men were well fed and all had somewhere dry and warm to sleep. The Master-at-arms Andras, and all the other men he had brought with him from Kingshome worked the men without mercy, every daylight hour was spent in turning them into a force capable of fighting and winning a battle. After much thought, and consulting with each other, Alexis and Andras had both decided that due to the lack of time and weapons all the men in this camp would either be archers or pike men. The archers needed the least amount of training. They could already use the bow to a high standard, all they needed was time to grow the extra muscle that the new weapon required. A few days before the newly knighted Earl of Greenburg (Lord Denis) had returned with a shipload of Tashmar pikes, a fearsome weapon that when fitted to a stout shaft was capable of stopping a horse in full flight. This was to be the weapon used by the largest and strongest of the men, a crucial part of their battle plans.

On the battlefield they would be used only in static defence. When set in their positions they needed the raw strength to hold their pikes at the correct angle, and the yet greater amount of courage needed to stand firm as a wall of horses and armoured nights charged down on them.

In the other camp two hours ride away were the hidden horses, over eight hundred of them along with their riders. Here again Alexis influence was everywhere, he organized blacksmiths from the estates and local hamlets to shoe the horses, saddle makers to repair and alter saddles. Along with bakers, cobblers and every other trade that was needed. His attention and knowledge of detail left everyone in admiration of his abilities.

The next day Alexis told Robert that he now had a price on his head. He reacted just as Alexis had predicted, with a laugh. But he insisted that Livia should not be told of this new development, she would worry unduly for his safety. Alexis also told him the bad news about the size of Williams' army.

"We will be heavily outnumbered your majesty. We still have the royal army of some five hundred men, and the Darosi who will fight for you will have another three thousand or so. William will have over ten thousand. It is the same with the nobility your majesty. We have less than two thousand committed to our cause, William has over seven thousand. There are still almost as many who have not chosen, and I doubt that they will. They will wait to see what happens, and then almost at the end when the result is clear, will declare for the winning side"

Robert shook his head in despair

"Does my brother realize that the coming fight will finish the Darosi as a ruling class. Whoever wins, there will be so few of us left, that if the armies to the lands to the north invade, they could conquer us in a single day"

When the members of the High Council heard the news, they asked for an urgent meeting. Lord Avon was the oldest member of the council and spoke first

"We have discussed the situation among ourselves your majesty, and we feel the only courses open to you are ether surrender your throne, flee the Kingdom, or prepare for a long siege, with the hope that William's army will grow tired of waiting and return to their homes"

Alexis was shocked at such a suggestion.

"You cannot take any of those suggestions your majesty. To flee or give up the throne will give William a bloodless victory. To remain in Castle Kingshome would be just as bad. He would rule the Kingdom, while you would rule a rock in the sea. He would be free to do all that he wished, and we would be trapped within these walls, unable to interfere with his plans"

Lord Fellows rose to his feet, his dislike for Alexis was well known, and now he added his weight to the argument for Robert to abdicate.

"We cannot meet William on the field of battle Lord Monrell, he outnumbers us at least four to one. To do so would invite certain defeat and death for us all"

Alexis replied

"We *must* defeat William in battle"

He thumped the table with a clenched fist to drive home the point.

"Do you not realize the certain outcome if Robert follows any of your suggestions my lords? What do you think will happen to the Darosi who have pledged their support for Robert? They will have to recognize William as their King, or die as traitors. If we just hide like scared children in this castle he will carry out his threats, he will attack the towns and try to make slaves of all the outsiders. But even if he does nothing, the people of the lands to the North will know we are divided, and will see their chance to invade and conquer us"

Most of the council jumped to their feet in anger. Again Lord Avon spoke first.

"Scared children my lord, you call us scared children, how dare you. I have served on the high council since before you were born"

He gestured with his arm to the other members of the council.

"All of us had to serve the King for many years before elected to this high office"

He looked sourly at Alexis.

"All you did was exposed a minor thief of no great importance. You are not yet wise enough, or schooled in the art of leadership enough to give his royal highness the advice needed at this time "

He turned to Robert

"I fought with your father in many battles the last time the armies of the North tried to invade, and I will not be spoken to in such a manor"

Again he waved his arm at the council.

"None of us will"

Robert held out his hand as a gesture of calm.

"We all know you are a man of great courage Lord Avon, along with all others on this council. I'm sure Lord Monrell did not mean to suggest otherwise. Is that not so my Lord Chancellor?"

Alexis knew by the look on Robert's face what was expected of him

He nodded agreement.

"Of course your majesty"

He turned to Lord Avon and the rest of the council

"I am sorry my lords, my words were spoken in hast and I did not make my meaning clear. I ask for your forgiveness if I have offended you in any way"

Lord Avon nodded his head in acceptance of Alexi's apology, but it was a token gesture. He did not like the young lord, but for some reason he had the ear of the King. And Robert was also turning out to be a disappointment, he would act in a casual manor, and often utter words that made no sense to him and called it "humour". Robert never seemed to take his Kingship seriously. He was so different to his late father. He had been a true king in every way, and had always taken the advice given to him by the council. He ended his daydreaming with the thought that maybe it would not be so bad a thing if William did sit on the throne. The meeting went on for several minutes longer. It ended with Robert promising to give their suggestions a great deal of thought.

Chapter 34
A Little Hope

When they were finally alone, Alexis decided that if Robert was considering giving up his throne, he should first know about Ben Tiller, and the efforts that the outsiders had made over many months.

"We still have some hope your majesty, the people of the land will help us if we are prepared to treat them in a more equal way"

Robert acted as if he had hardly heard him, and was slow to respond.

"What was that you said, the people of the land help us, what could they do? They have no skill in matters of war. They have not been allowed to use or own weapons for two hundred years. I doubt there are more than a dozen or so that could wield a sword. No my young lord, for once you give me bad advice"

Alexis shook his head and smiled

"Perhaps your majesty would care to see for yourself what they could offer you in defence of your throne"

Robert paused for a moment, Alexis had never given him false advice in the past. And there was something in the tone of his voice along with a sparkle in his eyes that said he was not telling all there was to tell.

"What have you been up to behind my back my Lord Chancellor? You are too perky in your manor considering the bad news you brought me. And how do you know what the outsiders have to offer? You speak as if I am to be let into a long held secret"

Alexis shrugged his shoulders.

"Yes your majesty, It is perhaps time you knew, many of the outsiders have worked for several months to make themselves worthy to stand beside us, but it would be better for you to see for yourself, rather than just be told"

Robert was silent for a moment, what did he have to lose? At worst he would have wasted a few days, at best it might be that Alexis had found some magic solution for their situation. He slapped his hands on his thighs, a common gesture of his when he came to a decision. Later that day Alexis sent word to Ben Tiller that Robert would meet with them and see for himself the progress made.

Just past midnight that evening Alexis was awakened by one of his soldiers. There had been an attempt by some armed knights to enter the Kings' chambers, but the extra precautions he had put in place had foiled them in their efforts. He put on some robes and made his way to the Kings' chambers. He was met by Sergeant Hugo, the bodies of five knights lay in the passage way.

"They tried to enter the kings' chambers my lord,"

He added with a sad note.

"We lost one of our own men dead my lord, and another wounded"

Alexis ask what had happen, the sergeant replied

"When they first approached us we had no idea of their true purpose my lord. One of them held what looked like a message in his hand. He claimed it was of great importance and he must see the king at once. Our orders are to let no one enter the kings' chambers without your permission, so we refused to let them pass. Only then did they draw their weapons and showed their true intent"

He looked down at the bodies.

"Five have paid for their treachery with their lives, there are two others my lord who we disarmed, one of them badly wounded. They have been taken to the dungeons."

Alexis looked at those who had fallen. He recognized one of the dead by name, it was Lord Herman, the son of Lord Allard. His estates bordered the river Hunggot on the eastern side. Both he and Herman had come to Kingshome at the same time, but while he had prospered, the man now dead at his feet grew bitter at being overlooked for any post of interest. The others he vaguely remembered as minor nobles living at the court trying to gain favourer from the king.

"Was the king awakened by this disturbance?"

The solider nodded his head

"Yes my lord, the sound of steel on steel carries a great distance in the quiet of the night."

The sergeant looked down at the bodies.

"The fight did not last long. They thought their armour would keep them safe, but all armour can be overcome with a quick thrust of a blade, you just have to know the right place to strike"

Alexis nodded understanding. A night in full armour would think himself almost invincible against an ordinary soldier, but his men were not ordinary soldiers. Halsey had trained them in the same skills of fighting as himself.

"I will enter and reinsure the King that the danger in passed"

A few minutes later both men sat facing each other across a table. The king with his usual goblet of wine in his hand, the only sign that he was troubled was he took more than just a sip at a time. He looked at his Chancellor.

"You were right, as usual. You said there would be an attempt on my life. I thought to make a jest of it. I was sure I was brave enough to face any who tried. But I had not reckoned that if they killed me, they would also kill my Livia, and that does worry me."

Alexis shook his head in sorry.

"It was not hard to suppose that William would try to accomplish your death by any means he could, so when news reached me that he had put a large sum of money on you head I was not surprised."

Robert brought the goblet down hard on the table.

"So be it, if William can place a price on my head, then I can place one on his"

He took a deep breath and another mouthful of wine

"Let it be known that any man who takes the life of William, will be offered any estate in the kingdom as a reward, along with 100.000 gilders"

He ran his fingers around the rim of his goblet, as if he was already sorry to have wished the death of his brother.

"I do not want the queen to know about this, she has just told me she is with child again, and this news would cause her great worry"

Alexis looked surprised.

"The queen does not know, how did you explain the disturbance to her?"

Robert nodded his head from side to side.

"Fortunately I did not have to, because she is with child she has not been well lately and took a sleeping portion to give her rest, she slept soundly and did not stir".

Alexis bowed acceptance.

"It will be as you wish your majesty, news of this event will not reach her ears"

He returned to the guards outside the chambers, the bodies were already being removed.

"The king does not wish for what happen here tonight to become common knowledge. Not a word of it must pass your lips. It would greatly upset the queen to think that Robert was now in greater danger. Clean all the blood from the floor, and dispose of the bodies. As for those who surrendered, they can stay where they are until I can fine time to deal with them"

The solider nodded his head in reply

"Yes my lord, it will be done as you order. No one will speak of this night, and no mark will remain to show that any of this happened."

But there were others who would know of tonight's events within days. Early that evening a knight had rode out of Kingshome. Hardly anyone noticed his departure, he was just one of many who came and went each day from the castle. But he did not ride far, just far enough to hide behind some trees. There he dismounted from his horse to kept watch on the castle. He was waiting for a sign, a light from one of the windows of the king's chambers. He waited all night, the first streaks of dawn lit up the eastern sky before he wearily mounted his horse to ride north. He knew their mission had failed, the king still lived. Williams' only hope now was there were still others in the castle who were willing to risk their lives to secure the throne for him. There were rumours that such men existed, as he rode north he hoped they were more than just rumours.

The next morning with a strong escort the King along with Alexis left the safety of the castle before too many prying eyes were about. On their arrival at the camp Robert was greeted by the council representing the outsiders and estate workers. Ben Tiller gave a slight bow

"We are honoured that your majesty has paid us a visit"

He nodded to Alexis,

"The lookouts informed us a many minutes ago of your coming. As you suggested on your last visit my lord we now had all approaches guarded out to three leagues or more. Now no one will be able to ambush you again as they did last time"

Robert looked at Alexis with a puzzled look on the face.

"Explain yourself my lord chancellor, how were you in harm's way"

Alexis reluctantly told Robert about being followed by some of Grimswick's men, and the attempt on his life. Robert listened in silence as Alexis told him in a modest way that he had dispatched two fully armed soldiers in seconds.

Robert looked at his chancellor with a clear look of respect on his face.

"You never cease to surprise me Alexis, truly you have become a warrior that few if any could better. And of course you told no one on this?"

Alexis shook his head

"No your majesty, you were still unware that the outsiders were being trained to fight by our side, so I could not tell anyone of the event"

Robert remembering the attempt on his own life the previous night could understand Alexis' reluctance to speak about the incident.

"Firstly I thank the Gods for your survival, and secondly as you keep my secret from Livia I will keep yours from your young bride. Like my Livia she would worry greatly about your safety"

He gave a gentle laugh as he said

"It is good that a man should have some secrets from his wife. But be more careful in future my lord chancellor, I care much for you and your bride"

Ben Tiller had stood discreetly in the background during this conversation. Now he stepped forward and held his arm out in the direction of some chairs and a table with a bottle of wine on it.

"If your majesty would care to sit and take a glass of wine"

As Alexis passed he silently said sorry for his slip of the tongue

For the next hour Robert was first given a demonstration of the power of the new bow. He watched as a hundred men marshalled by one of the castle instructors quickly formed two rows. Targets were set up one hundred paces away for the men to fire at. The instructor gave the order to fire, almost every arrow thundered into the targets shredding several to pieces. Robert was impressed.

"That is fine shooting, but why are we using arrows. Are there no swords to use?"

Alexis shook his head.

"We do not have enough swords to arm them all your majesty, and even if we did, there is not enough time to train them in its use, but all country folk know how to use the bow"

He gave another signal, another set of targets were set up two hundred paces away. Again the order to fire was given. Perhaps a few arrows missed their target, but the result was almost as devastating as the first. Again many of the targets were shredded. Robert now showed much more interest in what he was seeing. The targets were set up for a third time, but now at a distance so great that Robert had to rise from his seat to see them. He turned to Alexis.

"This is impossible, there is not a bow in the kingdom that could carry that far"

Alexis smiled

"Then be prepared to see the impossible your majesty"

For the last time the order to fire was given, the arrows travelled straight and true. The targets were so far away that Robert along with Alexis and Ben Tiller had to walk closer to them to see the results. They were not shredded as they were earlier, but enough found their mark or landed close enough to impress. Robert stood and stared for several seconds. He had just witnessed something he had not thought possible. And more was to follow. The archers were replaced by men carrying very large pikes, a fearsome weapon some twelve or more cubits long. They marched up and down going through a few of the manoeuvres they would need on a battlefield. They ended their display in a defensive stance with the long pikes held at the correct angle to repel attack.

Robert was impressed, he turned to Alexis

"I see you had time to train them in the use of a weapon I have never seen before. Where do they come from, and why are they of such a size. Surly a nimble soldier could easily avoid the point of the weapon?"

Alexis had been afraid the Robert would ask this question. He was equally sure he would not like his answer, but the king had to be told the truth.

"They come from Tashmar, and you are right, they are not meant to defend against soldiers, they are meant to defend against horses. As for the training, they somewhat resemble a pitchfork your majesty, a tool all who work the land are familiar with"

Robert sat quietly, the jest of comparing it to a pitchfork was lost to him as the full meaning of the words filled him with sadness. It took several seconds before he could speak again.

"You mean to defend against the noble horse by killing it"

Alexis was silent for a moment

"We do what we must your majesty to save the Darosi from destroying themselves"

Robert took another sip of wine. He said more in sadness than anger

"Is this what we must do? Do we now defy the Gods by killing the noble horse as well as ourselves?"

Another sip of wine, another pause before Robert asked.

"How did you come by all this knowledge my lord?"

Alexis looked out over the camp as he answered.

"The knowledge of the bow and how to use it came from my squire. The bows themselves were mostly made by the outsiders, I only supplied the material needed. The pike I knew of from my trade journeys to Tashmar, they used it in their war against the horse soldiers of Lalang some years ago. And finally, the skill of the pike men in using the weapon is due to the training of our own Master-at-arm and his instructors from Castle Kingshome. So you see your majesty, many have helped to give you an army that William will not know exists. And even if he did, he would think little of it"

Chapter 35
Mounted archers to the fore

Robert looked around the encampment as he sat sipping his wine, slowly recovering from the shook of what he had just been told.

"You look after your recruits well my lord, I see only well fed and active men"

Alexis watched his King as he took another sip, always a sip, sometimes only enough to wet the lips, never more. He would often take hours to drink one glass.

The result was he always seemed to have a goblet in his hand which made many people think him to be a heavy drinker, while the opposite was nearer the truth. Robert waved his hand to encompass the surrounding and asked.

"But how did you find the funds to pays for all this?"

Alexis showed a reluctant smile.

"We bear the cost together your majesty. The food they eat comes both from the royal estates and their own, the tents come from army supplies, and the horses you will shortly see were a gift from you"

Robert made a low angry growl.

"How so my lord, I do not remember giving you permission to take from the royal purse"

Alexis looked at his sovereign with a surprised look on his face.

"They were bought with your express orders you're majesty. They were clearly marked on the list of war supplies I presented to you some time ago, the list you did not want to know anything about, I clearly remember you saying "Spare me the details my lord, I give you full permission to buy whatever is needed" Do you recall?"

Robert at first gave a gentle laugh, which quickly grew in volume as his humour returned.

"My Lord Monrell you are a man not to trusted, you trick your poor King into becoming even poorer"

He shifted his position on his chair, and again laughed as he added.

"It is good you fight for me and not William, your cunning ways are as far above me as the clouds in the sky"

Alexis nodded his head slightly.

"To serve you and be at your side is reward enough your majesty, I could never serve another with the same sense of honour as I have for you"

"You please me with your efforts Alexis, I think of us more as friends or brothers rather than a king and his servant, and long may it remain so"

Alexis knew it had been a lie to say that the horses had been on the list, but it was a lie his conscience could live with. It was also good to hear the king laugh again. He had been afraid the events of last night may have affected him, but he seemed to have recovered his full composure. Alexis thoughtfully watched the men all around them training hard for the coming battles.

"I'm sorry we have been forced to bear all this unnecessary expense you're majesty. There are many other things more worthy to spend the royal copper's on"

At last he heard the sound of horses close by.

"There is one other part of this army you have not yet seen your majesty, perhaps the most important part. There is another camp of men training for the defence of your throne, it is deep in the forest of Teal, out of sight of any eyes

William will send to spy on us. The men there are being trained by my squire in a form of fighting never seen in this Kingdom before. I just hope that if we ever come to use them William will be as equity surprised as you are about to be. He raised an arm, seconds later a dozen riders appeared, they rode past at a full gallop, and as each rider passed, he fired an arrow at a cut-out target of a mounted knight fifty or so paces away. Twelve arrows were fired, ten found their target of horse or rider. For the second time in almost as many minutes Robert saw that the horse would again be a target for death. But by far the greatest surprise was seeing men shooting arrows while at full gallop, and hitting their target.

"Archers on horseback, who but my chancellor would think of such a wonder"

He shook his head as he turned away and whispered.

"I hope the Gods will forgive us if we ever preform this deed"

They were joined by Ben and a few others of the council. Robert looked across the table at them.

"And if I agree to accept your offer of help to keep my throne, what would you ask of me in return?"

Ben began to stutter a reply, but he could not find the words to speak. He looked at Alexis for guidance.

Alexis nodded his head in acceptance to speak.

"They wish for an end to *all* slavery, outsiders must be treated as free men rather than the slaves some nobility think them to be. Many Darosi ties them to the land, making them stay and work for little or no reward, always under the threat of death if they try to run away. This must stop, they must be allowed to go where they wish, to work for whoever they wish, and be rewarded fairly for their efforts, and"

He hesitated for a moment.

"They also wish to have the right to own land, and in exchange for this they are willing to stand by our side in any future battles to defend the kingdom"

Alexis finished with the words.

"They terms are fair your majesty"

Robert sat silently for several seconds.

"For my own part I can see the justice in what they seek, but I am not sure that all Darosi, particularly those of the west and north would agree such terms"

Alexis shook his head.

"This fight is for more than just your throne your majesty, it is also for the survival of Santross. We have often said in the past that Santross had to change to survive. Well circumstances have given us the chance to bring at least part of that change about. And as for those of the west and north, they are the ones who have forced this war upon us. If we win they will be the defeated enemy, and a defeated enemy can have little or no say about the future"

Alexis pressed home his point as he touched the pommel of his sword.

"We know it is a certainty that the north will invade, it's just a question of when. And when they do, you will lead your army as any good king would, but without the help of the Outsiders we will be so greatly outnumbered that even with the great strength and courage of our warriors we will be swept from the field of battle. You and I will be among the first to die, and after we had lost the war those of the Darosi who had survived will either be enslaved or would soon join us in the next world"

Robert sat with head bowed and spoke in a whisper.

"I fear it is too much and too quick a change to succeed Alexis"

Alexis sat beside his king, he spoke in a quiet but firm voice.

"Yes it is true, we may fail, but one thing is sure, if we don't try and Santross remains divided than the kingdom is sure to fall. Do you want to go down in history as the last Darosi King to rule? The only chance we have to stop this happening is for all the people to come together. No more Darosi, no more outsiders, just one Kingdom, one people"

Robert gave a deep sigh. It was a sobering thought that he or his brother could be the last Darosi king to rule. What made it even more freighting was that in his heart he knew the words were true. After a pause lasting several seconds Robert nodded, as usual, the young lord was right. Not for the first time he silently thanked the Gods for giving him someone with such wise council. He slapped his thighs to signal the end of the discussion.

"So be it, we will with all certainty need to crack a few heads together, but with your bewitching tongue and wise words to guild us we may have a chance. Now let us put all our efforts into the coming fray"

Both men returned to Castle Kingshome, and for once they were greeted with good news. For some time a trickle of Darosi knights whose code of honour appeared to be greater than their wish for gold had come to Castle Kingshome to join Robert. Now a whole company of some two hundred men had deserted from Williams's army to stand by Roberts' side. Andras had been right, the deed of building the solders new homes had spread and had persuaded some soldiers to fight for Robert knowing they would be treated in a fair way.

Chapter 36
An Offer is made

The High Council again met to discuss the situation, they were told of the offer of the outsiders to fight on Robert's side, but not of the terms they wanted, nor any mention of their numbers. They were not impressed, Lord Avon again spoke for them.

"A complete waste of time your majesty, the outsiders cannot fight, it is not in their blood"

A general nodding of heads by all the others showed their agreement. Lord Barton added.

"Lord Avon is right your majesty, they would only weaken our army, not add strength to it. They would run away at the first charge"

Again a nodding of heads, Robert looked at each member in turn.

"Then what would you have me do my lords"

Lord Avon rose to his feet and picked up a parchment letter from the table

"Compromise your majesty, this arrived the morning after your majesty and your…Chancellor had left on your visit to our new allies"

He gave Alexis a look that portrayed his true feeling for him before handing the letter to Robert

"It has the seal of Baron Grimswick on it your majesty, he sent it by order of William. He offers you and your family very generous terms and a safe passage if you agree to surrender your throne"

He added in a fatherly voice

"To oppose him when the odds are so heavily in his favour is suicide your majesty, to meet in battle could only end in certain death for you"

Robert read the words that had supposedly been agreed by his brother. They were kindly written, and as Lord Avon had said, made very generous terms for his future. He would be allowed to take his family, along with half of the treasury gold and all his private possessions, very generous terms indeed. William clearly wanted a swift end to the affair.

He handed the letter to Alexis, he quickly made the same conclusion.

"Very generous, your brother has modified his terms greatly from the last time I saw him. Then he swore he would put you in your grave, now he offers you your freedom"

Robert sensed the uneasiness in Alexis mind.

"Do you doubt his word? He is still my brother. He offers me exile as I offered him"

Alexis had a worried look on his face as he replied.

"I wonder why William did not contact you himself your majesty. Why did it come from Baron Grimswick?"

Lord Avon made a grunting sound.

"Perhaps because William is too busy marshalling his army, or in a place too far away. It is not unusual for a King to send messages by one of those who serve him Lord Monrell"

He added with a slight smirk,

"If you were older and more experienced you would know such things"

The insult aimed against him was so trivial and of so little importance that

Alexis hardly noticed it, after a long moment of thought he turned to Robert.

"There is something about this does not ring true your majesty. William knows he outnumbers us many times over, with such advantages I doubt he has thought of anything other than a victory. To make such an offer makes no sense, for him to sit safely on the throne you would have to be dead"

He looked at Robert.

"Can you not see the strangeness in him making such an offer your majesty? While you live he cannot be sure that at some time in the future you will not try to reclaim your crown. He even offers you enough gold to raise an army to try"

He shook his head, a slight pause followed before he continued.

"He thinks we may be afraid to meet him on the field of battle, and stay safe in Castle Kingshome which even his army may be unable to conquer"

Alexis again nodded his head, at first he spoke directly to no one as he put his thoughts into words.

"Yes, I see it know, it is no more than a trap to remove your majesty from the safety of Kingshome"

Now he directed his words at Robert

"If you agree to leave this castle, you and your family will be dead long before you take ship to leave Santross"

Lord Avon rose to his feet

"You dare to suggest that a king to be would break his word my lord?"

He pointed to the letter

"That is the solemn word of a king to be, written with honour, delivered with the unbroken sealed of Baron Grimswick to prove its worth"

For a moment he stood as tall as he could.

"No Darosi would break his word, even less one who would be king"

Avon looked at Robert

"You know your brother better than any of us your Majesty, is he not a man true to his word? If William promises you your freedom, then so it shall be. He would not want to lose his honour or defy the Gods by playing you false"

Robert slowly nodded his head in agreement.

"What you say is true, whatever William is, he is first a Darosi, and a proud one at that. There is little love left between us, but even if there was none, I would still think him to be a man of his word"

Alexis placed a hand firmly on the table.

"You judge me wrong my Lord Avon, I do not question the honour of Prince William, I question the intentions of Baron Grimswick. I doubt that William knows anything about this letter, this is a plot by Grimswick to quickly end the war even before it has begun"

Again he paused as his mind raced.

"With each passing moment, I am more certain in my thoughts".

He turned to Robert

"It was the supposed confession from Lady Faustina of the house of Grimswick that helped convince your brother that he should be king. And now a letter with the Grimswick' seal on it offers you and your family safe passage from Santross. I don't know why, but Baron Grimswick appears to be in a great hurry to lay his hand on a large sum of gold"

Roberts's eyes widen.

"You mean the half of the treasury I would have with me on my journey?"

Alexis nodded.

"Yes your Majesty, you see it now as I do. It is just a clever ploy to deliver both you and the gold into their hands. I wager that you and your family along with the gold would disappear. All would think you escaped and were still alive. Hiding in a place far away, with the gold still at your side, no one would think to look for it in Grimswick's castle. At first William would be upset at the loss of half the treasury, but he would soon forget that. To ease his disappointment he would have the throne, which is the prize he wants most".

Alexis sat down as he continued.

"Somewhere on your route of march you will be met by a strong force of Grimswick troops. They may even be presented to you as your escort for a safe journey. But they would be your executioners. You and all your family would be dead, and Grimswick would have the gold he so badly needs for some reason"

Robert looked scornfully at Lord Avon.

"How say you now my lord, if I had agreed to your suggestion, I would have been arranging my own death"

Lord Avon opened and closed his mouth as if gasping for air.

"It cannot be true your majesty, no Darosi would dishonour himself in such a manor"

He pointed an accursing finger at Alexis.

"You do not know this to be true. Somehow you beguile the king with your tongue and make him believe you"

Lord Avon turned to Robert and shook his head.

"What the young lord claims to be the truth is a lie your majesty. One that he invents to keep himself safe behind these walls, and I will find a way to prove it"

Robert looked casually at him.

"How can you prove it my lord, short of seeking council with William himself? As for you accusing Lord Monrell of trying to keep himself safe it makes no sense. If I go into exile there will be no war, and if there will be no war then his life will not be in danger. Yet he councils me to stay, and will fight by my side in any coming battles, which is the only way his life can be in danger"

Robert sat down, the letter still in his hand.

"The words of Lord Monrell have the ring of truth in them. I will not surrender my throne while I live"

Robert and Alexis left together, leaving the rest of the council still sitting at the table in silence. Alexis returned to his chambers and summoned Conway and Stephan, he told them and war was now only weeks away. They had suspended sending suppliers' to the northlands some time before, now they had to arrange for these supplies to be used to feed the Kings army when they marched. As evening fell Alexis paid a visit to the dungeons. He learned that the man wounded during the attempted assassination on Robert had died. Now he interviewed the only remaining survivor. His name was Lord Hallard, due to overspending and bad management he had recently lost his estate to the money lenders. He had come to court and offered his sword to Prince William in return for shelter. Now he stood before Alexis with head bowed. Alexis began to question him

"Who give you orders to assassinate the king, was it Prince William?"

His question was answered by silent. Alexis shook his head in despair.

"Come come my lord, do you think we do not know who your masters are. You have been in the pay of the traitor William since you came here"

Lord Hallard suddenly came to life.

"You mean *King* William, yes, I serve *King* William. He is a strong king, a true Darosi who is worthy to sit on the throne. Not the wine soaked sop of a man that *you* serve"

Alexis was taken back with the force of his conviction and shook his head in sorrow, it was unlikely that even the threat of death would make this man surrender his beliefs.

"You know what your fate must be for the crime you tried to commit. I give you a chance to save your life. If you tell me what I wish to know, then I will ask the King to spare your life and offer you banishment. Now are there any more allies of Prince William in Castle Kingshome?"

The man stood in stony silence. The next hour was spent with Alexis continuing to question him. It would make his task to protect the king easier if he knew of any who would still try to take his life, but Lord Hallard either did not know or just refused to answer. Finally Alexis gestured to one of the guards.

"Take him away, perhaps some time spent in the dungeons' will help him change his mind"

Chapter 37
To Seek the Truth

The following morning Robert sent a message to Alexis to come to his chambers. He entered to find Robert standing by one of the windows with his hands behind his back holding a letter.

"You sent for me your Majesty?"

The letter in Roberts hand caught his attention.

"Is the letter more good or bad news your majesty?"

Robert turned towards him.

"I am not sure my Lord Chancellor"

He handed it to Alexis. Silence filled the room as Alexis read the letter. It was from Lord Avon and most of the High Council. They had decided to ride north under a flag of truce to confirm the terms offered to Robert were true. Alexis shook his head.

"I pry they meets William's men first. If I am right, and it is Grimswick or Fairchild who finds them it will mean their certain death"

Robert held his hands behind his back as he continued to look out of the window.

"I blame myself for their going, my remark about consulting with William was said almost as a jest. I did not mean for them to undertake the task. Whatever you may think about Lord Avon and the others on the High Council you cannot fault their devotion to duty or their courage"

Alexis nodded in agreement.

"I never doubted their devotion or courage your majesty, only their judgment"

Robert turned to face his Chancellor.

"It will add much weight to their advice to abdicate the throne if the offer turns out to be genuine. To stay and fight William, whether we win or lose will cost many lives, perhaps too many lives"

For many days both Robert and Alexis waited for news of the council, but in vain, it was as if they had all disappeared from the face of the earth. Far to the north at Castle Grimswick, the Baron listened to one of his Captains report on the demise of the High Council.

"It was easy my lord, they did not try to resist when we came upon them. They thought the flag of truce they carried would save them from all harm"

Baron Grimswick gave a grunt of approval.

"It is a good thing we found them first. William may well have suspected something was amiss if they had told their story to him"

He made a gesture with his finger.

"You are sure none escaped you?"

The Captain nodded his head.

"Yes my lord, not one, they came to us willingly. They asked us to escort them to William's camp, they wished to confirm the terms you offered Robert to surrender his crown"

Grimswick stroked his beard

"Did you question them before you put them to the sword?"

"Yes my lord, they resisted at first, but pain can wear any man's courage away in time. They told us that Robert has less than two thousand Darosi, and about four thousand in foot soldiers"

The Captain hesitated for a moment, then with a smile on his face he added.

"Robert must be very disparate my lord, some of the high council told us before they died that he may have recruited some outsider's to fight by his side, although they did not know how many"

Grimswick smiled at the news, his views on the outsiders were the same as most Darosi, everyone knew that they were cowards at heart and useless in the art of war. The Darosi had conquered them long ago, and for over two hundred years they had not shown any spirit or desire to oppose their masters in any way. He was confident they would prove to be more of a weakness than a help and would break and run at the first charge.

"Did you bury the bodies well?"

"As well as we could my lord, we had no tools to dig, so we hid them in the undergrowth. I doubt they will be found"

He added in a casual manor and a smile

"Even if Robert knew their fate, he does not have the time to do anything about it, I wager the first he will know of their death is when he meets them in the next world"

Both men laughed, they had not expected the High Council to try and make contact with William. If they had seceded them all their plans would have been in jeopardy, but now the danger had passed, they were safe, and everything was proceeding as planned. What they did not know was that they had killed a friend as well as foes.

Chapter 38
A Spy in our Midst

As the time of war drew closer Alexis was giver the good news that two of the many lords he had called on during his journey north had decided to join Roberts' army. Lord Simmons and Lord Ayers knelled before Robert and kissed the royal ring as they swore allegiances to his cause. Now the wait was almost over as the armies gathered and readied themselves for the war to come. Leon had returned with over a thousand Darosi and the same number of other troops. He told Robert that as they had just began their march to Kingshome they had stumbled upon a small raiding party of men from the Northlands. He had been too late to save the occupants of the farm they had raided, but they had paid for the deed with their lives. But before the leader had died he had boasted that they knew about the war between William and Robert, and were only waiting for Darosi to kill Darosi before they would invade. This was sombre news, but only confirmed beyond doubt what they had already suspected. A day or so later Lord Belmont arrived with another thousand Darosi from the south. A disappointing figure, Robert had hoped for three or four times that number, Alexis was not so surprised. At the coronation Prince William had proclaimed his brother to be an empty headed fool who drank too much, and not a true Darosi king. Few knew the king as well as he did, and many had believed this of Robert long before that day. Now they were showing their displeasure by refusing to defend a king they had little love for.

When the count was made, Robert would have only two thousand nobility on his side, William would have four times that number. Not counting the outsiders the different was even greater with the common soldiers. Although a steady stream of soldiers continued to flee south to join Robert, their number was still barely four thousand, while William had almost three times as many. Sergeant Moro now stood before Alexis, ready to give him the latest news from the north. Alexis looked at the man who was one of Sergeant Caius original squad of twelve. When he had first arrived at Castle Kingshome, he had been the one who pinched him on his cheek and asked for a kiss, but that was long forgotten. Now Moro, like all of Captain Caius squad had become his close friends over the last two years, each liking and respecting the other. Many like Moro had been promoted to sergeant and now had their own squads. The original twelve had expanded to more than sixty, and all of them had been taught in the basic skills of unarmed combat. The Sergeant told him that William had moved his headquarters south. He was preceded by a small trickle of outsiders as they began to flee, the land was being stripped of all supplies and anyone who resisted was killed without mercy. He had not yet invaded Roberts' lands, but that time could only be matter of days away at most. The report was full of facts as to the number of men with William, along with the Lords who rode with him. Alexis thanked the sergeant for a good report well delivered. As Moro turned to leave, Huggle entered to tell Alexis that Lord Ayers and Lord Simmons were here to see him. Alexis bid them to enter. Both the lords walked past Moro without a glance, a common soldier was of little interest to them. Alexis had asked them to come to his chambers to find out many men each had for the fight to come. Less than an hour later he had a request from Captain Caius for an urgent meeting. The sun was just sinking below the parapets when the Captain and Sergeant Moro entered. Caius spoke first.

"My lord, we have news that I think you should know. You had a visit early today from someone we have seen many times visit Baron Fairchild"

He nodded towards Moro.

"Tell the Lord Chancellor what you know"

Moro spoke in a clear voice.

"It is true my lord, the one you call Simmons have been an ally of Baron Fairchild from the start. We have seen him many times come and go from Castle Fairchild, I recognized him the moment he passed me to enter your chambers"

Alexis was silent for a moment before asking the sergeant if he also recognized Lord Ayres. He shook his head.

"No my lord, I do not recall ever seeing him before. But of Lord Simmons I am sure, I would stake my life that he is the same man"

Again Alexis was silent for a moment, he had trusted this man with his life often in the past, he had no reason to doubt him now.

"You have done well sergeant, it appears Prince William has succeed in placing a spy in our midst"

He sat down at his desk.

"I must think how best to use him"

Captain Caius stepped forward.

"Shall I arrest him my lord and bring him too you?"

Alexis shook his head.

"No, not yet, we will let him think he is safe among us"

He looked at both men.

"Not a word of this must be spoken outside this room, I will deal with Lord Simmons when the time is right"

He placed both hands on his desk.

"Time for some well-earned rewards I think"

He looked at the Captain.

"As from this moment you are now Commander Caius,"

He pointed to Moro.

"And you can sew another star on your tunic…Captain Moro"

Both men were gracious for their promotion. As they turned to leave Alexis had an idea.

"Commander Caius, did Lord Simmons and Lord Ayres have any men with them when they arrived?"

The newly promoted Commander thought for a moment before replying.

"Yes my lord, a small squad of about eight men each"

Alexis rubbed his chin.

"Are any of them heavy drinkers?"

Caius shrugged his shoulders as he inwardly laughed.

"I have never known many soldiers who were not my Lord"

Alexis nodded his head.

"I think we should honour our new allies with a barrel of fine ale Commander, I will arrange for one to be delivered to your quarters so you can…. share it with them"

Both men smiled at the idea. Commander Caius gave a mock bow as he said.

"I will make sure that their thirst is fully satisfied my lord"

Alexis smiled in return.

"Just make sure they tell us what we need to know while they still can"

"Yes my lord, if they know anything, then by the end of the evening so will we"

Alexis smiled.

"It will not be a small barrel Commander. So there should be some left over for other uses, like celebrations of promotion"

Caius smiled a thank you.

"Your lordship is most kind"

Chapter 39
Luck of the Gods

Alexis sat silently at his desk, he pondered on the one item that you cannot control, but can make the difference between success and failure…luck. If Moro had been just a few seconds early, or Lord Simmons a few seconds later the two would not have met, and he would be none the wiser about a possible spy in their midst, on such random occurrences are the lives of people decided, good luck…bad luck, easy life…hard life, such is the fate of us all. But his daydreaming did not last long, the knowledge that at least one spy was in their midst was unsettling. If there was one, there could be more, now he needed to think hard on how best to use this information. He unrolled a large map of the north showing where the main roads and castles were. He remembered both castles well, but it was Lord Simmons' castle that interested him the most. It was built on a plateau at the edge of a steep valley, the front walls overlooked Edmond Way while the rest of the castle was surrounded on three sides by steep cliffs. The walls were not of a great height, but it would take a large and very determined force to overcome its defences, and the cost would be high with many casualties. He studied the map carefully, the castle was close to the junction where Tennyson's Way splits from Edmonds Way. He took in a deep breath. The Gods, or luck, had given him an opportunity to induce William to willingly walk into his trap. The position of the castle was the key. It was in the ideal place if you wanted to hold up an invading army. William was an experience commander in the ways of war, and would not be easily fooled. For him to believe any information of Roberts's intent it would have to have military merit or he would be unlikely to believe or accept it. The plan in his mind was nearly complete, he would add the final touches in the morning.

The next morning his first visitor was Commander Caius, the barrel of ale had done all they had hoped it would. Before they had passed out, two of Simmons' soldiers had boosted in their drunken stupor of the promise of great riches from Lord Simmons when William sat on the throne. There was no doubt, Lord Simmons was William's man. Either Lord Ayres was innocent in his intentions, or he kept better council than his companion, his men said nothing that could be held against him, but in his mind Alexis was still not totally convinced. The Commander had left long before the next visitors arrived. Alexis was sitting at his desk writing when Huggle showed Lord Ayres and Lord Simmons into the room. Alexis bid them to sit while he finished his letter. He looked up when he had finished his task.

"The waiting in nearly over my lords, William has started his march south. We are only days away from the battle that will decide who will be king"

They walked over to a table with a map that showed the main routes from north to south.

"It is a blessing you both joined us my Lords. You and your castles will play a large part in our plans. I can tell you now that William will outnumber us. We don't know his strength for sure, but we think he has between three or four thousand nobility, and maybe the same in common soldiers"

Alexis deliberately underestimated their numbers. At least one of them was a spy, it would do no harm for him to think Robert had little information about the true size of William's forces, Alexis continued.

"You will both return to your castles. You have a key role to play in this war. Both of you must raid all of your neighbouring lords who have declared for William. You must be bold and when you attack you must attack together to show a large force. We want William to believe that all our army is camped around the area of your castles. You will send us word when you know for sure he has committed his forces to attack you, that will be our signal to move. Until then King Robert and the main army will be camped here on Tennyson's Way, hidden out of sight"

Alexis pointed to a point on the map just short of where the two roads joined.

"Then he reaches the gates of Lord Simmons castle, both of you will hold his advance long enough for us to come up behind and attack him from the rear"

Alexis smiled as if very pleased with himself.

"We will rout him, his army will be in total confusion. But, it is most important that he takes the Edmonds Road. If he was to find out that our forces were camped on Tennyson's way, he could meet us head on and destroy us. Our only chance is to take him by surprise. All the raiding of the surrounds estates will be done by your men and your men only. We are too few in number to give you any help in this. But I am confident you will both succeed, you know the area best and will be fighting on your home ground"

He then addressed both lords.

"You must make William think you are the main force, if you succeed, I promise you will be amply rewarded. When we win, the estates of Grimswick and Fairchild will be offered to those who have served Robert the most "

Lord Ayers was the first to speak.

"An excellent plan my Lord Chancellor, a pity your men cannot share in all the fun, but I'm sure my Lord Simmons and I will cause William enough trouble for him to think we number in the thousands. How say you my Lord Simmons, are you up for it?"

Lord Simmons had a smile on his face as he said.

"We will have great sport that day my lord, yes indeed, great sport"

Ayers slapped him on his back.

"That's the spirit my lord, fear nothing, and go to it with gusto"

Alexis sat quietly at his desk, the trap was set, now he needed the luck of the Gods to make it come true. Later that day both the lords along with their escort left to return to their Castles. Both Robert and Alexis watched their departure from one of the many balconies that overlooked the courtyard. As the departing knights passed the outer gate to the causeway they turned to walk back inside, an arrow hit the wall in exactly the place where Robert had been standing just a split second before showering him with stone chipping. Even before he realized what had taken place Alexis had unceremoniously pushed him to the floor, then pointing in the direction he thought the arrow came from called out to the guards standing close by.

"Up there! Go quickly, we have a traitor among us who just tried to kill the King."

Robert tried to rise to his feet, but Alexis held him down

"Do not move your majesty until we know you are safe. I would be a poor protector of my king if I allowed whoever shot that arrow to have a second chance"

A few minutes later the faces of the guards appeared on the balcony above.

"There is no one to be seen my lord, he has fled"

Alexis helped Robert to his feet

"It is as I feared your majesty, William has made the task of keeping you safe much harder. Now as well as those who wish you dead so William can sit on the throne, we have others whose' main object could be to do it for gain."

Robert brushed the dust from his cloak.

"I thank you and the Gods for once more keeping me safe, but I must confess that staying alive in my own castle is proving a much harder task than I thought it would"

Both men now surrounded by guards walked quickly to the royal chambers, only when the King was safely inside did Alexis allow himself to relax. Now he took even more precautions, more men were placed on every approach to the king's chambers, while every rampart than a would-be assassin could use was guarded day and night. The next day he again made his way down to the dungeons where Lord Hallard was still a prisoner to again try to find out the names of any who would want to take Roberts' life. He spent over two hours interrogating him, but still he refused to say anything that would help him in his search. He began his return journey to his chambers. He was not alone, Robert had forbid him to go anywhere without an escort, an order he largely ignored. Now with only Sergeant Hugo as a companion he walked the last few paces down a narrow passage, two knights in armour without their helmets due to the poor light but with swords drawn appeared from a side passage to block their way. Alexis looked behind to see two more knights blocking their escape. Both the knights blocking their way advanced towards them. Alexis drew his sword and dagger as Sergeant Hugo did the same and turned to face the two knights advancing from the rear. He gave a little grunt of a laugh

"Only two each my lord, we will make them pay for thinking so little of us as warriors"

Alexis faced those advancing toward him. He danced on the balls of his feet as they came near. The knight on his left made the first move, he raised his sword high above his head as he advanced. Alexis feinted to the left only to move swiftly to his right as the knight drew close. His sword struck his enemy in a slashing movement hard across his face. The Knight recoiled dropping his sword. Blood spouted from the deep cut that had almost split his face in two. He fell backwards and slid down the wall to become a crumpled heap on the floor. If the man lived he would spend the rest of his life in darkness. The second knight hesitated as he saw the ease with which Alexis had dispatched his companion. Now he recovered his wits and advanced slowly and with great caution towards him. He quickly proved himself to be a skilful swordsman but grew frustrated as Alexis avoided his blows with ease. Then for the briefest of moments Alexis lost his footing as he slipped on the blood still flowing from the first knight. His opponent hoping to strike a death blow charged wildly at him. Alexis ducked beneath the attack and thrust his sword between the advancing knight's legs tripping him up. He came crushing to the ground and before he could recover Alexis thrust his sword deep into his throat. The man quickly died choking in his own blood. Sergeant Hugo had already dispatched one of his opponents, now with Alexi's help the fight ended swiftly. Hugo had suffered a small nick to the side of his face, just deep enough to leave a scar. Both men laughed as Alexis pointed out that he would have something to remind him of his day for the rest of his life. The knight Alexis had disabled was still alive then his body along with his companions were moved.

He lived just long enough to confess that all four had recently arrived at Castle Kingshome. They had come to kill Robert for the reward offered by William, but the king had been too heavily guarded, so had switched their attention to Alexis. The whispers they had heard from some said that he would be an easier target, but would still bring them a sizeable reward. Alexis did not want Gaia to know about this second attempt on his life, so only Robert and a few others would know about this event. Robert laughed and said that soon both men would have more secrets from their wives than fleas on a dog. On a more serious note he now ordered more steps to keep his Chancellor safe. From now on Alexis was to have an escort of at least eight men with him at all times, and like the King his quarters would be heavily guarded day and night.

Chapter 40
The March Begins

Alexis lay in his bed, it was past midnight at the end of another long and tiring day, but still he was unable to sleep. The army was due to march in the morning and his mind would not rest. He went over their plans again and again, praying that he had not overlooked anything. Prince William was an experience commander, and he had the added advantage of outnumbering them many times over. The whole of Santross was expecting him to be victorious. Few had any faith in Robert as a fighting man. None of the Darosi who rode to the kings banner were told of his plans for the coming battle, he was afraid many would refuse to fight in such a manor. The secret army of outsiders was also unknown to all but a few. Now thinking they were faced by overwhelming odds, all but the most optimistic had already resigned themselves to just one more glorious battle before their deaths.

The next morning all was made ready for the march. Earlier Alexis had said a tearful farewell to his new bride. Like all the men before and those since he promised to return, and with a final kiss they had parted. Now they waited for King Robert to make his farewell to Queen Livia, Alexis watched his king embrace his wife for maybe the last time. He was one of only a few that knew the Queen was expecting another baby, a major reason for keeping the assassination attempts a secret. So far she was mother to three girls, all who knew of her condition now hoped that it would be the long awaited son to inherit the throne. Now in the last few moments before the march Alexis looked at the inspiring sight all around him. The knights sat silently, the sun reflecting off their shining armour as they waited for their king. Their mounts neighed loudly as they pawed the ground as if impatient to be off. He was surrounded by the pageantry and splendour of men about to go into battle, a truly magnificent sight. And everywhere he looked was a riot of colours as every knight marched to his own banner. He could feel his own blood rise with the excitement of it all, and for the first time in his life he had some understanding of why the Darosi were so addictive to war. Then the thought came to him, a way that perhaps could help to bring all the kingdom together. But this was not the time or place to do anything about it. Robert had said his farewells and now mounted his horse. And with a finally wave to all those watching a very proud Alexis rode alongside his King as the small army of six thousand or so troops headed north.

After consulting with Andras the Master-at-arms, Alexis had decided that the army of outsider which now numbered over four thousand men, would leave two days after the main body and take a different route. It was though that the different route along with the time delay would keep them safe from any spies that William would have send. The two day delay would not cause any problem, the mounted archers could cover as much ground in a day as a marching army could in two. And it was the same for the other troops riding in horse drawn carts, they could easily make up the lost time and distance.

The plan for the coming battle was already known to those who would command the outsiders. For several weeks past every man had been trained in the task that would be his, For the battle, the mounted archers would split into two columns. One column would be led by Commander Halsey, his ex- squire. The other column would be commanded by Lord Denis, the Earl of Greenburg. The archers who rode in the horse drawn carts would be commanded by Ben Tiller, along with a few of the instructors who had trained them. The command of the important pike men who would take the brunt of the first change of horse and knights was given to Andras, the Master-at-arm who by now was a familiar face to all the men. His calmness and great ability to inspirer courage in others would help hold the line together. all that was needed was for William to oblige them by doing what they wanted. From the start it had become very clear just how effective Ben Tiller had been in organizing the outsiders as scouts and spies. The reports they had received so far proved to be very accurate, now once again such people were proving their worth. In small groups that sometimes even included their children they roamed the north acting as peasants with false papers of transit travelling from village to village, they kept Alexis informed as to where Williams's troops were and in what number. It would take the best part of a week to reach the ground Alexis had chosen for the battle. Robert could ride with the certainly that William was still many leagues to the north. His progress was slow due to his army spending as much time foraging for supplies as they did marching. It would still take him a week or more before he arrived at the important junction of Tennyson's Way, only then would it become clear if he would fall into the trap. Robert's men did not have the problem of lack of food, Alexis again proved he had mastered the logistics of war as each day wagons arrived with fresh supplies. The day before the intended battle, one of the many spies Ben Tiller had sent north delivered a message to Robert with gruesome news. The bodies of Lord Avon and other members of the High Council had been found only a few leagues to the north. All had their throats cut, and their killers had attempted to hide their bodies in some undergrowth. Robert ordered their remains to be taken back to Castle Kingshome to be given proper burial, he promised himself that he would find whoever was responsible for their deaths and would make them pay in full.

That night a sad Robert called all the commanders to his tent and told them of the gruesome find. His disgust that the high council travelling under the flag of truce should be killed in such a way was plain to see. His anger had a personal edge to it, he felt guilty that it had been his words spoken in jest had caused their deaths. For once it was a very serious and kingly Robert who addressed all present. After the meeting ended, both Robert and Alexis walked among the men as they went about the business of filling their daily needs. Robert was proving himself to be a good leader of men as he gave words of hope and encouragement to all about the battle to come.

"This is a better life to have Alexis. In Kingshome I did not know who was friend or who was foe, but here I feel safer than in my own bed"

Some men close by were cooking the carcass of a sheep over an open fire. They paused as the heavy smell of roasting meat quickly made them both feel hungry. Robert made his hunger known to the men who eagerly agreed to the honour of eating with their king. A few minutes later Robert and Alexis stood enjoying a plate of the well cooked meat washed down with a flagon of soldiers' ale. Suddenly Robert cried out in pain and slowly sunk to his knees. Alexis held his King in his arms to stop him falling further. His fingers touched the shaft of an arrow embedded in Roberts' shoulder. The unknown assassin had followed them on their march, and this time his arrow had found its mark. Alexis immediately looked to the trees close by, a movement caught his eye as a man turned to run further into the forest. He called to the men close by.

"Someone has tried to assassinate the King"

He pointed to the nearby trees

There, he ran there, quickly men, don't let him escape"

Even as he spoke the words, two men had passed him in a full run. Within second's dozens of soldiers followed.

Alexis called to other soldiers close by.

"Help your King, carry him back to his tent"

Robert was half carried and half walked gently back to his tent and put to lie on his side. One of the Kings doctors had already arrived. Together they removed Roberts's armour to examine the wound. Robert soon had his usual goblet of wine in his hand. He looked up at a worried Alexis

"What was that I said "safer than my own bed" this will teach me not to say such foolish things. Don't worry my Lord Chancellor, the armour you insisted I wear under my robes took most of the impact. It will take more than this scratch to keep me from the coming battle."

The doctor soon confirmed the wound was not in any way fatal.

"You were lucky you were wearing your Armor you majesty, it made what could have been a serous wound into something far less. You will be without your sword arm for some weeks, but I'm sure of a full recovery"

Robert looked up with a smile on his face.

"May the Gods always be so kind to me"

A loud jeering noise made everyone look to the tent entrance, a knight entered.

"Your Majesty, we have found the man who tried to take your life. But the Gods have already punished him for his cowardly deed. I fear he has not long to live"

Robert tried to get up from his bed, but Alexis put a gentle restraining hand on his good shoulder.

"Stay as you are your majesty and rest, I will see to what has to be done"

He gestured to the soldier

"Bring the would be assassin in"

Alexis and Robert looked eagerly as a man was carried in on a litter, he did not move and appeared to be unconscious. Robert made a gesture with his hand.

"Lift his head up, let us see who this villain is"

One of the soldiers pulled his head up by his hair. Both Robert and Alexis let out a gasp of surprise. With his head raised the cause of his impending death also became clear. The whole of the left side of his head was cut open to the bone, blood slowly oozed out of the multiple wounds making his robe dark with the stain of blood.

Robert looked to the Captain who had brought him to his tent.

"Do you know how these wound came to be?"

The Captain nodded

"We think so your majesty, we found him at the foot of a large tree with branches that reached almost to the ground. It is almost certain that in his hast to escape and in the darkness of night he rode his horse into then and was knocked to the ground"

Robert ordered the soldier to splash some water on his face. The man regained conscious slowly, it was several seconds before he realized his surroundings. Robert looked at him with a stony face.

"So my Lord Fellows, those on the high council are sworn to serve both the King, and the kingdom, and you dishonour yourself by committing treason to both. Why did you seek my life?"

Lord Fellows answered in a whisper

"It is you who have betrayed the Kingdom"

He went on in a soft and weak voice

"You will never be a true King of the Darosi, William is much better suited to the task ahead than you. If there is a coming war with the lands of the north, we could not have a better King than he to lead our troops into battle. I am just sorry my aim and strength were not great enough to complete my task. If I had, many Darosi lives would be spared in the morrow".

Then his voice took on a stronger tone

"But my sadness is not complete. I know that where I failed he will succeed, and you and this accursed chancellor of yours will soon lie dead on the battlefield"

Just then Robert cried out in great pain as the surgeon removed the arrowhead from his shoulder. Still in great pain he waved his good arm in a dismissal way.

"Take him away, the Gods have saved me the task of deciding his fate. Tie him to a stake in the forest so he cannot run, the smell of his blood will bring many wolves to feast on his carcass. If I look upon his traitorous face any longer I fear I will want to finish the punishment with my own sword."

The soldiers picked up the litter and left to carry out his orders. Robert was silent for several moments as the doctor applied a paste like substance to dull the pain. As his discomfort eased he turned to a solider standing close to him.

"Go after them, I change my mind, he served my father well in the past, tell them to place the traitor in a tent so he may die in peace"

Alexis sat beside his King as the doctor bandaged the wound to his right shoulder. He was proud to serve Robert and have him as his king, he could show mercy and kindness to everyone, even those who would take his life. More of a worry to him was that Robert would not have the strength to hold his sword in the coming battle, he would have to arrange to guard him well. Few would know by his appearance that all was not well. Both had been shocked by the actions of Lord Fellows. With hindsight it was easy to see that he had been working in the interests of Prince William from the start. He had been the most outspoken on the high council that Robert should renounce his throne in favour of his brother. And more than once he had counselled the futilely of going to war against such odds, a course of action he maintained throughout. Alexis did not know it, but William's last hope of assassinating his brother before the battle had passed, now the fate of both brothers was in the hands of the Gods.

Chapter 41
Let the battle begin

The next morning Robert and Alexis had two scouts report to them. One confirmed that neither Ayres, nor Simmons had attacked any of their neighbouring lords. For Alexis this was the proof that the information Captain Moro had given him was correct. The other said that William had camped last night less than two leagues from the all-important fork in the road. From the start Alexi's problem had been to find a reason for William to take the Tennyson's road, now that task being was done for him by Williams own men. Simmons and Ayres thought themselves the heroes by discovering Roberts' plans. Instead they were sending their master straight into the trap that had been set for him.

A small force of Darosi led by Lord Duncan now proceeded just past the point where the road narrowed. They would be the bait to draw William on into their trap. The rest of the army took up their positions. The outsiders arrived within an hour. All through the march they had camped miles away to the rear of Roberts's army to lessen the chance of discovery from William's spies. The Darosi knights at first were alarmed to find that outsiders were to fight by their side. A few confronted Robert that they had not been told about this arrangement, but the King quickly calmed their fears.

"My lords for many months my instructors from Kingshome have trained this army of outsiders in the art of war. I have seen for myself the skills these men possess, they are worthy to stand by our side, and will give a good account of themselves in the battle to come"

Some at first were not convinced by his words, but it soon became clear that their new allies were far from being a rabble that would break and run at the first charge. Now led by the instructors who had trained them they marched and behaved like the well-trained soldiers they had become. Some Darosi began to cheer as more and more arrived to boost their numbers and lift their spirits. Now all was ready, and William did not keep them waiting long. He soon reached the important junction in the road and without a moment's hesitation took Tennyson's Way. The small forward force waited until he was less than 1.000 paces away before retreating with a great show of haste and confusion. At the sight of the retreating troops William urged his mounted army forward at the gallop, leaving the foot soldiers to follow as best they could. If he could reach the main part his brother's army within seconds of him being warned he could catch them unprepared for battle and in a state of confusion. He was supremely confident that in such matters as war he would beat his brother every time. He was even more confident when word reached him that Robert had perhaps recruited some outsiders, a sure sign of a desperate man clutching at straws. Such cowards of men could only make his brothers' army weaker, not stronger. He doubted they would even have the courage to stand for the first charge, and would run as soon as his army advanced.

He had been disappointed when news that the assassination attempts had failed. But when Lord Simmons and Ayers had informed him of Alexi's attempts to rally them to Robert's cause, a chance of having two spies in his brother's camp was too good an opportunity to miss. He ordered them to join Robert's forces to find out his intentions, and they had done their task well. Now everything was working out as he had planned, they had delivered Robert's forces just where he wanted them…at the point of his sword. From the start he'd had little regard for Robert as a military man, although the plan to attack him from the rear had some merit, and may have worked, if Simmons and Ayers had really been on Robert's side. But they were his men, and their knowledge of Robert's plans would surely give him victory. Now the vanguard of Robert's pitiful small army were in full retreat. He was sure that by the end of the day he would be King, and his brother would lay dead on the battlefield. Soon he came to the point where the road narrowed. He slowed down, as an experienced commander he was ever conscious of a trap, but the road narrowed for only a short distance, and he could see the ground opening on the other side. An extra comfort was that although the road was slightly uphill, it was straight for as far as the eye could see. And still Robert's men were in full view as they rode in retreat. For a few moments there was a certain degree of confusion as too many tried to pass at the same time, but slowly his army formed a narrow column and passed through. Now they were out on the other side and in full gallop after their enemy.

Chapter 42
The Trap is Sprung

Out of the corner of his eye William noticed men riding at an angled as if to join the column. For a moment he paid them no heed, thinking they were his men, but then he heard a cry over the thundering of horse's hooves. He looked to his right just in time to see a knight fall from his horse, an arrow in his chest. The riders who he thought were his men were riding parallel to the column at a distance of 50 paces or so, and they were shooting arrows at him. He was dumfounded, Men riding horses and shooting arrows? Never had he seen such a thing before, no one fought this way on Santross, Robert must have hired foreign soldiers. He looked again, and took a deep intake of breath, they wore no uniforms, and judging by their dress were not soldiers but mere outsiders. So the stories about Robert having outsiders join his army were true. The shock of this was almost as great as seeing archers on horseback. Now another knight became a victim, and another. He looked at the other side of his column, more mounted archers were attacking that side as well. They pressed close on both flanks forcing his men to remain in a column. William was now filled with anger, the archers were killing horses as well as riders, surely the Gods would punish Robert for breaking the ancient code of honour and give him victory. As more of his army passed the narrow point in the road and reached the open plain they were greeted by more archers. Now they numbered in the hundreds as they attacked his column continuously and they were scoring hits, he was losing men with every forward stride they took. It was clear that he had walked into a trap, and he boiled inside with anger. He'd had so little respect for his brother as a leader in battle that he had never contemplated anything other than a quick victory. Now he was paying for his over confidence with the lives of his own men. A dozen or so of his knights, tired at being sitting targets left the column and tried to close with their enemy to engage then with swords. But all warhorses are descended from shire horses, they are built for strength, not speed, so the archers easily outpaced them. He watched as the dozen were quickly reduced to six, then four, the last knight fell just as they disappeared from his view. Now other small groups of knights tried to close with the archers, but immediately they left the main column they were quickly surrounded and suffered the same fate as all the others. William's army was being chopped up little by little, and there was nothing they could do about it. And all the time the retreating men of Robert's army stayed just a few hundred paces ahead, leading them on and on. Now to add to their plight the effects of the long uphill chase began to show. In a normal battle, both armies would line-up a few hundred paces apart, so the charge would be a short one. But they had ridden their mounts hard for many times that distance uphill. Now carrying both men and heavy armour almost all their horses were close to exhaustion. Some were already reduced to little more than a trot and fell far behind the main body. They became even more of an easy target for the archers who now came so close that every arrow was finding its mark. The archers peeled away just as they reached a sharp bend in the road. A field full of high wheat stood directly before them, and for the first time he saw Robert and the rest of his army. They were already formed up waiting for him. As soon as he saw this he realized he had walked into yet another trap. He had hoped to find his brothers' army still in their camp and unprepared to fight, now he knew the retreating knights had just been bait to lead him on a long chase. With their horses exhausted, their charge would now be a weak one, but he could not afford to wait, he must strike now. He gave the signal to halt as he looked back at the retreating archers, what he saw appalled him. Their route of march was clearly visible. Now there were two roads, one built upon the other, and the new one was made with the bodies of his men and many of their horses, in some places they were so thick on the ground that they piled one on top of another. It was impossible to know how many had fallen, but he could plainly see his army was smaller.

As William mourned the loss of so many, in the far distance he could see the first of his foot soldiers beginning to emerge after the narrow opening. What happen next was yet another surprise, now dozens upon dozens of large carts filled with more archers raced out of the trees of both flanks and using the carts as protection they quickly formed into ranks to send wave after wave of arrows onto the advancing troops. Even at this distance he could clearly follow their passage as the arrow heads glinted in the sun. The mounted archers now also added to the carnage as they began to ride up and down the flanks scoring hit after hit on any who tried to break ranks. On seeing this Williams let out a roar of anger, the trap that had been set for him was a good one, and so far he had no idea of how to overcome it. He would have been even more upset if he could somehow have witnessed close up the full carnage that was befalling his foot soldiers.

As they passed through the narrow gap they were confronted by many hundreds of archers who suddenly appeared from the flanks. The standard method of attacking or defending against archers was to form a wall of shields and advance from behind it. This they quickly did, but to their dismay, they found the arrows hit with such force that their shields made of wood and leather were of little value. The first line of soldiers charged to try and close the gap between the armies, but the attack quickly failed. Whole rows of men died as the arrows passed through their shields as if they were made of parchment, not a man got to within 50 paces of the enemy lines before they fell. Try as they might they could not live long enough to close with their enemy. Now to add to their woe men on horseback began to join in the killing. They rode up and down their flanks firing arrows into their midst stopping them from running to the nearby trees for cover. Their resolve to advance grew smaller as the mountain of dead grew bigger. Slowly at first they began to retreat to try and get out of range. But even that was not an easy task, so great was the carry of the arrows that no matter how much ground they give up, many still found their mark.

Chapter 43
A Lesson Learned

William was too far away to know the full extent of his soldiers' plight. He turned to look front again just as the last of the retreating knights disappeared behind a small but steep bank on which the rest of Robert's army stood. The bank marked the edge of the field on the road side, and continued along the entire width of the wheat field at the back. He cautiously made a rough count of Robert's army. He had already been surprised more than once today. First by the mounted archers, who somehow had been able to remain hidden from all the many spies he had sent to Castle Kingshome , and then by the use of large wagons to transport troops, but they seemed to have got the number in Robert's army right. They had all told him than Robert had less than two thousands Darosi, and double that number of common soldiers. So he was not surprised that this small army lacked the numbers to make a united front. He studied Robert's army for several minutes, looking for any weakness in their formation and quickly spotted that both flanks were lightly held. Robert had packed the centre of his front with Darosi at the expense of his flanks, where they were only one or two deep in places, this mistake would cost him his throne and his life. In a test of courage and skill he was going to win. He tried to rally his men after the ordeal they had already suffered.

"Robert has defied the Gods by killing the noble horse. For this they are sure to grant us a glorious victory"

He quickly gave the order to form into four lines of battle on the flanks, but only two rows in the centre. If Robert did not have enough men to secure his flanks, then that was where his main attack would fall. Four lines of mounted knights would cut through one or two enemy lines as if they were not there, and if he could turn the flanks of Robert's army he was sure of victory. William was riding his favourite warhorse, a huge black stallion called "Tempest" He raised his battle-axe above his head and called to his troops

"Victory will be ours, forward to glory and death to Robert"

He dropped his arm, and as one they charged their enemy. Both wings of Williams' army kept pace as they raced through the high wheat. Now they were within a hundred paces, then fifty. Just as they braced for contact, a whole army of men appeared as if by magic. Row upon row of men had lain hidden in the tall wheat, now as one they rose to stand before them. The men in the first few rows each held a heavy pike already anchored firmly in the ground. Behind them stood hundreds of archers, ready to deal out death to the attracting force. The first wave of charging knights was unable to stop in time, and the air was suddenly filled with the unholy scream of injured horses and men as those the arrows had missed impaled themselves on the long pikes. All along the entire length of the wheat field Williams forces suffered the same fate. In some places the second wave was so close to the first that they joined them in death. William himself was lucky, Tempest swerved sharply to his right to try and avoid the pike which had suddenly appeared a few feet in front of him. By doing so William was thrown from his saddle sideways to the left. He landed heavily and rolled forward under the raised pikes. For several seconds he just lay there, too stunned to move, the hooves of many horses were only inches from him, but the umbrella of pikes kept him safe from being trampled on. Finally he found the strength to roll back from the pikes and stand up, the point of a pike waved only inches short of his face. Tempest lay on his side, his legs still thrashing as with the motions of running. But he would never run again, the ground was covered with his blood that spurted out from a long gush in his chest. Even as he watched the motions became slower and fewer as its life ebbed away. Now in anger William hacked at the pikes with his battle-axe, but there was little one man could do against such a defence. He could do nothing more than jump out of the way as horses passed him to die just feet from where he stood. He cried out in despair as he watched almost the entire first line of attacking knights' fall victim to the long pikes. William was now completely filled with rage and frustration. Robert had broken every rule of honour that the Darosi had lived by for centuries. It had never occurred to him that Robert would fight in any way other than the Darosi tradition way, but this battle was completely foreign to him and his men. First archers on horseback, and now pike men with weapons that were strong enough to stop a horse in full gallop. It was impossible that all this could have been Robert's plan, this was the work of someone else, someone with great military knowledge and ability. He retreated the way he had come, using his heavy shield to avoid the shower of arrows that seemed to follow him. His remaining men mulled around in confusion with no one to give them orders. Lord Carsell recognized the retreating William and a spare mount was quickly found for him and the remaining Darosi gathered to him.

Chapter 44
Another Plan

If his foot soldiers were nearby William would have ordered them to attack the pike men and clear the way for another charge, He looked in their direction, but they were in no position to help his cause. And far from making progress it looked like they were in full retreat from the deadly arrows that constantly rained down on them. For a moment he thought to turn his army and ride back to attack the archers from the carts. But that would invite the mounted archers to attack again, and they had already proved themselves to be more than a match for mounted knights. He quickly dismissed the idea, to do so would also expose *his* rear to an attack from Robert. He was too experienced to fall into that trap. For the moment his foot soldiers must look after themselves, his battle was here, where Robert was. If he could kill him then victory would be his no matter how many men he lost. He viewed his brother's army again. Robert's right flank only reached to the end of the embankment. The road at this point was some twenty paces wide and looked to be unguarded before another steep bank formed the other side of the road. To order another frontal attack would be suicide, mounted knights had little chance of success against this kind of defence. He needed to try something else to turn the flanks of Roberts' army and win the day. After much thought he split his remaining forces into three. Baron Fairchild and Grimswick were nowhere to be seen. So he ordered Lord Carsell to take command of his left flank and use the gap in the road to try and attack Robert from the rear. The centre part under Baron Hendy would attack straight ahead, but not to press with any great desire, to do so would mean their certain death. Their task now was to keep the troops in the centre under threat so they would be unable to reinforce the flanks when they came under attack. He would take the remainder of the army and try to work his way around Robert's other flank. Once more William raised his battle-axe above his head.

"Ride for glory, death to Robert"

His arm dropped, and the charge began. The first attack to falter was that of Baron Hendy. The rows of pike men had held firm in the first attack. Some had fallen, but had been replaced by others. Now boosted by their success of holding the first charge they held their ground again. They thrust their pikes out before them, almost daring the knights to press home their attack, but the famed Darosi courage did not show itself and the knights just milled around out of range. The charge of Lord Carsell suffered a worst fate. The gap across the road had been deliberately made to look unguarded. But this opening led only to packed ranks of pike men supported by archers on three sides. The carnage was terrible as the left flank of William's army almost ceased to exist. Knight after knight fell before the strong defence. Lord Carsell was one of the first to fall, and with his death went the last of Darosi discipline and courage. They had never encountered archers before in battle, nether mounted or on foot, and the way this war was being fought was alien to them. They had suffered surprise after surprise that had reduced their number greatly. Now just like their horses they were a spent force, all the strength and courage had been beaten out of them, and they began to retreat. Slowly at first in ones and twos, then by the dozen, finally in mass they pulled back from the killing ground.

The only one to have any success was William himself. At this point a line of trees came within a few feet of Roberts left flank. William now led his men into these trees and moved around Robert's flank without being seen. Outsiders had joined Roberts's army up until the day they had marched, some of the newest recruit's had only a few days training, and by chance William was attacking the one place where most were gathered. The rear of Roberts' left flank had not been involved in any of the fighting and had been spectators, and like all spectators their eyes and attention was drawn to the main battle just a few feet from them, rather than looking to guard their rear. William now took full advantage of their lapse of discipline and concentration. Without their pikes in the proper position they were almost defenceless to his charge. He ploughed through their ranks with ease. Within minutes he was attacking the packed centre body of Darosi from the rear, the sight of Robert's banner close by acted on him like a red rag to a bull. He fought with the strength of ten men, none could stand before him as knight after knight fell beneath his flashing axe. Slowly he moved forward and sensed that victory could still be his.

Alexis had been directing the defence against Lord Carsell when word reached him about William's attack on the other flank. He rode to the rear where Lord Duncan and the troops that had been the bait to lure William on were resting. To help them keep ahead of Williams' troops none had worn any armour to lighten the load for their horses, so had not been involved in the defence of first attack. Now with their armour again in place they were being held in reserve to give them and their horse's time to recover after their long ride. He quickly rallied these men for a counterattack to close the gap William had forced in their ranks. Lead by Alexis and Lord Duncan they charged into the rear of William's men and slowly drove a wedge between the defenders and attacking forces to give fresh pike men the chance to make good the gap in their defences. The battle wavered back and fore for several minutes before the defenders gained the upper hand. The charge of William's men was beaten back, and those that were still outside the lines of pike men began to retreat with Lord Duncan and his men close behind. William and the few men with him became surrounded as the gap behind them began to close, but just before it did Alexis spied the distinctive helmet of Prince William as he cut a path of death straight toward where Robert stood. With his sword arm heavily bandage he would be unable to defend himself. He urged his horse forward and began to attack from behind those who had succeeded in penetrated their lines of defence. Alexis fought as he had never fought before, killing without any hesitation or pity, but in such a congestive space progress was slow. And all the time William narrowed the gap between Robert and himself. Although now being attacked from all sides William was in no mood to surrender, one brother would die today, and he fought with all his might for it to be Robert. He alone moved forward, encouraged by the sight of Robert's banner coming ever closer, while his men behind him grew fewer and fewer.

Chapter 45
The End in Sight

And suddenly he was through the ring of defence around Robert as the last knight fell to a blow of his axe. Now Robert was clearly in his sights, still unaware of the danger that was closing from behind. Alexis was still too far away and could do nothing to save his king. But as William had delivered the death blow to the last knight barring his way the sound had at last alerted those near the king to the danger. Now one of the knights at the side of Robert wheeled his horse around in the small space to confront William. Alexis immediately recognized the colours the knight wore, they were the colours of the house of Monrell. For a moment he thought it was his father, but even encased in armour the body was too slim to be his. The truth was clear. His younger brother Leon was about to give his life in defence of his sovereign. Alexis redoubled his efforts. He knew his brother had little or no chance of defeating William, in reality it was man against boy. At best his life would buy only a few seconds grace. But Leon was a true Darosi and did not lack courage. He charged at William and swung his sword with all his strength. But the blow lacked the cutting edge of a seasoned warrior and glanced harmlessly off William's shield. The return blow from William had much more purpose about it. It landed with so much force that it sliced Leon's shield in two and drove him backwards several feet. Before he could recover another blow knocked what was left of his shield from his hands. At this point Alexis had to turn his attention to one of William's men who blocked his way. The knight had recognized who he was and made a determined effort that he should go no further. Out of the corner of his eye he saw Leon's helmet fly through the air, he prayed that his brother's head was not still in it. By the time he had dispatched his opponent with a quick thrust to the throat the battle between William and Leon was over. Alexis let out a mournful yell, Leon had disappeared. Vanquish by William and now buried under the medley of so many men fighting in so small a space. Alexis urged his horse forward. But there were still the last few survivors of William's men blocking his way. Then another knight wheeled his horse to confront William. And this time he was sure who the knight was, it was his Father Damon. The old warrior urged his horse forward, determined to protect his king and gain revenge for his son despite the pain he must be in. William wheeled his axe above his head to strike a death blow. But Damon was the veteran of many a battle, and he maneuvered his horse skilfully so the blow found only clear air. In turn he brought his sword down on William's head. Twenty years before that one skilfully delivered blow would have won him the fight. But age and his injures had robbed him of much of his strength, so the armoured helmet took the blow. The two men circled each other looking for an opening. Again and again Damon parried Williams's blows aside. In return he thrust and slashed with his sword looking for a weak spot between shield and body. But William blocked the blows easily. Then at last William found a way past Damon's sword and brought his axe down with great strength. The blow cut right through the corner of Damon's shield, and wounded him on his arm. Encouraged by his success and Damon failing strength the younger man surged forward. A series of heavy blows rained down on the Baron from every angle, driving him and his horse backwards. Alexis urged his mount forward, but there was still one knight and several feet between them when William finally breeched his father's defence. Williams' axe cut through what was left of Damon's shield and bit deep into his shoulder almost severing his arm from his body. The Baron fell to the ground and lay still. The last line of defence had fallen. Alexis cried out in anguish as he dispatched the last of William's men. First his brother, now his father had fallen in battle to the same man. He was filled with rage. William must pay for those deeds with his own life. In anger he dug his spurs deep into the flank of his mount and the horse leaped forward with a burst of speed. William held his axe above his head and gave a cry of triumph for his victory over Damon. Now he eyed his brother just a few feet away. He was still looking forward and moving as little as possible to ease the pain in his wounded shoulder. He just sat there, still unaware of the danger close behind. William paused for a moment savouring the victory to come, in his mind's eye he could already see his axe remove Robert's head from his body. But by celebrating the act before it was done he gave Alexis the few seconds needed to close the gap between them. Just as William was about to start his charge Alexis drove his horse at speed into the flank of William's mount pushing both horses to the edge of the bank. They scrambled for grip as the ground crumbled beneath them. William had just enough time to turn his head and see who was attacking him before horse and rider disappeared over the edge. With William still sitting in the saddle the horse rolled over on his back, his full weight pressing down on William's chest. The horse seemed to hang there for several seconds with his legs franticly kicking the air in fright before it rolled over only to be replaced by Alexis mount who repeated the act. Alexis had nimbly dismounted just as the horses made contact, now he slid down the bank with dagger in hand, but the weapon would not be needed. He found William lying on his back, his body had been crushed by the rocks beneath him and the weight of the heavy horses and saddles above. A small trickle of blood came from his month and a fine shower of blood filled the air as he coughed. Alexis looked down at his beaten foe. William's eyes flared as he recognized his conqueror, and said just one word as the last breath left his body.

"Yyyoooooouuuu"

Alexis watched as the darkness of death triumphed over life. The eyes tell all. In life they are bright and clear and with depth. But in death they become opaque and ugly, dead men's eyes. He sat looking at William's body for several moments, almost expecting him to somehow come back to life. For over a year the spectre of this man had haunted his every thought. He had put his whole life aside, including his love for Gaia to find ways to counter his ambitions. And now it was over. His enemy lay beside him, a danger no more. Slowly his thoughts returned to the present, and the sound of battle became loud in his ears again. There was still men fighting and dying only feet from where he sat, and they were dying when there was no need for them to die. He leaned across and removed Williams Helmet before scrambling back up the bank. The first person he saw was Leon, he had survived his fight with William, but the side of his head was bloody from the blow that had both removed his helmet and knocked him from his horse. There were tears in his brother's eyes as he held the head of their mortally wounded father on his lap. Robert stood close by, aware at last to the danger that had just pasted. Alexis handed William's helmet to a knight at his king side

"Proclaim the victory your majesty, and let us put an end to this slaughter"

Robert silently nodded and remounted. The knight placed Williams' helmet on the tip of his sword, and together both began to ride up and down the lines of battle shouting time and time again

"Put up your swords, he battle is over, William is dead"

The call was quickly taken up by others, within seconds the words were echoing up and down the line of battle to be followed by a loud cheer from Robert's men proclaiming the victory.

What was left of William's defeated army quickly melted away when they saw their leader's helmet as proof of his death. Robert watched them go. He gave no orders to pursue them, death had already claimed too many today. And later there would be all the time needed to decide who to forgive and who to punish.

Alexis knelt beside his father, his breathing was now short and shallow as the blood of life drained from his body. Damon looked up at Leon

"Follow your brother Alexis, he is now head of the house of Monrell"

It took him a moment to find Alexis as his sight began to fail, he griped his arm tightly.

"Know that I am as proud of you as any father could be of his son. You are truly worthy to be called Darosi and you have my gratitude for the honour you have brought to the house of Monrell. Your way is the way forward for all of us, but I was too stubborn and too blind to see the truth"

A great surge of pain swept over him before he said in a much quieter voice

"You have been touched by the Gods, and they will…"

His voice died away and his head dropped to his chest as death celebrated another victory on this the most bloody of days.

Leon gently lowered the body to the ground before covering his fathers' face with his own cloak

Both brothers stood on the small bank looking out over the battlefield, the dead and injured were all around them, in some places they piled so high that it was impossible to tell which was man and which was horse. Leon watched as the pike men put their weapons down and began to help those who until a few moments ago they had been trying to kill. He looked at Alexis with a face of sadness.

"Is this what war is, death and more death, where is the glory in this?"

He looked down at his dead father

"He made it sound so different, as if it was something to enjoy, like some kind of sport. He spoke of honour and glory and the rich rewards that came with victory"

Again he looked over the battlefield.

"Well we won the battle, victory is ours, so where is the glory and rich rewards he spoke of? All I can see is death and destruction"

Alexis put a hand on his young brother's shoulder.

"This has always been the way of the Darosi, but it must change, and you and I must do all we can to show our people another way to live"

Chapter 46
Another Ghost put to Rest

As they looked out over the battlefield Alexis noticed a few dozen people suddenly appearing from the woods, men, women, and even young children. They went from body to body, searching each in turn. Alexis became anger, they were committing one of the most evil of crimes…. robbing the dead,

He called out to some soldiers close by to ride out and guard those who had fallen, and to use their swords if necessary. He watched the robbers scattered before the advancing soldiers, all except a young boy who refused to leave the body he was robbing. Alexis had the boy brought before him, his mouth was so full he could not speak. Alexis looked into his eyes, they told of a life of hardship, poverty and starvation, and even though he must in great fear surround by men with swords drawn he refused to stop eating. Alexis spoke to the solider who had caught him and asked.

"What did he take from the dead"

The solider shrugged his shoulders.

"Just food my lord, a crust of stale bread"

Alexis again looked at the boy, a moment ago he was so angry he was willing to have these people killed, now he could see the truth. These people were from the north, they had probably been following Williams' army, with so many men there would always be scraps of food thrown away, these people had been living on the little they could find. He ran his hand through the boys' hair in a playful way.

"Don't be afraid, we will not harm you"

A woman in a tattered dress ran up and holding her hands as if in pray knelled before him

"Please my lord, I beg of you, do not harm my son, we take nothing of value my lord, only the food which the dead have no further need for"

He looked down on the woman, judging by the age of the boy she was probably just past twenty at the most. But a life of hardship had made her look old and haggard, without any of the beauty she might once have had.

"Don't be afraid, no one is going to harm any of you. Call all your people to come near"

He turned to a nearby Captain.

"Use some of wagons to take these people back to camp, and tell the cooks that it is my command that they should be given food until they can eat no more"

The woman looked up in disbelief

"Thank you my lord, a thousand blessing on you and your family"

The Captain led her away with her son by her side as she still shouted out her thanks

"Bless you my lord, may the Gods always be by your side and keep you safe"

Alexis and Leon continued their walk over the battlefield. A few minutes later Commander Caius reined in his horse beside them.

"My lord, we have found the bodies of Lord Giles and Lord Ravenhead, they are some 50 paces further on and to the right"

Alexis asked if they had found the bodies of Baron Grimswick or Fairchild

"No my lord, not yet, but the field of battle is large, and we have covered only a small part so far"

A few minutes later he found the body of his sworn enemy. Ravenhead lay on his side. An arrow had found its way through the open vizier of his helmet and penetrated to the back of his skull, the remainder of the shaft still protruded from the helmet. There was little or no blood which confirmed he must have died quickly. Alexis stood for a moment looking down at him, he had wondered before the battle had begun if fate might bring them together again for the last time, but fate had decided otherwise. He moved on a few paces to find Lord Giles, half-brother to Gaia and therefore related to him by marriage. The body had been ridden over by so many horses that it was unrecognizable, only the colours of what was left of his tunic confirmed it to be him. And so it went on, step after step, body after body. In life each had been a father, son, or brother, perhaps the head of a family with history that went back to the old kingdom, now they were nothing. Many thousands of Darosi had died this day, never again could they regain the power they once had. They themselves had brought about their downfall, they had paid the ultimate price for their love of war and power that had lead them to this day of reckoning. He looked at the sun sinking in the west. As if in sympathy with the day just ending it was a deep blood red, surrounded by deep red clouds. Alexis stood for a moment in silent thought, this was more than just the end of a day. This was the beginning of the end of a way of life, and in more ways than one, tomorrow would be a new day.

Chapter 47
The Truth is out

Hours after the battle Alexis was given the news that as well as his father he had lost other close friends that day. His brother-in-law Denis, the newly promoted Earl of Greenburg had also died in the battle. While he was leading the mounted archers under his command his horse had stumbled throwing him to the ground. Some of Williams' men sensing an easy victory had dismounted and killed him where he fell. It was of little comfort to know that they had quickly followed him to the next world. It was a sad loss of a brave man. He had stood unarmed alongside him when William had tried to stop the coronation, and had done more than many to insure their victory today. Lord Ashdown had also fallen, he had died with almost the last blow of the battle while helping Lord Duncan drive back those who had breached their defences. Alexis had liked the old warrior. He had been a close friend for all his time at Kingshome, and had been the one to warn him of Lord Ravenhead that now seemed a lifetime ago. He and his wife the Lady Anna were among the few to treat him with any respect, even before the incident with Ravenhead. A man of great mirth, he would truly miss his company.

Denis' death would be sad news to Gaia, as full brother and sister they had been very close. Despite a thorough search the bodies of Baron's Grimswick and Fairchild were not found. So it was reasonable to suppose they had survived and returned to their castles. After allowing a few days of rest Robert and Alexis rode north with their army to confront the two Barons. They arrived a week later at Castle Grimswick to find it occupied by a prominent money lender from Ergon. He had claimed the castle in lieu of debts owed to him. They rode on to find a similar situation at Castle Fairchild, it too had passed into the hand of a group of money lenders.

A few days later news reached Alexis from Ben Tiller that both Baron Fairchild and Grimswick had taken passage by ship from Baruron. He did not know their destination, but with a few questions and a little gold they would soon find out.

Lord Fellows surprised everyone by surviving for many days. When Alexis first told him that William had been defeated, he refused to believe it. It was only after Alexis presented him with William's helmet that he accepted the truth. With a shrug of his shoulders he proclaimed that without William the Darosi were doomed. They would be swept from the field of battle when the armies of the north attacked the Kingdom. Alexis shook his head in denial

"You judge Robert wrongly my Lord. He is a true Darosi, but one who is willing to rule all the people of the kingdom without favour for the few, and with fairness for all. The army that defeated William was not just made up of Darosi, but thousands of outsiders as well. They fought for their freedom and for Santross, and their number will grow by many thousands more if needed. With Robert as king, we will be strong, so strong that no one would dare to attack us. The fear of invasion would be no more. With William as king, only the few Darosi that are left would take the field to defend the island, none from the land or towns would fight for a king or country that only wanted to enslave then."

When Alexis first asked why he came to serve William, he showed only hostility and would not answer any of his questions. But slowly as death approached he became more willing. He maintained that what he did, he did for the good of the kingdom. Like Alexis, he knew that the Darosi had lost almost all control of the island. He saw William as the best chance to regain that control, and make the Darosi great again. He raised himself on one elbow and said in the loudest voice he could.

"We cannot allow any outsiders to be free. Wither of the land or the towns, they must all serve the Darosi. We are the only true rulers of Santross, the island is ours"

His answer made Alexis sad, like his father and all others, Lord Fellows was blind to the fact that the time of the Darosi had pasted. Like a growing child, the Island kingdom was changing, it had moved forward while they had stood still. For the Darosi to survive they had to except the fact that the few could not rule the many by sword alone, and a new way of living together had to be found. For a moment, Alexi's voice took on a serious note.

"It was you who signalled my departure from Kingshome, you hoped that the men in your pay would take my life"

Lord Fellows shrugged his shoulders

"I underestimated you, I did not think you were capable of bettering Grimswick's solders If I had known your true ability's I would have sent many more men to make your death a certainty "

Alexis looked down at him without pity, not a word of regret that he had tried to assassinate him, only the sadness that he had failed. He asked why he had not counselled Lord Avon and the others not to travel north. He was silent for many seconds as the memory of their deaths returned, he slowly shook his head.

"We did try to stop them, we both knew the letter was not from Prince William, but how could we tell them that without exposing ourselves. We thought that Baron Grimswick was only trying to lore Robert away from Kingshome to end the war before it began. I was as surprised as you when it was found that Grimswick and Fairchild were playing their own game and they had all been executed, including Lord Basil"

Alexis was surprised and confused when Lord Fellows used the word "we".

"Was Lord Basil part of the plot to make William King?"

Lord Fellows smiled.

"You never knew about him did you. We both held the same views as to the best king to sit on the throne. When Lord Basil did not contact me, I knew something was wrong. By then I also knew that both Fairchild and Grimswick were not true allies of William, I tried to contact William direct to tell him of their treachery, but the castle was surrounded by many spies in the Barons' pay, I doubt any of my messages reached him"

Again he slowly shook his head.

"Their deaths are the one thing I regret, those on the council had been my companions for many years, and they were all my friends."

He lapsed into silence, his broken body lacking the energy to continue the conversion. That was the last time Alexis saw him alive, he died two days later from his wounds.

For the next two months the army camped in the north, ready to repel the expected invasion. But none came, it took the return of the many spies who were sent north to supply the answer. Just as the Kmaree armies had gathered in the south ready for the invasion of Santross, the tribes from the neighbouring Kingdom of Basshem had invaded the now undefended north. A long and bloody war was now being fought, so for the moment the kingdom was safe.

On their return to Castle Kingshome Alexis sat in the company of Robert and revealed all the facts to him as he thought them to be. And the honour that the Darosi cherished so must was prominent by its absence.

"Like all Darosi in the west they had to employ an army of guards to keep the outsiders from running away, and most of those were mercenaries hired from the northlands that had to be paid for their services Over the last few years the harvests had been so poor that the estates had produced barely enough food for their own needs, so there was little or none to sell for profit. We do not yet know who first thought of the plan to make them rich, but you can be sure that Grinswick and Fairchild were in from the beginning"

Robert still found it hard to believe all that had happened was the work of only a few men.

"They played my brother for a fool. They knew he was unhappy that it was I who would sit upon the throne, and they used this to suite their own ends"

Alexis nodded

"Just so your majesty, it was a simple but clever plan. Everyone knew of the events when you and your brother were born. But only the ladies who attended the birth knew that the young girl they questioned had chosen William as first born. There can be no doubt that over the years Lady Faustina had told Baron Grimswick of this. When they had decided on the plan they may even have arranged her death. It was then easy to write the letter and claim it to be a deathbed confession. Your brother was eager to believe it to be true, and when the other ladies who were present confirmed it had been so he would believe nothing else"

Robert shook his head again

"So the war and all the deaths was brought about by just a few men. Men who thought to cancel their debts by killing those they owned to. And to fill their coffers with the gold they would plunder at the same time"

Alexis nodded

"And by making all the outsiders' slaves, it was not necessary to have an army of guards. The kingdom itself would become their prison with nowhere for them to escape to. The greed of a few will end up changing the way that all Darosi must live"

Chapter 48
A new Beginning

The next few months saw many changes, many more than either man could have imagined. One of the first proved to be one of the greatest. When Alexis had ridden away from Castle Kingshome he had noticed that the King and all the knights had flags and banners to show who they were, all were represented except Santross itself. On his return he consulted with those who were most experience in such matters. Alexis wanted a flag that all could rally to. And now that flag flew proudly alongside the royal banner on Castle Kingshome highest towers. At the centre of it was the black outline of Castle Kingshome, surrounded by a red circle to represent the lava that made the island, and then an outer ring of green surrounded by blue to represent the land and sea.

To make the flag more acceptable to the Darosi, Robert allowed all those who had stood with him against William permission to include their own coat of arms in one corner of the flag. To the Darosi any symbol of honour was much sort after, and all flew the new flag with pride. The outsiders had also quickly embraced the new flag. It was a symbol that now they severed a country, not a single person. The towns and cities felt the same way. For many years they had resisted being ruled by a king who did nothing to help them increase their wealth, but wanted to take a share of it. But this flag was not that of a king, but of a country.

With the death of Lord Fellows and the others, the high council was reduced to one. Lord Tay had been unable to travel north with the others due to failing health. Alexis suggested that a new council be formed, but not one on the lines of the old. In the past, the high council had been the only contact the king had with his subjects, and then only with fellow Darosi. The new one was to be called "The Council of Santross" and it contained not only Darosi noblemen, but also outsiders like Ben Tiller who had been made a minster of the crown as a reward for his part in the war. Josh Cooper and Tom Halyard, two of the founder members of the workers council were also elected to the council. A recent addition to their number was a representative from Egion. Like all towns it suffered from a higher rate of crime than the countryside. It wanted a royal force to be formed to patrol their streets to make them safer, in the hope that trade could prosper even more. There was no upper limit to the numbers who could attend, so it was hoped that in time all towns and large settlements would be represented. Now everyone could have a voice in deciding the course that the kingdom should take. Robert also granted them the power to act as a people's court, their power second only to his and Alexis. Anyone who felt they had been treated unjustly could appeal to them to hear their case. Both Robert and Alexis were blind to the fact that unwittingly they had laid the foundations for a democracy. A democracy that perhaps one day would rule what was fast changing from a feudal kingdom into a country, but that was still far into the future.

Now just over one year after the battle the change was plain to see. It must continue for many years if they were to survive, but the journey to a better tomorrow had begun.

A short time after the battle the first post-war crises had been upon them. Many of the estates in the north and west of the kingdom had lost its lord in battle, and it turned out that the Barons Grimswick and Fairchild were not the only ones in debt. Almost all the Darosi from the west had been owing various amounts of money. This was a serious matter, an estate needs constant attention to keep it as a going concern. If left unattended the land will quickly return to nature, and buildings are always in need of repair. To compound the difficulties for the surviving lords, they had also lost their workforce. Given freedom the outsiders quickly left the places of enslavement. A few of the money lenders decided to become landowners and keep the estates for themselves. But the majority saw the land just as another item to pass on and make a profit from. The whole of that part of the kingdom was in danger of becoming a wasteland. There were many more estates for sale than buyers able to buy. The saviour of this situation came from an unlikely source. It was the council of workers that Alexis had first set up who came forward with the solution. Now free men who could own land, they came to agreements with the money leaders to work the land for themselves. They would use the profits from each harvest to pay back a part of the debt, so in time the land would be theirs. Estate after estate passed into their hands in this way, and the results could be seen instantly. Almost overnight the land was transformed from one of despair into one of hope. A few Darosi of the west reluctantly accepted the situation, and like the Darosi of the east offered their former salves a share of any profits if they stayed and worked the land. But there were many more that resisted. Unable or unwilling to give up the old ways they fought to keep the outsiders on their estates as slaves. They fell one by one to an army made up of Roberts' troops and outsiders. Two separated events finally ended the troubles. First the most outspoken and troublesome of the Darosi still resisting were killed in battle. Then a few weeks later the Barons Grimswick and Fairchild were captured and brought back to Santross. Many saw them as their last chance to overthrow Robert and bring back the old ways. At their trial they confessed that when the mounted archers had withdrawn they had slipped quietly away to hide in the trees even before the battle proper had begun. This act of betrayal cost them the respect of all the surviving Darosi. Many of their men tried to save their own lives by telling all they knew of their crimes. The evident against them was overwhelming. They and the men involved with the killing of the council were found guilty of all their dirty deeds, and along with the prisoners from Kingshome were duly beheaded. It was almost as if the last **chapter** of the past had been written, and the book closed.

Now there was no going back to the old ways, and all must live for tomorrow. And just to make sure that peace would rule, a company of the King's guard made their base in the area.

Alexis noted with satisfaction that although Kmaree had survived their invasion, the raids on the north coast had stopped. Their new style of fighting that had brought such a crushing victory over William had become common knowledge. Now much weaker after a long war of their own, Kmaree had as much to fear from Santross, as Santross had from them. To his delight, the threat of invasion had been replaced by overtures of a peace treaty. Alexis sat in the company of his king as they discussed the latest situation. Such was their closeness now that in private each called the other by name. The sun sunk below the ramparts as the afternoon wore on and the failing light began to make the room dark. Soon their meeting would come to an end for today. A few months before Gaia had presented him with a baby boy, out of respect for his king and father was given the name Robert Damon. Queen Livia had not been as lucky. The child she was carrying when they had marched off to battle was another girl. Robert still did not have an heir to the throne, and Livia was now at an age where she was unlikely to conceive again. It was a long way in the future, but both men had already talked that perhaps the two babies would make a good match for each other. But it would not be the only joining of the two houses. When Leon had returned to Castle Kingshome he had succumb to an infection that brought him close to death. Princes Charmaine was the oldest of Roberts' daughters and had stayed by his side day and night to nurse him back to full health, and what patient does not fall in love with his nurse? It was clear that both had become very much in love and married as soon as Leon had recovered. Now according to the latest message from Castle Monrell, if all went well, Robert and Livia would be grandparents by springtime. As for the kingdom, both men knew that there were many hurdles to overcome in the future, tasks that would push them to the limit, but the time would come soon enough to worry about those. For the moment Alexis was content. Gaia and his child would be waiting for him in his chambers. The look of love would be in her eyes and the feel of love in her arms, and for the moment that was enough for him.

The End

The Loyal Assistant
Chapter 1

Kevin sat quietly looking out of the window, his body quite still apart from the constant twitch in his right eye and the tremor in his right hand. The tremor was not new, it had been with him longer than his fading memory could remember, but the twitching eye had started only a few hours ago. A young girl had a tantrum about the style of shoe her mother had bought for her, and in a fit of rage she had thrown one of the offending shoes as hard as she could. The steel tipped heel hit Kevin just above his right eye. Only the child knew if Kevin had been the deliberate target or just unlucky to be in the line of fire. Either way it made no difference to the result. He had collapsed into an uncontrollable fit that had lasted for several minutes as his body reacted to the blow. Now he sat waiting patiently to be examined by a specialist, and his wait was about to end.

The door opened and two men entered. The first was the specialist wearing a long white coat, his pockets filled with various instruments to the point of overflow. The second was Kevin's boss, a concerned looking Mr Bloomer. The examination began, the white coat spoke to Kevin in a reinsuring soft voice as he held his hand to feel the strength of the tremor, then he used an instrument with a beam of light to examined the damaged eye. After a few minutes he began to use the other various bits and pieces from his pockets to conduct other tests that lasted several minutes before a final look again at the damaged eye. He nodded to Mr Bloomer,

"I have a full picture of his condition now"

He carefully returned the instruments to his coat pockets and began to walk towards the door. Mr Bloomer tried to look cheerful as he give Kevin the thumps up sign.

"We'll have you fit and well in no time"

He gestured toward the retreating specialist and with a smile added

"He's the best in the business, you'll probably end up as good as new"

And with those few words he quickly left the room and closed the door behind him.

With their departure Kevin returned to watching the raindrops make their way slowly down the window pane. It was a late November afternoon, and with the rain and heavy clouds the light was fading fast. The image of something old and wearing a shabby coat looked back at him from the glass. For a moment he was shocked by his reflection, did he really look like that? It was one of his mannerisms that when deep in thought he would often mutter softly to himself, and he did so now, over and over again.

"A lifetime of service….a lifetime of service and it comes to this"

He knew the blow to his head had caused damage. Now he could not control his thoughts for more than a few seconds before they drifted like gossamer on the wind between the present and the past. Uninvited memories of times and people long gone came flooding back. Memories are such wonderful things, they allow us to relive again and again the times we cherish the most. Now he sat silently, as in his mind the years rolled back to those happier days when he and the world were young, and the adventure of life was about to begin.

Chapter 2
The Beginning

The big day had arrived at last and he was excited, his training was complete and he was about to start his first day's work in his very first job. The vehicle he was in rolled to a stop outside the shop that was to be his place of work. He took a moment before entering to look up at the impressive shop front. The name of the establishment was embossed in golden gilt letters a foot high on a black background.

J T Bloomer & Son, Purveyors of High Quality Footwear

And the richness of the premises did not stop with just the sign, the whole appearance of the shop including the window displays of fine shoes had an air of wealth and grandeur about them. Kevin was impressed, no one could have any doubt about the kind of clientele they served there. He entered through the double doors and was totally surprised by what he saw. He just stood there for a moment to gather his wits, he had expected to find the interior of the shop the same or similar to what he had been trained on, but this was completely different. The area was divided into a series of three-sided cubicles containing chairs and tables so that they each resembled a small room, all the cubicles appeared to be occupied by customers. Several were having shoes fitted with the help of the shop assistants. Many others were sipping tea or other forms of refreshment laid out for them on the tables as they sat and commented on the style and suitability of the shoes being offered to them. His conclusion that the shop served a high class of clientele had been proved right, and high class clientele demand a high class service.

He turned his attention to the assistants, there seemed to be so many of them, they outnumbered the customers at least two to one. They were all dressed in what was obviously a shop uniform, a black lose fitting all-in-one with gold piping down the seams with the name Bloomer written in gold letters across their front, another point he noticed was that they all appeared to be quite elderly. He began to walk aimlessly across the deep pile carpet, unsure of who to ask or where to go, but that dilemma was quickly resolved. He had only taken a step or two before he was approach by one of the shop assistants.

"Can I be of service to you sir?"

Kevin was taken by surprise; this assistant had mistaken him for a customer and not recognised him as a fellow worker. For a brief moment he enjoyed his new found status and thought to play the role a while longer, but that idea quickly past. It would not please his new boss to have the assistant waste time on him, when he should have been serving genuine customers. He bowed his head slightly

"Thank you, I was told to come here and report to Mr Bloomer, I'm to be a new shoe shop assistant."

The man beamed a smile

"You are very welcome" he looked around the busy shop floor. "There are times when we could do with half a dozen new assistants. But now you'll want to see Mr Bloomer senior and introduce yourself to him. Follow me and I will take you to his office"

He walked to the rear of the shop, then up a flight of stairs that led to the administration centre of the shop.

Kevin followed a few steps behind, and moments later he was sat outside Mr Bloomer's office door. He twiddled his thumbs as he nervously waited to be introduced to the man who could make his life a heaven or a hell from now on. He wondered what he would be like, would he be a fair man, or someone only interested in making maximum profits from his labour. The twiddling of the thumbs grew quicker as he pondered the unknown future. He was so much on edge that the soft click of the door release mechanism made him jump. A secretary sitting at a desk opposite had watched him with amusement as his obvious discomfort increased. Now she nodded towards the door and said in the softest most lyrical voice he had ever heard,

"Mr Bloomer will see now, please go in."

Her voice had such a hypnotic effect on him that for a moment he just sat there as if in a trance. She looked at him still with the amused smile on her face

"Did you hear me? I said you can go in."

Kevin stuttered like someone waking from a deep sleep.

"Yes, what, I…I mean yes, I did hear you"

He cleared his throat, thrust his shoulders back like a soldier about to go on parade, and walked smartly into the office.

Mr Bloomer sat head down behind a large walnut desk writing a letter or note of some kind. Without looking up he gestured towards a chair with the tip of his pen.

"Please sit down, I won't be a moment"

Kevin did as he was told and looked around the room, he could hardly believe what he was seeing. Everything looked like something out of an old history book, including the man sitting at the desk.

For several seconds he could not help but stare at the top of Mr Bloomer's head, it was completely bald, the first he has ever seen. Thanks to gene replacement therapy baldness was almost extinct. Now only the very poor had to endure that condition, and he was sure Mr Bloomer did not fall into that category.

The old fashion pen in Mr Bloomer's hand made a soft scratching sound as he wrote real words on real paper, again Kevin was amused, nobody actually wrote anymore, they just dictated into any number of machines and the machines did the writing for them.

Kevin had already seen enough to know that this man along with his office and the entire shop and staff should be an exhibit in a museum, they really were something out of the twentieth century. He wondered what twist of fate had sent him here. He had been schooled in all the latest and most efficient methods of running a shop, there was no job he could not do, no knowledge he did not have. As shop assistants go he was the crème de la crème, and they had sent him to work in a museum.

After a few moments Mr Bloomer completed his task and looked up, and Kevin had a good look of his new master for the first time.

Mr Bloomers' face was as round as the top of his head, and reminded him of a full moon with a body to match. If you added some makeup he would make the perfect circus clown, or perhaps with a white beard an even better Father Christmas.

He rose from the desk and walked to one of the large windows that filled the room with light. He stood with his hands behind his back and peered down to the busy street below.

"I wanted to have an informal talk with you before you began your duties"

He turned and smiled at Kevin

"A sort of get to know kind of chat"

Kevin nodded his head in agreement

"Yes sir, I understand".

Mr Bloomer paused for a moment before going on.

"You are the first new assistant to start here for over twenty years"

His head gently shook from side to side as if in disbelief

"Twenty years, where does the time go?"

Mr Bloomer gave a little shrug of his shoulders to signal the end of his moment of nostalgia and returned to his desk.

"Very good err"

He paused as he began to read some official looking documents on the desk
"Kevin is it?"
Again the nodded of agreement
"Yes sir."
Mr Bloomer continued to read through the papers for a few moments longer.
"I see you have been instructed in the latest methods of accounting and stock control"
"Yes sir, along with the latest form of statistics analysis on stock rotation"
Mr Bloomer had a mystified look on his face, Kevin quickly added.
"It means that sometimes with the minim of information I can predict what will be a best seller"
Now Mr Bloomer's face split into a huge smile
"Well, well, well, I'd be blowed, you new chaps are getting smarter all the time."
He gave a little chuckle
"Before long you will be sitting behind this desk, and I will be the one on the shop floor"
He returned to the window
"I'm going to tell you a story, well, its more than just a story really, it's the truth of how Bloomers came into being."
Over the next twenty minutes Kevin learned how the original Mr Bloomer, a cobbler by trade had come to this country as an immigrant. He found the shoes that people wore were of such poor quality that he decided to make and sell his own. It was from these humble beginning that Bloomers' had grown to be more than just a shop that sold shoes, it had become a byword for quality and service. People came from miles around just to buy their footwear from the famous Bloomer & Son. And always, from generation to generation the shop had retained the high tradition of quality and service. Mr Bloomer looked intensely at Kevin
"There are many who would think that just running a shoe shop is of little or no importance compared with other pursuits in life, but my family thought otherwise"
He tapped his desk softly as if applauding those who had gone before him
They set standards, and now the responsibility of maintaining these standards are in your hands, do you think you are up to the task Kevin?"
Kevin had listened to every word Mr Bloomer had said, and had been inspired by them in a way he never thought possible. Now everything became clear to him, the layout of the shop, the office, even the appearance of Mr Bloomer himself, the whole establishment belonged to the distance past. The path they trod had been laid down for them by their fathers, and their father fathers. His

assessment had been correct, they were history, but they were living history, and that made a difference. And now he was to be a part of that living history, to be part of a family with roots going back hundreds of years. It made him feel humble, but at the same time so full of pride he could almost feel his chest get an inch or two bigger. He decided that from this moment on his fate and that of the shop would be as one, he would honour the history of bloomers as if it were his own, and he would serve Bloomers until he could serve no more. He answered in a calm and clear voice

"Yes sir, I am"

Mr Bloomer was surprized by the firmness and sincerity of Kevin's' reply, and give him a long hard look before slowly nodding his head

"Yes Kevin, I believe you are"

He rubbed his fingers over his chin gently.

"I have a good feeling about you Kevin, I think you are going to fit in here very well, and perhaps develop in ways that even you would not think possible."

He pressed a switch on his desk

"Miss C, will you ask Mr Abraham to come to my office please, I've finished interviewing Kevin"

He heard a faint "yes sir" in reply.

Mr Bloomer signalled the end of their time together by gently guiding him towards the door.

"Well, I suppose you'll be wanting to start work straight away"

Chapter 3

To your post

The office door opened at their approach to reveal Mr Abraham already waiting to receive the new recruit

"Ha…here is Mr Abraham, he will take change of you now"

He turned to his senior shop assistant

"Teach him well Mr Abraham, teach him well, I have high hopes for him, yes indeed, very high hopes for him"

He put his hand on Kevin's shoulder,

"You could be a star of the future my lad, yes indeed, a star of the future"

He pointed a finger at Kevin in a gesture of warning

"If you work hard enough and apply yourself with your best efforts"

With that he turned and the door to his office closed silently behind him.

Kevin looked at Mr Abraham, he was dressed as all the other assistants were, and looked just as old.

"My name is Mr Abraham, I am senior shop assistant here. You take your orders only from me or either Mr Bloomer senior or Mr Bloomer junior. But of course if either Mr Bloomer gives you an order you must obey them first"

Mr Abraham handed him a new top coat in the same colours as his own.

"Here, this will do for now, I was not informed that you would be so much taller than the rest of us, so you won't have a new suite until tomorrow"

Kevin could see over Mr Abrahams' shoulder to the young secretary still at her desk. She was speaking to someone on the phone and again the beautiful tone of her voice captured his attention. Just at that moment she looked up and their eyes met, and for some reason he felt guilty to have been caught staring at her. He hurriedly dropped his glaze to the floor and with eyes down followed Mr Abraham as he walked towards the rear of the shop, but as he passed her desk he stole a quick glance. She was looking directly at him with a smile of amusement mixed with surprize on her face, and somehow that smile made him feel much better. As they walked Mr Abraham said

"Mr Bloomer wants you to start in the stock department so you can learn the different styles and where they are kept"

Kevin was disappointed not to start on the shop floor, but even he could not argue with the logic of the decision, so be it, he would do as he was told, but promised himself that he would learn everything he had to in the shortest time possible, he would not be any old stock assistant, but the best there had even been. From now on "Mr High Quality" would be his middle name. Mr Abraham rounded a corner and stopped

"Ha, here we are, this will be your place of work until told otherwise, well, I must be getting on, we are re-dressing one of the windows tonight and I must get everything ready"

As he started to walk away he called over his shoulder

"Get to know where everything is as quick as you can."

Kevin looked around, there were stock assistants cress-crossing the area in every direction, some putting away new deliveries to replenish stock, while others were filling requests from the shop floor. Two assistants were nearby and both approached him. Keven was not impressed, like all the others they were definitely past their best. To his young eyes they looked at least a hundred years old, especially standing next to him with his new coat on.

"Ah ha, new blood at last, you are very welcome here, my name is Martin"

The other took a step towards him and shook his hand in a limp way.

"And I am James"

Over the next few days Kevin exploded every inch of his new surroundings. It was exactly as you would expect a stock area to be with shoe boxes stacked in every available space, but what surprized Kevin was that it was done in a very disorganized way. All the different lines of stock were allocated their own number, but they were not being stored in any kind of numerical order. It quickly became very clear that none working in the area had been trained in the skills needed to organize and run stockrooms in the correct way. They had all started out selling on the shop floor and had only been relegated to the stock area due to their increased age and failing ability. Within days Kevin was seeking permission from Mr Abraham to organize the stock in a more logical manor. At first Mr Abraham refused his request. He had always run the stockrooms this way, and he saw no reason to change. But Kevin persisted, and one day Mr Bloomer senior was in earshot as he once again made the request. He thought it a good idea and immediately gave Kevin permission to proceed.

Kevin himself retrained those that were still capable of leaning new methods, sadly, the others that included Martin and James were just too old and had their employment terminated.

He worked long and hard and within a few weeks the transformation was complete.

Chapter 4
A job well done

Mr Bloomer was highly delighted with the result and patted Kevin on his back,

"I knew you would do well here, I just knew it, well done young man, well done"

It was inevitable that within a short space of time Mr Abraham found himself under increasing pressure from the new recruit and his new ideas, so it was no great surprise when within months Kevin replaced him as head assistant.

Some said that it was the shook of this that caused the demise of Mr Abraham.

He had held the position of head assistant for almost all his working life, but soon after the changes his lifeless body was found slumped on the floor in the stock area.

Now under Kevin guidance the running of the shop began to change rapidly, all the staff were retrained and given the new skills needed to run the shop in the most efficiently manor, as a result of these improvements the number needed fell by almost half thus saving a fortune in overhead costs. Mr Bloomer senior was particularly delighted at the way Kevin performed his duties, and treated him almost like a son. As a mark of their esteem for him Kevin was given a suite to wear, rather than the livery all the other assistants wore, and given the title of Shop Manager. Kevin took great pride in his new position and renewed the promise he had made himself the day he started at Bloomers, along with another to never allow his standards to drop for a moment.

Now every day he would see one or both of the Bloomers to discuss the running of the shop, and this meant he got to see a lot more of Cathleen, the young secretary with the beautiful voice which always affected him in such a pleasant manor. This was a source of much amusement to Mr Bloomer junior, and he often asked Kevin why this should be, but Kevin was unable to supply an answer. Kevin would sometimes find reason to visit the office when he knew Mr Bloomer was unavailable, just so he could sit by her desk. Cathleen was almost as amused with his interest in her voice as Mr Bloomer, and she would often read out loud some of the daily correspondence of the shop just to please him. The two grew to be unlikely friends, and it was one of the saddest days of Kevin's life when a few years later Cathleen left to get married and start a young family.

On more serious matters both his bosses quickly recognize his uncanny ability to judge what shoes would be big sellers, and what styles not to stock. This alone helped to increase turnover by as much as 20%.

The next ten years saw even more changes, Kevin was given his own office as his control grew, now all the decisions on the day to day running of the shop were his to make alone. And as Kevin's' authority advanced, the Bloomers involvement retreated, now they had so little to do that one or both would spend days or even weeks away from the shop.

Kevin was now at the peak of his skills as year after year the profits of the shop continued to rise. He even developed a taste in music, particularly that of females and the sound of their singing could often be heard coming from his office.

There were minor disasters, one time he damaged his knee falling off a ladder, but the Bloomers arranged for an operation to replace the offending joint and return him to full fitness. Mr Bloomer senior had jokingly scolded him that he was too precious to the running of the shop to be climbing ladders and he should delegate such tasks to others. Kevin promised not to do it again, and so time continued to pass. In the world outside the doors of the shop thousands of events happen each day, wars were fought, fortunes won and lost, but all this pasted Kevin by. He lived in his own world, and that world only had room for J.T Bloomer & Son. For him this was a golden era that would never end, but it is a sad fact of life that **everything** comes to an end sooner or later.

For Kevin the real world invaded his private domain in the most traumatic way when Mr Bloomer senior passed away after a short illness. He'd always had a very close relationship with the elder Mr Bloomer, but Mr Bloomer junior was still pleasantly surprized by the genuine remorse he showed for his death. It became clear over the coming month that the event had hit him hard and he found it difficult to adjust to him not being there.

Chapter 5
A setback

Now Mr Bloomer junior became Mr Bloomer senior and brought his eldest son Thomas into the business, it turned out to be a big mistake. Less than a year later Mr Bloomer senior had an illness that kept him away from the shop for many months. Thomas used his time in control to introduced new lines of cheaper shoes that temperedly boosted the profits, but were totally unsuited for the shops usual clientele. Soon many customers began to take their trade elsewhere, while others complained about the fall in standards. Kevin tried hard to persuade Thomas to go back to the old ways, but he flatly rejected any advice given to him and was determined to run things his way.

Mr Bloomer senior returned just in time to save the shop from total disaster, and after some harsh words with his son, Thomas left the family business never to return.

Mr Bloomer senior overturned all the decisions his son had made, and with Kevin's help returned the shop to its former condition, but the damage had been done, and the shop never fully recovered its former reputation or level of trade.

The years marched on, the shop still showed a profit, but now no matter what Kevin did that profit grew smaller and smaller.

The reasons for the decline were many, taxes were increased so the rich were suddenly not as rich as they used to be. Staff came to the end of their working lives but with falling revenue could not be replaced.

But the real nail in the coffin was that the shop and their traditional style of quality footwear just fell out of fashion with the public. Now the rich no longer wore fine clothes and shoes to show off their wealth, but adopted a much more casual approach. In an effort to keep the name of Bloomer alive five years ago they had moved to smaller cheaper premises. It had worked, the shop still survived as a going concern but only with Kevin working himself into the ground by running the shop almost single handed.

His mind slowly drifted back to the present. With his one good eye he watched the tremor in his right hand in a detached way as if looking at someone else's body. He had punished himself with too much work for too many years, and now he had nothing left to give. Even before the incident with the child his ability to perform grew less with each passing day. He somehow knew that his journey through life was coming to an end, and that made him sad, but he also felt proud. He had fulfilled the vow he had made all those years ago to be a guardian and servant of Bloomers' and no one could take that away from him.

Mr Bloomer tiptoed up to the door of Kevin's room. He watched him through the glass opening for several seconds, but made no attempt to go in. The news he had just received from the specialist had been like a hammer blow to him. The bitter truth was that Kevin was at the end of his working life. His whole body was just plain worn out and already beginning to fail, he had added.

"He will show less signs of movement as one by one his life systems cease to operate. Finally the last function will fail and he will be gone. He could at best last a few more days, but the chances are he will be gone by morning"

He had half expected this, and without a moment hesitation had decided in his own mind to close Bloomers for good. The truth was that for many years Bloomers had been kept alive by Kevin's efforts alone, and without him he had neither the strength nor desire to continue. He remembered the prediction his father made when Kevin had first started that he would be someone very special, and he had been right. It was as if he had fully understood from the beginning that Bloomers' was more than just a shoe shop, it was an institution with standards set by his ancestors of long ago. And Kevin had maintained those standards with more diligence than anyone had the right to expect. He had often wished his son Thomas could have thought about the business in the same way as Kevin, but he never did. After his short but disastrous time in charge all those years ago he'd had no contact with him, and in time he had come to look upon Kevin as one of his family.

Finally he turned and started to walk away. As he walked he looked down at Kevin's registration papers, now yellow with age. He'd had to show them to prove he was the legal owner of Kevin before they would examine him. He read the words slowly, this was only the second time he had seen this document and somehow his mind refused to register the full meaning of the words.

ROBOT SHOP ASSISTANT
Made by KENTAR ELECTRONICS
KE series VI model N
Series name - Kevin
Model number 1673493
Operate date 6/6/2157
New Owner J.T. Bloomer and Son

He spoke his thoughts out loud.

"I will miss you Kevin, I will miss you a lot. Mr Abraham and the others were good, but you were in a class all of your own. You were the best, the **very** best robot we ever had"

He crumpled the papers up into a ball, with KE-V1-N gone there was no need to keep them and he casually dropped them into the nearest waste bin on the way out.

The Chosen Ones
Chapter 1

Richard Gough sat watching the bank of monitors spread out before him, he was constantly giving instructions to change from one camera angle to another as the two newscasters read out the latest stories in turn. As Director of the News Department he would normally never preformed the lowly duties of a producer, he had passed that rung on the ladder many years ago. But tonight was a very special occasion. It marked the end of a remarkable career of someone very close to him. And just to emphasize how important it was, before transmission he had made it clear to everyone that a mistake tonight, however small could end their broadcasting careers, at least with him. It was so typical of the man to treat the people under him in such a way, because Richard Gough was a work driven tyrant. A perfectionist who maintained his professional standards no matter what obstacle or difficulties confronted him. He was recognized by even his most ardent enemy's as a formable opponent for truth, and because of him many including high government ministers had paid the ultimate price for their transgressions. As Director of the News Department he had a certain amount of respect shown to him, but on a personal level his methods and attitude made him disliked by many. This was in stark contrast to the person he was honouring who had the love and respect of all.

Angela Morrow was regarded as a legend by both the public and those she worked with. Early in her career she had interviewed the dictator of a country who only stayed in control by killing all those who opposed him. When he had agreed to be interviewed he thought the questions would be gentle in nature and show him in a good light, but he was wrong. At some risk to her life Angela deviated from the agreed script and tore into him about his record of genocide, and his many accounts in foreign banks totalling millions of dollars. The whole world saw him fall apart under her searching questions. Angela was immediately regarded as a brave champion for truth. She became known overnight as "The People's Reporter" a title that stayed with her for the rest of her career. As for the dictator, when he returned home he lost power the same way he had achieved it, under a hail of bullets. Of even more importance to Richard was that in a very small circle of people he called friends, she was at the very centre. When he had first started in national TV nearly thirty years ago, it was Angela who had unexpectedly taken him under her wing. She was already well established as a TV celebrity, so it was quite a coup for him to have her as a patron. At first his young arrogance let him think she found him attractive and her interest was of a romantic or sexual nature. But when she had arranged for him to produce a series on the wildlife of Africa, neither emotion made even the briefest of appearances between them. She did however meet a cameraman called David Callan who made quite an impact in that direction. They seemed to feed off each other, and in the end Angela's inspiring commentary and his superb camerawork played no small part in the success of the series. He had tried to compete with David for her affection, but quickly lost the battle and was best man at the wedding he had hoped to be the groom. But the friendship survived, and many years later it was his sad duty to report David's death while covering the troubles in Somalia. He had hoped that maybe a romance between them would grow after a suitable time, but by now his work had become his master, and that never left him time for other pursues. There was always something that had to be done, and done now, so his half-hearted attempts had fallen on stony ground. Now after nearly a decade any thoughts in that direction had died a long time ago. But he still loved her in his fashion, and paid homage to the debt he owed her for all her help and guidance in the early years of his career.

Now he watched her perform as she always performed, with the calmness and grace that others imitated but none equalled. All too soon it was over, the last piece of news delivered, followed by Angela thanking the public for all the kindness and support they had showed her during her career. And that was that, her time before the cameras ended probable the same way it began all those years ago, with a smile.

At the end of transmissions, he joined in the ripple of applause that quickly grew to a sizeable crescendo as everyone on the studio floor paid tribute to a long and distinguish career that had spanned four decades.

Angela made her way through the crowd of handshakes and backslapping to a side office where some bottles of champagne appeared. For the next hour she was the centre of attention as she listened to tributes and antidotes from co-workers that seemed to grow higher in praise as the stock of bubbly grew smaller. Finally, the last toast was drunk, the last firm handshake endured followed by a quick but quiet exit through a side door. Within a few minutes she was sitting safely in the back of her chauffeur driven car on her homeward journey.

It was that time of year when the evening gives a hint of the winter to come. Angela pulled the lapels of her coat closer together and dozed in the cosseted warmth and luxury of the limousine.

"Take the long way home Gerald, and go slowly, tonight I'm in the mood for a long drive."

The next morning her alarm went off at the normal time of six thirty. Angela half opened her eyes and reached across to switch it off. All her life she had been a slave to time, but not today, or any other day from now on. No more deadlines, no more eating a sandwich in the back of a taxi as she rushed from one appointment to another and no more panicking that everything was ready just before they went on air. From now on the pace of life would be as she wanted. For a moment she smiled like the famed Cheshire cat at the thought, and in a playful but very unladylike manor, she poked her tongue out at the clock, turned over and tried to go back to sleep.

But the habits of a lifetime are hard to change so quickly, her inner clock also said it was time to get up, so an hour later she was in the kitchen making a cup of coffee. In the past she referred to this as her "To do today time" when she had decided what was so important that she had to do herself, and lesser things that she could afford to delegate to any assistances. But now that part of her life was over, the only big decisions she would make from now on was what to wear when she went out, and what to eat when she didn't. And somehow whatever meal she decided on it was never going to be as tasty as intervening the Prime Minister about the latest scandal to hit the government.

A week or so later she again entered through the marble double doors that were such an imposing feature of the TV building. Word quickly spread of her arrival and many found excuses to visit the News's Department's offices. It seemed they all wanted to say one last farewell to her. Angela refused no-one as she made her way through the handshakes and autographed hunters to her old office to collect the last of her personal things. The first item she carefully packed away was a picture of her and David taken just after they married. It was over nine years since his death, without conscious thought she added the seven months and 23 days to make the date complete . She had two great regrets in her life, the death of David, and their inability to have a family. When they had first found out they could not have children there was much sadness, but they had drawn solitude from the love they had for each other. But David's death had taken his love away and left her with nothing more than memories. What made his death seem even more unfair was he was not due to go to Somalia. He was going to cover the visit of some American government official, but the wife of the original cameraman had just given birth to their first baby, and so as a favour David had swapped assignments with him. Three days later he was dead, killed in a roadside ambush, and the memory still hurt as much now as it did then.

Richard arrived just as the last items were safely packed away. She smiled
"Hello Richard, you're just in time to carry this box to my car."
Richard picked it up, it was heaver than it looked.
"Perhaps it would be better if I got one of the manual staff to carry this"
Angela playfully felt the muscles in his arm and said in a light-hearted way
"Oh don't be such a wimp, that's nothing to a big, strong, man like you. And besides, you know you can never find help when you need it."

Richard picked the box up again with a small sigh, he had never found a way to say no to Angela, and it was too late to start trying now.

All her early admirers had returned to their posts, so Angela was able to walk slowly and without interruption along familiar corridors and offices once occupied by former friends and colleagues' each with a story to tell. The first one had been occupied for many years by Sam Wallice, although only a short man he was known as "Big Sam" to all his friends. A no-nonsense northerner as hard as the steel his birthplace was famous for. He earned his knick-name when he was interviewing a Police Inspector in the middle of a works dispute when one of the demonstrators' tried to attack him. Sam saw him coming and without breaking the conversation he knocked the man out with a single blow and carried on as if nothing had happened. Now she drew level with Peter Crain old office, one of her closest friends and ally now long retired. His secretary Evelyn had been the most accident prone person she had even known. Peter had soon found out that a desk top with cups of coffee and important papers plus Evelyn equalled disaster. One time she had bought Peter a new cigarette lighter for his birthday. The first time he had used it a jet of flame a foot high had stringed his eyebrows and set fire to his hair. Needless to say the gift was quickly returned to the shop as unsuitable. But they must have had good feeling for each other because they ended up getting married. She sighed at the thought of leaving behind so many memories, there had been a few sad ones, but mainly it had been a time of happiness. It was here that her romance with David had first blossomed. Before and after their marriage he would often sneak into her office and steal a quick kiss, at the time it made them laugh as if they were two naughty school children misbehaving in some way. And even after all these years there were times in her office when his presence was so strong she could almost feel his arms around her.

It was also a time when her word had come first, even senior directors bowed before her every wish. But not now, in just a few days her status had gone from a major player to one of no real importance.

The change did not bother her, she had decided many months ago to retire from her role here. She had achieved as much as she could and was ready for the next challenge in her life. A short time after David's death she had used her position as a TV celebrity to help set up a charity for families who had lost their husband or breadwinner due to war. Over the last few years the organisation had grown and had helped thousands of families in distress. Now she was leaving her well paid position to devote all her time to helping other people who were less fortunate then her.

They returned to the main foyer where she was confronted by a man who had obviously been waiting for her.

Richard was beginning to struggle under the weight of the box, and if this turned out to be a long farewell he needed to relieve himself of his burden, even if only for a few minutes. He spied the lobby desk a few feet away and without any ceremony pushed everything aside to deposit the box there. The young receptionist was upset at seeing her area of authority treated in such a disrespected way and give Richard a look of displeasure, but Richard was immune from such attacks. He returned her look of displeasure with one of his own.

"You can have your desk back when I've finished with it. This box is so heavy that if I carried it much further my arms would be as long as an orang-utan."

He shook his aching arms from side to side to encourage the return of feeling to his fingers. To the young receptionist it looked as if he was imitating the creature. The idea of seeing the great Richard Gough in the guise of an ape brought a smile to her face, yes, the image fitted the pompous old fool perfectly. Richard, seeing the girl smile though his sense of humour had won her over. What a blessing for all of us that mindreading is still out of our reach. The waiting man beamed at her.

"Hello Miss, didn't think you could go without me saying goodbye did yer."

She smiled at the warmth of his greeting

"Hello Alf, if you had not found me, I would have looked for you."

He shrugged his shoulders as if embarrassed and proud at the same time.

"You always know the right things to say you do Miss, a proper lady you are, and that's no mistake."

She gave a modest smile in reply.

Alf was a short slim man of indeterminable age who seemed to been there for all eternity, everyone knew him only as "Alf" and a more wise and happier sole you are never likely to meet. As a doorman he had welcomed her on the first day of her TV career, and now still as a doorman he was wishing her farewell.

She leaned forward and gave him a hug followed by a kiss on his cheek. For a moment he went red in the face, then with a cheery smile added.

"Cor, how am I going to explain to the Mrs's when I don't wash my face for the next two weeks."

She gave a little chuckle.

"You always knew how to make me laugh Alf, no matter how sad I was."

In a more sombre mood she whispered

"Thank you Alf, I shall always remember you, and if you ever need any help, you know where to come."

He whispered back,

"No, it's me who's saying thank you, it's been a real honour knowing you Miss, it really has."

Angela gave him one last hug before turning to leave. As she reached the door

Alf called after her.

"Don't leave it too long before you come back and visit your old friends."

She nodded

"Every time I'm in the neighbourhood"

Richard was silent as they walked to Angela's car, he had just witness a conversation between a senior newscaster and a lowly doorman that bordered on intimacy. In all the years he had known her she had never hinted that she even knew Alf existed. Now his curiosity got the better of him.

"You seem to know him quite well, and he you."

Angela knew he was fishing for the story but said nothing. They had barely gone ten yards before he tried again.

"Well come on, don't keep me in suspense, spill the beans as they say in all the best movies."

They reached her car and with a sigh of relief Richard deposited the box in the boot. Angela opened the driver's door

"I was wondering how to go about telling you, but you insisting makes' my task easier"

Richard nodded

"Yes, every little detail, now stop acting like it's a state secret and tell me"

"OK my curious friend, I don't suppose it would do any harm now for you to know the full story, seeing that almost everyone involved is either dead or long retired."

She touched his arm, and said

"And its time you knew. It goes back long before I met you"

She nodded towards the TV building.

"In fact it started the very first day I walked through those front doors, or I should say nearly walked through them. I was a very young, very nervous twenty-two year old. Just as I was about to enter the building I bumped into my new boss, only I didn't know he was my boss at that moment. Nor did he know I was to be one of his underlings. His name was Frank Garman, but I always called him Grey-suite. He was looking over his shoulder dictating a letter to his secretary, a Miss Carlisle when he marched straight through me, and I mean through me. He was a big man, a **very** big man, and my books and papers ended up on one side of the entrance, and I on the other. To make matters worst, instead of him apologising to me, he demanded that I apologize to him. Well, new girl or no new girl, there was no way I would do that, and I told him so in no uncertain terms."

Richard burst out laughing

"You had a stand up row with your new boss, on your very first day?"

Angela nodded her head in agreement.

"Yes, but like I said I didn't **know** he was my boss, and he didn't **know** I was due to start in his department. Anyway he stormed off shouting all kinds of threats. Alf acted the gentleman by picked up my papers before pointing me in the right direction."

Richard finished rubbing his hands to restore circulation.

"And I suppose he was not well pleased when he found out."

Angela gave a little sigh.

"He made my life a hell, I had hoped that I could work in news or current affairs, but instead I was given every dirty mucky research job in the building. I went home every night and cried myself to sleep. I was just about to pack in all in when one day Alf found me in the corridor after one of his tantrums made me cry. He took me into his little office and over a hot cup of tea I told him everything."

Angela had a faraway look in her eyes as she relived the memories.

"Anyway, Alf said he would fix it that I could get my transfer so all my troubles would be over."

A small frown creased Richard's brow at the mention of Alf's name and the offer of help, and the very faintest of memories stirred for the first time in over a quarter of a centenary. He smiled as he gave a little grunt.

"You're not telling this story very well Angela, I can see the punch line coming a mile off."

Angela gave a gruff laugh

"Well you did ask what the story was, so the least you can do is listen to it"

Richard nodded his head in agreement.

"Ok, I'll shut up,"

He wiggled a finger in her general direction before adding

"But if anyone else was telling me this I would file it under "fiction.""

Angela gave a small sigh and shook her head in mock disappointment.

"You can be a very decent man when you try Richard, but you have never paid much attention to the little people of this world"

Richard waved his arms in the air.

"I seem to remember having this conversion with you many times in the past, you're like a cracked record going on and on about how we should pay them respect"

He spoke with a little steel in his voice.

"One day you will understand that its people in authority that are the ones that matter, people like us. Your "little people" should be grateful we are willing to make the decisions for them. If it was not for organized authority the world would be in utter chaos. Your little people should stop whining about how hard life is for them and just get on and do their jobs"

Angela looked at him with a calm look on her face.

"Just listen to my story, then decide"

Richard nodded his head with the smug look of someone who had made his point.

"OK, carry on, Mr Fix-it doorman was just about to make you the most famous TV presenter in history."

Angela ignored the sarcasm in his tone.

"Yes, well anyway, a few days later he asked me for an old photograph of myself, I give him one taken of me at a gymkhana when I was about thirteen or fourteen. It was a bit blurred, but you could just make me out under my riding hat. Then again nothing happen for a few days until a very elegant lady came and sat by me in the staff restaurant. For a moment everyone seemed to stop doing what they were doing and looked in our direction. All the time we were together I could feel hundreds of people staring at us, including Miss Carlisle who was sitting only a few tables away. She introduced herself as Kathleen Harrington. I had no idea who she was, but I knew she must be someone of real importance. She kept touching my hand as if we were old friend who had known each other for years. We chatted happily all through my lunch break, and afterward she insisted that we leave together"

In a rare act of humour Richard hunched his shoulders up and rubbed his hands together like a character out of a Charles Dickens novel.

"Ah ha, the plot thickens, I smell murder afoot."

With a smile on her face Angela gave him the kind of look a mother would give a naughty child

"Little boys will play their silly games, even fifty year old."

Richard held a finger up and said in a mockingly way

"Fifty-one, not fifty if you please, you know how I like to get the facts right, then what happened?"

Angela shrugged her shoulders,

"Alf told me a week later that a vacancy had suddenly appeared in the news room, and if I applied I would get it."

She slid her slim body into the driver's seat.

"So I did apply, got the job and the rest as they say is history."

Again that dark faint memory stirred a little more as Richard looked at her sideways

"You're not seriously trying to tell me that Alf the doorman arranged all that on his own are you?"

Angela shook her head.

"Well, not quite on his own, but he did arrange it"

Richard paused for a moment in deep though

"How could he do such a thing, I mean, did he blackmail someone high up, you know, being a doorman you can get to know a lot of secrets about people"

Angela laughed at his disbelief

"Dear Richard, you really are the original doubting Thomas aren't you"

She made herself more comfortable in the driver's seat.

"The trouble with you is that along with your other faults you are also an intellectual snob. You think unless someone has been to Oxford or Cambridge they can't be very intelligent, and if they had not been to Eton they could not be very important."

He looked at her with a hurt expression.

"That's not true, I'm as liberal as the next man"

Angela made a snorting kind of noise

"Yes, as long as the next man is Attila the Hun"

Richard conceded he was not going to win this argument.

"Ok, just tell me how Alf the Mr Fix-it doorman managed to do that"

Angela looked up at him,

"It was quite simple really, the elegant lady who came to sit by me in the canteen was the personal secretary to the then Director General Sir Charles Bendell. And by the end of that day everyone in the building was convinced we were old friends. Some even claimed they had seen us out shopping together"

She looked up at the sky for a moment.

"You know we always keep files and folders about some important people just in case they pop off suddenly."

Richard nodded,

"Yes, the obituary files, so what?"

Angela gave a little chuckle,

"Well Sir Charles's folder turned up the very next morning on the desk of Mr Grey-suit himself, with instructions to update the contents. And one part of the file said that he had a grand-daughter about my age who wanted to make a success in news media without any help from her family"

Now it was Richards turn to give a chuckle.

"Don't tell me, the picture you had given Alf somehow found its way into the folder, and he thought you were the big chief's grand-daughter incognito"

Angela nodded

"I often wondered who thought it first, Miss Carlisle or Grey-suite himself. Anyway the plan worked and in the two weeks before I left his department old Grey-suit could not do enough for me"

Richard took a deep breath, the dark thought was now rising faster, but still he tried to ignore it.

"But how…I mean why did those people help you, did you know any of them or pay them for their help?"

Angela shook her head,

"I had never met Kathleen Harrington before she sat down at my table, and it was ages before I persuaded Alf to let me thank personally the lady who had placed my photo in that file."

Richard stuttered

"But..but why would people who didn't know you risk their jobs by doing such things?"

Angela looked at him with sadness in her eyes

"You really don't know do you? The reward is the joy you feel when you have helped someone in need, not for financial gain, but for the love of mankind. I was not the first person that Alf had helped, and when Kathleen was helping me she was only paying back a debt she owned for the help given to her."

She smiled,

"We became a band of little invisible superhero's, helping others who had suffered an injustice, or needed help, as we had"

The dark thought now took shape and form as it filled Richard's mind with details long forgotten. As he silently watched Angela close her car door, his memory went back to the very beginning of his time here. Being a junior in the department, one of his duties was to pick up any special deliveries and mail from the front desk, while the items were collected and signed for he would often chat for a few minutes to the doorman, telling him about his ambitions to be a producer in the news department, along with a promise to always tell the truth. The very words he used came back to haunt him

"If the fish are rotten, I will tell people they are rotten, right down to the smell."

And the doorman telling him he would help him all he could. Now the face of that doorman was as clear as a bell, it was Alf. He had not given the promise any weight at the time, after all, he was no-one of importance, only a doorman. He had let the friendship die with-out a backward glance as he quickly moved up the ladder of success. Now he had a question that had to be answered. Richard gripped the car door and looked at her intensely

"Please, I need to know, when I first started here, why did you give me all the help you did?"

Angela looked into his eyes,

"I think you know the answer to that already"

Richard looked distraught

"It was Alf, wasn't it, he asked you to help me….am I right?"

Angela nodded slowly

"Yes, it was Alf, he saw in you an overwhelming desire to always tell the truth, and the inner strength to carry out the task. And he was right, in all the time I have known you, I have never known you to tell a lie, or back-down from telling the truth. No matter what pressure you were put under. But I was not the only one who helped you, do you remember Peter Crain? He arranged to have you produce the African series"

Richard nodded his head slowly as if he was in a trance, the wildlife series had set his career on the first step to fame. Without that opportunity his career would have gone nowhere. All his life he had thought of himself as someone special, one of the elite. The chosen ones destine to rule the world through their superiority over the ordinary people. Now all his feeling of being superior, his arrogance, the very inter core of his character began to crumble. It had not mattered all these years to think that he had been helped by Angela, because she was clearly a chosen one herself. But to owe his career to a lowly **doorman**, this was something completely different, his ego could not accept it. He tried to convince himself that without any help he still would have made it to the top. But even as he thought such thoughts he knew them to be untrue. Because of his abrasive attitude many of his colleagues, including his immediate superior had disliked him from the start, so the chances' of promotion were as close to zero as you could get. The truth was undeniable, if Alf had not enlisted Angela and Peter's help he would not have had any kind of career. For several seconds he just stood there with head bowed, all his feeling of being superior and the arrogance thoughts of being a chosen one lay like the rubble of a broken wall at his feet. And for the first time in his adult life Richard Gough was truly a humble man. Angela sensed his dismay and leaned out of the car to hold his hand.

"This was the right time to tell you, I'm surprised you did not ask long ago."

When they had first met the thought that Angela had found him desirable was plausible, to his overblown ego at least. But now in the light of day and the passage of time it seemed so ridiculous he could not bring himself to utter it out loud. He slowly looked up,

"Why is this the right time to tell me?"

Angela smiled, even as upset as he was, it had not taken him long to question the meaning of her words.

"I told you so you could understand better what I'm about to ask of you. You have a young man in your department called Michael Knight, and you are about to let him go"

Richard nodded,

"Yes I vaguely remember something about the man, he started here on a six months trial. As far as I know his work is alright, but Personal recommends dismissal because of excessive time off"

Angela nodded,

"Yes, but no one has taken the time and trouble to find out the true facts. His

Father and sister were killed in the same road accident that paralysed his mother from the waist down, and he has looked after her from the age of fifteen. She is just recovering from pneumonia, which is why he has taken so much time off."

Richard knew what was coming next

"And you want me to keep him on."

Angela shook her head,

"I want you to do more than that, I want you to take him under your wing, I want you to do the same for him as I did for you all those years ago."

Richard sucked on his teeth for a moment

"And what reason to I give Personal?"

Angela scoffed at his question

"Since when does the great Richard Gough give reasons? Just do what you always do, give them a telling off for not finding out all the facts"

Richard was still in too humble a mood to argue.

"OK, I will do as you ask."

Angela looked sideways at him

"There is one other thing I want you to do. Alf needs people in high places who can help those who need it. I want you to join his little band of helpers."

Richard rubbed his fingers over his chin.

"I don't know about that, he might not want me after ignoring him for all these years"

Angela held his hand again,

"He will want you, and you will want to help him, I know you will."

Richard shrugged his shoulders

"Why are you so sure?"

Angela started her car and fastened her seatbelt as she answered.

"Because at heart you are a decent man, you also have much pride, and that pride will make you want to pay back the debt you owe him."

Again Richard bowed his head, Angela knew him too well. She was right, his arrogance may have taken a blow from which it might never recover, but his pride was still intact, and that pride would not allow the debt to go unpaid.

"Your right, as always, I will go and see him the moment I return inside and offer him my help and support"

He added with a familiar firmness in his voice

"The debt will be paid"

He leaned forward and kissed her gently on her cheek. He looked longingly at her.

"Don't forget what you promised Alf, come back soon and visit your friends"

Angela laughed and gave a little smile

"I make you the same promise, every time I'm in the neighbourhood."

He stepped back as the car quickly pulled away. His last sight of Angela was of her waving as the car disappeared around the corner.

He stood there looking first at the spot where the car had disappeared, then back towards the TV building. In just the last few minutes his life had been completely turned around. His assessment about who were the chosen ones in life and who were the little people required a total rethink, and for certain a new conclusion. He had left the building as a giant, he would return to it the size of an ordinary man. To complete the sombre mood it began to rain, he turned the collar of his coat up and started walking back towards the building. And as he walked he realized just how big the debt was he owed to Alf. Without him Angela would never have known he existed, and without her help all those years ago he would never have achieved anything.

"Well, I may have been wrong about myself, but Angela truly is a chosen one."

He looked up towards the approaching entrance,

"And I think I'm about to meet another"

Dirty Gutter Rat
Chapter 1

It was a warm summer's evening, the kind of that makes you want to relax after the heat of the day. But when you have been hunted for thousands of years and half way across the galaxy you are never fully relaxed. You see, the entity we shall call Galan was not of this planet, in essences "it" was made up of billions of individual particles of pure energy that stayed together and worked as one, much as a colony of ants would do. This meant that even at rest part of "it" was alive and seeking out any danger that could threaten its existence. The first few tenuous thoughts that touched Galan's' mind were enough to rouse him to full consciousness. There were at least four, no...make that five males all with a single thought. That thought took the form of sexual desire and was focused on the one they were chasing, a young female. He could feel the fear in her voice as she called out hoping for someone to come to her aid.

"Help me, please help me."

But she cried out in vain, his sensors were now fully deployed so he knew that apart from him there was no one near enough to hear her.

She tried to lose her pursuers by making a sharp turn into the empty shell of the building that was his adopted home, but they were too close to be outfoxed by the move.

She was still a little ahead of them when they came into view. But the lead did not last. Just a few feet short of his hiding place they caught up and cut off her escape route. She retreated until the cold bare wall of the building was against her back, but still she squirmed from side to side as if trying to find some secret passage to escape through.

Galan looked down from his high vantage point. The girl had the look of a young animal that had been run to ground by a pack of predators. She looked at her five tormenters, her fear so real that Galan could almost taste it. Her chest rose and fell as she gulped in air and the sweat from her running glistened on her face and neck in the dim light. The tallest of the five showed himself to be the leader as he smiled a sickening smile.

"It's ok baby, we just want a little fun with you."

As he spoke he thrust his groin forwards and backwards, much to the amusement of the others who quickly copied his actions,

"Yeah, just some fun."

More laughter,

"Just like you were going to do with your boyfriend back there,"

Another peel of laughter echoed around the empty shell of the building. One asked in a mocking voice

"I wonder if he's alright lying back there in the gutter."

The leader smashed one fist into the other and shook his head

"Nope, not anymore"

And still they laughed. Galan lightly probed the girls mind to find out the circumstances that had brought her here. It played out before him in a set of moving images. He saw her kissing a man, a man she was in love with and about to marry in just a few weeks time. They were on their way home and as many young lovers do had used a dark doorway to steal a kiss. They were just about to continue their journey when the five men came out of the darkness and began to taunt them.

"Come on man, move over. If kissing is as far as you go then let someone show you the **real** fun you can have with a slut like her."

He saw the fiancé strike out at then, one, then another fell to his fighting prowess, but even as the second one fell, the tall one clubbed him from behind. Two held the girl by her arms as the others continued to kick the body long after all movement had stopped.

The girl screamed and threw herself across his still form, she cradled his head in her lap and felt wetness at the back of his skull, she looked at her blood-stained hand and screamed

"You've killed him!!"

She held her hand up to the light so they could all see. And cried aloud again

"You've killed him."

The mournful sound of her crying echoed up and down the empty street as they began to talk between themselves. The leader looked at her young sharply body with hunger eyes as he said.

"To the victor go the spoils,"

Another added,

"I'm as horny as hell, come on, get her back into the doorway."

One or two had begun to unbuckle their belts as they started to argue.

"I'm first"

"No you're not, I'm first."

But the leader shook his head.

"Not here you idiots, the police will know for sure if they catch us next to the body. We'll take her someplace else, then we can all have her as many times and as many ways as we want."

She screamed with fear as they lifted her to her feet, but the fear give her enough strength to break their grip and she began to run, a run that would end just a few feet away from him. Galan had seen this scenario or something very similar play out many times, on many different worlds, and it was always the same result. The weak always lose, there would be only one winner…the strong. Justice and fairness had no part in the outcome. A great many species in the universe pray on their own kind, and unfortunately "humans" were one of them. It was one of many reasons he had chosen not to adopt their life form when he had first arrived. He had neglected to break all contact with the girl's mind, now the calmness of his thoughts had a tranquil effect on the girl's fear. She regained some of her composure and looked at each one in turn.

"I can't stop you from doing to me whatever you want, but someday I will make you pay in full, both for this and what you did to my fiancé."

Their laughter echoed around the empty building

"How are you going to do that princess?"

Her eyes blazed,

"I will remember you and what you look like as long as I live"

They laughed again as the leader said.

"Well you know, you might not live for as long as you hoped."

The five exchanged knowing looks between each other, some laughed the same sickening laugh as he went on,

"You know I said we only wanted to have fun with you?"

He chuckled,

"Well I lied."

Now all five were laughing, the girl took in the full meaning of the words he had spoken, she was a witness to a murder and they would not let her live to tell the tail. She was surprised by how calmly she accepted her death sentence by turning on the leader and said in a clear voice.

"You're nothing but a dirty gutter rat,"

She waved an arm to encompass all her would be executioners,

"All of you, your just dirty gutter rats."

She looked skywards as if praying.

"Please God punish these evil men, make them all burn in hell for their sins."

All were quiet for a moment, as if waiting for something to happen. Then the silent was broken as more laughter echoed around the building.

"I guess he didn't hear you princess"

The taunting started again, they played with her as a cat would a mouse. Her newfound composure began to crumble as they reached out in turn as if to grab her. She would react, but as quick as she would knock one hand away, another would try from a different direction. Again the leader spoke

"That's good princess, we like it when the woman fights back, it makes it more fun"

At first their touches were no more than just a slap, but within minutes the slaps became punches as they beat her into submission. Soon the top of her dress lay in tatters on the floor. The sight of her naked breasts brought more jeers and crude remarks about what was about to befall her. She struck out blindly with one hand while trying to cover her body with the other. But she quickly grew weaker under the relentless onslaught. But her pain and obvious distress did not touch their conscience, and their laugher never stopped as they continued to enjoy their "aperitif" before the real evil began.

Chapter 2

Only then she was barely able to stand with all her strength gone did they make their move. Both her arms were pinned to her side as they wrestled her to the floor, two more pinned her legs apart and held her there.

While this had been going on Galan was also involved in a fight, but for "him" it was a fight with his own conscience. All his life he had fought against injustice. It was his fight against the injustice of his own kind that had made him an exile, someone to be hunted down and eliminated. And now he faced the dilemma of deciding if his sense of justice included other species, the fight did not last long. An injustice was an injustice wherever and whenever they occurred. With his mind made up he needed to act fast if he wanted to save the girl from real harm. He could have killed the men with a single thought, but the act of taking the lives of others appalled him. And there was always the slim chance that his enemies may be close enough to pick up the energy signature used that was unique to his species. No, he must find a more subtle way to save the girl. He looked into her mind to find someone with enough authority to intimidate the men but she would recognize as a friend, perhaps someone who kept the law. There were many she respected, but there was one image that stood out very clearly over all others, even down to how his voice sounded and the way he dressed. He quickly assumed this person's identity.

The girl saw him first and cried out in joy as he slowly descended from the high beam he had been hiding on.

"He has come, he has come!"

The men followed her gaze upwards to see a figure slowly descending towards them. Their reaction was completely opposite to their victim. They let the girl go and cowed around each other, their eyes wide with sudden fear in the dying light.

His choice of identity was a good one, they recognised and accepted him as person of unlimited power. Their fear was so great and their thoughts in such turmoil that they offered no resistance to his probing. He quickly read each man's thoughts gathering information of their past deeds. Then he spoke to them with the strong voice that was part of the girl's image of him.

"All your lives you have inflicted pain and suffering on others, but no more will you pray on the weak for your own pleasure."

He called each man in turn and told in full some foul deed from their past, and as he spoke they cowed even lower. His voice grew louder.

"Know that I am everywhere and see everything at all times"

Galan again entered their minds and tore them apart as you would demolish an old house. He moved quickly without being gentle in his work, finally he was done. He had rebuilt the pathways in their minds. Now every evil thought, every wish to do wrong would bring great pain. There was some anger and satisfaction in his voice as he said.

"As you have given pain on others, now I gave pain to you."

He raised a finger and as one the men covered their heads with their hands and rolled about the floor crying out in agony.

Galan went on

"You must pay in full for all the harm you have done, with every good deed you do the pain will lessen. If you see an injustice you will try to correct it, if you meet others who are in harms way you will go to their aid **for you will be your brother keeper**, now go and do my bidding."

All five men staggered to their feet and still crying out in pain and fear half ran and half stumbled back the way they had come. All the time he had been speaking to the men the girl had been on her knees looking up at him. He reached down and raised her to her feet. She was still trembling from her ordeal. He covered her body with his robe and held her in his arms to comfort her

"There is no need to have fear now."

He placed a hand on her head and gently over the next few minutes took away all the trauma and fear and replaced it with a deep calmness. When he had finished he held her at arms length.

"Now go to your loved one, he needs you."

At the mention of her fiancé her eyes widen.

"Is he?"

She could not bring herself to ask the question. Galan made a gesture to calm her.

"He lives, when you coved his body with your own you saved his life, a good neighbour who lives nearby heard and saw the fight and contacted those who keep the peace"

He smiled,

"Even as we speak a vehicle has arrived to take him to a place of healing."

He pointed to the way she had come from.

"Go, do not be afraid of the men who tried to harm you, they are already safely in the care of police officers."

Chapter 3

Galan watched as she ran back the way she had come. He sent a small part of his consciousness to hover invisibly just a few feet above and behind to guard her. He stayed with her until she was met at the entrance of the alleyway by two policemen coming to find her. Seeing her dress in tatters one of the policemen took off his jacket and rapped it around her shoulders. She was now safe, his guard duties over he quietly retreated.

The policeman who had given her his coat helped her walk the last few feet

"I'm very pleased to find you mostly unharmed miss"

He pointed to the five men a short distance away sitting on the floor with their backs against a wall.

"We know what kind of men they are, you are very lucky to be still alive"

He lead her towards a police car parked nearby, as they neared the street lights he saw her clearly for the first time. From the state of her battered face and her tattered dress it was obvious she had a hard time. But instead of looking haggard and in great trauma after such an ordeal, she looked radiant. Her eyes were filled with a brightness that gave her almost an angelic look. She saw the look on his face and guessed the reason for it. She smiled as she said

"God placed his hand on me and took away all my pain and hurt, just like it says in the bible."

The policeman looked even more surprised

"You saw God?"

She nodded,

"Yes, I prayed that he would come to my aid, and he did."

The policeman persisted

"How did you know it was God?"

Again the smile answered him.

"It could not have been anyone else, he looked and spoke exactly as I knew he would."

She pointed to the five men

"Who but God could make them confess their sins. He told them that from now on they must do only good, and that he would watch them all the time to make sure they did."

The policeman shook his head, this was too much for a simple man like him to understand. God saving girls from rape, and young men from being murdered, all on his patch. It was almost unbelievable, he nodded towards the prisoners.

"That's what they have been telling us for the last five minutes. Not only have they confessed to trying to rape you, and assaulting your fiancé, they've been telling us about every crime they've ever committed. We already have enough evidence to send them away for a long time."

The girl looked past the police officer

"Please let me see my fiancé, I will answer all your questions later."

He pointed to a nearby ambulance.

"He's in there miss, he's banged up pretty bad, but the doctor thinks he'll make a good recovery"

She smiled the same smile.

"I know he will, God told me."

He watched her disappear into the back of the vehicle before turning back toward the five criminals. As he drew near one tugged his trousers leg. He looked down at the sorry wretch, his face twisted with pain and anguish and for a brief moment despite knowing what the man had done he felt pity for him. The man began to talk with long pauses between words.

"I saw him…came...down… from heaven. He's….he's real… you know, I … never…thought ...he was real…but he is"

He pointed to the back of the ambulance and with a trembling hand said.

"Ask…ask her…s…she saw him...she…saw him too."

The man lapsed into a moments silence before tugging his trousers leg again

"And…and…he's…everywhere…everywhere…all…the…

time.. he knows…we…can't escape...can't escape."

He lapsed into silence again, a small stream of saliva dribble from his slack jaw. The police officer shook his head in sadness, It was plain he had suffered some form of mental breakdown, all of them had. But what had made them this way? They all said they had seen God, and he had punished them for their past deeds. Even the girl said the same story, and there was something about the way she looked. He struggled find a word that fitted, the word "holy" popped into his head, yes that just about right. She had been touched by the hand of God, and came out after a rape attack looking better than any film star. He shook his head again as he looked up at the now dark evening sky.

"Tell me Lord, how the heck am I going to write all this in my report?"

Back at his hiding place Galan again assumed his adopted shape. He felt a sense of wellbeing and satisfaction of a good deed well done. He had saved the girl from death and punished the men with very little effort needed from him. He had also sampled again the simple pleasure that comes with contact of another living being, something he had forgotten during his long flight from tyranny. He had dived deep into her mind and found that her ideas of good and evil were not so different from his own. It occurred to him that he may have been a little hasty in condemning the whole of the human race, and should investigate further.

Galan had many senses and abilities, including the ability to create any form of matter out of the very atoms that surround us, but to be able see future events was out of his reach. So for the moment he was blissfully unaware that because of his ignorance of human culture and religion his hideaway would now be considered as holy ground. As the events of the evening become common knowledge a steady trickle of people would come to his hideaway to pray. All would believe that God himself had descended to this spot to save a young girl from death, and punished her wrongdoers. Within weeks that trickle would become a torrent, and within months sermons and services would be held at a newly build alter. But he would have been driven out long before that. For now a slight stirring in his stomach told him it was time for dinner.

The faint aroma of pizza from a restaurant a hundred yards away reached him, they must have just thrown out the leftovers from the evening meals. His tiny feet made a scraping sound on the metal beam as he headed off in the general direction. He held his snout up high and his whiskers twitched as the smell grew stronger. He felt safe, after all who would think that he Galan, would hide away on such a small insignificant planet, and even more unlikely *chose the life form of* a dirty gutter rat.

Who is Galan?

There are many reasons why all the secrets of the universe will never be known, but the lack of living organisms is not one of them. The universe is full of life, almost every planet that can sustain life will be populated, but the life that evolves is not always of the kind that would ask any questions or seek any answers. For most the mere act of surviving is enough. Longevity is another obstacle to the gathering of knowledge, not just the life of an individual, but of a whole species. In the scale of the universe whole worlds or born and die in the twinkle of an eye. So there will always be secrets, events that none will witness, and wonders that will never be seen.

The two giant stars had circled each other like dancing lovers from the time of their creation, but it was the attraction of gravity not love that brought them closer and closer together. The dance went on for many millions of years, but it was inevitable that the relationship could only have one ending.

Their meeting was marked by an outpouring of energy and matter that surpassed many supernovas, and at the point of first contact a new element was created. It was not a life form in the accepted sense, but a high energy particle that was unique enough not only to exist, but to have the ability to absorb energy and constantly renew itself. In time "it" would grow larger by joining with others. Many icons later the ability to think and retain knowledge appeared, and so a new form of intelligent was born. This is how Galan came to be created. His species had an inner core made up of billions of particles that remained individual but acted as one. This core would stay in place for as long as it had energy, and each core has certain characteristics. In human terms you might say it sings a tune. If it is a "good" tune then it will attract other particles floating in the void which give it more energy, and more energy meant more power to attract yet more atoms. Galan rebelled when some of his species started to consume more power than they needed, so created "super beings" that would "feed" off the weaker of the species and in the end totally consume them. So in fear of his existence he fled into space, to roam the cosmos, hiding from those who would destroy him, until he could find a safe place to call home.

Deep in the heart of living stars is not the most likely of places to find life, but it is in such places' that all the building blocks of life are formed… including us…we are all made out of stardust.

Three Lives

I had woken in my usual manor, lying on my bed still more drunk than sober. I was still wearing the same clothes from last night. They smelled of spilled alcohol and one of my shirt sleeves was ripped. I must have fallen on my way back to the hotel, but I had no memory of the event. Now it had taken a long cold shower followed by several cups of coffee to make me feel almost human again. Today was the third of February, my thirty-third birthday, but the event had little meaning to me. I had stopped counting birthdays over a decade before, and the cups of coffee had long been a daily routine. The last birthday that had good memories was my twentieth, my twenty-first birthday was the far the saddest and marked the end of my first life.

My first life had been a good life, full of achievement, happiness and love, all of the very best things that could happen to a person. My second life has been completely opposite, full of unhappiness, despair and torment. I rubbed my aching left arm, a sure sign that if it was not raining now it soon would be. I smiled a rare smile, that arm was better than any weather forecast, and it was never wrong. I looked at my watch, it was past eleven o'clock. I should have left hours ago, just because it was my birthday it didn't mean a day off work. I still had one deal to make before I could return to England. My target was a winery over two hundred miles away, not far from Gaillac in the Armagnac area. Not the best known area in France for wine, but occasionally you can find a diamond in the most unlikely of places. They were a small fairly new winery that we had never bought from before, but they had a red wine that had just won third prize in a one of the largest wine contests in France. Such a wine deserved our attention, so I was meant to check if it was up to the high standard of wines that we stocked.

To understand my tale better, it would profit you to know something about myself and my family. My name is Anthony Stevens. I doubt you would have heard the name before, my moments of fame had ended almost before they had begun. My family originally came from Austria, the land of great composers and music. We moved to England in 1903, and quickly changed our family name from German Schmidt to English Stevens when the First World War started. The strongest memories I have from my childhood are sitting at my grandfather's feet as he played his violin. He told me many times in a voice full of regret that when he was a young man, he wanted to play the violin in some grand philharmonic orchestra. It was his misfortune to be the only son in a family that had been wine merchants for two hundred years, so he was forced to give up any idea of a musical career and spent his life tied to the family business. His love of music had passed my father and older brother by and landed squarely on my shoulders, and to my grandfather's delight I showed a natural ability in playing the violin. Perhaps thinking of his own sacrifice to the family tradition, he persuaded my father to allow me to follow my dream of a musical career. When I became old enough I was able to attend one of the finest musical schools in the country. It was quickly followed by an invite to join the National Youth Orchestral, it was here than I met Emma, it was the start of a courtship that lasted many years. As time went by my reputation as a violist grew. I could see my future stretch out in front of me, my goal was to be recognised as the best violinist in the world. Anything less than number one would be a failure. I would have sold my soul to the devil if he would have granted my wish, but the future changed for me on that fateful twenty-first birthday. I had just signed a contract for a worldwide tour that I hoped would be a big step up in my career. To celebrate I had taken a ski holiday at the Austrian resort of Sölden. I had two companions with me, my older brother Peter, and a cousin from the Austrian side of the family called Karl, who was by far the better skier. Karl had easily outpaced us on every run thus far, now I set myself the task to as least try to match him. I rashly set out at a fast pace, far too quick for my skill level. I was just in front when the accident happened, and to this day I can remember nothing. I was later told that I lost a ski on the fastest part of the steep downhill slope and crashed into an outcrop of rocks. The result was that almost every bone in the left side of my body was broken, and although I did not know it then, my career as a violist was over.

It was nearly eight months before I was able to practice with my violin again, and from the start it was clear I had lost much of my ability. My left arm had suffered too much damage in the accident and I had lost the full use of my fingers. Before they had been supple and agile, now they felt like lumps of clay, slow to respond to my wishes. I finally had to accept the truth that I would never fulfil my ambition of being the very best, and in my eyes that amounted to failure. I was utterly devastated, I had failed in my lifelong quest and felt my life had ended. I would have gladly climbed into my coffin and sealed the top down myself if I could have. I was blind to the fact that life still had a much to offer. Emma had rallied to my side soon after my mishap, and her love kept me sane enough not to commit suicide. We married three years after my accident, now with a wife to support I joined the family business. Soon our marriage was blessed with two beautiful children, a boy and a girl. Our son we named Michael after my father, and give him Friedrich as a middle name after my grandfather, we named our daughter Sophie, after Emma's mother.

With no financial worries and the love of a good wife I should have been thankful for my good fortune, especially as it was my own bravo that had cost me my musical career. I would tell myself almost every day that many men had suffered greater loss than I, and they had set about living the rest of their life with some kind of purpose. But it was no good, I just could not overcome the loss of my greatest quest in life and move on. A big turning point was when Emma made a successful return to her music career after Sophie was born. Her involvement in a philharmonic orchestra only reminded me of how much I had lost. I became very bitter about everything and to everyone, and over time I filled a bath with tears of self-pity and sank deeper and deeper into it. I felt betrayed by life itself. In my despair I turned my back on Emma and the children and began to drink almost as much wine as I sold. I constantly asked "why me?"

Emma pleaded with me many times to moderate my drinking, but her words fell on stony ground. Finally after years of heavy drinking and endless quarrels Emma could take no more. She and the children moved to Manchester to live with her parents. That had been just over a year ago. After the loss of my marriage I began to drink even more. I became trapped in a downward spiral, the more I drank the more depressed I became, and the more depressed I became the more I drank. As you may have already guessed, I was not a happy person on the morning of my thirty-third birthday. Looking back now I was heading to an early grave, but lacked the will or desire to change my lifestyle.

I finished another cup of coffee and rose from the table, it was well past the time I should have started my journey. The part of France that was my destination is a very rural area, with few people and even fewer good roads. The rain my arm had promised begun to fall not long after I started my journey, and with it being February the heavy overcast sky would hurry the end of the day. As the last of the light faded it became even more difficult to see the unlit road clearly. I was still many miles from my destination and driving faster than I should have when I came to a bend where the canter of the road had allowed unseen water to collect. The car aquaplaned across the road to end up in the road side ditch. As my car came to a sudden stop I was thrown upwards to strike my forehead on the car roof and knocked myself out. I don't know how long I was unconscious, but when I came to my senses it was total darkness outside. I was lucky, apart from the bump on my head I had escaped intact. I walked around my car to look for any obvious damage but in the dark I saw none. What *was* plain to see however was that I would need a breakdown truck to tow the car back onto the road. I looked around for any sign of life, there was none, no lights or any signs of houses close by. At first I decided to sit in my car and try to flag down the next car that passed. An hour later and with no sign of traffic I give up on that idea. I got out of the car, it was still raining heavily and started to walk in the direction I had been travelling. I walked for over twenty minutes and found no sign of life. The cold rain soon chilled my body, so I turned and walked back to my car. I thought that perhaps I would have better luck in the opposite direction, but if the worst came to the worst, I would spend the night in my car out of the rain. For the first few hundred yards it was no different, no houses, no lights, nothing. I began to think that maybe I was the only person in this part of France. Then I saw a dim light blinking through the branches of the roadside trees. I could not see the house clearly, but moving further along I came to a small garden gate. I could hear the sound of music coming from the house, a violin and a cello in a duet. The gate opened with a loud screech of protest from the hinges. Now I could see the house better. Like many country homes, the walls were painted white, and had a wooden poach with thick pillars painted black that glistened in the dim light. The music stopped the moment I knocked on the door. After a few moments the door was opened by a lady, I could see little more than her outline as she was framed by the light from inside.

"Apologises *Madame* for interrupting your music, but I have had an accident and my car is stuck in the ditch at the side of the road. I need to telephone a local garage with a breakdown truck to recover it, I am more than willing to pay for the call."

She answered in a soft voice with a strong local accent.

"Of cause *Monsieur*, please come in out of this terrible weather."

She called out to someone in the front room

"Andre, we have a visitor"

She stepped aside to let me pass

"Please go in *Monsieur* and warm yourself by the fire"

A man sat by the window, a violin still in his hands. The room was lit only by oil lamps, they produced a calming and somewhat romantic mood, but not a great deal of light. I introduced myself and give a brief account of where I was going and why.

"You are welcome *Monsieur*, it is a bad night to be travelling, my name is Andre Durand"

He gestured to the lady

"And my wife Angel"

They looked to be about my age within a couple of years or so. They insisted I take my wet coat and jacket off. Angel took them away to dry. I could not stop myself from admiring his violin, it looked to be of excellent quality, and to find such an expensive instrument in the middle of nowhere surprised me. Andre noticed my interest.

"You admire my violin *Monsieur* with the eye of an expert, are you yourself a violinist?"

I nodded my head

"I used to be, but I give music up a long time ago"

He shook his head

"That cannot be *Monsieur*, music has been mankind's companion from the dawn of time, it is as necessary as the air we breathe. It can inspire us to do great and noble deeds that we thought were beyond our reach. We serenade the ones we love with music, and always we have music at times of great joy. And when life has ended it is with music we bid farewell to those we hold dear"

He opened a draw in a nearby cabinet. He took from it a violin and bow which could have been a twin for the one he was holding. Without turning his head in my direction he handed them to me.

"Of all my violins this is my favourite."

At first I was reluctant to accept the instrument, but Andre insisted in a way I found hard to refuse. When I give up the idea of continuing my career I had never touched my violin again, and with my mind full of twisted logic had begun to blame music for promising so much fame but only giving me pain and despair. Now It felt a little strange to hold a violin again after so many years. I played a few notes, it had a beautiful tone. It took several attempts, but at last some of the ability learned over so many years returned. Just then Angel returned with a tray holding three cups of coffee

"I phone the local garage monsieur, the man is out attending to another breakdown at the moment, it will take maybe three hours for him to get here, but his wife promised me he would come as soon as possible"

I sipped the hot coffee slowly, it was very welcome after my time spent in the cold rain. Andre spoke with a smile on his face.

"Our visitor is a musician Angel, he plays the violin, I think tonight we will have a rare treat and play as a trio"

Angel smiled acceptance as she retrieved her cello from a stand in the corner and made ready to play. Andre looked at me and said just two words

"Vivaldi, Winter"

I nodded in agreement. We started to play, at first I struggled to stay in tune and played as many wrong notes as right ones, but slowly I picked up the rhythm and my playing improved. For the first time since my childhood I was playing just for the pleasure of playing, rather than having to practise or perform for an audience. Now I began to remember why I had first been drawn to music, it was more than just the pride of being able to play, it was the harmony and beautiful melodies written by the great composers of the past. What happen next is almost impossible for me to explain, but within seconds I felt the power of the music began to act on me like some magic portion. I could feel it sweeping through me like a great tidal wave of sheer enjoyment. I sensed as if we were slowly turning as if on a giant roundabout and leaving our oil lit room far behind. In the corner of my eye I could see row upon row of shadowy figures joining us, but all were dressed differently. It was as if all the musicians from all the ages past had come to join us until we were no longer just a trio but part of a great orchestra. If there was such a place as a musical heaven then we had arrived. Now the music not only held sound, but colour as well. Shades of every colour imaginable mixed in perfect harmony with the music. Flashes of light on the short notes and rivers of colour that filled my vison on long notes that faded to just a subtle shade when the music became gentle. We played with great joy and touched many of the great masters of the past, Mozart, Beethoven, Stravinsky to name but a few. For hour after hour we played, and all the time the joy of the music flowed through my body like electricity bring back to life something that had died long ago. Finally we returned to Beethoven and entered the calmer waters of Moonlight Sonata. Now the tempo slowed, and as it did the shadowy figures and the flashing colours faded away. When the last few notes sounded we were just as we started, a trio in a lamp lit room.

For several seconds we sat in silence, it was as it the music had cast a spell over us that no one wanted to break, finally Angel rose and returned her cello to its resting place, then turning to me said

"It is time for you to go *Monsieur,* the breakdown truck is not far away, I'll get your things"

With that she left the room. Andre had a knowing smile on his face, it was as if he knew in full the wonders I had just experience, he said only one word.

"Better?"

I nodded agreement, the music had completely overcome me in a way I never thought possible, it left me exhausted, but at the same time stronger than I had felt in years, and best of all, with a great feeling of happiness and contentment. Angel entered and helped me on with my now dry jacket and coat. Both still held some of the heat that had dried them. I felt snug as if I was covered in warm blankets. I followed Angel as she opened the front door and stepped outside. The rain had stopped and stars shone brightly through holes in the thinning clouds. I started to thank them for all their help and hospitality, but Angel held up a hand to stop me

"Please, we need no thanks, we are only too pleased that we were able to help"

As I turned away Andre said

"Remember Anthony, wherever you find people, you will find music. For some it is no more than the beating of a hollow tree with a club, or the rhythm of many drums, but we all have a need for music, no matter what form it takes. It is food for the soul, once tasted you cannot live happily without it"

Again I nodded agreement and promised I would remember always. I stopped by the garden gate and waved a last farewell, two hands were raised in return. Again the horrible screech of the hinges as the gate closed behind me. I began to walk back to my car, but within seconds my walk turned into skipping, jumping and waltzing as my mind filled with some of the music we had just played. I reached my car just as two headlights showed the approach of the breakdown truck. The driver expertly hitched my car to the winch on the truck. A clatter of metal sounded as the car was removed from the ditch, not a good sign. The exhaust system must be extensively damaged. A quick inspection by torch also showed one front wheel to be buckled and the tyre deflated. He quickly loaded my car onto the bed of his truck. As soon as the journey began the friendly driver asked me why I was in this part of France at this time of year. I told him about my intended destination, and that my family had been wine merchants for many generations. With a laugh he said like many French men he was more interested in the drinking of wine that the making of it. I mentioned that with my car out of action I would need a place to stay overnight. He replied that there was a hotel only a few kilometres or so from here, and that he would drop me there on the way to his garage. He then apologised for taking so long in coming to my rescue, I told him there was no need for him to be upset, a friendly couple who lived close by had taken be in out of the weather. I asked in a casual manor in he know *Monsieur* Andre Durand and his wife Angel. There was a long pause before he answered, he said he did not know them, but he had heard of them. He was strangely quiet for rest of our journey. Within 10 minutes or so we arrived at the Hôtel de Jardin (Garden Hotel) I entered to be greeted by the owners, Madame Adele and Madame Yvaine, two elderly ladies who I quickly found out to be sisters. At this time of year the hotel had few guests, so I had no problem finding a room. I phoned the winery I should have visited that day, and was able to tell them a sort of truth that I had been in an accident and that was the reason I had not kept my appointment. I told them that if my car was roadworthy I would visit tomorrow. It was now getting late, and supper had finished some time before for the guests, but the two ladies were kind enough to make me a bowl of hot broth. As I sat eating my meal, my head was still full of the magical music I had played with Andre and Angel and I hummed a few notes from Vivaldi "Spring" Madame Adele surprised me by joining in, she added that Vivaldi's "Four Seasons" had been one of her favourite pieces of music from childhood. I told her of the couple who had taken me into their home and treated me with such kindness. As an after though I mentioned that both Monsieur Andre Durand and his wife Angel were excelled musicians, and Vivaldi had been the first piece we played. Even before I had finished speaking the air was filled with the sound of breaking china. Madame Yvaine had dropped a tray full of dishes, breaking every one. Out of the corner of my eye I saw Madame Adele and Yvaine exchange a look of distress, but not for one moment did I suspect that my words could had been the cause of the accident, or that the look of distress was caused by anything other than the dropping of the tray. They hurriedly cleaned up all of the broken glass and retreated to the kitchen. I saw little of them for the remainder of the evening. It had been a long and eventful day, and now fed and warm I wanted nothing more than a good night's sleep. For the first time in a very long time I went to bed cold sober and even with a slight headache from the accident slept the sleep of a young child.

 Next morning my headache was gone and I received a phone call from the garage, apart from the need of a new exhaust and wheel my car would be ready for the road. A couple of hours later the car was parked outside the hotel ready for me to continue my journey. I paid my bill to a very quiet Madame Yvaine, exchanging hardly a word, her attitude completely different from the first time we meet. I arrived at my destination by early afternoon. It only took one taste of the wine to confirm it was every bit as good as we had hoped. We signed a deal, and by the end of the day I was on my way home to England.

It did not take long for Peter to notice the change in me. Now free from the twin demons of drink and depression I realized just how badly I had treated Emma and the children. I wrote her a long letter of apology for the years of misery and unhappiness I had inflicted on her. I did not know that Peter had already phoned her telling of my new-found attitude, and he confirmed that I no longer had a drink problem. In April I received a phone call from Emma, it would be Sophie's sixth birthday in two weeks' time, and would I like to attend, I jumped at the chance. It was marvellous to see the children again. Children can be far more forgiving than adults, and Sophie greeted her daddy with a big hug and lots of kisses. The visit went well, and was repeated two months later when it was Michael eighth birthday. I had stayed at a hotel on both occasions, but come late summer Emma trusted me enough for us to go on holiday for the first time as a family. Finally Emma give me the best Christmas present she could have by agreeing to us becoming a family again. On Christmas morning Emma and I serenaded our children with a selection of carols, it was the first time they has seen and heard me play my violin. They were so surprised and impressed they stopped unwrapping their presents for all of ten seconds, then they returned to the more serious business at hand, namely the filling of the room with discarded wrapping paper. Year one of my third life started on that day, and this time I was determined that nothing would be allowed to spoil it for us.

A little over a year later I found myself again in southern France, not far from the place that had changed my life so completely. I now realized just how big an impact that evening of magical music had made on me, and was determined to fully thank Andre and Angel for what they had done. The only guide I had as to where they lived was it had taken only about fifteen minutes to reach the hotel I had stayed at, perhaps about 10 to 15 kilometres at most. I came to a bend in the road that I recognised as the place where my car had ended up in the ditch, I stopped and started to walk back the way I had come. I had gone about two hundred yards before I found what I was looking for, the small garden gate, now almost completely hidden by the spring growth. It opened with a loud screech of protest from the hinges that I remembered so well, this was the place. I stepped past the trees guarding the front of the house, and there it was. At first glance it looked the same, but at the same time different. First the garden could not be called a garden by any stretch of the imagination, a patch of wild forest was more of a truth. The path was completely overgrown and only visible in parts, and the house looked different, older and shabbier than I remembered. On the night of my visit I could clearly remember the white walls of the house and the rain reflecting on the painted porch pillars, now the white was a dim grey, and the pillars faded and old, I placed a hand on one of them, and a large piece of rotten timber came away without effort. This house had not been maintained for many years and was close to falling apart. I knocked on the faded front door, the echo of an empty house was my reward. I tried to look through the windows, a thick covering of dirt hindered my view. I rubbed away a small patch from the glass, but still could see nothing inside. I started to knock the door again when I heard a voice from behind me.

"You can knock all day *Monsieur*, but you will never get an answer. No one has lived in this house for thirty or forty years"

By the way he was dressed and with a dog sitting by his side he was clearly a local farm worker. He leaned on the only part of the boundary fence what was free from trees and undergrowth. I asked him if there were any other houses close by, he shook him head

"Not another house for five or six kilometres in any direction. A few farms, but they be far from the road and out of sight"

I told him of the happening of the previous year, and that I had found shelter in a house close to the roadside. Again he shook his head.

"I've lived round these parts all my life, and I can tell you *Monsieur* there is no house like you say anywhere near. You must have the wrong place"

His was clearly telling the truth about the house, it had not been lived in for many years. Again I shook my head, and told him I was totally confused, I had been sure this was the house I had stayed at, I added that I had played music with the young couple who lived here for most of my visit. When I mention the playing of music he stood bolt upright as if the fence had suddenly become electrified and took a step back.

"Music you say, I don't know nothing about that, well I've got me work to do, so I best be on my way"

He turned out of sight, but returned a moment later

"There be a hotel a few kilometres from here called Hôtel de Jardin , it be run by two sisters, ask them about this house, they were born here"

With that he disappeared for good. I hurried over to the fence, he was already many yards away. I shouted my thanks, he replied with a wave of his arm but did not look back nor stop his hasty retreat. I slowly made my way back to my car. There was a mystery here. If the sisters were born in this house they must know something about the people who had lived here. I suddenly remembered the incident when Madame Yvaine had dropped the tray of plates, it was at the exact moment I had mentioned Andre Durand and Angel by name. and then there was the frosty way Madame Yvaine had acted towards me when I checked out the following morning. It was clear to me that the sisters could tell me a great deal more about this mystery, and I wanted to know all there was to know.

I arrived at the hotel, a young woman sat in reception. I told her my name asked to if I could see Madame Adele and Madame Yvaine. She returned a few minutes later with Madame Adele. She did not look surprised at seeing me again.

"My sister and I wondered if you would come to see us again *Monsieur* Stevens, please follow me. She led me to her living quarters at the back of the hotel. Her sister sat by an open fire. My eyes went straight to a silver framed photo on the mantel piece. It showed Angel with Andre wearing a uniform. They looked a little younger than I remembered, but it was clearly them. I pointed to the photo and told the sisters this was the couple who had given me shelter when my car had broken down the year before. They both looked at each other, Madame Yvaine said

"We might as well tell him Adele, I think Mama and Papa would want us to"

Her sister shook her head in agreement. Madame Adele pointed to a nearby chair

"Please sit down *Monsieur* Stevens, the story I am about to tell you is hard to believe, but I promise you it is all true"

She pointed to the photo.

"That photo of our parents was taken in 1916, just before our father went to fight the Bosche". (German)

At first I did not realized the full meaning of her words, when I did I shook my head in disbelief. This was not possible, I had meet this couple only one year before, and had looked to be about my age, now she was telling me the photo was taken over 70 years ago. She took the photo from the mantelpiece and held in her hands, gently touching the frame.

"Our mothers' family name was L'hernault, they could trace their heritage as far back as the crusade's   Our Grandfather was Charles L'hernault, one of the biggest landowners around here. He owned all the land for miles around, including this hotel and most of the village. Like many rich men at that time he was also a patron on the arts, so when Mama showed an interest in playing the cello he did all he could to encourage her. One of the men working on the estate had a son named Andre of about the same age, and he was already known by many for his talent of playing the violin. When my grandfather heard about this he invited the boy to visit. From the very first time they met the two children became friends and played together almost evert day. When Andre was 14 his father died in an accident on the estate, his mother had died when he was a child, so our grandfather took him in to live as one of the family. As time went by our future mother and father became well known as musicians, and were invited to play at gathering in all the great houses, along with wedding and birthday parties. By 1914 the war with Germany had begun, and the young men of France were being killed in their thousands. Within two years over a million men had fallen, and still more were needed to hold the Germans back. So in 1916 Andre went to war like many other boys of his age, that was when this photo was taken. His war lasted only a few months, the Ambulance he was driving was hit by a shell and caught fire. He survived, but with terrible injuries. The left side of his face and neck were horribly disfigured from the fire, and shrapnel from the shell lodged in his chest too close to his heart to be removed. He returned home in a sorry state and was not expected to live. With death so near Mama begged her father to allow them to marry, and he thinking it would be no more than an act of charity to a dying man agreed. For many months Papa's life hung on a knive edge, Mama stayed by his side, not knowing if today would be his last. But helped by the great love they had for each other Mama slowly nursed him back to some kind of health. Now because of his disfigurement Papa became a recluse and hid away from everyone. He never left his room in daylight, only under the cover of darkness would he sometimes walk in the gardens on the house. Grandfather L'hernault was sad to see such unhappiness, and built them the house you visited the night of your accident. He also give them all the land within five kilometres so no one could live close to them. Now Papa could go outside whenever he wished without anyone seeing him. In the years that followed we were both born there. We had a happy childhood, every day was filled with love and laughter, and always in the evening Mama and Papa would play us music until bedtime. We had a garden at the rear of the house where we grew most of our vegetables. At first we used to help Papa tend to it, but as time went on he grew weaker as the shrapnel in his chest moved closer to his heart. For the last few months of his life he was so weak he could not play his violin or leave his bed. He died on the morning of February the third, his thirty-third birthday"

My eyes opened wide when she said the date, was it just another coincidence that my new life had started and his life had ended on the same date and both at the same age? She paused as the memories of long ago came flooding back, now Madam Yvaine took up the story.

"Mama was never the same after Papa's death, she pretended to be happy for our sake, but there was always sadness in her eyes. She would often play her cello in the evening, but the music always sounded sad. After the war there were many men who like our father who had paid a heavy price for defending France. Mama always said it was the sprite of Papa that made her want to help those as she had helped him. Over time some of the local women also joined her and began to help. They would visit all who were sick or disabled and made sure they always had food to eat and clean clothes to wear. She did this every day for the rest of her life. As Adele and I reached adulthood Germany again attacked France, and this time we could not hold them back. I think the shock of seeing them march through Paris was too much for Granddad L'hernault, and he died a few days later. He left Mama some property in the village, including this hotel. He had always given Mama a weekly allowance so she could live without poverty, now with his death the money stopped. Adele and I took over the running of this hotel to earn a living for ourselves and to help support Mama. We begged her to come and live with us, but she refused. She always said that the happiest memories of father were in the house, and to leave would be like leaving him. She lived there alone until her death, and when she died *Monsieur*, the church was too small to hold all those who came to honour her. Soon after her death we began to hear stories that people passing Mama's house in the dark heard the sound of a cello and violin playing. At first we did not believe them, but as time went by more and more people said their heard the music play, but it always faded when they approached the house to investigate. You know how superstitious country folk can be *Monsieur* Stevens, soon all believed the house was haunted. Now for as long as I can remember no one will go near the house after dark"

Madam Adele added

"You are an honoured person *Monsieur* Stevens, over the years there has been rumours that a few were allowed entry, but you are the first person that we can be sure of, do you know why this should be?"

At first I had listen to the their story with disbelief, then I began to remember little things than had felt odd at the time, like Andre always sitting with only the right side of his face towards me, he had not turned his head even when he handed me the violin I was to play. Then there was the driver of the pick-up truck who acted so strangely after I had mentioned I had spent the evening with them, quickly followed by Madam Yvaine and the tray of dishes. And just today it was the farm worker, as soon as I mentioned the music he reacted with real fear. I told them the full story of how my evening with their mother and father had changed my life so completely, and helped me regain the love of my wife and family. When I finished both smiled. Madam Adele spoke for them both

"The sprite of Mama and Papa must have felt your unhappiness, and decided to help you as they had done for so many others".

I returned to England more confused than when I had left. Then I had set out to thank a couple for giving me a new start in life only to be told they were ghosts from the distant past. I told both Peter and Emma of my discovery, Peter dismissed it out of hand. He said in a firm voice that there was no such things as ghosts. He reminded me of the car crash, and that I had hit my head making me unconscious. He argued that my night with Andre and Angel had been no more than a dream. It first it was a plausible answer to what had happened, but did not stand-up under closer examination. Firstly if it had all been a dream, who phoned the garage to tell then that my car had been involved in an accident and where it had happened? This was a time long before the age of mobile phones so I could not have done it. And how did I know Andre and Angel names, and was able to recognise the photo of them? To these questions he had no answers. Emma was less concerned of how I had changed so completely, she was just grateful the transformation had happened. Over the years that followed the mystery of that night was like an itch that refused to go away, I *had* to try to find out more. Emma and I had talked about it so often that gradually her curiosity became as great as mine. We decided to visit the house and hotel again in the hope that we might learn something new that could help solve the mystery. As before I stopped at the bend where my car had left the road. We walked back until we found where the gate stood. It was still there, but now was bent and pushed half aside leaving a much smaller opening. We ducked under the drooping branches of the trees guarding the entrance only to find the house in ruins. At some point in the past fire had totally destroyed it. There were only two ways the fire could have started, either a lighting strike, or more likely an act of arson by one of the locals who wanted to end the ghostly music. We walked among the ruins, but there was little to see, nature had already reclaimed most of it with small trees and other greenery. We drove on to the hotel, a middle age woman of amble girth sat in reception. I asked to see Madam Adele or Yvaine, she replied with a sad face that both the sisters had died within weeks of each other three years before. With their deaths and the burning down of the house a drama that had begun decades before came to an end, and an important chapter of my life passed into history with questions that now will never be answered.

However there is no mystery to the happy ending of my story. Not long after we became a family again Emma decided to give up her musical career to be close to our children as they grew up. She did not turn her back on music completely however, and spent the next twenty years as a music teacher at the local school. Our marriage has been one of love, and it is as strong today as it was 50 years ago. Peter and I retired from the family business some time ago, now his son James and my Michael are in charge, and doing a very fine job of it. Another highlight in our lives is due to happen next week. Emma and I, along with our daughter Sophie will attend a performance of the National Youth Orchestral. The music they play will be of little interest to the three of us. We will be there to encourage the latest member of our family who has chosen a musical career. Our granddaughter Amy will not however be playing the violin, as a fitting tribute to *Madam* Angel she has chosen the cello, and so the music plays on.

Music is food for the soul, once tasted you cannot live happily without it.

The End.

The Picture Restorer
Chapter 1

The woman walked with the weariness of old age, her strength taxed to the limit as the small bag of shopping she carried became heavier by the minute. And now to add to her discomfort it started to rain. She opened her umbrella, the effort needed to hold it in the wind only added to the drain from her small reserve of energy,

Across the street a man in a dark coat matched her progress, stopping when she stopped, and walking at the same shuffling pace when she walked. At first glance he looked no different from all the other people as they hurried about their business. But if you could have looked closer you would have seen a look of sadness on his face. Sadness caused both by the distress of the old lady, and by the callousness of a society that had grown unseeing and uncaring to the plight of the poor and the old. At last she reached her front door and after spending a few moments to find the right key she disappeared inside. The man stepped back into the shadow of a nearby doorway. After just a few moments, he turned and walked quickly away with a smile on his face. He had found another who was worthy of his efforts, so he best be getting on with it.

Mrs Toms hurried the last few yards to the front door, her haste was due more to the weather than the fact that she was late. She had a habit of speaking her thoughts out loud, and now she muttered to herself as she turned the key in the lock.

"This weather is really getting me down, when the hell is this rain going to stop, that's what I want to know"

She closed the door behind her and shook the water out of her umbrella before placing it in a stand in the corner. As she undid her coat she looked around at the old and faded furniture.

"This place could do with a bit of money spent on it, getting more like a pigsty every day it is. I'm sure I don't know how much longer I can stand working in these conditions."

She nodded her head in agreement with herself

"Lots of jobs around for a good experienced worker like me, oh yes, plenty and with more money you can be sure"

Not for one moment did it occur to her that she was part of the reason for this decay. She was employed as a cleaner but discharged her duties in the same disorganize way she lived her life. And so most of her work was either not done, or done so badly that the house continued in its downward spiral. She walked over to the living room door and tapped gently as she opened it. Mrs Elizabeth Martin was sitting in her usual chair holding a photo in her hand, others were scattered on a small table in front of her. Mrs Toms nodded her head

"Good afternoon Mrs Martin, terrible weather out there, would you like me to make you a cup of tea before I start my cleaning?"

The old lady looked up

"Oh good afternoon Mrs Toms, yes thank you, a cup of tea would be very nice"

She lowered her glaze back to the photos. Mrs Toms turned to go to the kitchen, she muttered to herself,

"The old dear going senile, that's all she does these days is sit in that chair and look at those old photographs"

She filled the kettle and put three teabags into the teapot, and then looking over her shoulder to make sure she was alone she slipped a dozen or more into her open handbag. Next stop was the fridge, her eyes lit up,

"She must have done a bit of shopping"

Every item was looked at in turn

"This is a nice bit of ham, me and Bert will have that for tea tonight"

She placed the ham into her bag as she muttered

"She'll never notice it's gone, and what the old dear doesn't know won't hurt her"

The next day found Elizabeth sitting in her favourite chair, in her hand a faded photo of her late husband Peter. It was now five years since he had passed away, five long lonely years. The tips of her fingers lightly touched his image, her heart still ached with his loss. Their love for each other had lasted a lifetime, and she loved him still, even in death. This photo of him was one of her favourites, she had taken it herself. It was just after they had been married. They had gone down to stay with one of his aunts for the weekend. Elizabeth smiled at the memories the picture brought to mind, they were such good times. She remembered thinking as she pressed the camera button that she must be the happiest, luckiest girl in the world to have found such a perfect man to love, and best of all, that he loved her deeply in return.

Her mind drifted forward a year, their joy at finding she had become pregnant, but then the sadness that quickly followed as she lost their baby and nearly her own life as well. The doctors had told them that she would probably never conceive again, but they put their trust in God and hoped that one day the miracle would happen, but it never did.

But still their love endured, even as her sister had children and they were left childless. They ignored their personal sadness and set about becoming the best aunt and uncle a child ever had. The years had swiftly passed, they had grown old together but their love was still strong and they were content with each other's company. Then Peter was diagnosed with cancer. He had fought hard, unwilling to leave the woman he had loved for nearly fifty years, but finally he had succumbed to the disease. She touched the photo again, life was so hard without him. A knock at the front door broke her train of thought and she fussed for a moment wondering who it might be. In the past she and Peter had many callers, but those days were long gone. She opened the door slowly, a man stood on the door step, he tipped his hat to her.

"Good afternoon madam"

He tapped his chest with a finger

"John Higgins is the name, and picture restoration is my game"

The old lady shook her head

"I'm sorry, but I don't have any pictures that need restoring"

She started to close the door, the man leaned forward

"No, no good lady, you misunderstand me, it's not framed pictures, but the photographic type of pictures I restore"

She hesitated, a little unsure of what he meant, he spoke again.

"Perhaps the good lady has some photographs she would like to repair, or bring back as new of a loved one, a husband perhaps?"

She turned her head towards the living room with the faded photos of Peter still lying on the table

"Well maybe I do have some,"

Again she hesitated

"But they are very precious to me, how do I know you won't lose or destroy them"

The man laughed in a jolly kind of way

"My good lady, I've been doing this for longer than I care to remember and I've never lost one yet"

Elizabeth studied his face, it had an open and honest look about it that reminded her of one of her favourite uncles, now long dead like all her family. But again she hesitated.

"But I am just a poor widow, I doubt that I could afford the cost"

Mr Higgins beamed at her

"It just so happens I have a special offer on at the moment, I do the first order for no charge, and in return you tell all your friends about me"

He added quickly

"But only if you are satisfied with what I do"

He at last won her over, and a few minutes later left with many of her favourite photos, promising to return in two days' time.

Two days later, almost to the hour, the old lady heard a knock at her door, she opened wide to find Mr Higgins standing there with a brown package in his hand, he handed it to her

"Here you are then Mrs Martin, returned as promised and as good as new to look at"

Her eyes lingered for a moment on the package.

"Thank you Mr Higgins, would you like to come in for a cup of tea?"

She looked up, and for a moment a look of astonishment covered her face, he had disappeared like a puff of smoke. She looked around the corner of the door, then up and down the street, but he was nowhere to be seen. Slowly she turned and went back into the house with a bemused look on her face,

"What a strange man to go without saying goodbye"

She placed the package on the table excited to see the results of his efforts. Her less than nimble fingers struggled for a moment to undo the string, but finally she was able to open the package wide. There were two stacks of pictures, one the original photos, which she put aside, the other were the repaired ones. She held one up, it was as fresh as the day it had been taken, quickly she looked at another, the same. Her face beamed with joy

"Oh thank you Mr Higgins, you are a man of your word"

Now her joy was complete as details and memories long forgotten became clear again.

Finally she came to the photo she had taken of Peter. Her eyes lit up as she held it her hand, she sighed like a young girl, the colours were as vibrant as if it had just been taken. She had forgotten the flowers were such a deep shade of blue, and the sun light on Peter's hair that made it shine like gold, now thanks to the photo she remembered it all. But wait, there was something not quite right here, and then the truth dawned on her. No wonder she had forgotten the colour of the flowers, the photo had been taken in black and white, now it was in glorious colour. She wondered what magic Mr Higgins had to bring about such a change, but even as she looked at the photo, more magic began to happen. Were the flowers moving in the wind? The photo seemed to have a hypnotic effect on her, she felt as if she was falling head over heels. She started to scream, but before she could make a sound she was looking up into the eyes of Peter. He was smiling at her

"Hello Beth, it's been so lonely without you"

She could not believe this was happening, she must be dreaming, but Peter answered as if he could read her thoughts

"No my love, it is not a dream, we are together again"

She looked around; everything was exactly has it had been on the day the photograph had been taken. They were both young again sitting on the bench in his Aunts' garden. She could feel the warmth of the sun and the light summer breeze on her face. Butterflies danced above her head. She cried as she touched his face then flung her arms around him

"And I have been lonely without you Peter"

They kissed in a long embrace. Again she spoke with wonder in her voice

"But how can this be?"

Peter held her closer

"I do not know Beth, but somehow I do know that this is our new world, a world for us alone"

They both stood up

"Come my love; let us explore our world for eternity"

Beth cried the soft tears of joy, she was safe in the arms of the man she loved, she whispered in his ear,

"Eternity is not long enough for me"

Mrs Toms arrived late as usual the next day, she was a little concerned that Mrs Martin was nowhere to be seen, and when she found her bed had not been slept in she sent for the police. They searched the house and the surrounding areas for more than a week without finding a trace. Now over a month had passed and Mrs Toms sat in Mrs Martin chair as a police officer questioned her yet again to try and find a clue of what could have happen to the old lady.

"And you're sure she did not have any family she might have visited?"

Mrs Toms shook her head,

"She only had one sister and she's been dead for years"

The policeman persisted

"Did her sister have any family?"

Mrs Toms leaned to one side as if to perform a well-known body function. The policeman guessed what she intended and gave her a stern look of disapproval. Mrs Toms quickly sat upright again with a guilty look on her face before continuing

"Yes, she had two sons; there are some photos of them in that lot there"

She pointed to the clutter of photos on the table She paused for a moment before shaking her head

"But they were both killed in the army"

"What about friends or callers, did she have any she may have gone to visit?"

Mrs Toms picked the inside of her nose in a casual way as she answered

"Come to think of it, she did say she had a visitor the day before she disappeared, something about offering to make her photos like new she said, but I never saw him, and there is no new photos in that lot, so nether she was mistaken or he didn't come back"

The police officer shook his head in sorrow.

"You would be surprised how often people go missing. Mostly they run away because they are in debt, or they're in trouble over something else. Many are never heard of again, but I don't think that is the case here"

He closed his notebook and rose from his chair

"Best give me any house keys you still have and we'll pass them on to the solicitor who is handling the estate"

He dropped the offered key into his top pocket and moved towards the door

"Well I don't hold out much hope for the old dear still being alive after so long. Perhaps one day someone out walking his dog will find a body in some undergrowth, and the mystery will be solved"

Mrs Toms bowed her head and for a moment felt more sadness at the loss of Mrs Martin than her job. Her eyes flicked over the photos still scattered on the table, one caught her eye, she held it in her hand as she turned to the departing policeman

"Isn't it strange, I've looked at these photos almost as much as Mrs Martin over the years, and I could have sworn this one was of her husband only?"

The policeman leaned over and looked at the faded picture of a happy couple sitting on a garden bench

"You must have been mistaken"

Mrs Toms nodded

"Yes I must have"

She placed the photo carefully back on the table.

"What will happen to the house now?"

He rubbed his chin with forefinger and thumb

"I expect they will try to find her nearest relative and pass it on to them, but it could take years for that to happen"

He turned to leave

"Well there's nothing more we can find out here, so we best be off"

He held the door open for her

"After you Mrs Toms "

Mrs Toms shook her head

"No, not yet, I'll be a couple of minutes, I just want one last look around"

There was something about the way she said the words that made the policeman suspect her motives.

"Ok, just make sure the door is locked when you leave"

He added with a knowing look,

"The solicitors were in last week doing a complete inventory"

He looked around at the faded furnisher, all of it well past its best.

"Not that there's much worth the taking, but if there is anything missing….."

His voice trailed into silence, but Mrs Toms knew the real meaning of his words. He turned and a few seconds later she heard the solid cluck as the front door closed. She looked around the room that had been part of her life for so many years. Her eyes lingered on the fireplace that had always held warmth and given the room such a cosy glow. Above it the heavy wooden mantelpiece with the old gilt clock that marked the passing of time with slow steady steps that could be heard anywhere in the house. She remembered what the policeman had said and muttered under her breath,

"Bloody policemen, I only wanted the clock as a souvenir to remember the old lady by. To take something as a souvenir isn't really stealing, not in my book anyway"

She looked around the room, in the corner was a large black wooden screen, a prize from some foreign war fought in the dim and distant past. It was the only other item that might be worth the taking, but that was far too big and heavy to carry home. And finally her eyes came back to rest on the photos. She shook her head

"Funny that, I could have sworn"

A blast of cold air interrupted her thoughts as it made a whistling sound down the empty chimney, a chill ran up her spine, and suddenly she felt uncomfortable to be in the house on her alone.

"Time you wasn't here my girl, no good catching a cold now without having anyone to pay you sick leave"

She opened the front door just as the first raindrops began to fall. Within seconds the rain was so heavy she tried to retreat back inside the house, but a gust of wind from inside firmly closed the door in her face almost taking the tips of her fingers off in doing so. Mrs Toms had the strange feeling as if it had been done deliberately. She scowled at the heavy front door

"That's a fine how-do-you-do after all the years I spent cleaning you"

Only the wind answered her as it whistled around her legs.

She turned away and began to open her umbrella, but immediately a strong gust of wind took her hat from her head and the umbrella from her hand. The hat was sent flying high over the nearby houses never to be seen again. The journey of the umbrella was much shorter, it reached only as far as the front wheels of a passing car.

Mrs Toms stood on the edge of the curb looking down at its shattered remains as it lay in a quickly forming puddle. She began to curse her luck with such force that the English language plunged to depths that would have made the worldliest sailor blush. The outburst only ended when a car travelling a little closer to the curb then others drove through the now deep puddle and sent its content high into the air to thoroughly drench her. For several seconds she could only stand with clenched fists and gasp as the shock of the cold water left her speechless.

Finally, a bedraggled and now very chilled Mrs Toms turned and started what would be a very uncomfortable and long walk home. And as she walked she endlessly complained in a voice loud enough to be heard on the other side of the street about the unjust fate that had befallen her.

Just as Mrs Toms started on her homeward journey, many miles away an elderly widower answered a knock on his door to be greeted by a stranger in a dark coat who tipped his hat in greeting

"Good afternoon sir, John Higgins is the name, and picture restoration is my game"